MY OWN
WORST
ENEMY

ALSO BY LILY LINDON

Double Booked

MY OWN WORST ENEMY

LILY LINDON

HEAD
of ZEUS

An Aria Book

First published in the UK in 2023 by Head of Zeus
This paperback edition first published in 2024 by Head of Zeus,
part of Bloomsbury Publishing Plc

9 7 5 3 1 2 4 6 8

A catalogue record for this book is available from the British Library.

ISBN (PB): 9781801107631
ISBN (E): 9781801107648

Cover design: Nina Elstad

Printed and bound in Great Britain by
CPI Group (UK) Ltd, Croydon CR0 4YY

Head of Zeus
5–8 Hardwick Street
London EC1R 4RG

WWW.HEADOFZEUS.COM

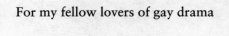
For my fellow lovers of gay drama

PROLOGUE

I'm crouched backstage, about to throw up.

Come on, Emmy. Touch your toes. Shake out your arms. Pray with a tongue twister and spin your lucky earring.

I *can* do this. I *have* prepared enough. I *won't* get stage fright and ruin my one chance to ever achieve my dreams.

Behind the curtain, my fellow drama school graduands complete their own rituals, avoiding each other's eyes.

Of course, everybody hates actors. But the people who hate actors the *most* are other actors.

We've spent three years together. Daily sessions of ritualised touching, trust falls, and sharing how our characters' traumas relate to our own have done their job, and we're all dangerously bonded. But now it's final term. A deep, unspoken suspicion has arrived. We've become dreadfully aware we're about to be thrown from the nest and expected to fly into The Acting Industry.

My fellow actors are not my friends anymore. They're my enemies.

At this showcase, we're not only performing to friends and family, but to agents. Agents who will make or break our careers.

I peek out at the crowd. You can tell who the agents are, not only because they have an aura of godliness, but because their faces are lit up by their open laptops. The rumours are true, then: agents will have the program with our contact details open on their armrests, and they'll send emails offering representation before you've even finished your monologue. Or, crucially, they won't.

Supporting friends and family have picked up on the tense vibe. It's deathly quiet out there. Normally I want to strangle people who cough in the theatre, but right now I'd be grateful for a few phones going off.

I don't have any friends or family here. My dad's working, obviously, and so's Pete. Ruth is preparing for an interview, and Raphy is on a meditation retreat in Uzbekistan. I didn't invite Mum.

A cold hand squeezes mine. In the dim backstage lights, I look into the painfully beautiful face of my best friend, Thalia. Everyone else may have become suddenly distant and menacing, but Thalia's exactly the same. She's the only one I trust to never, ever let me down, even when she inevitably rises to stardom.

I clasp her hand in both of mine, trying to warm it. I know she's trying to be comforting, but the thought that she'll be watching always ramps up my nausea. I want to impress her even more than I want to impress those agents.

Thalia tugs me in the direction of the green room.

I glance out towards the stage. There's three monologues between now and my performance. Yes, technically that means fifteen minutes, but what if someone speaks superfast, or quits?

But Thalia strides away, so I follow.

In the empty green room, I turn up the speaker that feeds through the audio from the stage into the room and angle the screen showing who's on the stage. It's still Ben, doing his modern. I squint at his technique. His left hand is swinging. I know he's meant to be my rival now, but my stomach clenches in sympathy.

Thalia yawns. 'Shall we place bets on who isn't going to get any offers?'

I can't join in with her laughter. She rolls her dark eyes at me.

'Emmy, how are you going to be a professional actor when you get *this* nervous before a performance?'

Thalia doesn't have to be nervous. She already has an agent – one of the best. She's even already been offered a major TV role, which she turned down. Unlike me, raised on a diet of theatre, musicals and pantomime, Thalia has always set her sights on Hollywood.

I try to breathe.

'They don't *care* about your performance,' she says reassuringly. 'They're businessmen. They'll just choose people based on their casting type.'

She pouts in the mirror, tossing her ponytail. With her athletic physique, spotless brown skin, sharp cheek bones and bold eyebrows, Thalia has sarcastically said that her casting type is 'they couldn't afford Zendaya'.

'You'll be fine,' she says, patting my arm. 'It's not like many agents already have a short-haired lesbian on their list.'

'Most agents don't *need* a short-haired lesbian on their list,' I mutter. 'It's not like the industry has hundreds of "leading lady" roles for anyone remotely butch.'

Thalia tuts.

'OK, but the industry needs *one*. You can be that one. The best. You're top of the year! You got, like, the highest mark ever on that Shakespeare thi—'

'We both know good exam results don't matter on stage,' I say, pacing.

God, was twenty times enough times to practise my monologue this morning? I mutter it again at supersonic speed under my breath. Damn, damn, damn, I knew I should have gone for the other one. Maybe I still have time to change it. I do have two others memorised, just in case. Maybe I should—

'Emmy. Chill out. You'll put them off. It's like horses, they can tell when you're scared.'

I gape at her and start hyperventilating.

'Jeesh, OK,' she says, swinging down from the table. 'I'll see you after.'

I try to steady my breaths. She's right.

3

'Wait, wait,' I say, grabbing her hand. 'Thank you. I just...' I look down at her fingers in mine. 'Please don't forget about me when you're a star, OK?'

Thalia smiles and tosses her ponytail over her other shoulder.

'How could I forget about you, you dummy? We're going to be living together, and flying round the world doing all our filming. Who else is going to roll my celebratory cigarettes?'

After a successful performance, Thalia and I always go to the smoking area to have one celebratory cigarette. Well, I don't actually smoke myself, but I roll it for her in a celebratory way. Of all my theatre rituals, it's my favourite.

I stroke her fingers.

'I'll roll you a whopper on graduation day.'

She grins and pulls away, flopping over a chair.

'It's so soon, I can almost taste it. No more stupid lectures, no more pointless exams, just being an *actual* performer.'

She closes her eyes in pleasure.

'Picture the scene. Graduation day. The others are stuck in the foyer, making fake promises to stay in touch, and singing from like, *Hello Dolly*. But you and me, we're out in the smoking area, sipping champagne and signing contracts. It's going to be so good, we're going to want to do it every year.'

I watch her laugh, reflected a hundred times in the green room mirrors. And I know, without a doubt, that she's going to be famous one day. One day horribly soon.

'Then *let's* do it every year,' I say urgently. 'No matter what happens with... Every year on June 29th we'll come back to The Boards, and see how far we've come.'

Thalia looks up at me.

'Urgh, you're *such* a thespian.'

But she smiles, that rare, unpractised grin that shows the gap between her teeth and makes my pulse do stupid things. When she smiles at me like that, I can almost convince myself that Thalia likes me back.

Graduation day, I promise myself, June 29th, in The Boards

Theatre Smoking Area, I'm going to finally tell her how I feel.

Applause thunders through the intercom. On the screen it's suddenly Aoife, and she's bowing.

'*Shit*,' I say, and dash towards the door.

'Good luck!'

I gasp and trip.

'Thalia!' I say, crossing myself, and knocking on the wooden door frame three times.

'What?' she laughs. 'I thought it's only bad luck to say that during a performance of Macb—'

I scream and hold my finger out to silence her, then point urgently at my trousers.

'*Break a leg*, then, whatever.' She yawns. 'You don't need to care about that crap. Superstitions are for people who can't rely on their own talent.'

I wish I could believe her. Thalia waves lazily as the green room door closes.

I sprint up to the wings, our teacher already announcing my name.

There's just time to take a deep breath and twist my earring. Then I step out onto the stage.

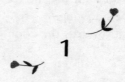

1

Nine Months Later

'Emmy Clooney,' announces the casting assistant.

'No relation,' I apologise.

The four panellists look at me. I know exactly who each of them is: the director, head writer, producer, and casting director. I memorised all their IMDb pages. Let's be honest, I memorised all of their social media pages too. You can never be too prepared.

I've done all the sniffing around about the project possible before it's in production – it's a TV drama called *High School* about sixth form students on drugs. It would be my first TV part.

I try to keep my voice calm.

'Thank you for the opportunity to read for you.'

They nod and shuffle their papers. Four printouts of my acting CV stare back at me. My upside-down headshot doesn't look happy.

For auditions, I try to look exactly like my headshot: no make-up on my pale skin (except a secret dot of white eyeliner which Thalia once told me makes actors' eyes more expressive), black T-shirt (loose enough to be androgynous, tight enough to showcase breathwork), black jeans (soft enough to allow for choreographed movements), one earring (silver hoop from my mum, supposedly lucky), and my signature short back and sides (cut last weekend so that today I would have optimum fresh-but-not-raw look), quiff gelled carefully back. The aim is to be neutral, a blank canvas to showcase not my own personality but that of my character. And also to look explicitly gay. I am confident I have at least succeeded in that.

The director, Laura Brooke (white, blonde, 38, attended Kent Grammar School, father also a successful director, had muesli for breakfast) frowns at my CV. My pulse surges with anxiety. I've spent approximately one thousand hours trying to perfect the best structure and wording for it, but whenever I'm in an audition room, I'm convinced I got it wrong. My first-class degree from Saint Genesius School of Drama is surely the most important part so I've got that at the top. But does that make it look like I am embarrassed about my unimpressive professional work? Surely, they're thinking – hang on, this person graduated nine months ago, why hasn't she had her big break yet? Why are we even bothering to see her in this audition if she hasn't already had multiple lead TV roles?

'Whenever you're ready,' says Laura.

The camera is on a tripod next to the panel, already recording me. I instinctively angle my face so that it will be capturing my best side.

Unlike theatre, where you must exaggerate your expressions for the audience, good television acting is about reducing your emotions to minute details. Instead of showing your emotions, you should hide them. Fortunately, I'm well-practised at that.

I put down the script. I always bring it so that I can revise my annotations beforehand, but of course I would never *dream* of auditioning without knowing it by heart.

Deep breath in through my nose, and out again. I close my eyes and let my own gait drop from my body. Just like I practised a hundred, a thousand times over the weekend, I adopt a whole new physicality.

I'm no longer Emmy Clooney (no relation). I'm now... Lesbian Number Two.

'Fuck off, Christina,' says Lesbian Number Two. 'You never seen two women kissing before?'

And... that's the end of the lines. I hold the silence for a second, all Lesbian Number Two's pent-up frustration and insecurity tense in the air. Then, controlled, I let all my muscles relax into my own posture. Well, into the character of Emmy Clooney, a professional actor, awaiting feedback.

The panel whoop. One of them does a spontaneous little round of applause.

'You're perfect!' squeals the producer. 'It's like you were made for the part!'

I bow my head graciously, but my eye twitches. Damn it, I hope they've turned the recording off. I remind myself that being put up for the role of 'Lesbian Number Two' doesn't mean they think that I'm a 'second-best' lesbian actress. It will just be because Lesbian Number One is being cast as a more femme lesbian (likely with long hair, lipstick, and other more audience-pleasing stereotypes).

Fictional lesbian couples must either be one femme and one butch, or two femmes. The question of whether two butches have the capacity to fancy each other in real life is irrelevant. The Media rules that two butches cannot be a couple – how else would audiences know which one wears the trousers?

My spiral must have lasted too long, because Laura looks aghast down at my CV.

'Oh my God, I'm so sorry,' she says. 'You *are* a lesbian, aren't you?'

I rehearsed a thousand scenarios for this audition, but none of this is playing to my script.

'I… What?'

Laura's forehead is crinkled in genuine distress. 'You are a – er – a woman who – umm – sleeps with other women?'

I'm not sure if I'm thrown because of the weirdness of being asked that outright by strangers, because of the binary implications of that phrasing, or because I'm taken aback that she even needs to ask. Normally it's enough to just have short hair and do a monologue from Oscar Wilde.

'I am gay,' I say, managing to avoid adding 'duh'. 'But—'

Technically, I don't sleep with other women, I avoid saying. I am a woman who has in the past had embarrassingly few half-hearted fumbles with other women. I haven't even *kissed* someone since graduation – except onstage.

'Thank *God*,' says Laura. 'No wonder it's so authentic! You're a natural!'

My eye twitches again. I spent one hundred hours practising so that I could look this natural.

I swallow and remind myself what my drama teacher used to say: the sign of a true actor is complete control over your emotions. Whatever I am feeling right now is not relevant. All that matters when the camera is on is the interior life and complex motivations of Lesbian Number Two. Now the camera is off, all that matters is performing the well-rehearsed role of Emmy Clooney, the world's next great lesbian thespian.

I smile and bow.

'Thank you so much,' I say, hand on heart. 'I really identify with this part.'

The casting panel beam back, radiating the confident glow of good allies.

'Well done, Emmy,' says Laura. 'We'll be in touch.'

2

Fade out on the audition scene. Or ideally there'd be some kind of fun special effect like they used to do in the noughties – a clunky dissolve, perhaps, or a whoosh.

New establishing shot: a surprisingly nice flat in Walthamstow. The front door is large and green, the marble steps are clean, and there's a well-kept garden patch with unusual fresh herbs that a witchy viewer might recognise as potion ingredients. The general viewer will question how attractive the flat is given that my character is a clearly unsuccessful actor. They might wonder if the film is going to be unrealistic, or if I have some other source of income, or if the story is set in an alternate universe that is not in the midst of several economic crises.

Emmy fumbles for her keys, and she – er, I mean, *I* – am about to open it when it swings from the inside. Two gorgeous men are standing flushed in the doorway. One I don't recognise, wearing designer yoga pants, was about to go in for a kiss. The other is my flatmate Raphy, wearing just a towel. His brown skin is tattooed with abstract shapes in rainbow colours, and his voluminous sun-kissed curls are in a loose bun.

Raphy opens his naked arms to me.

'Welcome home!' he says, completely unphased. The man I don't recognise throws his hands up and runs out into the street.

Raphy waves to him and closes the door behind us. He smells of the aloe vera and ginger scrub he makes himself. As I lean into his glistening chest, I try not to think about how embarrassing it is that I'm more physically intimate with my best friend than I've ever been with a romantic partner.

We go arm in arm into the inner flat, which features light wooden floors, tall windows, and an inordinate amount of house plants.

He puts our keys in the clay dish he made and says, 'I'm so glad your audition went well!'

Raphy insists he isn't psychic, merely in conversation with the universe's frequencies.

'Can you please just tell me if I'll get the part?' I ask.

'Honey, you know it doesn't work like that.'

But he wiggles his eyebrows at me. I grin back.

'Time to nourish,' he says.

In the kitchen, Raphy clicks open a mason jar of rice and opens paper bags of fresh vegetables – courgette, tomato, kale, red onions.

'He seemed... nice?' I say.

'Oh, he's the nicest,' he sighs. 'Sweet Ferdinand. He's got a serene cat pose. We met at the cacao ceremony last night.'

That would explain the uninhibited noises coming from Raphy's room last night.

'Do you think you'll see him again?'

Raphy starts chopping. 'No, I think we learned what we needed to from each other.'

'Seemed like he wanted you to teach him some more...'

'Sometimes we don't get what we want,' he says, soberly, 'but we get what we need.'

He pours two large glasses of red wine, just as the front door slams. Multiple digital devices are dumped on the entrance table, and Ruth strides in, looking as fresh as a photoshoot for *Forbes* 30 Under 30 list. She's wearing a crisp white shirt under a magenta broad-shouldered suit and matching lipstick. Her stilettos are as sharp as her smooth black bob, but as Ruth is about five foot, she still only comes up to Raphy's chest. She pokes it hard.

'I nearly *yawned* during my pitch today. If I don't get this client, I'm blaming you.'

'Sorry, my love,' he says, and holds out the second glass of wine to her.

Ruth softens.

'At least someone is getting laid around here,' she says, taking a large sip.

'Oh, like you're one to complain!' he laughs, whipping her with a tea towel. 'You've been working very late at the office this week.'

'Urgh,' says Ruth. 'Not any more. He's started sending GIFs on our team Slack, and honestly? Ick.' She kicks off her shoes and rolls her eyes. 'Straight white marketing dudes in suits. Em, are you sure you don't have any hot actor friends you can introduce to me?'

'Never date an actor,' I say darkly.

'Oh, for God's sake, they can't *all* be unreliable. You're the most chronically committed person I know.' She shrugs. 'Except me.'

'I'm the exception that proves the rule, I promise you,' I say.

Ruth's watch beeps with the signal for the start of the hour. I flop my head on the table and groan.

Raphy pats my head. 'Can I get you anything else before your shift?'

I realise I'm being melodramatic.

'I'm OK, I'm OK,' I say, rolling my shoulders back. 'I'll send them your regards.'

'Well, do try not to be *too* late for your shift,' says Raphy, putting his apron back on. 'You can tell Pete I'm trying his recipe for garlic bread tonight. With naan, though, so Mum doesn't disown me.'

Raphy's mum is Indian, his dad's Nigerian, and they're both competitive food snobs.

On cue, Ruth's stomach rumbles, and she starts typing. 'My parents must never find out the only Greek food I eat these days is from Deliveroo…'

'I'm making more than enough for two,' says Raphy, 'if you'd like to join me for dinner?'

Ruth gives him a rare smile, but then her work phone starts ringing. They both flinch.

'I'll leave it in the oven for you,' says Raphy, as she heads to her bedroom to take the call.

He turns away and puts on a melancholy birdsong playlist. My stomach knots. I feel responsible for their friendship, because I'm the mutual who brought them together. Ruth's my best – and only – childhood friend, a friendship forged by the two of us being the most intense geeks in our primary school. I met Raphy last year on an 'Acting and Community' workshop that I should have known would be irrelevant for my actual career. But it's the best thing I ever did for my non-working life. Raphy said I had a gold-coloured aura and that it was in our destinies to be friends. I, bizarrely, believed him. Unlike my drama school friends, I trusted him to stick around, regardless of my external success. So far, he's proved me right.

Raphy says he wants to live in a commune, but his dad is a property developer and gave him landlord duties of this flat. (Yes, Raphy is one of those hippies with significant family wealth.) I assumed he would have a million Pilates partners clamouring to move in, especially as he had convinced his father to charge mate's rates. But, when living with Thalia after drama school fell through, I contacted him on a whim and he said yes. He even asked if I had a friend to invite into the third bedroom. Specifically, he asked if I had a 'friend who has just got a high-flying promotion in London which means she can move out of her family home and is looking to complete your childhood promise of living together'. Ruth messaged me a few minutes later.

When Ruth and Raphy first met, it was weird. It was as if they thought that to be on their best behaviour they should be the opposite of themselves. Ruth kept trying to smile (creepy) and Raphy, inexplicably, wore a suit. We spoke about the weather until our pizzas arrived. Then Ruth went into business mode.

'If we're to consider this arrangement, we should clarify our positions. Emmy told me you're into all sorts of'– she waved her hand dismissively – 'hippie spirituality. Well, you do you, but I shan't participate in it. I don't believe in the supernatural.'

I froze with my pizza slice suspended in mid-air, horrified.

Raphy slowly undid the top button on his collar. 'Well, Emmy told me *you're* into all sorts of… workaholic careerism. You do you, but I shan't participate in it. I don't believe in capitalism.'

I put the pizza down and buried my face in my greasy hands.

But then, to my complete astonishment, I heard them laughing. I looked up to find them pushing each other as if *they* were the old friends. They even shared a sorbet. It's as though they're so opposite to each other that they've somehow gone full circle and ended up on exactly the same wavelength.

By the end of the evening, we'd already arranged our move-in date. To sign the deal, we created a handshake, crossing over our hands to shake the three of us at the same time. When our hands united, Raphy looked dramatically into the middle distance.

'I have had a premonition. I prophesy that cohabiting will bring great love into all of our lives. This is for the best.'

'Well then,' said Ruth, shaking our hands, 'maybe your powers aren't complete bullshit.'

'For the best of times,' I said, squeezing hard, 'with the best of friends.'

Still, even though we've lived together in harmony for nearly half a year now, I still get the sense they prefer hanging out as the three of us rather than just the two of them.

I know it sounds bad, but this is absolutely fine with me. I'm very happy being both of my best friends' best friend. Forever and ever, amen.

I dry our plates, slotting them neatly into the rack, and smile when mine fits into the slot perfectly between theirs.

3

Heart-shaped transition fade. Then the camera pans to a scene-setting shot.

We're on a street in Finsbury Park. It's not yet *entirely* gentrified, and we're in front of a row of family-run establishments. To the sides we can see the edges of a newsagents and a bakery, but in the middle of the screen is a pizzeria.

It could not be more obvious that this shop sells pizza. In fact, it doesn't merely sell pizza, it is dangerously obsessed with pizza.

The round tables are painted with different pizzas in cartoonish shades. The stools surrounding them are shaped like toppings: tomatoes, mushrooms, peppers, and pepperoni. The exposed red-brick walls are decorated with yellow triangle-framed illustrations (you guessed it: they're pizzas), and there's a sign legible from the street reads, in a circle, THE BEST PIZZA AROUND. The overall impression is of a fever dream brought on by too much late-night mozzarella. It probably was.

Camera tilts and lingers on the embossed red and yellow shop sign: PETE'S'ZAS.

This is where I – the main character and narrator in this movie (progressive!) – would start doing my voiceover.

'Yes' – I'd say, in my best romcom heroine voice – 'that's pronounced "pizzas".'

Pete's'zas is named after the Head Pizza Chef, Pete. Pete's my dad's best and only friend. They're co-owners of this place and the flat above. Dad tried desperately to include a pun on his own name for the company brand, but unfortunately he's called Julius.

Pete's'zas is busy tonight. The Italian classical music is already difficult to hear under the sound of clinking glasses and tippled customers. Even though it's barely seven o'clock, five of our thirteen round tables already have customers. Bert – one of our regulars – is seated at Table Number 4 (decorated like Pepperoni) and waves at me. It sounds disloyal of me, but I'm still surprised that the restaurant does such reliable business. Who knew? People love pizza.

I glance over at the corner. Table 13 is empty, as usual. Table 13 is decorated like a Marinara (tomato, basil, garlic, no cheese), because Mum was vegan even back in the 90s when they opened. Somehow the restaurant never gets *quite* full enough for either my dad or I to seat someone there.

And there he is now. They say a good waiter is like a good butler – invisible – but it's impossible not to notice my dad when he's working. He's a blur, whirling around the restaurant like a flamboyant Swiss-army knife. His salt-and-pepper quiff never has a hair out of place, and his maroon shoes tap with the efficiency of Fred Astaire. In his left hand he's waving around a tray stacked with way too many wine glasses, while with his right hand he's tucking chairs, straightening cutlery, pulling out cloths from about his person like a magician's extending handkerchief and wiping everything else down. All the while, he's charming the first-time customers and gossiping with the regulars. Even as I watch, the payer in a group of four, laughing at something Dad has said, presses a twenty-pound tip onto the bill.

I keep my head down and dash to the staff room at the back. Raphy was right: I'm late. I grab my uniform and check the staff notes whiteboard. Dad's scrawled that Carmella, the new waitress, is off sick. Damn, just me and my dad on front of house, then. I try to tell myself a busy shift is a good thing – more money for my dad's business and the continuation of my flexible part-time employment. But it also makes it more difficult to run through my lines for my next audition if I have to actually interact with people.

I can cross my fingers about the *High School* part, but the reality of trying to be a working actor is that you are in a perennial state of job-hunting. I'm grateful that I have another audition tomorrow, but it means I'll only have ten hours to prepare for it. Will that be enough?

I tighten my Pete's'zas tie round my neck. Of all the costumes I've ever worn, the pizzeria waiter uniform is the worst. Beige trousers, a red button shirt, and a yellow tie and waistcoat with Pete's'zas pizza-shaped logo in basil green. Mine's too big for me, which at least means it's more androgynous than the scarily tailored 'women's version' that Carmella and the other waitresses wear. Dad keeps offering to get me one made that fits, but that would feel like an official commitment. An admission of failure.

I check Pete's scrawled list of today's Specials, and smile. He's got the 'Emmy Special' on there again: three types of olives, rocket, olive oil, chilli, and vegan feta. My stomach rumbles just thinking about it.

I'm heading out when Dad swings in through the restaurant door.

'Deduct thirty minutes from your pay cheque,' he says, picking up a dustpan. 'And reset Table 12.' He swings back out again.

'Hello, Emmy, my precious only daughter, how are you?' I mutter to myself, doing an impression of his melodramatic gestures. 'Oh I'm fine thanks, Papa! Had a really good audition actually!'

But then I hear the bell going from the kitchen for service and hurry over to the window.

'Evening, Uncle Boss,' I say to Pete.

He's not technically my uncle, but he might as well be. Dad and Pete bonded in their youth over Neapolitan pizza. They're both Italian. Well, Dad's half-Italian (his mum never left Stoke Newington) but he overcompensates so much you'd think he was triple Italian. I swear he exaggerates his accent and gestures in public because he thinks it's what the customers expect. Pete's as serene as Dad is fiery, and Pete's pale under the kitchen lights, whereas Dad's a big fan of sunbeds.

Ruth and Raphy used to hope Dad and Pete were having a secret love story. I should clarify that (as far as I know) they're both straight bachelors. Pete used to live above the restaurant with his wife Sally, who was actually the mutual friend who first introduced Dad to my mum. Sally passed away when I was about twelve. I'm ashamed to say I don't remember her much, just that Pete used to laugh a lot around her, and that her favourite pizza was Hawaiian. Pete's'zas no longer serves pineapple.

Pete nods towards the ready pizzas, and I check their toppings as I load them onto my arms.

'Three Emmy Specials,' I grin. 'Add it to the regulars, already!'

Pete winks and returns to his dough balls.

I'm still terrified every time I try to carry more than two pizzas. I try to will myself into the character of a brilliant waitress. If these were prop pizzas, I'd be fine. Hell, I could perform a stylish stage fight involving pizza shields and breadstick swords. But the fact that they're *real*, and this is a real restaurant, with real human customers, renders me useless.

I take them over to Table Five (decorated with mushrooms), exceptionally slowly.

'Hi, I have your—' I look up at them. One shaved head, one mullet, one blue bob, all wearing plain white vests.

Lesbians! In Pete's'zas!

I'm so thrown, I forget all my waiter lines. I don't hold my balance properly, and one of the olives nearly slides off into mullet's lap.

I plonk them down, avoiding all eye contact. 'Bon appétit,' I say. Idiot, we're an Italian restaurant! 'I mean, buon appetito.' Idiot, what if they don't understand Italian? 'I mean, er, good eating.'

Mullet is blushing, presumably out of shame at how much I'm letting down queerdom.

Panicking, I slam the huge pepper grinder on their table and run away.

I really, really should be a better waiter by now, because I've basically worked in this pizzeria all my life. Dad started me on shifts before it was legal. Presumably he thought a cute child waitress would result in good tips but, unfortunately, I was not a cute child. I looked even more awkward than I do now, bug-eyed and bony, with long plaits that seemed to belong to someone else. And there was the fact I was so nervous around strangers I could barely speak. It's the same now: either I don't speak at all, or all the wrong words come out at once. It's only when it's scripted that I can get them right.

'*Mi scusi bellissime*, are you possibly finished with this pepper?' Dad graciously collects the grinder I wasn't supposed to leave behind me and, when their backs are turned, pokes me with it. 'Bert wants the Specials.'

We share a brief smile. The only thing I have always been able to do well is recite the Specials. Even when I was five or six, I could reel them off word for word, usually resulting in a round of applause. My first taste of showbiz.

I head over to Bert and perform it from Pete's list. I nearly bow at the end. I'm still disappointed I don't get a clap.

Bert considers, then orders a pepperoni, like always. I catch Dad's eye over his head and he shrugs in faux surprise. Pete already has Bert's order in the oven.

At eight, the party table arrives. Dad makes a big show of getting out pizza-patterned paper hats for them to wear. They're the same he used for my fourteenth birthday when Dad decided we'd have my party here at the pizzeria, perhaps to prove that he could host without Mum. I'd just been in the school's production of *Little Shop of Horrors*. (I played Audrey 2. I can't sing or dance to a professional standard, much to my chagrin, but that doesn't matter if you're performing from inside the papier mâché puppet of a man-eating plant.) I summoned up the courage to invite everyone in the cast. Dad and Pete closed the rest of the restaurant, and set eleven place mats with pizza party bags. Of a cast of eleven, only two showed up, wishing they hadn't. The only person who seemed glad to be there was Ruth, who had bought me a present of some revision cards. It was the first, but not the last time, I learned that actors are only your friends while you're doing a show – not before, and not after.

As the rest of the shift passes in a monotonous blur, I try to surreptitiously practise for the audition. I do my usual trick of cleaning the empty tables, muttering to myself.

I'm auditioning for an indie short film which reimagines the Victorian male-impersonators from Sarah Waters' novel *Tipping the Velvet* as a modern-day queer couple, performing in a gay bar. I'm up for the role of Nan, a drag king who falls in love with her co-star, Kitty. It could be my first-ever main part, and the director has enough kudos that if I got it, it's just possible that Thalia would hear about it. *And* I'd get to wear a top hat.

The last customers to leave are the three gays. As I'm clearing their table I notice they've left something on the bill tray, and for a mad second I think Mullet left me their number. But no, when I open the pizza-shaped card, all I see is a single five pence piece.

I sigh and put it in the tip jar. To be fair, it's more than I've earned from acting this month.

I flip the CLOSED sign with great relief. The other staff manage to escape before Dad changes the classical music to Semisonic's 'Closing Time'. Dad sings along loudly while I mop in silence.

Pete comes out from the kitchen and removes his chef's cap. Visually it doesn't make much difference as his hair is permanently moulded to its shape.

'Thanks for your work today, Emmy.'

I salute.

'Thanks for your employment today, Boss.'

He chuckles and gives me a doughy kiss on the cheek. 'Not

your boss once the cap's off,' he says, and starts switching off the kitchen appliances.

Dad grabs his end-of-day items from the counter – the shift calendar and the tip jar. He tucks the jar under his arm, the coins and notes swishing like sweet music. He takes a well-worn pencil from his waistcoat pocket and licks the lead, looking up at me efficiently.

'Now then, Patata,' – (that's a relief, he only calls me potato when he's happy with me) – 'how many shifts do you need next week? I've currently got you with Carmella on Friday and Saturday, but your rent's due next week, isn't it? Shall I add you in for Monday and Tuesday?'

I shift uncomfortably.

'Well, Dad... I actually had a really good audition today.'

His pencil hovers.

'It's for prime-time TV!' I add. 'I think this could be *it*!'

Dad, in his pizza-themed uniform, looks at me pityingly.

'Right...' he says. 'And even if you do get it, when will they pay you?'

I bite my lip.

The amount you get paid for acting roles is notoriously difficult to predict, and the paperwork can take a hideously long time. But damn it all, I'm nine months past graduation; surely I *should* be earning enough to live off my acting work by now! If Thalia could see me, still serving pizzas in my dad's house...

'Monday and Tuesday sound great,' I mumble.

He pats my head and I watch him happily scribble my name into even more boxes on the calendar. One of these days, I tell myself, one of those days will be my last shift. Then again, I thought the same thing years ago...

Dad shuts the calendar and then opens the tip jar. He rummages and holds out a handful of money to me, including the prized twenty he got earlier.

'Dad, I absolutely did not earn that. All I got was five pence.'

'We're a team,' he says, pushing it into my pocket. 'We all contribute, we all benefit.'

'No, Dad, we're individuals,' I say, pushing it into his. 'This is yours, *you* earned it, not me.'

'Emmeline,' he says sternly.

I meet his eye. I think I understand his expression. What's he going to spend this on – another board game for him and Pete? It would just go back into the pizzeria.

I swallow, then nod and mumble a thanks as I slip the glistening twenty into my pocket.

Dad pulls me into a hug and then holds me at arm's length, studying me with unusual sincerity.

'Polpetto,' – (when he's sorry for me, I'm a meatball) – 'if things don't work out with – well, if you ever need a proper full-time job, you know there's always a place for you here, don't you?'

I wriggle out of his grip.

'Yeah, Dad, I know.'

He's not done. He coughs uncomfortably.

'Has, er, has your mother been in contact with you recently?' I freeze.

'No. No, of course not!' It's not technically true, she still texts every few weeks. 'Nothing new,' I say. 'Nothing important. And even if she had, you know I wouldn't reply.'

'Oh, my little Prosciutto.' He shakes his head and squeezes my cheek. I think he's always at his most affectionate towards me when I'm stating my fealty to him, or insulting Mum.

But then Pete calls out. 'Time for me to win back that Monopoly money.'

Dad turns away from me, looking relieved.

'Get ready to lose your day's wages, Chef.'

They walk up to their flat, trash-talking, just like every other night. I watch as they close the novelty meatball doorknob behind them.

4

No matter how many auditions I do, I still feel petrifyingly sick beforehand. But it's especially nerve-wracking when it's a project that actually sounds good.

On the morning of the *Tipping the Velvet* audition, Raphy makes me a green smoothie, and Ruth makes me an espresso. I force them down. Then I have a choice between whether to do a yoga pose with him or a power pose with her. As usual, I take the latter, smiling apologetically at the former. He says namaste disappointedly.

The audition itself is in a rundown gay bar. Instead of a bouncer, the casting director is on the door with the list of actors.

I've arrived my usual forty-five minutes early. I join the queue with three other actors, who are all classic 'girl-next-door' casting types: one blonde, one brunette, one red. They all smile white smiles at me. Oh God, I never know what to do back. We might end up colleagues, so I want to be professional, but I don't want them to think I'm coming on to them or something equally business inappropriate. In the end I just freeze and look away.

'If you're here for the part of Kitty, please sit on the left – you'll audition in room 1,' says the casting director to those in front. Then, spotting me, says, 'Phew, a Nat! You'll be on the right.'

I haven't been inside a gay bar since Raphy took me to his short-lived drag debut. It feels wholesome during the day – the rainbow bunting isn't hidden by gyrating bodies. The bar tables have been pushed to the sides and two rows of chairs are laid out facing each other. On the left, there are two more girl-next-doors. On the right, the chairs are all empty. I sit on one, feeling like the loser at a school disco.

The next-doors are reading their lines, or even, *quelle horreur*, talking to the other actors. I spend ten minutes with my eyes shut, rehearsing in my mind. I'm only momentarily distracted when another Nat auditionee arrives. I recognise her: Sandy Lopez. We've been up for the same roles before, and I've always beaten her. I used to be secretly reassured by this and think my training must have counted for something, but now I wonder if it's because she's an unclear type. She has a buzz cut, chiselled bone structure, and a medium-large dick energy, but she's wearing a dress and make-up. Offstage, it's a great look. But for being typecast in the acting industry? Rookie mistake.

When Sandy sits down next to me, I stand up. Seeing competition makes my nausea even worse, and I can't be distracted from my pre-audition habits. I'm not *superstitious*, exactly... I simply believe that if any part of my ritual is off, my audition will burst into flames.

I push open the door to the toilets, still marvelling at why other actors don't use loos the way I do. It's like my own private green room.

I breathe out slowly, scrutinising myself in the mirror. My audition uniform matches my headshot, as usual; all black denim for an archetypal 'androgynous butch' look. I carefully dampen my fingers from the dripping tap and tame one loose hair from my quiff back into its rightful place.

I go into a cubicle for privacy and shake out my muscles. I swivel my tongue around my mouth clockwise and then anti-clockwise. I pull a section of my hair like a puppet string to centre my posture.

I place my hands on my abdomen and breathe deeply. On the exhale, I violently push my diaphragm out, with a 'ha' sound.

'Ha! Ha! Ha!'

I take another deep breath in.

'Ha! H—'

A creak; I freeze. But after a few long seconds holding my breath, all I hear is the tap dripping, so I move on to my articulation exercises.

'Unique New York,' I say, enunciating every syllable. 'Unique New York.'

There's another creak, louder this time, recognisably the bathroom door. I break off, my mouth frozen in 'oo'.

Has one of the other actors found my spot? Or does someone just need a wee?

A slow tap of soles on linoleum. The door next to mine creaks plastically open, then shut, then locked.

I have to decide whether to make my presence known, pretend I'm weeing, and therefore rustle some loo roll (commit!). But the moment passes and I've stayed quiet too long. I glance at my watch: ten minutes until I'm scheduled to go in. I'll just have to creepily wait for this person to do their business and then carry on. I twist my earring to ward off bad luck.

But there's no rustle of clothes from next door. Only the lid of a loo seat being flicked closed, and the slight scuff of trainers on sticky linoleum. Then, like a renegade saying the password at the door of a speakeasy, a voice says,

'Unique New York.'

The articulation is effortless and flawless. The voice is slightly higher and brighter than mine, and the accent is unusual – New Zealand, with something else. Irish?

I hold my breath. Am I being mocked, teased, or challenged? Could this be a bizarre coincidence?

Very seriously, I ask, 'A proper copper coffee pot?'

There's a pleased chuckle from the other side of the wall. A tingle dances along my spine. I'd have to practise a *lot* to make a laugh as charming as that.

'Peter Piper picked a peck of pickled peppers,' they say.

I say it back, faster. But halfway through they join in with me, so that we're saying it in unison.

I start again, trying to accelerate to the end of the line to beat them. But they keep up, laughing, with perfect diction in that unusual accent. Yes, definitely New Zealand and Irish, but there's still something else, like they've picked up inflections from multiple places. And I swear it's familiar in some way, but I can't place why.

'If Peter Piper picked a peck of pickled peppers…'

I urge my mouth forwards, fumbling slightly but faster, racing through the last line to the punch and *just* beating them. We're both shouting now.

'Where's the peck of pickled peppers Peter Piper picked?'

We break off triumphantly and their laughter is infectious. I bark and then feel self-conscious at how ugly my laugh is compared with theirs.

'Well,' says the voice, 'I have never felt so warmed-up.'

Damn it. What am I playing at, fraternising with the enemy before an audition? But wait, it might be all right. This could be the person who plays Kitty opposite my Nat… I could be signing up to perform opposite that voice.

'You're not here for the part of Nat?' I ask.

'No,' they say, and my heart soars. 'I'm here to do a massive shit.'

I laugh in surprise, then stop. The echo in here is not flattering.

'Yeah, I *am* actually here for the part of Nat,' they say. 'You?'

'Oh…' I say. 'Me too.'

There's a pause.

'We can practise together,' they say, at the same time that I say, 'We're rivals.'

There's another pause. Then we both, at the same time again, say, 'Jinx.'

They laugh. 'We probably just cancelled each other out.'

The wall next to me wobbles, as though they're leaning

against it on the other side of the cubicle. I have an image of leaning against it too, like in a music video where the lovers are in different bedrooms thinking about each other.

I'm going mad. I stay seated.

'I'm Em, by the way. Emmy Clooney. No relation.'

They laugh again, that delightful laugh.

'God, I'm sorry. Do you have to say that every time?'

'Yeah, it's difficult not having a famous actor for a parent.'

The voice pauses for a moment and I fear my joke hasn't landed. Then the angelic sound comes again and I smile to myself.

'I'm Mae. Mae Jones.'

'Mae Jones,' I echo, then blush. God, why am I being so embarrassing?

'My pronouns are she/her,' she adds.

'Oh! Yes! Sorry, I should have – me too,' I say, glad she can't see me flustering. 'It's a pleasure to, er... Does this count as meeting you?'

'Well, I don't know about you, but I'm planning to leave this bathroom stall at some point.'

She clicks open her lock. There's the squeak of her shoes, and then I can see them under the gap at the bottom of my door. Well-worn, outrageously chunky multicoloured trainers, their soles so large they're practically platform, turn towards me.

The tap drips.

'What's wrong?' Mae asks with a laugh. '*You* need to do a pre-audition shit?'

'No, I...'

I don't want to break the spell. But that's stupid.

'Well then,' I say, to force myself, 'I'm coming out now.'

'Proud of you.'

I laugh and take a breath. Then I open my cubicle door.

Looking out, I lock eyes with myself in the mirror.

But something is wrong.

Yes, my dark brown hair is short, my face is pale and slightly flushed, my eyes are blue. But it's all... Off. It's like a game of spot the difference. I'm wearing the wrong clothes. In the mirror, my professional black audition outfit has become a clashing pink and red oversized shirt, over baggy blue jeans. My ear is pierced in the wrong ear, and instead of a hoop it's a glittering stud. Where my face is usually long and chiselled, in the mirror I have adorable dimples. I'm holding out my hand to shake, but in the mirror, I'm going in for a hug. And the smile in the reflection – a smile that's broader, straighter, more mischievous and charismatic than my own – is quickly dropping.

For a second, I have a sense of an alternate universe, a universe where I'm like myself, but better in every way.

Then I realise it's not me at all.

But Mae is *exactly* my type.

My pre-audition routine is in flames.

I sit on the right side of the room, hyper-aware of Mae next to me. Her knee is centimetres away – a knee that is surely the same but better than mine.

The Kitty auditionees are staring at us. It's different, being variations on a mainstream casting type. We've all seen two pretty 'girl-next-doors' sitting next to each other. But in an audition room, two – whatever you want to call us – overtly androgynous, masc-of-centre, 'soft butch' women – are a rarer exhibit.

I feel my seat starting to shake and think that, of course! Now there's an earthquake. Then I realise it's Mae, next to me, convulsing with silent laughter.

I slowly turn to look at her.

'Sorry, sorry, I always laugh when I'm—' She catches my eye and sets herself off again, clutching her belly as if she's in agony. I stay very still. I feel in pain too.

'You look like you've seen a ghost,' she splutters.

'This is bad luck,' I whisper.

Mae's bluer-than-my eyes stare at me.

'It's bad luck to meet your doppelganger,' I say. 'When it

happens in fairy tales, you and your lookalike are destined to fight to the death. Only one can survive.'

I don't know the specific ritual for warding off this kind of omen – I'll have to consult Raphy. But in the meantime, I knock on the side of my head three times.

Mae's eyes twinkle. She leans into me and says, 'It doesn't feel like bad luck to me.'

I look away, my cheeks burning. I can feel some kind of dark magic working on me already, deep in my stomach.

The audition room door opens, and the casting director calls out, 'Emmy Clooney?'

I know I need to stand, but I'm stuck to my chair.

It's official. Mae has cursed me.

Mae softly touches my elbow. 'Hey, are you OK? Want me to go first?'

I blink at her hand, then force myself to look back up at her face. Her better-than-my face. Her photogenic, cinematic, ready-for-a-close-up face. Why would any casting director choose me when they could have her?

I have no shadow of a doubt that Mae Jones will beat me to this part, and any others she wants.

I stand suddenly. All the audition preparation papers that were in my lap fall to the floor. Mae and I both duck to pick them up, and bump heads. She clutches at hers, laughs, and moves back to grab the papers again. I try to snatch them away. Each of us grapples with half the pages of my worn-out copy of the acting Bible (*Constantin Stanislavski: An Actor Prepares*). The book rips in two.

We both stumble back slightly, then look instinctively from the pages up at each other.

If my eyes are an overcast blue, hers are a clear summer afternoon. They search mine, and then, for just a fraction of a moment, flicker down the rest of my body. She must be doing exactly what I'm doing: comparing us, sizing up the competition. Like me, she'll be cataloguing all the ways in which she is superior.

She frowns at my face, no doubt seeing all my inferiorities. Then her face splits into her effortless grin.

Blood powers up my cheeks. It's clear. We both know she's the alpha, and I'm the pathetic beta.

I turn on my heels, and walk as calmly as I can down the room.

'Emmy?' call two voices behind me, but I'm already at the door.

As soon as I'm outside, I break into a run, dumping all my preparation for the part in a bin.

5

'She's going to take everything from me!' I scream.

Ruth and Raphy stare at me. We're in my bedroom, which looks like the makeshift office of a renegade detective who is obsessed with tracking down a criminal thespian. My walls are plastered in heavily annotated theatre tickets, playscripts and audition monologues, connected by theme with colour-coded strings. Above my bed are signed show posters of my idols – Olivia Colman, Viola Davis, Cate Blanchett, Annabel Finch.

Ruth and Raphy don't seem to understand how terrible the situation is. I try to be clear.

'The only way I can get cast in anything is if I'm the *only* short-haired lesbian actor on the scene. Don't you see? Suddenly we're going to be in all the same audition rooms.'

'Em,' tuts Ruth, 'you got a first-class degree from the best fucking drama school in the country. Give yourself some credit.'

'Evidently exam results don't matter! Look at me! Nine months later and my biggest role has been the understudy to *Orlando*'s understudy! I never even stepped on stage! There aren't enough parts for two of us.'

Raphy steeples his fingers. 'What I'm hearing is that scarcity mindset is affecting your sense of security.'

'Security?' I blink at him. 'Oh God, you're right! If she takes all my parts, I won't be able to make rent and I'll have to move out and you'll stop being my best friends and I'll have to live with my dad and he'll take it as proof that acting isn't a viable career choice, and Thalia will know I'm a failure and I might even have to talk to my mo—'

Ruth plays a loud alarm sound.

I stop.

'Right.' She turns it off and smooths her hair. 'Stop spiralling. You don't have enough data to know if Mae is even a real competitor. You self-sabotaged your audition. It could be that she's utterly abysmal. Maybe you would have got the role if you'd auditioned.'

'I...'

Damn it, she's right. I was so thrown by Mae that I ruined it myself. I can't rationally blame her. It definitely still feels like her fault though.

'So, what am I meant to do now?'

Ruth shrugs her shoulder pads.

'Maintain business as usual. Audition for good parts, and do a good job. Most likely thing is, meeting Mae Jones today was an anomaly and you'll never see her again.'

I nod, pacing, pulling at my quiff.

'I'll never see her again,' I mutter. 'I'll never see her again.'

That should be reassuring. So why do I also feel so... disappointed?

'Honey...' Raphy coughs. 'Your energy is... a lot right now. How about we do a little meditation?'

'Raph! I can't sit still right now!'

'Exactly,' he says. 'Look, even Ruth will join in.'

Ruth rolls her eyes but seems to accept it's for the greater good. She pulls me onto the living room bean bag.

'Breathe in... and out... In... and out...'

My fidgeting stills gently. Annoying as it is to admit, Raphy might be right. Breathing makes you feel slightly better than not breathing.

Then Ruth's watch goes off. I open my eyes, suddenly panicked again. Raphy sighs, but bows graciously and helps me up.

'Darling,' he says, moving us through to the kitchen, 'maybe your acting career wouldn't seem quite as all-consuming if you had... Other interests?'

I feign offence, but honestly? Being single-minded in my ambition is something I'm proud of.

'I agree,' says Ruth. 'And you know, the best stress release is a good fucking.'

I choke on an olive. Raphy has the audacity to nod.

'Raphy! You said that after Ferdinand you had taken a vow of celibacy!'

Ruth scoffs loudly. 'Sure, he's going to be "celibate" until some sexy yoga pants come along and do downward-fac—'

Raphy snaps back, 'At least I'm not simulating feelings for my colleague to aid my career.'

'I'm not screwing him to get promoted! I'd get promoted anyway!'

R&R fold their arms and face away from each other. I look at them and decide it's now my turn to act for the greater good.

'OK, what if I was open to dating...?'

R&R's arms immediately unfold. I try not to let my smile show. This is why three is the perfect number for a friendship group.

'But how am I meant to find time to go on dates?' I say to Ruth, then turn to Raphy. 'And how am I meant to find a real connection with someone?'

They look at each other, then shrug. 'Date an actor?'

I gag.

'Of course, you would suggest she dates in the workplace,' mutters Raphy.

'I'm suggesting she shares deep conversations about the art of faking an—'

'Guys. Stop. Actors are the number one veto.'

Ruth shakes her head at me.

'Em, you've got to accept that not all actors are going to be like—'

Raphy hurriedly presses Ruth's lips together. 'Her name is not to be said in this house. Bad juju. We'd have to get the sage out again.'

Ruth bites at his fingers.

'It's not just *her*,' I say. 'All actors are the competition. Especially lesbian actors. It would be literally sleeping with the enemy.'

My mind has the audacity to think about Mae Jones. I groan.

'And why would anyone ever want to date *me*, when there are so many better options out there?'

The constant rejection of dating would be like doing even more auditions.

Raphy puts a hand on his jutted hip.

'I will *not* accept negative self-talk in this house. And it simply isn't true. You're very attractive.'

'Raphy, you think literally everyone is hot.'

'I do believe everyone has been blessed with their own unique magnetism, and that, yes, if the stars aligned in the right way I could form an intimate connection with near any consenting adult *but* –' he waves his hand in a characteristically abstract gesture over me, '– even lay people fancy you. You have a – *je ne sais quoi*.'

'Maybe on stage,' I say tentatively, fiddling with my quiff. 'When I rehearse enough.'

'Only because you have more self-confidence when you're onstage,' says Ruth. 'Other people see it offstage but you just never give people a chance. Remember that woman who kept following you round asking for your autograph?'

I blush. 'She just wanted to be an actor herself.'

'Em, she asked you to autograph your number!'

'To ask me about getting an agent.'

Ruth throws up her hands.

'Honestly, why did you become an actor if you can't stand people looking at you?'

'Because they're not looking at *me*, they're looking at my character.'

'Very noble.' She rolls her eyes. 'But it'll still be your name up in lights.'

I shrug sheepishly. It would be lying to say I didn't want the validation of fame. If my name was in lights then my dad would have to accept that acting is a real job. And if the lights were shiny enough, maybe Thalia would message me again.

'You're so sure that no one is interested in you that the energy you give off comes across as if you are not interested in them,' says Raphy. 'You know, sometimes you assume no one wants to talk to you so you don't talk to them? It's a self-fulfilling prophecy.'

It's part of the job to get feedback on the way I present my characters – from my agent, from directors, from reviewers – but I always find it disarming when someone describes the way I come across in 'real' life. I don't want to deny my friends' impression of me, but I'm sure Raphy's just trying to spin my failings into a positive light.

'Yeah,' says Ruth bluntly. 'First impressions? Your personal brand of awkwardness comes across as aloof.'

She starts touch-typing on her phone while maintaining the conversation.

'If you were my client, I'd say you need to be less polished, it'll seem more human. Work on your public relations. Didn't you say your drama school friends have a party tonight?'

Ruth has an uncanny memory for schedules, even other people's. But I know what she's going to suggest.

'No?' I lie.

'Excellent,' says Ruth. 'And she who must not be named won't be going, will she?'

'She's shooting in LA,' I mumble.

'Perfect. Then your mission is just to go to this party and flirt with someone.'

Raphy squeals and makes spooky gestures.

'Destiny calls,' he says. 'I foresee it. You will form a powerful connection at this party.'

'Why is it that my destiny always seems to correspond to what *you* think I should do?' I grumble. 'Why should I bother trying to find a relationship when I already have you two?'

Ruth looks up from Deliveroo.

'Because we don't want to have sexual intercourse with you.'

'OK,' I say. 'Please stop there.'

'Because despite how attractive you are, *even offstage*,' continues Ruth, 'I'm still tragically straight.'

Raphy stands and stretches his leg back in an arch. 'It's so sad that Emmy's sexual identity is, like, the only one that doesn't overlap with mine.'

'Guys, please, you don't have to justify why you don't fancy me,' I say, watching him teeter. 'We're three friends. Best friends having the best time.'

Raphy wobbles. Ruth instinctively lunges to hold him. Raphy clings to her shoulder and they stare into each other's eyes to communicate stability via telepathy until they refind his balance. They continue to stare at each other for a moment, until Ruth's watch beeps and they jump away from each other.

'You need to stop sitting in lotus with the same left foot crossed over,' Ruth snaps, tapping at her wrist. 'It's messing up your posture.'

'Well,' Raphy says, tossing his hair, 'your watch is messing up your circadian rhythms, so—'

I take up my peacemaker mantle.

'Fine, fine, I'll go to the party tonight.'

They immediately cheer.

'But only if you both help me get ready. And we listen to musicals.'

Ruth rolls her eyes, but I know she secretly loves *Hamilton*. Raphy claps and goes to get his make-up bag.

6

I realise this is the first party I've been to since graduation. That's sad, isn't it?

I press the buzzer and Toby answers. 'Yaaaas, who is it?'

'Emmy.'

'Who?'

I turn around to leave.

'Wait, Emmy *Clooney*?!'

He seems to have forgotten he's still on the intercom because he shouts to the room, '*Clooney* is coming!'

The door buzzes. No way out now.

It's easy to follow the stomps of *Chicago*'s 'Cell Block Tango'. Toby opens the door, blinking as if I'm a hallucination. Behind him, half-naked thespians pause mid-straddling chairs, shooting imaginary guns and slut-dropping to stare.

I hand over a bottle of Pete's'zas House Red.

'Thank you for having me,' I say.

'Oh, I… You're so welcome!' blinks Toby. 'I think the idea of BYOB is to drink it yourself, though?' He hands the bottle back to me.

Going through, I spot one of the cliques of my Saint Gen's class – Ben, Aoife, Will, Colin and Enrico.

They all wave and scream extravagantly in the universal language of an actor's welcome.

'Emmy!'

I wave the wine bottle to create a force field so they don't feel they have to hug me.

'It's so nice to see you! How *are* you? Are you still even *on* the group chat?'

Everyone else shares news of their casting successes and failures on a group chat called BAFTA NOMINEES 2k??. I avidly watch every update, judging my own progress by theirs – but I would never actually *participate*. It's the same reason I'm not public on social media. What if I typed something wrong and then my mistake is immortalised forever on the dark web?

'Is *Thalia* coming?'

'Oh.' I swallow hard and try to look nonchalant. 'I'm not sure if she can make it.'

'Well, that's fair,' says Ben. 'If I was as famous as her I'd throw all you suckers under a bus.'

The others slap his arm in camp outrage. I'm not sure if he's joking.

'How *is* she?' asks Toby. 'I haven't heard from her in ages! She's doing so well, isn't she?'

'Mm-hmm!' I nod.

'Isn't she in that new film... Oh, what's it called?'

Aoife supplies, '*My Best Friend Wants to Kill Me.*'

My eye twitches. 'Excuse me. Bottle opener.'

I escape the kitchen and pour myself a slow glass, trying to do my breathing exercises. Ruth and Raphy would be disappointed – I can't even talk to my old classmates, let alone flirt with someone new. Maybe I can will myself into the character of someone else, someone who is the life and soul of the party. Someone confident, gregarious, funny, charming—

My eye is caught by the door opening.

And there she is. Mae Jones.

Her party outfit is a knitted vest decorated with big sheep. Her cargo trousers are weighed down with a heavy ring of keys, and she's bouncing on the same chunky colourful trainers.

Her hair's a little wet; the messy curls spring like happily watered plants. I swear the entire party turns to gaze at her. She says something with a grin, and everyone laughs. She lifts a bashful hand to ruffle the short hair at the back of her neck, and everyone tries to hand her a drink. She takes a beer and toasts the new friends around her, and, just as she looks up, our eyes meet.

The light changes to a red strobe. The speakers play *Wicked*'s 'What is This Feeling? (Loathing)'

Mae misses her mouth, spilling beer all over her vest.

Her (very gorgeous, femme) friend laughingly shepherds her to the kitchen. Mae tries to resist but she's pushed towards me. I am cursed again, unable to move.

Her friend dabs at her, then looks up at me, then to Mae, then slowly backs away. Mae doesn't seem to notice. Clearly she's not a very attentive girlfriend.

'Well well well,' she says finally. 'Are you here for the audition?'

I'm in such a state of anxiety that for a second I don't realise she's joking.

Mae tilts her head at me and starts to smile. I look back, willing myself to say something witty. Nothing comes. I try to cover it by taking a gulp of my wine.

'Sorry,' she gestures behind her, 'would you prefer to have the rest of our conversation in the toilet?'

I choke. Still, I don't have a reply quip. Her eyes are twinkling.

'I didn't get the impression you'd be so desperate to see me again that you'd follow me to a party.'

How is it she's said multiple quirky greetings and I haven't said a single thing back? It's like she can't help rubbing in how much more charming she is than me.

She takes a sip of her beer, looks round at the party, then glances back at me.

Now I'm thinking about what R&R said, about how I come across as aloof. God. Say *something*. I swallow.

'Nice vest.'

Mae blinks at me, as if working out if I'm being sarcastic or not. I try to smile. Her face breaks into a wide grin.

'Isn't it! Guess what? This is *so* queer of me,' she says, touching my arm, 'but my ex knitted it.'

It has the note of a line that's been used many times before. I have no right to feel this way, I know, but I resent that she's saying the same things to me that she says to others. She thinks I can't see through her script, but I know better than anyone what it sounds like when you've practised the same lines too many times.

I pull my arm away. We stand in silence for a bit.

'Are you here with someone?' she asks.

I blush. Is she asking if I'm here with a date? R&R should have warned me how weird it is to come to a house party by yourself.

'I – I know Toby,' I say. I gesture to the BAFTA clique, who I swear are watching Mae. 'I went to drama school with that lot.'

'Oh! The Big Toe! I love him!'

Of course Mae has nicknames for my friends that even I'm not aware of. I top up my wine, which has somehow already disappeared.

'Where did you go to drama school?' I ask.

'Oh, I didn't,' she replies.

I blush harder. This is why I should never go to real parties. I must seem like such a snob.

'So how did you get in?' I ask. 'I mean, to this party? Who do you know?'

Mae looks around.

'Kind of... Everyone?'

Across the room she waves at Louisa, a former performer who has now become my agent's assistant. She waves joyously back. Several people behind her wave too, then look at each other jealously.

I frown at her.

'Why haven't I seen you before?'

'Oh,' she laughs, touching the back of her neck, 'I haven't been in anything big. I only started acting relatively recently. Accidentally, to be honest. I've been a bit of a, you know, a drifter I suppose – pubs, cafés, studios. I only moved to London a few months ago. Hence the stupid accent. No one can ever guess where it's from.'

Without thinking, I say, 'New Zealand and Dublin, but recently lived in New York.'

Mae blinks at me, then breaks into a slow smile.

'I'm impressed.'

I look down.

'Any actor should be proficient in accents,' I mumble. 'And actually, umm, I realised one of my favourite actors has a very similar voice type to you. Maybe you've heard of her – Annabel Finch?'

Mae stares at me. Do I have stains on my teeth? I plough on.

'I saw her live once, with my mum, when I was a teenager, and she was absolutely... She's got that –' I click my fingers '– that stage magic, you know? She's magnetic. I aspire to be like that, to be like her.'

Mae's looking at me so strangely, I realise I must have sounded violently stupid. I forget that stage presence is something I talk about with my mum – *used* to talk about with my mum. It isn't something people discuss at parties.

'I just think she's good,' I mutter, and gulp more wine.

Out of the corner of my eye, I watch Mae pick at the label on her beer. Then she shrugs.

'I don't think she's *that* good.'

Oh my God, is she jealous? Is it that Mae can't stand someone else being complimented for their stage presence because being effortlessly charismatic is *her* thing? If her ego is wounded even from a casual comparison to someone else's talent, she must be a true actor.

Mae taps her head. 'She struggles with acting from her brain, not from her heart. But acting isn't a science, it's an art.'

My jaw tightens. I don't know if I'm more offended on behalf of my idol or myself. Does Mae know this is a personal attack? Is this to get me back about the drama school comment earlier?

'Acting is a craft,' I say stiffly.

Of course, I'm proof you can just about be a working actor relying on preparation and research, even if your drama teachers were always telling you to get out of your head. Even if you still haven't worked out the formula to engineer that elusive magnetic spark.

'Agree to disagree,' smiles Mae. 'So how long have you been crafting?'

'All my life,' I say immediately.

'Oh, are your parents actors? I mean, I know you're not actually one of George Clooney's children.'

Wow, she has an incredible ability to say exactly what's going to poke at the chips on my shoulder.

'No,' I snap. 'My dad doesn't even think acting is a real job. I'm not a nepotism baby.'

Mae, for the first time, seems lost for words. I take a sip, trying to calm down.

'How long have you been working as an actor then?' I say, trying to sound casual and not like I'm data gathering on my enemy.

'Oh, er... I guess... a few weeks?'

I spit out my wine.

'Well, I did improv a lot, growing up,' she says quickly. 'Improv isn't considered to be weird in the US. It's seen as pretty cool actually, especially New York, which, as you guessed, is where I spent the last few years. And I had, like, actor friends, I guess, so maybe it kind of, I don't know, sank in organically?'

'So how did you get into the audition room today?'

'Oh, from Sandra!'

I blink at her. She seems to realise that information isn't sufficient.

'Someone came into the café I work in at the moment and

– this is so embarrassing – but I was doing a stupid joke for my—' She stops and points over at the person she came to the party with. 'For Rowan, there, in the white skirt, and Sandra was waiting for her coffee and saw and turned out to be the casting director.'

'You… You got talent scouted?'

I thought that was a myth.

Mae laughs delightedly, her hand going to the back of her neck.

'That makes it sound a lot more exciting, but I think it was just cos I looked right for the part. I mean, there aren't that many performers who look like us, are there?'

I twitch. So it's not as though she hasn't noticed that we're the same casting type.

'That's how I know that lot,' she continues, gesturing her beer to the party. 'A lot of the other people who work in the café are performers, so I met them through that and going to their parties and stuff.'

I bet Mae doesn't need to have her friends force her to go to parties to attempt to flirt with someone. I bet Mae flirts with people effortlessly and successfully.

I'm suddenly aware of how long we've been talking. Surely she wants to talk to other people. She must be desperate to get away from me. I must have not been giving the right cues for her to feel like she could leave. Urgh.

'Well, I won't keep you,' I say.

'Oh,' she blinks at me. 'OK! Well… Maybe I'll see you around, right? On the audition circuit? Maybe we'll get cast in the same thing!'

'That seems unlikely,' I say.

Mae peels off the last bit of her beer label.

'You think you're in that different a league to me?'

I frown.

'The opposite.'

She frowns back.

'What do you mean?'

How did I get a rival who doesn't even understand she's a rival? I fold my arms.

'Mae, we won't get cast in the same thing because no shows need more than one person who looks like us. We'll be going for the same parts. We're in competition.'

'There's room for more than one queer woman in showbiz,' she laughs.

I don't laugh back.

Has she really been so sheltered up to this point that this comes as a surprise to her? How can she be, whatever our type would be labelled, 'a butch woman', and not know this stuff? Was her otherness not rammed down her throat at school, at work, in the street?

My chest hurts. Maybe her charm has saved her from all that. Maybe if I wasn't so awkward, I'd be allowed to swan through things too.

'Well, OK,' I say. 'But the statistical majority of queer female roles will be in a more traditionally "femme" casting type. They're more audience-appealing and less threatening to the status quo of Hollywood beauty standards. There isn't room for many "butches", not when we're only ever there as a novelty, or a back pat for representation, or an easy plot twist. So there's *certainly* not room for more than one white, slim, cis, non-disabled, short-brown-haired, twenty-five-ish-year-old butch to get their big break.'

'But… but that's not fair,' she mumbles.

'In a very small pond, there's only room for one fish,' I explain, my stomach churning. 'Otherwise, the fish will starve. And then they will eat each other.'

Saying it makes me realise just how devastating Mae's existence is to my career. Feeling shaky, I put my glass down, twisting my earring.

'Maybe we should… Make some kind of agreement,' I say.

Mae eyes me suspiciously.

'What kind of agreement?'

'Well, we don't want to be bumping into each other at every audition, do we?'

She picks at her beer label. 'Would that really be so bad?'

I look at her profile – her button nose and neat chin, both clear upgrades on mine. I don't want to be the one to break it to her. She's only been acting for a few weeks. She still doesn't understand how dog-eat-dog it is. I, on the other hand, know that if she continues to audition for my parts, she'll win them, and destroy my career. Plus, she'll distract me so much with her... her *vibe*, her dark magic, her ridiculous charisma that my pre-audition routines will never be the same again.

'Well, yes,' I say. 'I really do think it would be awful.'

Mae's expression changes. Surprise turns quickly to disdain, then anger. The change is sudden but complete, like a flicked switch.

She squares up to me. She's only centimetres taller than me, even in her big shoes, but exudes the energy of a giant. Her face is so close to mine, it's even more clear in which ways our faces are similar and different. For one thing, she has offensively cute freckles across her nose. For a mad second I want to touch them.

Mae jabs at my collar.

'Fuck you,' she says. 'If you want a competition, you've got a competition. Who are you to try to control my life? I finally accepted it's my stupid destiny to be an actor, and now you think *you* can stop me?'

She laughs.

'Oh, you think it would be "awful" to see me in auditions. Well, strap in for the nightmare of your life, Emmy Clooney. I'll be there. I'll be doing all the self-tapes, all the auditions, all the callbacks. Wherever you are, I'll be there too.'

Suddenly she presses herself close to me. Her proximity makes me breathe in sharply. She smells like the cologne I've been looking for all my life: peppery bergamot and bright citrus. She whispers into my ear.

'But I'll be the one who makes it. I'll be the one on all the screens, all the billboards, all the grand stages. And you'll be in the audience. Watching me. Clapping.'

She storms away and puts her arm around my old drama school friends, leaving me breathless in her lemon-scented air.

7

'So *now* we're in this deadly competition for parts.'

'Hot,' says Ruth, crunching her breakfast toastie.

'No!' I shout. 'Not hot! Career destroying! Life destabilising! Ego devastating!'

'Factually, nothing has changed from when we spoke yesterday,' Ruth says.

'Everything has changed! You *said* I'd never see her again. Then I saw her within a few hours!'

The room is swimming. Maybe I'm just not used to being hungover, but I feel as though the room is closing in on me. I swear my porridge looks like Mae's gloating face.

'Argh!' I drop it and cover my face. 'She's *everywhere*!'

'Told you it was destiny,' says Raphy, sipping his smoothie serenely.

'How can I escape? How can I… OK. I'll have to change my look.'

'Emmy,' sighs Ruth.

'I *know* this is what I "feel comfortable in",' I say in heavy air quotes, 'but what's the point of being true to myself if I don't have a job? OK, so I'll grow my hair out. No, that would take months. OK, so I'll wear a wig. Yes, and I'll change my name, and my voice, and I'll start going for all the boring straight girl roles like – like Juliet, and Cossette, and I—'

'Emmy,' sighs Raphy.

Damn it, he's right, I would never be able to compete with

the entirety of wannabee actresses. I will only ever be able to compete for tiny short-haired lesbian parts.

'No. Fine. You're right. OK. I keep my identity but I escape to – to America! Yes, I move to Hollywood, and I walk right into the— Wait! Mae used to live in New York, the Americans will all know her and—'

'*Emmy*,' they say together.

'What?'

'Snap out of it!'

Ruth steeples her acrylic nails. 'So you have a rival. Great! Rivals are great for business. Competition encourages innovation.'

'Innovation…' I say. 'Innovation. You're right! To win, I need to go harder. I need to pull out all the stops. You guys need to help me.'

Ruth checks her watch and then clicks her knuckles.

'All right. I can smash this in five minutes.'

On her laptop, Ruth sweeps through hundreds of tabs to create a new virtual brainstorm board.

'This is classic crisis management. You just need to update your business model to hit her weaknesses. Gather as much information about her as possible. Does she have a website?'

The name 'Mae Jones' doesn't bring up anything. Believe me, I tried. No Spotlight (the standard website for performers to list their CV), no agent affiliation, no social media.

'She did say she's only been acting "for a few weeks",' I growl. 'And I guess improvisers don't really need to showcase themselves online?'

'OK,' Ruth says. 'So what do we know? You're classically trained. She's not. You're a drama nerd. She's not. So do what you do best.'

She studies me over her laptop, flashing red icons reflecting in her eyes. It's just like when we used to study late in secondary school. I nod maniacally.

'Work harder.'

8

'Emmy, what have you been snorting, and how can I get some?'

My agent, Valerie, speaking over the phone. There's a sound of babies cooing in the background – her six-month-old twins, Judith and Hamnet. (It's nice to know I'm not *the* most pretentious person in this industry.)

'You've got three jobs in two weeks. That's incredible!'

Since my session with Ruth, I've done twice as much preparation, filmed twice as many takes on my self-tapes for twice as many roles. I thought I worked hard before, but I realised I'd really been slacking by sleeping for seven hours every night. Still...

'It's not *enough*,' I say. I auditioned for six parts. Even though I haven't seen Mae, and have no way of checking until the cast lists are announced, it must have been her who got the others. That means we're even.

'Aren't there *any* more I can go for?'

'I like your drive.' There's the sound of her typing and moving a rattle out of the way. 'There are some small things looking for your casting type, but I don't think they're...'

'I'll do them,' I say.

'Sure,' she says. 'If you want to exhaust yourself to make me more commission money, that's fine. Just don't, whatever you do – Judie, please!'

There's a sound of a bash and then a wail.

'Don't do what?' I say.

'What? Oh, I have no idea. Sorry, my brain is occupied keeping two of my literal flesh and blood alive. But think of it this way: commission from your acting jobs means I can hire a nanny which means I can work to get you more acting jobs. And maybe even stay slightly sane.'

The sound of screaming.

'Ham! Don't— Oh God. Right. I need to clean up their bodily liquids and then give them more bodily liquids. I'll leave the paperwork with Louisa. Keep up the great work, Kenneth.'

Ruth's advice was good, but clearly it's not enough for me to just be a supercharged version of myself – I need to change myself drastically.

I knock on Raph's open door. He's whittling.

'Raphy, can you pray for me?'

'What will be, will be,' he smiles, working at the old wood. 'As with all of life's seeming problems, it's not about trying to fix the world around us, but instead about looking inward to discover it was never broken.'

He shows me the wood which he's shaped into a heart.

'Maybe you would benefit from therapy.'

'Raph! For Christ's sake, I don't need therapy, I need to thwart my enemy! Can't I make an offering to acting gods or something?'

'You *could* try a Bacchanalia,' he says thoughtfully. 'But I always find I just come away with a terrible hangover.'

I get on my knees in front of him. 'Raphy. Please. You are *so* good at getting the universe on your side. Isn't there *something* I can do?'

'What about manifesting?' asks Ruth smugly, from the doorway.

Rare annoyance falls over Raphy's face.

'Manifestation as a power shouldn't be equated with… with mere wish fulfilment,' he says.

'Oh?' pouts Ruth. 'You mean one of your pseudosciences doesn't work? I'm surprised.'

Raphy glares at her, then at me. I quickly put my hands into a gesture of prayer. He ties his gorgeous golden curls up on the top of his head.

'Fine,' he says. 'But don't say I didn't warn you.'

I was hoping Raphy could just say some magic words and make me a celebrity with my foot on Mae's neck. Instead, he reaches over to a wicker chest at the end of his bed and pulls out scissors and a glue stick.

'You're going to make a mood board. If you are truly aligned with your desires and your needs, then this will act like a magnet out to the universe. Be as specific as possible.'

I love Raphy, and clearly spirituality works for him – I've seen him manifest size twelve sparkly heels in an Oxfam in Luton – but cutting up magazines with names like *Radical Candour*, *Om*, and *Ice Cream for the Inner Child* doesn't feel like the most productive use of my time.

Still, I try. I snip as fast as I can. I find a lot of gold rings (to be the best), roses (to be thrown at my feet during encores), and rainbows (international gay fame). I must have beginner's luck, because I open one onto an article about the role of the supernatural in Shakespeare, and there is an actress playing my dream role – Viola in *Twelfth Night*. I carefully cut her out.

Unfortunately, this inevitably makes me think about Mum. *Twelfth Night* is her favourite play too. The first time I saw it performed was with her. It was the moment I first knew I wanted to be an actor.

The glue stick slips and I end up mangling the cut-out Viola's foot. Trying to smooth it down, I tell myself I should *not* be manifesting Mum's return into my life. Not only is it definitely not what I want, it's also the last thing I need.

Still, as I look at Viola on my mood board, the memories start to ripple across my vision, like my brain has a low-budget cinematographer.

It was an Open Air production at The Globe, the year my parents separated. I was thirteen, and every weekend my mum collected me from the flat above Pete's, where I lived with Dad on weekdays, to stay in her new cottage in Hertfordshire. I was given a taste of her better life: her handsome new partner John to replace Dad (though Mum and John never officially married, and Mum kept the name Clooney even after the divorce), and her beautiful new daughter, Amy, to replace me. Amy's even the same age as me, but different in every other way – long blonde hair, good at sports, breezily popular. She made an effort to be nice to me, I'll give her that. But I wasn't allowed to like her, or John, or the wisteria cottage, or their pizza-free meals, or any of their adorable pets. (They have three rescue dogs, Watson, Robin, and Spock, and, genuinely, a pig they saved from slaughter. Her name is Piglet but everyone just refers to her reverentially as The Pig.)

No, I wasn't allowed to like anything about their parallel life – that would have been betraying my dad.

Mostly, those weekends, I hid in their second-best bedroom and tried to watch films my dad liked – violent tales of betrayal and revenge, like *The Godfather*, and *Scarface*, and other age-inappropriate gangster films.

But then Mum took me to see a play. I can't remember why it was that we went that first time – maybe Mum bought the ticket (with John's money) because she knew I liked acting at school, or because she felt guilty that we had once played all sorts of make-believe games together and now we didn't. Looking back, I suppose I could have refused to attend, but I argued in my mind that it wasn't *really* betraying my dad to go to see a show, because I would just be giving Mum the silent treatment for a few hours, which is what I'd been doing anyway.

It changed my life. I couldn't believe that these words – words that, when I studied them in school, were so unfamiliar and difficult I had to pore over footnotes and research their meanings – suddenly made sense. Here, in the mouths of actors, this seemingly foreign, dead language was alive, was *mine*. These weird old stories felt real. Relatable. Important.

I couldn't believe a woman could be, not just some man's lovely princess, but the main character. Here was a woman dressing in a man's clothes, saying brilliant speeches, getting the audience on her side, and I wanted to be just like her. In hindsight, yes, I probably fell in love with the actress playing Viola as much as I fell in love with the part. She had glimmers of that sparkle which I saw again with Annabel Finch (and, terrifyingly, in Mae Jones).

After the show, swept up in the magic, I forgot I wasn't allowed to talk to my mum. We raved the whole journey back, about the acting, the story, the set, the direction, trying to remember every detail. We wanted to pinpoint why it was that the actress who played Viola was so captivating, tried out different words to describe it: Stage presence? Charisma? We ended up calling it 'magnetism': that hypnotic, liveliness like an electric current that holds your attention; which complements the other actors' energy too. Mum and I spoke fast, as if trying to squeeze in all the quantity of words we hadn't said to each other the rest of the week. Then we pulled up to the cottage, and John and Amelia opened the door, and the pets all ran out to greet us. I almost stroked The Pig's big ears. Then I remembered I was a traitor, and didn't talk for the rest of the night.

But the next week, Mum bought us two tickets to a musical.

Those weekend shows were how I got my real education in theatre. They were an escape, sure, from feeling like I was always doing something wrong, that I hadn't found the right words, that it was my fault Mum and Dad didn't love each other anymore. But getting lost in those shows was also when I felt most myself.

Raphy's sounds of the sea playlist ends. My memories dissolve back into the present-day room.

I can't believe I've spent a whole afternoon on mystic arts and crafts. The Gods had better bloody show up.

Raphy steps back from my mood board.

'Did I do it wrong?'

'No,' he says. 'It's just... Very powerful... Too powerful.'

I hug him and rush to pin it above my bed, over the top of my posters and playscripts. I stare at it, trying to get it into my subconscious, or whatever. I force all thoughts of my mum and her new life out of my mind. That's pretty easy – I've had plenty of practice.

But no matter how hard I try to concentrate on the images of my personal success, my fantasies keep involving Mae. Mae's gloating face, in an audition room, or behind a camera, or watching from the wings, about to steal the show.

9

Unfortunately, I must be amazing at manifesting.

The next week, I get called in for the second round of another play about the AIDS crisis, and in the audition room, Mae's waiting for me. Smirking.

'Jones.'

'Clooney.'

We sit in charged silence. I had planned ten witty put-downs to say to her, but they've all gone from my mind.

The three other actors in the room – variations on the 'adorable twink' casting type – shuffle their chairs to turn away from us. Clearly the tension between us is putting them off their preparation as much as it's putting me off mine.

'You look stupid,' I say.

To be fair, her jumper *is* ridiculous. Orange and fuzzy. I don't know how she could think it's appropriate.

'Ouch,' she says, pretending to be stabbed in the heart. 'God, and I bet you worked so hard to rehearse that.'

She leans forwards, resting her head on her chin to look at me.

'So, how's our rivalry going for you? I haven't seen you on Broadway yet?'

'The West End,' I snap. 'I'm British, I'd be on the West End.'

Mae grins with the satisfaction of annoying me. One of the boys coughs. I lean forwards to hiss at her privately.

'How are we supposed to know who is winning the competition when I have no way of knowing what parts you've got?'

She shuffles her chair closer.

'Clooney, have you been Googling me?'

I roll my eyes. What does she take me for?

'Obviously. Thoroughly. But Mae Jones is nowhere to be found.'

She looks relieved, then cocky. She leans back, tilting her chair onto its back legs.

'Stage name,' she says.

I stare at her.

'You went to the effort of crafting a stage name and the surname you chose for yourself was... Jones?'

She swings on her chair.

'I don't need a memorable name to be a memorable person. Having a quirky acting name would be overcompensating, don't you think?'

I flush. I didn't *choose* to have the same name as the awards for excellence in the television industry, nor a surname that links me to one of the most famous actors of our age – although I have wondered in the past if it might work as subliminal messaging for casting agents. Evidently not enough.

Mae rocks back down in satisfaction, stretching her arms above her head.

Above her fluffy sleeves, I notice a small tattoo on her right wrist. I've always thought it's deeply unprofessional for actors to get tattoos – you should be a blank slate for whichever characters you're going to become. Hers is a navy blue wiggly line that I think for a moment might be an infinity sign, or a clumsy sea lion. But then I realise it's an '&'. I confess, having punctuation embedded into your skin appeals to me, but it doesn't correspond to my impression of Mae.

'What's so special to you about an ampersand?' I ask.

She glances at her wrist, then at me.

'I can tell you,' she says, 'but I promise you're going to hate my answer.'

I rear back.

'Oh God, it's not some kind of sex thing, is it?'

'Not exactly.'

Mae looks at her wrist, traces the blue line running over her veins.

'It's to remind me to be present in the moment I find myself in,' she says, 'and to say yes to whatever life presents to me...'

She looks up at me, her eyes sparkling.

'No,' I say.

'Yes,' she says.

I groan. 'You mean, "Yes, and."'

We both laugh, then remember who the other is, and abruptly stop.

'I cannot *believe* you have an improv tattoo,' I say, shaking my head. 'That is officially the saddest thing I've ever heard.'

'And you are an expert on sad,' she agrees.

I give her a sarcastic clap.

'I bet you don't have any tattoos,' she says.

'Because I'm an uptight loser,' I nod. 'Good one.'

'No, because you'd think it would be unprofessional.' She sits up rigidly, and does an impression of my RP accent. 'An actor is not allowed to be an individual, for an actor has the potential to represent every individual. Therefore, the key to a lasting career is to eliminate all trace of your life outside of the stage. An actor should be a blank slate for their characters.'

I blink at her. Then I realise I haven't replied.

'I don't sound like that,' I mutter.

'I don't sound like that,' she mimics, perfectly.

Mae gets the part.

10

'Emmeline! You're not concentrating!'

'I *am*, Dad!'

The problem is, I'm concentrating on my audition lines.

Dad's had to pull me into the staff room to tell me off, which is completely fair. I accidentally gave two tables the wrong pizza orders this evening, including Bert. Despite the fact he's ordered pepperoni every week for over a decade, I tried to give him a Portobello.

'Look, in the end, there was no harm done,' I say, sweating. 'And now we know for the future that Bert is very, very allergic to mushrooms.'

Dad throws his hands up.

'Sometimes I think you don't even *care* about pizza.'

I gasp. Admitting that I think pizza is merely one of many different kinds of nice food in the world would result in me being disowned.

'Of course I do, Dad,' I say with my rehearsed sincerity. 'And ours is The Best Around.'

He narrows his eyes at me.

'Emmeline, pizza is more than just bread and tomato sauce.'

'I know *that*, Dad. It's got cheese—'

'Pizza is *important*,' he says, slamming his fist into his palm like the football coach before a big game. 'Pizza is family. Pizza is history and pizza is modernity. People will always want pizza and pizza will always, *always* be there for them.'

'Yes, Dad,' I sigh.

Dad folds his arms and looks back at the restaurant.

'Go onto napkin duty.'

This is the restaurant equivalent of being put on the naughty step. I bow my head and go behind the counter to fold the napkins into triangles. They're patterned with pizzas that means when you fold them along the right line they look like an individual slice.

From her front of house chair at the entrance, Carmella sniggers.

But actually, despite the embarrassment, it's ideal. I'm left alone to mutter lines while I origami.

When I finish a decent size stack, I check my phone. I've had a Google alert. I set it to email me whenever there is a mention of 'Mae Jones' and apparently there's a new Instagram account: @therealmaejones. The poor last napkin gets crushed into a tight ball.

Omg hiiIiIii guys!!! reads the first caption. *An acting friend said it's important to be online to tell everyone about all the parts I'm getting, so here I am! I'll be posting updates NON-STOP. I'm counting on you to tell all your cool creative friends in the acting/casting/producing/directing biz about me. Let's get all those gorgeous, gorgeous queer characters looking like me!*

I hate her. I hate her, I hate her, I hate her.

But I also can't stop staring at the photo of her. It's a professional headshot, with a plain grey background, like the one I have in mine. But whereas I'm, of course, wearing black, she's in one of her garish shirts, a beetle green that clashes brilliantly with the intense blue of her eyes. In the first photo, she's flaunting her trademark 'cheeky grin'. She looks like an advert for orthodontists. In the second photo, she's more serious. She's leaning towards the camera, her lips are just slightly parted, as if she's about to tell you some incredible gossip.

I zoom in on her face, her horrible, better-than-mine face.

My finger slips. I like the photo.

I scream.

The customers around me look over in alarm.

I hold up a glass.

'Saved it!' I laugh, and duck back behind the counter to assess the damage.

Despite only making the account an hour ago, Mae already has nearly a hundred likes. Presumably she did that option to connect the numbers in her contacts, and all her love interests have been quick on the uptake.

She won't have noticed my like. And besides, it's for occasions like this that I don't have my name in my handle. It's all OK! It's all OK.

I click through to look at Valerie's audition list email with renewed desperation.

I had previously crossed through one of them, for a company called 'Saucy Sausages: a new meat experience'. They're sausages stuffed with curry sauce. The casting call says they're looking for 'a short-haired LGBTQ+ woman to share a sausage with a long-haired LGBTQ+ woman'.

OK, so it's against my vegan principles. And against my (admittedly low) self-respect. *But...* It's good for the CV because it's prime-time TV viewing. And commercials are usually very well paid. Most importantly, Mae will be going for it, and I refuse to let her beat me over a meat doughnut.

I'll just have to stay up late tonight to record the self-tapes. I'll ask Pete if I can take home some veggie sausages to cook as props.

My phone flashes with another notification with @therealmaejones. Surely she can't have announced a part *already*?

My stomach plummets. It's a private message.

@therealmaejones: *i thought enemies didn't 'like' each other?*

I do now drop the glass.

The restaurant cheers. I lean down to clear up the shattered pieces, trying to laugh along with them. Blood pounds in my ears.

I put the glass in the bin and take a breath before checking my phone again. I must have just been having a waking nightmare.

As I stare at the screen, Mae sends another message.

i know you're there, clooney

and i know it's you

who else would be enough of a loser to call themselves StanislavskyDevotee100?

I close my eyes. Damn, damn, damn! Point to Mae.

I press on the bar to reply, then immediately regret it. Will it show her that I've seen the message? I can't have her see the amount of time it would normally take me to craft a comeback. Breathing fast, I type:

Frankly, I'm surprised you know who Stanislavsky is.

Mae types back with no hesitation.

you left his book behind at the tipping the velvet audition

I blink.

well, half of his book

left me on quite the cliffhanger on page 120

I blink harder. Did she really keep it? I respond:

I'm surprised you can read.

And she replies:

i'm surprised you liked my photo

I type *I'm surprised I like it so much*, then realise that's just a compliment. I delete it. I bet Mae can't resist double-messaging.

She can't.

i bet you prefer the second one

My cheeks heat. I don't need to click onto the photos for them to appear in my mind. She's testing me.

I do, actually.

You don't look as offensively happy.

She replies:

i prefer the second headshot on your spotlight too

I know it's only out of enemy research, like me, but the thought of her, somewhere else, looking up my acting profile, at the same time as I'm looking at hers, makes me feel light-headed.

you look like you have a slightly smaller stick up your ass

I snort, then stop, as if she can see me. I type:

Thank you for the constructive feedback, which I will be ignoring.

And she comes back with:

so let me check i've got this right – rivals can't text, but they can dm?

I sneer:

You started it, Jones.

She replies:

can't help but notice you're not ending it

I stare at her message for a second, the blood deafening in my ears. Then I triumphantly turn my phone off.

I fold the rest of the napkins very fast, forcing myself not to turn it back on.

11

Valerie emails me a few days later. Saucy Sausages liked my self-tape! Or, more likely, they didn't even watch the self-tape that I spent the early hours of the night rerecording, but I'm the right 'look' for them.

Unusually for a commercial, they have hired a space for the actors to come in person for a group chemistry read because they want to 'ensure maximum sauciness between the talent'.

As I walk up the corporate workspace lobby, I notice my heart is pounding even more than it usually does before an audition. There's something about anticipating being in proximity to Mae that makes my blood boil, I guess.

We've been messaging since the other night, trash-talking and trying to put the other off their preparation. She hasn't posted about the Saucy Sausages audition on her Instagram, but that could be part of a ruse.

I wonder what colour of stupid shirt she'll be wearing today? I wonder what kind of smile she'll use when she insults me.

I look around. Mae's not here yet. Typical of her.

It's bizarre, being in casting commercial rooms. Typecasting is far more overt than for theatre, and even more than for TV or film. It's like walking into a scene from *Where's Wally?*. There are five variations on 'manic pixie dream girl' type on the seats opposite me, all with pink hair and dungarees. Then on my side, there are two other 'short-haired butch' types. Sandy Lopez and I nod at each other. I recognise the other from my late-night competition searching – El Kearns – and mentally scan their show reel. Neither of them are a threat like Mae.

A few minutes later the doors are closed and the director calls us all forward to receive the briefing.

She's not here. Did she not get through the self-tape round? Does this mean I've won? Why doesn't it feel like that?

'We'd like to see you interacting with the sausage,' instructs the director. 'Our brand is saucy, so we want you to deliver.'

I spent three years of my life at the best drama school in the UK, training in the noble art of acting. And here I am, watching a room full of queer people trying to seduce a sausage on a stick.

Some dance with their sausage. Some whisper sweet nothings. One strokes a finger along its side. Another nuzzles it against their cheek.

I wince at the thought of the fatty oil seeping into their pores.

But hey, it's easy to judge them. I'm worse. I haven't moved at all. I can't lose this part to someone who isn't even Mae. What would she do right now?

I readjust my stance. Then, sultrily, I drop to the floor. I land on the floor kneeling with my legs wide apart. Holding the fork in two hands, I lick along the full length of the sausage and then, looking right down the lens of the camera, I take a big bite.

OK, I haven't eaten meat in several years now, but I hadn't remembered it being so... sawdusty? Triumph flares through my mind: carnivores truly are idiots; even a Linda McCartney's better than this.

On the other side of the camera, I see the faces of the audition panel. They're all open-mouthed, watching *me*. I'm impressing them. Keep going.

I try not to let the disgust show on my face, instead imagining it's one of Pete's finest Emmy Special pizzas. I chew slowly and deliberately, questioning what exactly the 'sauce' in the centre of these sausages is, because honestly, it tastes like glue.

That's when I realise the casting panel's faces are not impressed – they're horrified.

'That's a prop sausage,' someone says.

Then the casting panel start yelling.

'Spit it out! Spit it out!'

The other lesbians stop and stare. In my shock and horror, I gulp.

There's a moment where no one moves. I remain kneeling on the floor, the half-chewed sausage on a fork in front of me. Now that I've eaten it, it is very, very clear that the brown casing is paint over newspaper.

The cameraman turns the camera off respectfully, and takes his hat off. I start heaving and, with a sprint start, stumble to the toilet.

As auditions go, I'm not sure this one should be written up on a blog for my old drama school success stories. Nothing shouts 'give me a BAFTA' less than throwing up a fake currywurst.

After I flush, I remain on the floor, staring at the fake marble tiles.

This is all Mae's fault. If it weren't for her, I would never have put myself through this. And she isn't even *here*.

I gargle water from the tap, frantically chew three pieces of gum, and avoid my own eye in the mirror.

By the time I summon up the courage to leave, the other actors have gone, but the casting team are still there. I would usually shake their hands and thank them for the opportunity – not today. But as I'm trying to sneak past, they turn to me with a mixture of revulsion and awe.

'Emmy Clooney? You're hired.'

12

Valerie speeds the contract through. The commercial will be paying me half upfront, and it's more money than I've ever had for an acting job. I've also finally had the full *High School* contract, which I'm due to be filming as Lesbian Number Two next week.

Sure, acting should never have been about the money. But now I don't know which is sweeter: being in the green in my bank account, or imagining Mae's face when she sees me on prime-time television.

I cook a leftover vegan sausage casserole for R&R to celebrate.

But then Raphy comes out of his room, doubled up in pain. I run to him, but he holds up a martyred hand.

'I've never been better,' he says, clutching his belly. 'I've had a lot of encounters with my demons today. At Equinox laughter yoga, we danced for thirty minutes each while our partner just…' He shakes his head. 'They just stared. Bearing witness. I danced and danced and wept and wept and no one said anything. It was incredible. Awful, obviously. In an incredible way.'

I pour the rest of the red wine from the casserole into a glass for him.

'Thank you,' he gasps. 'But *then* I had reiki and discovered my heart chakra is completely imbalanced.'

He looks at me as if that explains everything.

I say, 'Oh!'

'Right?! No wonder I've been having shifts in my emotional

experiences lately. I need a radical realignment. It's too wild a time to be thinking about love.' He shakes his head. 'Global politics. The climate crisis. Mercury retrograde.'

Even *I* know that one means something bad.

I say, 'Oh no!'

'No, it's good,' he says, earnestly. 'Change is not the enemy. Change is the only constant.'

I taste the casserole, but something's missing. Without trying it himself, Raphy adds in a spoonful of Marmite and a hearty dash of paprika.

The front door clatters and there's the clop of Ruth dismounting from her high heels. She strides into the kitchen, slams her laptop down on the table, and does a power pose.

'I had a huge day!' she says. 'I am up for promotion! And if I get it, I would have even more responsibility! I'd be managing twice as many people and have twice as many clients! Twice as much work as now!'

Ruth is smiling. It's unnatural and terrifying. Raphy and I look at each other.

'Congratulations?' I try.

Ruth starts crying.

We're both at her side in a flash, guiding her to the sofa. Raphy hands her a very used linen handkerchief. She waves it away, pointing to her make-up.

'I just…' She sniffs angrily. 'Urgh. I know it's the best thing for my career but…'

Raphy uses the handkerchief to carefully dab at her beautiful eyeliner. This makes her sob harder.

'Sometimes it's just all so *much*. Every night I tell myself that tomorrow, tomorrow is the day I'm going to catch-up on all my work, get to the end of my to-do list, have one hundred life-changing ideas, finally *arrive*. And instead, every morning when the alarm goes off I already feel like I'm behind. Something goes wrong, or I lose focus, or purpose. I've never done enough. I never do enough.'

I stroke her back.

'You work so hard,' I say. 'It's no wonder you're burnt out.'

She screams.

'I don't have time to be burnt out! Other people have it together. I bet Mike never feels like this.'

'Everyone needs to have a break sometimes,' I say.

She wheels round to glare at me. 'And when was the last time *you* took a break?'

I swallow. 'Well… Acting is different.'

'Why?' she demands. 'It's still work. Just because it's not in an office. You're still packaging yourself to make money for someone else.'

I pretend I need to go and stir the casserole.

'You sound like me,' jokes Raphy. Ruth blows her nose.

'Even when I'm not at work, I'm still thinking about work. Even when I'm with you guys, or with my family, or lying in bed trying to sleep, I'm still going through my fucking inbox in my mind. I dream about ticking off those little red flags. It never stops. I just want one day, one *hour*, where I can… Stop. Do absolutely nothing.'

Ruth's watch alarm beeps. She stares at it. Then she suddenly screams, rips it off and throws it across the kitchen. It knocks Raphy's hand-made Buddha statue, which wobbles like a surprised jelly.

I go to set it straight. Raphy picks up her hand, stroking the place where her watch has left a mark.

'Ruth, I feel like I'm being called to help you,' he says. 'I truly, truly believe I can. I can help you find calm, and peace, and fulfilment…'

'Yeah? Well I truly, truly believe I can help *you*,' she snaps. 'I can help you find success, and ambition, and purpose, and money, and—'

'What would I do with money?'

She pulls her hand away.

'Raphael, you love to pretend you have nothing to do with

money because your family is rich. You don't *have* to work to exist. Please don't claim you're some kind of ethical superior because it's a choice the vast majority of people don't get to make.'

Raphy pushes the curls out of his eyes, looking bewildered but earnest.

'I understand that I have a huge amount of privilege, and that no one can control the circumstances they're born into, for better or worse. But this isn't about me. You're saying you wouldn't work if you didn't have to have money. So we need to work towards abolishing the capitalis—'

'No, I'm *not* saying that!' Ruth shouts, starting to pace. 'It's a lot, and of course there are ups and downs, but I *like* my job. My parents are proud of me. I *want* to be challenged. I *want* to learn. I *want* to give back.'

She picks up her watch from the corner and clips it back on, stopping the Buddha's vibrations. 'I mean, you claim you're living such a noble life, Raphael, but you spend all your time working on yourself. You make it seem like I'm selfish for having a career, but the pursuit of personal enlightenment is *more* self-absorbed. At least I actually make things for other people. You sit around doing yoga all day – what are *you* giving back?'

Raphy slowly unfolds his legs from lotus position.

'I'm not hurting anyone,' he says quietly. 'And I'm not knowingly contributing to systems that harm others.'

Ruth throws her hands up. 'It's not my personal responsibility to reform the world.'

'That's where we disagree.'

'I'm doing the best I can!'

'And that's all any of us can do,' Raphy says. 'But sometimes, to be the best version of yourself, you have to be willing to listen to other people's ideas, even when they're different.'

Ruth folds her arms stubbornly.

'Fine,' she says. 'Convert me.'

Raphy closes his eyes and takes a deep, meditative breath in through the nose and out through the mouth.

'I'll do everything you tell me to,' Ruth continues. 'Or, sorry.' She puts her hands in a sarcastic prayer sign. 'I'll do everything you "invite me to practice".'

'Ru, you know I find it difficult to be kind when you're unkind.'

Ruth pauses. Then she nods, and crouches on the sofa in front of him.

'You're right,' she says. He sighs. 'I'm serious,' she insists. 'It's sensible to look at what your competitors are doing, but you should also look to businesses with completely different models. That's how progress happens. So. Help me.'

Raphy considers her, fiddling with his witchy rings.

'But in return,' Ruth says, '*you* have to listen to *me* too. You need to get out of your apathetic bubble and join the real world. Oh, you can keep all your hippie beliefs, but at least try to enlighten other people too. Practise what you preach, but also preach what you practise.'

While they've been talking, they have gotten closer and closer to each other, and they're breathing heavily. They both seem to have completely forgotten I exist. Not wanting to get caught up in committing to teach either of them about acting self-tapes or stage directions, I stay quiet, stirring the bubbling pot.

'Come on,' Ruth says, with her deal-broking confidence. 'Maybe a secret part of you has been trying to manifest this ever since we met.'

Raphy presses a hand to his heart chakra and gives her a rueful smile. 'This is not exactly what I put on my mood board, no.'

'Well, change is the only constant.'

She holds out her hand for him to shake.

Raphy tilts his head, a curl breaking free from his bun. Then he takes Ruth's hand and kisses it.

'Then it's agreed,' she says, looking a little flushed in triumph.

'6.30 a.m. tomorrow, we'll have an agenda meeting where we set our project goals.'

'Fine,' says Raphy. 'But in return, at sunrise, we meditate in the garden.'

'Guys,' I call from the hob. 'Sunrise is *at* 6.30 a.m. at the moment. Can I join?'

They jump, then zealously invite me along.

The casserole does taste better than the prop sausage.

13

I can't believe I'm finally on an actual television set. It's a tangible next step on the road to being a legitimate actor. Sure, I'm only in one episode, and sure, I only have one line ('Fuck off, Christina,' to be said in between canoodling Lesbian Number One), and sure, it might get cut in edits, but still.

Not to be creepy, but I'm also excited by the promise of kissing someone today, even if it is only a stage kiss with a fellow performer. I've forgotten what it feels like.

I've read hundreds of (smug) acting blogs about what it's like to be in a TV shoot, but the thing that surprises me most about the *High School* set is just how many people there are milling about. Runners run, wobbling trays of flat whites. There's an industrial-size coffee and tea vat, and a water cooler with triangular paper cups. There are catering staff, restocking cling-filmed plates of sandwiches, crisps, and massive bowls of liquidy fruit salad. Two sad little paper plates have individually cling-wrapped pastries, hurriedly labelled 'gluten-free' and 'vegan'. I chew mint gum instead.

I look around with my gaydar on, trying to work out who will be playing Lesbian Number One and apply another round of lip balm (unflavoured and nut free, just in case).

Everyone is gravitating to Amber Lenowitz, the actress playing the lead drug-taking teenager. She is already a B-lister and by far the most famous talent attached to *High School*. Those acting blogs also told me the importance of networking, that the closer you get to success the harder you should throw yourself at people – but I can't bring myself to talk to her. Or indeed to anyone else. Everyone looks so confident and self-contained.

I bet Mae would be talking to Amber. Amber would probably fall in love with her.

The thought makes me think about how, however awkward I feel being here right now, I have a great excuse to send Mae a gloating message at the end of the day. My brain starts trying to craft witty quips.

After what feels an age of silently chain-chewing gum, the showrunner gathers everyone together.

'Morning, all,' she says, both weary and upbeat. 'We've got a tight schedule, as per bloody usual, so we need to get straight on with—'

The door behind her opens and in walks Mae Jones.

My whole body slackens.

She's wearing the same *High School* costume as me – a red-and-pink-striped tie over a white shirt and black trousers – but where my tie is neatly tight (as ties should be), hers is fat and cropped, worn low over her half-unbuttoned shirt. Her hair has been gelled into a punkish explosion, and her eyes have been made-up with carefully amateurish green liner. She reminds me of the popular secondary school girls who bullied me.

'So sorry,' she mouths, and runs into position behind the group.

My neck hurts at how quickly I turn my face away so that she won't spot me. My brain is struggling to compute.

If Mae is here, she must be Lesbian Number One. Lesbian Number Better than Me.

'Oh, Mae! Hi!' The producer waves chirpily. 'Grab a snack!'

I dare myself to look back. The other extras around the food table move along to give Mae a path, grinning back at her as if they're old friends. Maybe they are. I see her take the cling film off the vegan plate, and start eating my pastries.

Now I *have* to glare. I don't care who else sees me. I'm glad I practised it in the mirror to make it the stoniest, coldest frown possible for the next time I saw her. (Yes, it also happens to make my cheekbones look good. Coincidence.)

Mae glances back across the room, and our eyes meet. For a moment, she just stares back. Then her mouth spreads into the slow, smug smirk that I know she reserves only for me. She is not surprised to see me.

She knew! She knew I'd be here! Damn her! She must have seen it on my agent's website. She deliberately didn't post about being involved in this show so that she'd have the upper hand.

I do a performance of being unfazed, and turn back to the show-runner, who talks through the line-up. I'm finding it incredibly hard to concentrate, sensing Mae sliding through the crowd.

'— chemistry class – camera close-up Christina – they all snort the—'

But wait. Mae *can't* be Lesbian Number One. If I'm Lesbian Number Two, Number One *has* to be femme. That's the rule of portraying queer couples in the media, isn't it? You *can't* have two short-haired women kissing—

Shit. Mae and me. Kissing.

The gum nearly falls out of my mouth.

'Well, hello, Clooney,' says a low voice. 'Fancy seeing you here.'

I turn to glare at her, forgetting to craft my stony cheekbones. I point at the showrunner and mime zipping my lip.

'Oh, chill out,' she says, ripping off a segment of the vegan croissant that should be mine. 'It's fine. Have you not been on a set before?'

It's too much. I don't know why my body decides to act out this way, but I slap the pastry out of her hand.

To my horror, it flies far. As if in slow motion, I see it hit the head of Amber Lenowitz. Defying gravity, it lodges in her hairspray. Amber reaches a slow arm round to her painstakingly groomed hair, and squeals, then spins to us. The rest of the group follow her lead.

In a split second, I turn to stare at Mae too. She does a double take, looking at me, then the others. I register the moment where she realises I'm passing the blame. In a flash, she adopts an impression of an adorable bumbling Hugh Grant.

'Crumbs! Amber, I am *so* sorry,' says Mae, stroking pastry flakes off Amber's shoulders. 'I'm an incorrigible klutz. Could you ever forgive me?'

Amber does not scream in outrage, or demand that Mae is fired.

'I'm clumsy too!' she giggles. Mae runs a practised boy-band hand through her hair and Amber's eyelashes flutter. My blood goes from cold to boiling.

The showrunner coughs amusedly. 'If we're all done food fighting…?'

Amber and Mae nudge each other in cahoots, then the showrunner continues as if nothing happened.

I watch as Mae glances back at me and, smiling like a shark, tips the crumbs from her plate into her mouth.

I don't hear any of the showrunner's instructions after that.

'Lesbian Number One and Lesbian Number Two, over here please,' someone calls.

I take a deep breath and start to walk over. Mae turns too, matching my stride.

She holds two fingers out in front of her. 'Remind me, which number comes first, one or two?'

'Not surprised you have difficulty counting, Jones.'

I'm grateful for my brain supplying a comeback while I'm in panic mode. A stage kiss is not a real kiss, duh, I'm not a child. But still… Does Mae know?

I glance at her. She keeps reaching up to scrunch her wild hair, her hand barely leaving it alone.

'It's ironic, really,' she says. 'I'm not even a lesbian. I'm bisexual.'

'What?'

I nearly fall over.

'Wow,' frowns Mae. 'Not surprised you're biphobic, Clooney. Adding it to the list of all your other charming qualities.'

'No,' I flush, 'I…'

Mae isn't even a lesbian, yet she's still cast as a 'better' one than I am! Jesus Christ, it's so humiliating.

'It really has nothing to do with me,' I say stiffly, 'who you are or aren't attracted to.'

Mae raises her eyebrow.

The person who called us over introduces himself as Robbie.

'I'm the intimacy coordinator, here to ensure that filming scenes of a sexual nature are done in a way that's comfortable for all involved.'

I learnt about intimacy coordinators at drama school, but I've never been involved in a project that needed one before. It adds a feeling of legal formality, like a wedding contract. Porridge writhes in my stomach.

'Now' – he checks his notebook – 'there isn't any specific act required for you guys. You don't need to touch any particular parts of each other's bodies, over or under clothing, and there's no contracted nudity.'

Mae starts to laugh.

'I didn't realise the Lesbians were hooking up. I'd have worn my best underwear.'

My mind, unbidden, flashes with images of what might constitute Mae's best underwear. Calvin Klein boxers and sports bras like me, or pink lace and—

'That won't be necessary,' says Robbie, unphased. 'What are you comfortable repeating in multiple takes?'

'Oh, I'm up for anything,' says Mae, chirpily. 'Tongues, dry humping, full-on intercourse.' There's a wild tone in her voice now. '*Apparently* I just broke up with my "girlfriend", so I should take any action I can get!'

I glance at her in surprise. I can't imagine Mae being anything other than an impeccable girlfriend. Not to my personal taste, obviously, but—

'Emmy?' asks Robbie. 'What about you?'

I blink, still staring at Mae's profile. Now I'm noticing her red-rimmed eyes and pink-tipped nose... She looks back at me, no longer joking. I suddenly realise that Mae has a whole life outside of our rivalry that I know nothing about and for some reason that makes me feel... ill.

'Number Two?'

I know I've frozen, but the more I think about it the more stuck I become. Who was her girlfriend? The girl at the party? Or someone else even more talented and beautiful? This whole time me and Mae have been texting, trash-talking, competing, she's been holding hands with someone. Did they ever laugh about me? Is Mae heart-broken? Was she in love with her?

Behind Robbie I see the director having a hurried conversation with technicians, wiping sweat from their brows. Amber Lenowitz is in her newly touched-up hair, waiting for the command to have a choreographed manic hallucination.

This is a professional television set, with hundreds of people involved in creating a take, and I'm just one tiny part of the machine, my job simply to kiss someone in the background. But I can't do it, just because of some weird thought I've had about my co-star. Oh my God, I'm clearly not cut out to be a professional actor after all.

'Actually,' says Mae suddenly, 'I just remembered. I have a cold sore. Many cold sores, actually. Really nasty. We absolutely should not kiss.' She laughs self-deprecatingly. 'Sorry.'

'Oh, wow,' says Robbie, veering back, then remembering himself. 'Don't worry, this happens all the time.'

I start to unfreeze. I glance at Mae's mouth. I can't see any cold sores. But if she doesn't have one, then why would she...

My cheeks burn. She must have been so horrified at the thought of kissing me – even stage kissing me – that she would rather humiliate herself on a professional set than come too close.

'In that case, Lesbian Number – sorry – Mae, you hold

Emmy's face in your hands, Emmy, you hold Mae's waist. Then after Emmy says her line, go back to stroking each other.'

Mae nods. After a moment, I do too.

'So,' says Robbie. 'Say what you're going to do?'

'I'm going to reach my hands out and stroke your cheek,' says Mae, not meeting my eye.

'I'm going to hold your waist,' I say quietly back. 'Then after I say my line, I'm going to touch your neck.'

There are sounds around us of the scene being ready to roll.

Still not looking at me, Mae tentatively holds her hands out to my face. I take them and place them on either side of my face. Her hands are as cold as my flushed hob rings of cheeks are hot.

'Happy?' asks Robbie. We both nod, infinitesimally. 'Lovely, now hold until the take.'

Mae's hands have warmed now, or maybe my cheeks have cooled. I wonder what she does to get those gentle callouses. My actor's hands are only ever roughened from script papercuts.

It proves impossible, at this proximity, not to look at her.

I know from endless self-tapes that my eyes are grey-blue, blank, reflective, like a mirror. But hers. Bright cobalt, textured with intricate patterns, irises ringed with gold, swirling with warm, living flames. Hers contain a universe.

Now, though, I also see the still-lingering redness of her blood vessels, the wetness of her eyes, the new swollen bags under them. Mae's girlfriend – ex-girlfriend – must have hurt her badly to make her cry this much.

The thought of it makes some vengeful demon inside of me rise with sudden and wild violence. *I'm* Mae's enemy. Only *I'm* allowed to make Mae feel bad.

Mae's still staring back at me, and she asks quietly, 'Are you OK?'

I just nod, my jaw tight. 'You?'

She meets my gaze, holds it there steadily.

'Yeah,' she says. 'I am.'

There's a tiny bit of tissue caught in her hair. Seeing it there makes my chest ache. Without planning what I'm going to do, I reach for it slowly, and remove it. Touching it releases a waft of citrussy shampoo. Her hair is softer than mine. Superior in every way. But, just this second, I don't mind.

I suddenly remember that this was not on the approved intimacy list and remove my hand from her hair like it's electric.

'Sorry,' I say. 'You had a…'

I show her the tissue to prove my innocence.

She looks at it.

'Right. Right,' she says. And then, so softly I'm not sure if I misheard, 'Thank you.'

There's a call for silence on set. We hurriedly look away from each other, shake out our arms.

'Ready for take one,' calls the director.

We readopt our position, hands on either sides of our faces, and reconnect eye contact.

'Action.'

In theory, three high school girls sashay down the corridor next to us, passing pills between each other. But I don't notice it at all. I don't notice anything except Mae's face.

It doesn't feel like looking in a mirror anymore. Now I'm noticing all the things that are different from my own face – the infinite small improvements that build to an almost unrecognisable finished product. It's like the changes from the base layer of a painting to the one that hangs in a gallery. Mae's face is the finished draft of mine; hers had feedback from professionals until it was perfectly polished. Sure, at a distance, if you're squinting and not really paying attention, we look alike. But right now? It's embarrassing to think I ever compared myself to her.

I'm dimly aware of sounds nearby, someone shouting. Mae's expression changes from sarcastic to hesitant to… suddenly alert, trying to signal something.

'Cut!'

That wakes me from my stupor. Rustles of frustration from camera crew and cast.

'Lesbian Number Two? Where was your line?'

Oh my God.

'I am – *so* sorry.'

'Come on, let's be professionals here, OK?' She sighs and shouts, 'Reset!'

In the next take, I'm so alert and scared of forgetting my cue, I can't concentrate on anything. Mae's eyes stare into my own in mutual panic.

When the time comes, I am premature in my shout, cutting off Amber's cue line before it's even out of her mouth.

'*Fuck off, Christina*!'

In my palms, Mae winces. Even I'm aware I sounded like a pantomime villain.

'Cut! This is television, Number Two. Do less.'

I nod, swallowing hard. I try to remember my training. I am a canvas for my character. I am a mask. My emotions are not my own. I will not cry.

'Going again. Lesbians, can you look more natural, please?'

All my planning. All my research. It isn't working. I'm going to mess it up again and no one can recover from being a tiny extra messing it up a third time. I'll be axed and I'll never work again.

A soft touch on my cheek.

'Come back, Em,' whispers Mae. 'It's OK. Be here. Whatever you're feeling, that can be what Lesbian Number Two is feeling. Just go with it.'

I should be outraged that Mae is giving me acting lessons. But it feels strangely helpful. What am *I* feeling? Confused. Frustrated. Ashamed. And something else, something that's making my whole body hot.

Mae licks her lip. Still no cold sore. The vengeful demon rises. I let my shoulders press into her, put my hand on her lower back and pull her closer towards me.

'Action.'

I'm half-conscious that I'm acting, and that this is my enemy.

But I also know, completely, that this is the most alive I've felt in forever.

So when some popular bitch tries to start a fight, I pull Mae protectively out of the way. Her hands slip from my cheeks to round the back of my neck. I look the irrelevant girl up and down, mutter, 'Fuck off, Christina,' then turn back to Mae, against the locker under my arm, and dip my mouth down to kiss her neck.

'Cut.'

I pull away as if electrocuted. The taste of Mae's citrus perfume is on my tongue. I hold a hand over my mouth, in shock, in horror and to stop it from doing anything else it's not allowed to.

'Got there in the end,' shouts the director. 'Moving on. Shoot 23E.'

Everyone immediately disperses to set up for the next scene, and I look anywhere but at Mae. She hasn't moved from leaning against the locker.

What's *wrong* with me?

'That wasn't very enemies of you,' says Mae quietly. Her cheeks are flushed. I can still feel the ghost of how they felt in my hands. Her salty neck. I'm so ashamed I want to be vaporised.

'It wasn't me, it was my character,' I say, not meeting her eye. 'Just doing my job.'

She doesn't reply for a second.

'Right,' she says. She folds her arms and laughs a dark, nasty laugh. 'Just doing your job. Silly me. Because kissing me would be even worse than losing some stupid rivalry game.'

My chest tightens. Is that what she thinks our careers are? Is my livelihood a joke to her?

'Jones,' I say, 'this isn't a game.'

'No,' she says coldly. 'You're right. Games are meant to be fun.'

14

In the living room, Ruth and Raphy are 'learning from each other'. Ruth is trying to meditate, Raphy is trying to make a LinkedIn page, and I'm trying to do both. Impressively, I'm failing worse than they are.

Ever since the *High School* shoot I haven't been able to concentrate. It's bad. In fact, it's existential. I haven't got another acting job lined up, unless you count my full-time commitment to checking if Mae has messaged me.

But when I click the screen on, a different horror awaits. I have a message from my mum. Raphy senses a shift and frowns up at me over his screen. I avoid his eye and open it.

Good afternoon, Emmeline, are you well? I hope you won't mind, but I saw the update on your agent's website that you have been cast in a lot of exciting roles recently. I just wanted to let you know we'll all be watching High School *when it's out, and keeping our eyes peeled for your commercial too. I know how competitive those are, so I hope you're enjoying celebrating your wins. Hello to you and Pete and Julius from all of us.*

And then she sends me a picture of a big pink blur, with wild eyes and gnashing teeth.

The Pig is very proud of you.

I swallow hard and press at my eyes. I'm usually adept at controlling my tear ducts, but Mum's always had a knack for disrupting that process.

My thumbs hover over replying. I very nearly do. Then I remember myself, shake my head, and close the one-sided conversation.

Instead, I text Dad guiltily, asking for more shifts at Pete's'zas. He sends a thumbs up and a pizza emoji.

Well, I can tell I won't be making any progress on my supposed career for the rest of the day. I sigh deeply and open up Instagram.

It starts playing a video at the top of my feed: it's an animated stage poster from Thalia Brown.

Ruth screams at me for interrupting her peace. I don't reply. I'm too busy staring at Thalia.

'Emmy,' says Raphy, an amount of time later. 'Are you doing what you want to do with your one wild and precious life?'

'Mm-hmm,' I say, zooming in.

Gorgeous, distinctive, inimitable Thalia – her treacle eyes looking straight down the lens, her gap teeth biting her lip indecently. She's straddling a chair, completely assured, with her legs spread horizontally wide. On her top half, she's wearing a turtleneck under a blazer; on otherwise bare, long, glossy legs, she's wearing crisp white boxers. On the waistband is the repeated title of the show: BRIEF.

It's already got stars from all the right places, a mix of reputable and edgy. The biggest quote is from the notoriously hard to please Alice Sefton at *The Atre Online*: '*Thalia Brown is the nation's new darling.*'

Thalia's caption reads: *Lovely Londoners! I am beyond humbled to be bringing my one-woman show* BRIEF *to my favourite Boards Theatre next week!*

My jaw drops. Boards? Our old stomping ground? The last place we saw each other?

I've never written a stage play before, but it's been the most incredible experience to share MY journey in MY words. I've never been so candid about something that's very close to my heart... I would be so grateful if my precious friends – old and new and yet to be made – came to support me. I love you all. Links to buy tickets here x

I read it again and again. 'Old' 'friends'? I know it's *not* a message directed at me. But... What if it is? What if she's trying to reach out? What if there's some reason she can't reply to my WhatsApp messages for half a year but she *can* tell me how much she loves me through the medium of an Instagram caption? Oh my God, what if her play is all about *me*? Our too brief—

Raphy snatches my phone.

'Your energy is scaring me,' says Raphy. 'You need to purge that website.'

I scream and grab it back from him. What if he liked the photo or somehow revealed my obsession to the world! Or saw that I was on forbidden Thalia's page! It took Ruth and Raphy long enough to persuade me that what Thalia had done was ghost me, and that was a really shitty thing, and not a sign of a good ongoing friendship. They wouldn't understand. I never admitted that our bond had been more than just a friendship. For me, at least.

I scuttle to my bedroom and hide under my blanket to study her poster in more detail. The light from the screen glares directly into my brain. But the poster of Thalia has been replaced – replaced with a photo of Mae. A selfie of Mae, with Amber Lenowitz.

Oh fresh Hell! Mae has her arm around Amber, who is gazing adoringly at her. Mae is looking gloatingly at the camera, as if the photo is just for me.

Can't wait to take a lot of (definitely not real) drugs with this one! ;)

It has hundreds of likes, including several verified accounts of idols I follow: Emma Watson, Jordan Peele, and Annabel Finch. My heart throbs in jealousy. *How* is she this well-connected?

I'm astonished to see that Annabel Finch has also commented underneath.

Look at you two! So at home on set. Can't wait to hear all about it xx

Hang on. Have I just gone fully mad in my paranoia, or is there something about that message that doesn't sound like an actress complimenting a colleague? It sounds almost like...

The blanket falls from my shoulders. I look up from my desk at my poster of Annabel Finch. She smiles warmly back at me, with her supernaturally bright blue eyes, round dimples, and charismatic energy.

I look at Mae's headshot, which I printed out and stuck up above my bed with drawing pins in her eyes.

I slowly unpin Mae, and hold it next to Annabel.

I gasp and drop them.

Mae's unusual accent. Her stage name. Her weirdness when I mentioned Annabel at the party, and her prodigal familiarity with the industry and high-profile contacts despite having only worked as an actor for months.

With trembling fingers, I check Annabel Finch's Wikipedia page, scrolling to the section I never usually bother with: Personal Life.

Annabel Finch has two daughters: Avril and... Mae.

For a moment I just stare at the posters of them both. Then I rip up Mae's headshot into tiny pieces and scream.

'*I HATE HER!*'

The world is red as I pick my phone up and, pulse in my ears, furiously type a message.

@StanislavskyDevotee100: *I know your secret*

Mae sees the message instantly.

@TheRealMaeJones: *oh yeah? which one?*

I jab each letter out hard.

Your mum

This time, the typing dots pause, then:

isn't that insult a bit pre-pubescent even for you?

And I say:

I'm not playing
I know the identity of your celebrity actress mother
I know that you are a nepotism baby

I know that any success you have or have not secured in this industry is as a result of your family and your networking, not your own talent

I watch the screen triumphantly.

Then, to my astonishment and alarm, I see that Mae is calling me. I didn't know you could even *do* that on Instagram. Like a bomb disposal unit, I carefully but quickly press the cancel button. She must have pressed it accidentally and be just as horrified as I am.

But then she calls again.

I let it ring out.

clooney i will not stop ringing until you pick up

I look around me, as if she might have cameras in my room. I do a power pose, check my door is shut, and pick it up, leaving the video off.

Then Mae's voice is in my ear. 'What do you want from me, Clooney?'

My breathing becomes shallow. It's so strange, hearing her voice as if she's right here. I stare at her holey headshot, the printed smile not matching the malice in her voice.

'I… Wait, you're the one who rang me!'

She pauses, then, 'You're the one trying to blackmail me!'

'Christ!' I say, appalled. 'No I'm not.'

I look out of my window at Raphy, showing a reluctant Ruth how to harvest lavender. I wonder what Mae's looking at right now. I wonder what the view is. Is she in her bedroom, like I am? Is her ex-girlfriend there?

'Why not?' she asks.

I don't answer. Damn it. She's right. Why didn't I think of that? This could be exactly my trump card. I could insist that she stops acting, or I'll sell her whereabouts to the papers. Or something? I start pacing.

'What's your plan?' Mae demands.

But for once in my life, I don't have one. I had just… Messaged her. Without thinking it through.

I swallow.

'That's for me to know,' I say, 'and you to find out, when you least expect it.'

'If you reveal my parentage to anyone in the acting industry or the media, I *will* find out all *your* secrets and I *will* make you pay.'

'Oh, who's blackmailing who?'

'I'm serious,' hisses Mae.

'Well, that makes a change, doesn't it, Jones? Or should I say... Finch?'

It's as if the phone is suddenly on fire.

'Don't you *dare* call me by that name,' she hisses.

I sit on the bed. The intensity of emotion in her voice right in my ear is breaking my knees.

'I am doing my career completely independently, OK?' says Mae. 'I am doing everything, *everything* I can to make sure that my mother is nothing to do with it. So *don't* bring her in to this. She is *not* part of our rivalry, OK? She's off the cards. Veto.'

'OK,' I mumble.

'And if you *ever*... Wait, what?'

'OK,' I say. 'I get it. I agree to your terms.'

'I... Oh. Right,' she says. 'OK then. Thank you. I mean... Not *thank you*, obviously, but...'

'Yeah. I understand you.'

We listen to each other breathe for a moment. I can't tell if I'm in a horror film or... something else.

I hang up.

15

'Out! Out! Brief! Candle!'

Thalia is in the centre of the stage, holding a burning skull above her head. I can see the outline of the techie through the backstage curtains, primed with a fire extinguisher.

I didn't tell R&R that I bought tickets to see Thalia's new show. I didn't tell anyone. If Mae can have secret celebrity connections, so can I.

I'm sat in a restricted view seat at the back, to the side. Even though I had a very vivid fantasy about being in the front row, catching Thalia's eye, and her stopping her performance because she was so overcome with the emotion of seeing me again, I didn't want her to see me sitting on my own. Besides, I couldn't afford the front row. Even this ticket cost thirty pounds. Thirty pounds to see Thalia Brown talking about herself for an hour on a Saturday night. It used to be free.

When she first walked out onto the stage, wearing her Brief boxers and suit jacket, I nearly fainted. So she *is* still alive. She is a physical flesh and blood person who has thumbs capable of texting me back.

It turns out that no, the play is not about me. It's about how hard it is, being very, very successful. That's it, really, other than the spectre of an unspecified traumatic incident from her past. This has led, the play implies, to her seeking approval from strangers and having lots of ambiguously fulfilling hot sex.

Standing tall in black lingerie and pink heels, she is now overtly signalling a finale.

'Life's but a walking shadow, a poor player.'

Thalia does an elaborate gesture with every word, somewhere between spoken word and interpretive dance.

'That *struts*' – she struts – 'and frets' – she frets – '*her* hour' – she clicks her fingers in a gesture of feminist empowerment – 'upon the stage and is heard...' She takes a deep breath and shouts. 'No more!'

Blackout.

My eye twitches. I don't understand. Thalia used to be a good actor. Didn't she?

I remember an exam where we all had to pretend to be animals. I challenged myself to choose the hardest I could, finally selecting a frilled-neck lizard (*Chlamydosaurus kingii*). I went to the zoo's reptile cages every day for a month to study them. Thalia chose a lioness. They sleep twenty hours a day. When it came to exam day, she simply lay down and had a nap. I thought she was a genius.

Am I just viewing her performance in a poor light because she's hurt me? Or did I used to confuse my feelings for her acting with my feelings for her?

But when the lights come back up and Thalia returns to the stage for her bow, the audience rises for an ovation. Everyone around me is whooping. Roses are thrown onto the stage. I can't understand it. Maybe everyone is only cheering to try to get her attention?

I believe audiences should only give standing ovations if the show really deserves it, otherwise the whole concept is devalued. I've only given one in my life, and that was... Well, that was for Annabel Finch.

I swallow. Even over the applause, I swear I can hear Mae's voice in my head. She's saying, '*Don't* bring her into this.'

I watch Thalia – the gorgeous friend I used to think might, possibly, like me back – take a third bow.

I stand up and cheer.

★

After Thalia's performance, the audience file out into The Boards foyer. I feel as though I'm jostling with the ghosts of the times Thalia and I visited as drama students, gossiping about everything that was wrong with the show we'd just seen. This time, I look round in silence.

'She's just as beautiful in real life, isn't she?' someone giggles to their friend. 'Do you think she's selling those boxers as merch?'

The Boards' foyer is wine-coloured (actors can't resist a red carpet), and has impressively tall ceilings, with curling stairs that surround a glittering chandelier even the Phantom of the Opera would envy. Around the staircase there are larger-than-life photos of productions past. As you ascend the stairs, the renown of the featured actor also increases, until you reach the gods on the top floor: Judi Dench, Maggie Smith, Mark Rylance, and – God, can I never escape? – Annabel Finch, playing Lady Macbeth, her hands covered in imaginary blood.

Thalia's biggest fans head out to the backstage doors to get her autograph. I have *just* enough self-respect not to do that.

But I find my feet have walked me towards the smoking area. I hesitate.

Does Thalia still smoke one ceremonial cigarette after a performance? Who rolls them for her now?

If I really thought she was going to be here, I wouldn't open the doors.

But there she is.

Thalia's standing alone, smoking a pink e-cigarette. The air smells of stale ash and synthetic strawberries. She's still wearing her white boxers and lace bra, with her long blazer draped over her shoulders. I marvel at how her whole look is so different now – her make-up more 'classic' Hollywood, her hair out of its ponytail into long waves round her shoulders. Even her body is different – skinnier, less muscular. I guess it's natural to change when you have a full brand team.

But the pink summer sunset catches on her, and I have vivid déjà vu: the way her hip juts to the right, the way she holds her phone with her little finger poking out, the way she inhales like she's never needed anything more than that nicotine. It could be a year ago, or two, or three, about to gossip about all our classmates; about to get drunk and share our deepest hopes and fears; about to move increasingly close to each other until the theatre closes and throws us out.

Thalia glances up and her eyes flicker over me. My mouth opens. She turns away and returns to scrolling.

My stomach flops to the floor. I can make no excuses now. Thalia is officially ignoring me. She hates me. I've been cancelled, deleted, abandoned. I fumble with the doors.

But then I hear her voice.

'Oh my God, *Emmy*? Is that you?'

I turn back and mirror her surprise.

'*Thalia*?! No way! Hi!'

Thalia steps towards me and circles her arms around my neck. I breathe in, my chest aching. Chanel Coco. I clutch her, breathing in deeper, but her e-cigarette is in my face. I splutter away, cursing myself, choking the pink smoke down. I worry she's going to think I'm crying.

'What are you *doing* here?' she asks, long eyelashes fluttering in surprise.

'Oh, I...' I blink back. 'I was just having a meeting about a part.'

She smiles. 'Ooh! What part?'

'Oh, umm, it's... it's nothing really.' Her smile fades. I can't bear it. I put my hand to my face in a gesture of confidentiality. This was one of our in-jokes, back in the day. 'It's confidential.'

Her smile returns, and she tosses her hair behind dangling earrings.

'I *thought* you might have come to see my show.'

I know she's only pretending to be offended, but the feeling

I've let her down makes the blood rush to my cheeks. The fact that I *did* see her show doesn't make me feel any better.

'I... Oh! Yeah! Of course! How's it going? I saw your poster, it looks amazing. Great, umm, great font.'

I am making myself cringe, but Thalia doesn't seem to notice anything wrong.

'What's it called again?' I ask. '*Beach*? *Beef*?'

I want to slap my own face.

'*Brief*,' she laughs. She puts her hand conspiratorially to her face. 'It's not very good.'

I'm so overwhelmed by her doing our in-joke that I can barely concentrate on what she's saying.

'I put the whole thing together in, like, a day,' she says. 'But I just didn't have time between filming everything else. It was so last minute. You know how it is. When I was up for MBFWTKM,' (she pronounces each letter of the acronym separately, so it takes me a moment to work out she is talking about *My Best Friend Wants to Kill Me*), 'out in cinemas next summer, they said, "Thalia, darling, we love you, but we need your image to be more artsy and authentic and deep". So Walter – you know, my agent – set me up with this little run here. He said, "Thalia, darling, just make it a bit Shakespeare, a bit feminist, and a bit sexy." So I really followed that brief.'

'Ha!'

She blinks uncertainly.

'What?'

'Brief?' I say, questioning my own sanity. 'You followed the brief for *Brief*?'

'Oh,' she laughs, but I know it's one of her fake ones. 'Right!'

I remember in second year, getting Thalia a birthday card of two peas in a pod. How she squealed because she had already got me exactly the same one.

'Oh my God,' she says suddenly, touching my hand. My stomach twists. 'Emmy, do you remember what we said at our showcase?'

I stare at her. I can't believe it's *her* who is saying this. I played out so many hundreds of versions of this conversation with Thalia – increasingly surreal explanations of why she stopped messaging me, all the way to her completely ignoring me in person too – but never once did *she* bring up our showcase.

'Er… What in particular?'

'Emmy!' she squeals. 'Where's your super-brain memory gone? We promised to meet here, a year after graduation, to toast to our successes. Shit, it's already nearly that time, isn't it? When…'

'June 29th,' I say quietly.

'Right!' She clicks. 'June 29th!'

'I thought you'd be too busy,' I say.

She laughs and gets up The Boards' theatre website on her phone.

'I'm never too busy for my friends!' she says. 'It will be such a nice break from all this bloody *filming*. Look. The show that day is some gay Shakespeare thing.' She suddenly claps her hand to my arm. 'Wait – is that your exciting meeting from earlier?'

All I can do is shrug mysteriously.

'Maybe…' I do the conspiratorial gesture. 'Maybe not.'

Thalia claps her hands delightedly.

'Well, isn't this all just perfect! I'll come and see you! And then we'll toast to our careers afterwards, right here, at this very table. June 29th.'

She puts it into her horrendously busy phone calendar. It looks like Ruth's. Thalia sighs at it, then puts her hand back on my arm.

'You're lucky, you know,' she says. 'It's hideous, being in demand. Enjoy this time.'

She looks so at ease, so un-self-conscious, tapping away on her phone and waving her e-cigarette, as if she would be doing completely the same thing if I was here or if I wasn't. It's a blissful familiarity.

I misunderstood this whole 'ghosting' situation. I must be missing something. I must seize this opportunity.

'Thalia… Did I do something wrong?'

'What do you mean?' she asks, not looking up.

I stare at our shoes: my polished old Docs, her costume pink heels.

'I just…' My head's spinning with all the things I wish I could say, with all the things I'm not allowed to. Don't say I wish we were still close. Don't say I miss you. Don't say I was once in love with you. 'If there was something I had done, or if I could do better, or…'

'Oh Emmy,' she says, and puts an arm around me. The touch makes my throat painfully tight. 'You haven't done anything wrong.'

I sniff desperately, but I already feel a glimmer of hope. It *was* worth the risk. I'll finally find out why she stopped replying.

'I know I've been more successful than you,' she says, 'but it doesn't mean I'm *better* than you, necessarily. Walter always says: don't work harder, work smarter.'

She pats my shoulder.

'When I was about to go in for the third audition for MBFWTKM' – (Does she know it would take less time to say those one syllable words than to spell out their letters?) – 'Emma Thompson gave me some great advice. She said, "If you want to be successful, don't try to be clever, don't try to be different, just be exactly what they think you should be".'

This doesn't sound like Emma Thompson, but who am I to question what Thalia's celebrity friends say in private?

Her phone vibrates in her hand. I blink at her in increasing suspense as she checks the notifications before clicking the screen off and turning back to me.

'You're not doing anything wrong, but you could definitely do more right. Your look is solid, but it's a bit… Well, it's not that radical, any more, is it, to just be a lesbian? Even if you do have short hair.' She gives me an appraising glance. 'You could get a nose ring?'

The smoking area doors open.

'Thalia, darling, your adoring fans are getting impatient!'

Thalia rolls her eyes and picks up her things. I feel the moment slipping away, try desperately to snatch some of it back.

'Well, I guess I'll see you around,' I say. 'Or maybe I won't! It's fine either way! Congratulations about everything!'

'Emmy, why are you saying that like it's goodbye?' she laughs. 'You're coming to my after-party, right?'

A final ray of golden sunset pierces through. Thalia's lit up with a halo, her sparkly eye-shadow fluorescent, her lipstick as bright as her smile. Relief, triumph, joy, all flood through me. This is proof. Thalia *is* still my best friend, she's just been busy. God, why do I always have to be so dramatic?

Her after-party will be full of successful industry folk. The fact that she's asking me either proves that she thinks of me as a big enough deal in showbiz that I'm not cramping her style to be there, and/or that she likes me enough to have me there anyway. I can't decide which I'd prefer.

'Of course I'll be there,' I say. I do our conspiratorial gesture once again. 'Wouldn't miss it.'

Thalia's head tilts onto its side and she smiles her wonderful, real, gap-toothed smile.

She says, 'You haven't changed a bit.'

The Hollywood man coughs, and the spell's broken again.

Her autopilot celebrity voice comes back as she air kisses my cheek.

'See you soon, darling!'

16

I return to the Boards Theatre attic bar for eleven o'clock. I guessed the after-party details from scrolling back through the BAFTA NOMINEES 2K?? chat – someone else was a backing dancer in a production and explained how she could get others on the guest list. Turns out having acting friends *can* come in handy.

I'm in my Red Carpet Premiere outfit. I've never worn it before. It's a tailored white shirt and loose-fit black pinstripe suit, with my Doc Martens (polished again). I'm styling it with the chunky silver watch Dad got me for my twenty-first birthday, and a plain chain round my neck. My hair is extra-carefully quiffed.

The high-ceilinged room is dark but has bursts of multi-coloured light everywhere, like even at parties performers can't resist being under spotlights. A disco ball gives flecks to everyone's tipsy eyes, loosens limbs. Everyone is lavishing each other with praise, whether or not they were involved in this particular show, and just as eagerly insulting anyone who didn't make it here. Heads are thrown back in laughter, everyone definitely having more fun than anyone else and wanting them to know it. No one looks anyone else in the eye, always checking the room behind them in case there's someone else more impressive to talk to.

I can name every person in this room. I can name the shows they've been involved with; I can tell you their reviews; I can tell you how many online followers they have. All these people I'm supposed to emulate: their glitzy clothes and sparkling smiles, their well-performed confidence and affected humility.

But even more than those who are successful sharks, I notice the insecure fish on the fringes – the unsuccessful or uncool, and the tech crew, always ignored by performers until they're needed. Sure, they are almost definitely more skilful and nicer people. But I can't look like one of them, not in front of Thalia.

Mae would be great in this situation. She'd be magnetically drawn to the other most interesting people, schmoozing in the most endearing way, becoming everyone's fast friend. Worse, she'd probably be enjoying it.

So when I see Thalia's beautiful bare back through the crowd, I know what I need to do.

I down my champagne glass and impersonate Mae. I pull my shoulders back, smile broadly, tilt my chin roguishly. I ruffle my hand through my hair and walk with a bouncing lope towards her. Thalia's hugging a woman with dark blonde hair, tied into a complicated French plait. The Emmy part of me hesitates, waiting for them to part.

But then the woman pulls back from Thalia and meets my eye.

I recognise her immediately. Alice Sefton, a critic at *The Atre*. She's a few years older than me, perhaps approaching thirty, and holds herself with the assurance of someone who knows her reputation precedes her. Her thin lips are lined in a tasteful nude pink, and her eyebrows are neatly drawn onto her artfully matte forehead. She's wearing a figure-hugging emerald dress, belted at the waist, with silver heels that bring her to the same height as model-tall Thalia.

But what's weird is that Alice is staring at me as if she recognises *me* too. Which is impossible. She would never have seen any of the small-fry shows I've been in.

Thalia sees her expression and turns round. Surprised, she gestures between the two of us.

'Oh! Emmy? Have you two met?'

'I don't think I've had the pleasure,' says Alice, breathlessly, from under curved brown eyelashes. I'd place her moneyed accent along the Kent coast.

'Well then,' says Thalia, annoyed at not being the centre of attention. 'Allow me to introduce my absolute *best* friend in the whole wide universe–'

I flush with astonished pleasure.

'– the marvellous Alice Sefton,' Thalia finishes.

'You're too kind, really, darling,' says Alice, tucking a non-existent stray hair behind her dangly earring.

Alice holds out her hand with her knuckles on top, making it clear that what she's expecting is for me to kiss it.

Some instinct from watching old black-and-white films kicks in.

'*Enchante*,' I say, bowing over it. Alice smiles at me, a princess pleased with her new knight.

'This is Emmy Clooney,' says Thalia.

'No relation,' I say, before I can stop myself.

Alice clasps her manicured nails to her chest, throws back her head and laughs for an extended period of time. Thalia and I glance at each other and it's almost like the times when someone in one of our lessons was acting badly. But then Alice rests her hand on my forearm and Thalia looks at that instead.

'My goodness,' says Alice, sumptuously. 'Aren't you simply perfect? Thalia, where *have* you been hiding her?'

This woman could make or break my career with one stroke of her pen. And she's looking at me with what I can only describe as 'goo-goo eyes'.

'We *mustn't* keep the woman of the hour,' she says to Thalia. 'Emmy– is that short for Emmeline? Why don't you accompany me to the bar to get a *proper* drink.'

I look back at Thalia. For a second, I can't read her expression. But then she's engulfed in a wave of adoring fans.

Alice orders herself a martini, reeling off specific instructions for its preparation which I don't take in, and, without asking, orders me an Old Fashioned. This is absolutely not a drink I would have chosen for myself, but it seems like it would be rude to refuse. At least it's an open bar, so I don't have to worry about the etiquette or pain of paying for it.

I clink my glass to hers. She's one of those people who makes very deliberate, intense eye contact with you when glasses are clinked. The green of her jumpsuit must have been chosen to compliment her hazel eyes, piercing into mine.

'So tell me, Emmeline—'

I grimace.

'Oh, really, please call me Emmy.'

'*Emmy*,' Alice murmurs, as though it's a fancy flavour of ice cream. 'I'm afraid I can't return the favour, there isn't really a conventional nickname for Alice.' She touches my arm. 'Unless you'd like to give me a private one.'

A tentative prickle rises on my arm under her fingers. Is she...? She *can't* be interested in me, can she? No, she's so far out of my league that it's ridiculous for me to even consider it.

'How do you know our Thalia?' she asks, taking a sip of her martini.

'We were in the same year at drama school,' I say.

'Saint Genesius?' she asks, with clear approval.

I nod, taking a tiny sip of the whiskey, and trying to style out my choke into a neat cough.

Over her shoulder, I watch Thalia throw her arms around a handsome actor I recognise from a recent Bollywood sensation. He takes her hand and they walk off towards an exit. I wonder if he's going to roll her a cigarette.

'What did you think of her show tonight?' asks Alice.

I look back at her, wrong-footed. She said it with a mischief that implies her own thoughts are not positive. Alice is Thalia's 'best friend', isn't she? She gave that wonderful review that's all over her poster?

'Well, I respect your professional opinion more than my own,' I say, carefully.

'Please don't misunderstand me,' she says, touching my arm. 'I *love* Thalia. Dearly. As a friend. A *sister*. But as a performer... Don't you think she's lost her way?'

She takes a sip of her martini. She looks at me conspiratorially, companionably, like we're old friends, well-practised in gossiping. She hasn't removed her arm. I choose my words carefully.

'*Brief* didn't seem very... her.'

Alice stares at me in awe, as if I've just solved quantum mechanics. 'Exactly. That's exactly it, you're so right.'

I stand a little straighter. Maybe I should be a theatre critic? Maybe I'm a genius?

'She thinks she's on the brink of commercial success so she's trying to pander,' nods Alice, popping the martini olive into her mouth. 'This barely formed attempt at "modernising" Shakespeare, the nondescript past trauma, the underwear – it's so cliche! There's nothing of herself in that show. Nothing, ironically, of what made her successful in the first place.'

I kind of agree with her, but I don't want to say the wrong thing. What if this is some sort of test of loyalty?

I imagine the three of us, Thalia, Alice and I, discussing a new play. What if that's the way my friendship with Thalia is meant to progress? A holy trinity, like me, Ruth and Raphy?

'Fortunately for her career, it doesn't matter,' Alice is saying. 'After all, she's exactly what Hollywood is looking for right now. The industry can pat themselves on the back for diversity, while getting her to play the same old problematic tropes written by straight old white men.' She tuts. 'It's not Thalia's fault. It's nothing to do with her, really. Lord knows it's hard enough for anyone minutely "different" to break into this business. She's simply ambitious, and this is her way to success. It's up to her how she chooses to use it, once she's made it. But for now, she's playing their game, and she's playing it *marvellously*.'

She does a little ironic curtsey, then clicks for another martini and gestures for me to drink up.

I can't believe Alice Sefton is being so frank with me. It's as though we've skipped years of small talk and she's treating me as someone who has earned her trust. I'd always taken critics' reviews at face value, thinking that they were their honest, expert, somehow impartial opinion. Now I realise that was impossibly naive. They're a business, there to sell the paper and form industry connections.

When I meet Alice's gaze, her eyelids flutter again.

'But tell me about *you*,' she says. 'I want to know all about *you*. What are you working on at the moment?'

I'm too embarrassed to say that I don't have anything lined up, so I mumble something about a television shoot and a commercial in post-production, making them sound more impressive than they really are.

I'm surprised to see she's already finished her next drink and is clicking for another.

'Now look, er…' She hesitates for a second.

'Emmy,' I supply.

'Emmeline, yes. I knew that.' She slaps my arm again and demurely hides a burp. 'Emmeline Clooney. Forgive me if I'm misreading, but am I right in thinking that you are a lesbian?'

Actors dance on the dance floor beside us. Alice's eyes don't leave mine. I seem to be getting asked that an awful lot recently.

I nod. Alice smiles slowly and pulls out the stick with the olive on, popping it into her mouth.

'Well then,' she says, 'how would you like to see a *good* show sometime? With me?'

I choke, whiskey going up my nose.

'I get review tickets to so many shows,' she says, languidly. 'I'd like you to be my plus one.'

'I…' I swallow. 'I'm flattered, truly. But… Why me?'

Alice laughs a short, sharp bark.

'Emmeline,' she says, opening her clutch bag with a snap and pulling out the latest iPhone. 'I've been messed around by enough people in my time to want to be frank and upfront with people.'

She hands her phone over to me.

'I'm interested in you. You're an attractive woman, we share interests, and you seem to have a surprising amount of brain for an actress. I see it working out rather well for both of us to date.'

She waits for me to put in my number. I blink from her to the screen. She doesn't seem to consider any other option than for me to agree. Not that there's any sensible reason why I wouldn't.

As I type in my number, I think about Mae. This is surely a point to me in our rivalry. She might have a famous actress for a mother, but I can have influential friends too. An influential *date*…

I put my number into her phone and, for some reason, name myself Emmeline.

'Perfect,' she smiles. 'I'll be in touch. In fact, why wait?'

She opens up her calendar.

'How about Tuesday night? It's opening night of that Churchill play?'

'I…'

I'd have to cancel my shift at Pete's, but surely Dad would be pleased that I'm finally, *finally* going on a date – a real, grown-up date with a woman who is not straight, and who has explicitly told me she's interested in me.

'Tuesday night,' I agree.

Alice smiles and, as I watch, sends me a text.

Tuesday, 7.30 p.m., at the Old Vic xx

She looks up at me, at my mouth, and adds another x.

It must be a sign of how utterly inexperienced I am with dating, that even as this intelligent, impressive, beautiful woman is flirting with me, I don't… *feel* anything. I'm too in my head. My drama teachers would have told me off for not being embodied, not being in the moment. But I'm already thinking about how I'm going to tell this as an anecdote to R&R – how they're going to clap me on the back for succeeding in our agreement to get out of our dating comfort zones. And I'm thinking about how, even though I am finally in the same room as flesh-and-blood Thalia (a Thalia who doesn't seem to remember that she ghosted me for months), I doubt I will have an opportunity to speak to her again.

Most of all, I'm thinking about whether Mae would be jealous, if she was here seeing this.

It's that thought, really, that makes the blush rise to my cheeks as Alice leans in to me. She kisses my cheek, lingers there, and then kisses the other.

No one has ever kissed me like that. Like it's familiar. Like it's a promise.

'It's a date,' she says.

17

I summon Ruth and Raphy to the living room by blasting 'Omigod You Guys' from *Legally Blonde*. In unison, they both lean out of their bedrooms and skip in for a gossip update.

I can tell they disapprove of me going to Thalia's show, but don't have time to tell me off because I detail everything about Alice, and how she explicitly and enthusiastically asked me on a date.

'I *did* it! You said I should flirt with someone at a party and I did! Or at least, she flirted with me, which is basically the same thing. And she's… She's bizarrely cool? And very pretty. And I'll get to watch theatre for *free*! And she – she seems to actually be really into me?'

I don't add my hope that it might also be a way to re-befriend Thalia. (As predicted, even when I tried to be bold and find her, she had disappeared from her own after-party.) That can come naturally in time…

Raphy tilts his head, a curious smile on his lips.

'But how does she make you *feel*?' he asks.

I hesitate. To be honest, she makes me feel nothing except anxious about disappointing her. But that's how I feel all the time.

'Not much,' I admit, flopping on the sofa between them. 'Oh God, there's something wrong with me.'

'No!' coos Raphy quickly. 'There's no right or wrong way to feel. It's early stages. Just check in about it with yourself, when you're with her, so you know how you're really feeling, not how you think you "should" feel.'

'She isn't who I would have ever imagined myself with,' I say. I lick my lip carefully, trying to avoid Raphy's piercing eyes. 'I'm not sure if she's my – my natural type?'

Raphy waves his hand reassuringly.

'Oh, types don't exist. Why try to box individuals with labels?'

Ruth scoffs.

'You try to box individuals with labels based on their fucking star signs!'

'That's different,' he says. 'That's science.'

'And Raphael, you *do* have a type,' she says.

'How dare you!' he gasps. 'I am deeply pansexual.'

'Oh sure, maybe you don't have a *gender* type. But put anyone in flowy tie-dye in a silent retreat and a few minutes later you'll be silently retreating into the bedroom.'

Raphy opens his mouth in indignation.

'Th-that's – I—'

'Then as soon as they want to actually *talk* to you, you realise you never want to see them again.'

Raphy gasps, considers, then shrugs. 'OK, fair. But *you* do the same thing with your colleagues.'

Ruth's mouth opens this time. Then she folds her arms.

'Yeah, that's fair.'

'You guys need to break the cycle,' I suggest, smugly. 'Like I did.'

R&R look at each other over me.

'Huh,' muses Ruth, chewing on the end of her tablet stylus. 'Alternative tactics.'

Raphy nods his head slowly, then faster.

'Yes... Yes! It's the natural progression of trying to think outside of our entrenched views. Maybe this is what all my heightened heart chakras have been pointing to.'

'Date outside our usual types,' says Ruth.

'Date outside our usual types,' agrees Raphy.

'You can go on dates at the same time that I go on dates,' I add, delighted to be involved in anything that can bond the three of us. 'And then we can all share how it's going! Like best friends in romcoms!'

I nod enthusiastically and put out my hands for our three-way handshake.

Ruth and Raphy look at each other, then join in.

That night, I'm surprised when Alice texts me.

Still thinking about you, she types. *Hope you have sweet dreams! Xxx*

I look at it. That's nice, isn't it? I suppose I was also thinking about her.

I have been thinking about you too, I type. *Sleep well.*

I can't bring myself to put xs. It's not in my usual text language, even with my family.

I put the phone on my bedside table, but feel wide awake. Before I know it, I'm back on Mae's Instagram. Just for a little bit of late-night anger and angst.

She's posted a video on her stories. Amongst her other followers, she surely won't notice if I watch it? And even if she does, it's just keeping her on her toes, showing I've not forgotten her, or our rivalry, despite my recent absence from the audition circuit. I click on it.

It's a trailer. A full-length shot of Mae, dressed in a formal Victorian suit, doffing her top hat. Then Mae, in mirror image, now dressed like a modern drag king, nodding a crown in the same gesture. An old-fashioned font writes over the top, '*Tipping the Velvet*', then it flashes into a modern neon font, 'as you've never seen it before'.

I suddenly realise that, if you don't count our co-acting on the *High School* set, this trailer is the first time I've actually seen Mae act.

I can't tear my eyes away.

Mae is arm in arm with a gorgeous blonde femme. They're dancing on a stage, dressed in matching Victorian 'boy's clothes'. Mae is looking slightly off-camera, as if she is searching but hasn't yet spotted me. It cuts to a close-up of Mae, as she slowly pulls on white gloves. Then Mae is in the sweaty drag bar, about to kiss the blonde. It zooms in on Mae's thumb, stroking across a glossy lip. Zooming further still, on their mouths a centimetre away. Mae laughs, like she's amazed.

I slam my laptop shut, breathing heavily.

I'm so… I'm so…

I watch it again.

I'm so *angry*. Sure, sure, I'm jealous too – as in, I'm jealous of Mae getting this part.

But she's… She's doing it all wrong.

She's not *acting*. Oh sure, she's in costumes, and she's on camera, and she's saying lines. But she's just being… Mae. She's being completely, wholly, magnetically herself.

That's *cheating*. If acting was meant to be about being yourself then I wouldn't have had to get into lifelong debt to go to drama school.

I watch it again, several more times. Then I lie awake, staring at the ceiling, seeing Mae, laughing at me.

18

I meet Alice outside the Old Vic at exactly 7.30 p.m. I feel as if everyone is clocking her presence and, by extension, looking at me. I hate it.

I try to pull my shoulders back, as Mae would. Alice waves casually at agents, casting directors, actors and journalists, and she's generous with her introductions.

'This is Emmy Clooney,' Alice pronounces carefully. 'Remember that name. I'm placing bets on her being our next rising star!'

We stand at one of the tall tables – Alice chooses one right at the entrance – and I read the pink neon sign above us: 'Dare, always dare'. I turn my back to it.

I offer to get our drinks as she got the tickets (though technically they're free through her work). Alice smiles at me as though I've passed a test.

'My usual, please, darling.'

I go to the bar, wracking my brains for what she drank at Thalia's party. I think it was a martini, but I don't know if there are different kinds. I keep thinking about James Bond.

As I hand it over she frowns at it, and at my beer. My stomach cramps. But then she reaches her glass out to toast mine.

'So, what do you know about this play?' Alice asks me. 'Have I brought you along to a bore?'

We're seeing Caryl Churchill's *A Number*, a play I haven't

seen performed but which I know from studying contemporary playwrights.

'I find her pauses a little bit too...' I pause dramatically, 'much.'

Alice throws her head back and cackles loudly, holds her arm on my elbow. It wasn't that funny, but it's nice to have someone to nerd out with. She asks me more about the play, and it's as if I'm back in exams, using my old revision cards in my mind. I'm glad. Those hours of studying were worth something after all.

The bell goes off for the five-minute warning. I'm itching for us to be in our seats, and also wondering whether I have time for another wee.

'Oh darling, relax. It's only a play.'

Still, tiring of my agitation, Alice waves me over to pick up the tickets. I feel cool, standing in the VIP line, and when I say the name Alice Sefton the attendant nods with respect. I wish Mae were here to see it.

More bells go off for the start of the show. We're the last ones in the foyer now.

'Let me take your coat for you,' I say to Alice, as an excuse to escort her to the entrance.

'Oh, fine,' she yawns. 'Let's get it over with.'

I'm not used to being in the front row. I need to crane my neck to see the actors towering above me, can see the beads of sweat on their foreheads, the microphones tucked under their collars. I'm so close I feel as if I'm part of the show myself, the audience's eyes watching Alice and me.

She balances her notebook on her right knee and holds a pen above the notes she made from our conversation earlier.

The play is about a father and his two separated sons, who we discover are actually clones of each other. They worry about which of them is the 'original'. I try to lose myself to the story, but it's no use. I haven't been able to for years.

I used to find it deliciously easy to escape into stories, especially live theatre. Mum liked to recount the first time she took me to see a pantomime. I was nine and I didn't understand that the stage was something to be watched but not interacted with. She had to restrain me from running onto the stage to dance. When the villain crept behind the good guys and everyone around me sang 'He's behind you!', I was just full-out screaming. After the bows, Mum took me backstage. I watched as the princess took off her crown and was just Emily the drama teacher. Daisy the Cow was disembowelled and two men emerged from her insides. I was inconsolable.

Now, when I look up at the stage, all I see are actors, using the same techniques I learnt. False and hollow, trying to be more real by being less real. It's not even that they're bad – they're highly proficient. But to me, their 'spontaneity' seems forced. I hate to admit it, but the only time I've believed in someone's performance recently has been Mae Jones in the trailer for *Tipping the Velvet* – and that was because she wasn't *really* acting, she was somehow being completely herself. Faker.

On the stage, the actor playing the dad is saying a line about how being cloned damages his son's uniqueness, weakens his identity.

That's what Mae's doing: devaluing my uniqueness by being the same casting type as me. But I don't feel the same violent bitterness I had just a few weeks ago. Instead, I find I'm thinking about how Mae's voice sounded in my ear, when she thanked me.

She hasn't posted any new acting job updates since then and I wonder if she's lost her acting drive too. I mean, I suppose I should hope she has...

I wonder what she's doing instead. I wonder if she's on a date tonight. I wonder if she's still in touch with the ex who made her cry. I wonder if she's back with her, or if she's with someone else. Someone who treats her better.

I feel a sudden warmth on my thigh. Alice has slid her hand onto my leg, alarmingly high. I freeze, unsure what I'm meant to do. It's like knowing there's a fly on me, but I'm not allowed to bat it away. Starting under my knee, Alice slowly traces her pen along my trousers' inside seam. She has just reached the slight crease at the leg of my boxers when the show finishes, and she has to remove her hand to clap, and I sigh with relief.

Afterwards, we blink out into the theatre bar.

'Well,' she says loudly. 'I think we can all agree that the best thing about that show was that it was only sixty minutes long!'

I tense and glance around at the crowd, who are definitely family of the cast. They all look at her, some perhaps recognising her as a critic, and look hurriedly away again.

Before I can think of a reason to go home, Alice steers me to the bar, ordering a martini and an Old Fashioned.

She scribbles a few quick notes, saying them aloud – even more loudly – as she does so. She's talented at finding fault with every part of the production.

'As an actor,' she asks me. 'What did you *really* think of the son's performance?'

I look around. It feels like very bad juju to criticise an actor who a) likely has friends at the table next to me, and b) is tangibly more successful than me.

'I… I thought he was good.'

Alice looks at me, unimpressed. I need to give her more.

'He was solid. Professional. A safe pair of hands.'

Alice frowns at me, then starts to smile. 'I see what you're saying. Yes. He was so *safe*. He didn't take any risks. He was the worst thing an actor can be: boring.'

I wince.

'That's not—'

Alice snaps her notebook shut.

'Thank you so much for sitting through that with me, darling.

But don't worry, work time is over now,' she smiles. 'It's play time.'

'Well,' I say. 'Thank you so much for inviting me, but I should be going – I need to be up early to do some self-tapes and—'

'Oh pish,' says Alice, and gestures around at the bar. '*This* is the real work. I introduced you to the right people earlier. Stick with me and you won't need to go to work anymore – the work will come to you.'

I hesitate, and Alice takes this as permission to pull me to the far corner of the bar. The neon pink flashes: 'Dare, Always Dare'. I decide I'll try.

Three more cocktails later, Alice is leaning very close to me, and both her hands are on my legs. I can't tell if my heart is racing because I find it exciting or stressful or both. Maybe I'm just drunk. Whatever! At least I'm feeling something.

Alice hiccups, lifts the martini to her slightly smudged lipstick.

'I want you to tell me about every time you've had your heart broken.'

I look away from her stare.

'*Romeo and Juliet*,' I say. '*The Notebook*. The first ten minutes of *Up*.'

She raises a neat eyebrow. 'No heartbreaks of your own?'

I sip my whiskey. It's going down quite smoothly now.

'I haven't ever had a real relationship. I've had a few... What *I* thought were real but... In secondary school there was someone – we were in *The Crucible* together – who used to flirt with me after rehearsals. She said she didn't want to come out, that she was still deciding if she was bi or gay or not, so I didn't tell anyone, not even my best friend Ruth, and, you know, I get it, but it still didn't feel great to be completely ignored offstage.' I shrug. 'Then she started going out with the one straight dude in drama club and now they're married.' I shrug, and take a deep breath. 'And then at drama school, God, it was like the same—'

I suddenly remember I met Alice at Thalia's party. That they're friends.

'At drama school,' I correct, carefully, 'I was concentrating on my work.'

'What about hook-ups?' asks Alice, leaning over the table. 'Flings?'

I shrug awkwardly and pour myself some water.

'A couple. Unremarkable. Left the next day and never heard from again.'

'They never texted you?'

'They did, but… I knew they were just being polite.'

Alice raises an eyebrow.

'So Emmy,' she says suggestively, licking her glossy lip, 'what do *you* want?'

Her eyes are piercing in the dim light. They're pretty. Hazel. But they're not bright blue with golden flecks, and they don't sparkle.

'I want… I want to be more famous than George Clooney.'

Alice says seriously, 'I can make that happen.'

I laugh along. I'm about to say, 'I can make it happen myself,' when I bite my tongue. I've been trying for years and look at me.

'What do *you* want?' I ask her.

She doesn't answer for a long moment, then, alarmingly, I realise her eyes are watering.

'I'm so used to interviewing actors,' she sniffs. 'No one asks the interviewer anything.'

'I'm sure you're far more interesting than most actors,' I say.

She strokes my hand. I stay very still.

'I know it's not fashionable,' she says, 'but what I want is to be a wife and mother. I want a traditional family. I want to care for someone, and keep house, and… make my corner of the world perfect.'

I swallow. I must be so disappointing for her. I'm hardly wife material.

'But…' she says, 'you can't control whether someone wants to marry you!' She laughs, suddenly frenzied, then snaps back to her composure. 'So I'm concentrating on what I *can* control. My career.'

'How did you become a reviewer?'

'It was the only available slot in my school's newspaper. I thought I would move from reviews to a column to front-page breaking news. But then I realised you can influence more people with reviews. Sure, it's a smaller pool of people who read them, but they're more impactful over individual lives.'

She sucks her martini stick. 'I remember there was this boy, in sixth form. Full of himself. His "band" played at the school talent show. I wrote a review of it.'

She smiles up at me mischievously. The hairs on my neck prick up.

'He never played again.'

At that moment, a tall black man walks over to our table. I don't recognise him and assume that he's a contact of Alice's, but it's me he's wagging his finger at, like he recognises me.

'I'm so sorry to interrupt, ladies,' he says, with an accent I'd place in Manhattan. 'But I just had to say, I'm a huge fan of yours.'

My body tingles with delight. This *never* happens to me. I can't believe I get to look like a legitimate actor in front of Alice.

'You won't remember me,' he says, 'but I'm a performer too. I saw you a few months ago, and you were phenomenal. Really stand out. Darn, what was the show…'

I'm about to list my credits – it wouldn't take long – but he carries on.

'Man, it's so serendipitous to bump into you, actually. Someone's just pulled out of a gig next weekend. Would you be up for it?'

First rule of showbiz: if you're offered a part, say yes. If the performance is next weekend, I'll be expected to learn my part very quickly – but I don't have any other jobs this week. Raphy's manifestation gods are finally coming through.

'I'd be honoured,' I say. 'I've got some copies of my CV in my bag, if you'd like one? Or I can give you my agent's contact?'

'Don't worry about that stuff,' he laughs. 'Your performance is all the recommendation I need.'

He passes me his phone to add my number while he carries on explaining.

'You'd be doing what you did before,' he explains. 'You know, monologue from prompt, Harold format, a few short-forms to fill the rest of the time.'

I nod as I'm typing, though what he's saying doesn't make sense. Harold format as in the playwright Harold Pinter? I don't want to show my ignorance in front of him and Alice, who is smiling. I'll dig out my essays later.

'When are rehearsals?' I ask.

He laughs jovially and slaps me on the back.

'Good one. Oh hey, I've just remembered! It was at The Temple of Good Vibes. You know, up on Fifth Avenue?'

Fifth Avenue? But I've never been to Ameri—

My blood starts turning to ice.

'*Wild* vibe that night,' the man continues blithely, taking his phone back. 'Absolutely mad scenes. The prompt you got was, like, Trump and Boris Johnson fall in love.'

As he laughs, my stomach writhes. He's mistaken me for someone else. Someone who performed brilliant improvised comedy in America. Someone who would have a tattoo of 'yes, and' on her wrist.

I realise what's happening just as he clicks his fingers in remembrance.

'Isn't your name—'

'Emmy!' I say, shaking his hand and smiling the way I imagine Mae would in this situation. 'Emmy Clooney. No relation.'

He frowns, then shrugs. '*Emmy*, right. Well, I'm Dylan Bryant.'

'Aah, of course! Hi!' I say. This seems to satisfy him. I don't dare look at Alice.

'I'll send you the deets,' he says.

I try to stay in character. 'Yes, *and,*' I guffaw, 'I'll look forward to it!'

He laughs and walks away, whistling to himself. I take a huge gulp of Old Fashioned, in shock that I managed to get away with it. Maybe I am an improviser after all.

I take a deep breath, and turn back to Alice.

'Sorry about the interruption,' I say. I expect her to be impressed. Instead, her face is blanched.

'Alice, are you OK?'

'You do improvised comedy?' she says.

Oh, Alice is an improv snob. Like me. That's a good sign.

'No, I don't.'

Alice blinks in confusion. Oh great, now she thinks I'm a liar, or worse, unprofessional.

'I mean, improv is not my *speciality*,' I say. 'I don't prioritise performing it over my other work. But of course, I studied it at St Gen's.'

Alice doesn't need to know it was the module I got my lowest score in and the one I found by far the most difficult. But I still passed – proof that you can get good marks in any exam if you memorise the curriculum.

'I see…' she says, some pink returning to her cheeks. 'I'm afraid I'm not a great admirer of improvisation.'

'Neither am I,' I say quickly. 'But it's good practice to broaden my portfolio and… and it seemed like they really needed someone to fill in, and, well, to be honest…'

I should have just admitted that he'd got me confused with someone else. It would have been embarrassing at first, but at least she would still respect my acting integrity. And it would have been an excuse to message Mae…

Alice reaches out and strokes my cheek.

'You're very committed to your profession, aren't you, Emmeline?'

I'm flustered by the PDA, both because it's affection, and because it's public. Two tipsy lesbians, late at night, in a crowded bar. I tense. Maybe as a conventionally beautiful, long-haired woman Alice doesn't have to be as aware of how strangers will react? But she's being so sincere, it would be rude for me to break away, regardless of how I feel.

'That takes real dedication,' she says, keeping her hand on my face. 'Loyalty. Both admirable qualities.'

I can't stop remembering my cheeks in Mae's hands, against the *High School* lockers. My face warms. God, I'm a terrible person, thinking about my enemy while a date strokes my face. I try to concentrate on Alice's soft fingers instead.

'I'm sure you'll be an invaluable addition to their improvised theatre production. Bring some order to their chaos.'

I can't believe someone like Alice is actually interested in me. Is actually being kind to me.

If it was any other kind of show, I'd ask if she wanted to come and see me in it, as a second date. But she's just said she hates improv and, frankly, I'll need every bit of my concentration for the show, so I say 'Thank you,' and then dare myself to turn my head to kiss the palm of her hand.

Alice blinks rapidly, then smiles in pleasure.

'You're welcome, darling.'

I don't know how to signal that I want to go home, so I wait for her to do so. This means we stay until the bar closes.

Through the fog of whiskey, my stomach writhes with the joint fears of how the hell I'm going to prepare to be an improviser in a week and, more urgently, whether I'm meant to kiss Alice.

'How are you getting home?' I ask her, as I stumble down the steps to the foyer.

'Taxi,' she says. 'Will you be joining me?'

I clutch the handrail.

'Oh, that's fine, that's fine,' I say. 'Thank you, but I have my bike.'

She smiles ruefully. Even though she has had a lot of martinis, she seems to be very steady on her feet.

In the taxi bay, she looks at me expectantly, the moon reflecting on her jingling jewellery. She leans in.

'Is that a taxi?' I blurt.

Alice blinks and looks round at the empty road.

'Oh, sorry, I must have imagined it…'

Alice tilts her head, takes a step closer to me.

'Do you… do you have any feedback for me?' I ask quickly.

She frowns. 'I haven't seen you perform?'

'No, I mean as a date?'

She laughs.

'I have never been asked to give criticism to someone's face.'

'Well, I always welcome the opportunity to improve. I don't want to… I want to be a good dating partner.'

'All my feedback is positive so far.' She smiles, looks down, then up again. 'When can I see you again?'

Yes! If I try really, really hard, it turns out I *can* successfully date! I win!

'I'll text you?' I say.

'Promise,' she says. Her eyes are fixed on mine, glowing almost orange in the street lights.

I swallow.

'I promise.'

Alice's eyelashes flutter and she stares hard at my mouth.

I understand my cue. I'm Humphrey Bogart kissing Ingrid Bergman in *Casablanca*. I'm Leonardo DiCaprio kissing Kate Winslet in *Titanic*. I'm George Clooney kissing any of the actresses George Clooney kisses. I'm finally playing the romantic lead.

I lean down and kiss her.

I have memorised a lot of speeches in my time about the heady experience of kissing your loved one for the first time. I always knew that they were stylised, metaphorical rather than literal, but still. It's a little disappointing, to feel the same neutrality I feel kissing someone onstage.

After an appropriate amount of time, I pull back. Alice's eyes stay closed and fluttering.

'You kiss by the book,' she says breathlessly.

I'm so bowled over by someone using a Shakespeare quote on a date with me that my mouth automatically replies in an old woman's voice.

'Madam, your mother craves a word with you.'

Alice blinks at me.

'It's... It's the next line,' I say. 'From *Romeo and Juliet*. Act I Scene V. The nurse. I can do the rest of the scene if you like.'

I thank God that her taxi arrives.

'Next time, darling.'

19

The library won't be able to order in the improv books fast enough so, with the familiar twist of anxiety that comes with spending literally any money on anything, I order on express delivery *Improvisational Techniques for Theatremakers and Practitioners: Third Edition*, *Improv for Dummies* (a title I resent), and *You Too Can Be The Most Bonkers Improviser in the Whole Wide Universe!!!*.

When I asked Ruth to help with some improv scenes, she laughed wildly, showed me her work calendar with every twenty-minute pomodoro of her day blocked off until her upcoming pitch, and shut her bedroom door on me.

So I have Raphy, who I suspect will be a natural. That should be good for practising but makes me feel even more inferior. He hovers as I move my room around to create a mini performance space.

'Em…?' he asks, fiddling with a corner of my improv revision cards. 'You remember the other night when Ruth and I said we'd both try dating outside our usual types?'

'Yeah?' I say, moving my self-tape camera into the corner. At least for once my failed attempts won't be recorded.

'Do you know if – if Ruth has followed through on that?'

I glance at him.

'She hasn't said anything about it to me, but… I guess I haven't asked.'

I got back so late from my date with Alice that R&R were

asleep, and the next day I was so hungover I only really told them the fact that we'd kissed, and then about the improv debacle. I feel more positive about the date now – after all, Alice wants to see me again and has been texting me with even more kisses at the end of each message. It must have been a nice evening – I just felt weird on the night out of nerves, and whiskey.

Raphy nods, tucking hair behind his ear. He glances at the wall next to mine, from which we can hear Ruth's muffled focus playlist (screamo).

'Does she seem... Different to you?'

My stomach twists uncomfortably. Am I missing something? Is Raphy trying to tell me that I've been a bad friend?

'She seems really busy preparing for this promotion,' I say. 'But that's not different, is it?'

'Oh! No! You're right! Yeah! Must just be because I've been trying to, you know, understand her way of working a bit better that I'm noticing different things about her or something! It doesn't matter! Forget it!'

I shrug.

'OK,' I say, and open up *ITFTAP:3rd ed.*

Technically, as outlined in the first paragraph, 'an improvised show is one where the plot, dialogue, and characters are created collaboratively by the players in present time, without any recourse to a previously prepared script'. However, the thought of performing anything unscripted in public brings me out in hives. I've therefore spent the morning memorising fifty one-liners covering all the bases: food, animals, transport, sex, and the weather.

If *Mae* can do improv, I can do it better.

'Raphy, you'll need to be both an audience member and my other improviser.'

He retrieves two hats – a pink cowboy for the improviser, and woolly deerstalker for the audience member.

'Amazing, thank you.' I cough and go into emcee mode. 'So, please may I have a random word from the audience?'

Raphy puts on his deerstalker and raises his hand.

'The fields of Elysium.'

I blink at him.

'OK,' I say. 'Raph, how about a word that a lay audience member is more likely to say?'

'Oh…' He considers. 'Astral projection?'

I sigh. But what if someone in the crowd is as weird as Raphy? Given that it's an audience for an improvised comedy show, that's not impossible. Maybe I really do need to play by the rules of improv and throw the script out the window.

'OK,' I say, shaking out my tense arms. 'Let's start with a – a classic scene.'

'Yes!' Raphy says happily. 'I'm the shopkeeper, and you're the customer.'

'Yes!' I say. 'And…!'

Raphy nods at me encouragingly, but I don't have anything else to add.

'Great!'

I open an imaginary door.

'Ring ring,' sings Raphy.

'Cut,' I say. 'Raph, are you the door?'

'No,' he whispers, taking off his cowboy hat. 'I'm the shopkeeper, remember? I was just making the sounds of the door. To add to the atmosphere.'

'But why would a shopkeeper make sounds of a…' I shake my head. Not everyone spent thousands of pounds in drama school fees. 'Let's go again.'

Raphy puts his cowboy hat back on. 'Ring ring!'

I twitch, but walk through the imaginary door, close it carefully behind me, then walk forwards.

'Welcome to my shop,' says Raphy, in a Russian accent.

'But… wait.' I make a time-out gesture with my hands. 'Are we in Russia?'

'Maybe!' grins Raphy.

'Is my character Russian?'

'Maybe! We don't know yet!'

I gape at him in terror.

'OK, OK,' he says. 'It's OK. Yes. Your character is Russian. And he's called Herbert.'

I frown. Herbert feels unusual for a Russian. But still. I can work with that. An older gentleman, perhaps. Dad's age.

Raphy gives me a thumbs up. 'Ring ring!'

I walk towards him in an emulation of my dad's portly gait.

'*Shit*,' I scream. 'I walked through the door. I mean I walked through the solid wood of the imaginary door. Shit. Shit shit shit. I'm such a fucking idiot.'

'It's OK, Em—'

'Herbert!' I shriek. 'My name is Herbert!'

'Welcome to my shop, Herbert,' says Raphy, wide-eyed. 'Welcome to my shop of... of *dreams*. What can I get for you?'

We stare at each other in heavy anticipation.

In a few days, I need to do this in front of a crowd. I start to hyperventilate.

'Why would a shopkeeper say what kind of shop a customer has walked into?' I scream. 'Surely they'd know? *Urgh*! Why are we doing this? Why does anyone do this? What's the point if it's all just... random?!'

I think of Mae's stupid tattoo and her stupid smug face. It's all her fault I'm doing this. It's all her fault I'm going to embarrass myself on a stage while pretending to be her. It's all her fault that I'm a useless improviser, and therefore a useless actor, and therefore a useless person. It's all her fault she's better than me at everything.

Raphy pulls me into a hug. I sniff into his lovely aloe vera-scented shoulder.

'I could tell them I'm sick?' I sniff into his shoulder, but I know my professional instincts are too ingrained to leave a production without a replacement. It's the supreme rule: the show *must* go on.

Raphy rubs my back.

'Sometimes the only way to stop being scared is to stop running away,' he says. 'Stand and face your dragons.'

From Ruth's bedroom next door there are sounds of her slamming her laptop shut, then starting a very loud meditation podcast, played on double speed. Raphy chuckles, then sighs.

'Or, you know,' he adds. 'Maybe you can replace the dragon with a different dragon.'

A light bulb goes off in my mind.

'Raphy, you're a genius.'

He pats my head and then stands outside Ruth's door for a moment, listening to the super-fast wind chimes. Then he knocks.

'Ru? Want to watch a film and get drunk?'

@StanislavskyDevotee100: *Jones, I have a confession to make.*

We haven't messaged for days.

Mae sees it instantly. With trembling fingers, I paste the line I crafted and edited in my notes app.

A few days ago I was spotted by a producer who said he'd seen me perform and thought I was great, and offered me a job doing something similar.

Mae sends an emoji of a medal.

The job is tomorrow evening, and it's an hour of improvised comedy.

She sends back:

wait

YOU do improv?

how???

why haven't I seen u on the circuit?

Unfortunately, this is where my pre-scripted messages end. I stare at the screen, willing her to work it out for herself. For a while we are at an impasse of typing dots. Eventually I sigh and type.

Jones, he thought I was you.

There's a pause.

hahahahahahahahahahahahahahaha

god u must have HATED that

i love it

delicious

chef's kiss

imagine if youd said yes

I blink at the blinking cursor.

oh my god

I sigh as I type, *Yeah.*

oh my actual god

Yes.

did u try to teach urself how to improvise from a book?

Alas, my colour-coded Post-it notes let me down.

hahahahahahahaha

'Emmy, who are you smiling at?' asks Ruth.

'Nothing,' I say quickly, looking up from my screen. 'I mean, no one. I mean, Alice.'

'Cute,' she says, suspiciously.

The smile is quickly wiped off my face when I look back at the phone.

not that i don't love hearing about your biggest failures, but...

why are you telling your rival about this?

I type carefully.

Because I want to make a proposal.

Do the improv performance in my place.

...

whats in it for me

You get to do your beloved improv. Isn't that enough?

Also the hundred pound fee. And I will reimburse all your drinks and transport (keep the receipts).

I send it, then look at the list. Money doesn't matter to Mae Finch. Fingers shaking, I type:

And I will owe you a favour.

I imagine Mae sitting in a luxurious flat, considering my text.

I wonder what she's doing. Presumably sitting on a pile of gold, being fed grapes by scantily clad lovers?

are there any boundaries on what favour i can ask for?

I blush. God, my brain needs to get out of the gutter. Obviously Mae is just asking the genie if she's allowed to wish for more wishes.

Any equivalent favour, I type. *As long as it isn't stupid, like telling me to quit acting.*

can it be illegal?

I snort.

Being imprisoned could affect my hireability.

Our lawyers can draw up a contract.

hahahaha

I grin at her laughter. But then Mae deletes her message, and I stop. It's a reminder that I'm not meant to be enjoying this. It's a business negotiation.

let me get this straight...

you'd fess up to them about the mix up and make them hire me instead of u?

isn't that just a straight up win for me?

u lose a job, i gain a job?

I wince. Now I have her hooked, I need to convince her of the next step. I might never do improv again (fingers crossed) but the acting circle is almost as small as the lesbian one. My name is on their posters and their social media. I can't have my reputation tarnished as a liar or a fraud.

One of my conditions is that you perform under my name. Pretend to be me, but good at improv.

My heart beats in my ears.

clooney

riddle me this

why wouldn't i just say yes...

go on stage as u...

and then be deliberately shit?

Panic rises to my mouth.

like even worse than u would have been
i could say anything in your name
i could get u cancelled
and then ud never work again
and ud STILL be obliged to buy my drinks

She's right. How didn't I think of that?

I feel I'm sinking through the sofa cushions straight to Hell. Either way, my name is going to be tarred. I'll never work again. I need Mae to perform as me, but I also need to know that she won't use this as a way to sabotage me.

I swallow. I *do* have a trump card…

If you did that, then a story might get leaked to the press that Annabel Finch's mysterious daughter is trying to take after her mother…

How can I feel a mood shift so much over a screen? I can see, as if she's here, Mae's dangerous shark eyes, glaring with the hatred she reserves for only me.

W O W
so much for your understanding
thought you were being surprisingly decent about that
should have known i was wrong

I grind my teeth.

Let's not let this get dramatic, Jones. Remember the message scored into your wrist? I am merely inviting you to spend an evening doing your favourite thing in the world. Just… think about it?

Mae's typing dots are there for a long time. But then they disappear.

Desperately, I send another message.

Please?

She goes offline.

I can't concentrate the whole rest of the evening, staring at my phone as R&R laugh about trying on each other's lives. Raphy tries to make Ruth's espresso martinis (they end up with twice the normal amount of both caffeine and alcohol), and Ruth somehow burns Raphy's signature superfood salad. They giggle away through the whole of *Mamma Mia!*. Meanwhile, I don't even join in with 'Dancing Queen'.

'Wow, Alice's really got you hooked, huh?' says Ruth.

'Oh... Yeah,' I say guiltily. This prompts me to send Alice a message suggesting days for our next date, to which she immediately replies agreeing to the first.

I can't wait to see you again, handsome! Xxxxxxx

After we've all applauded 'I Have a Dream', I tell R&R I'm too tired to join in with their co-training tonight, despite being a jittery wreck of caffeine. I leave Raphy staring at an Excel spreadsheet titled 'Enlightenment: to-do list', and Ruth, in a stiff lotus position with her knees barely at ninety degrees.

I stare at the phone on my pillow, willing it to light up.

At around 2 a.m., it does.

@therealmaejones: *yes (and)*

20

I need to ensure that Mae follows up on her end of the bargain, but I also can't be seen by her, or Daryl. So (and I can't believe I'm saying this) I decide to attend the improv show in disguise.

Now, if Daryl got me and Mae confused before, presumably he won't remember me that well. But Mae...

I need R&R's help.

Ruth, seeming a lot calmer and jollier than she's been recently, wheels me into her bedroom, plays Lizzo and appraises me like one of her clients. The first thing that needs to be covered is my short hair, disguised in Raphy's high-quality pink bob wig. My own wardrobe is monochrome and androgynous, so she puts me in her pinkest dress (Raphy offered me his pink dress too, but he's too tall) and thick black tights to cover up my hairy legs from the patriarchy police. I draw the line at heels.

'The last time I put make-up on you was in Year 9, do you remember?' she asks. I smile and go to say that yes, her cat-eyes were so good she earned respect from the popular girls, but Ruth shushes me so that I don't ruin the lipstick. I squeeze her knee instead.

Raphy's looking on, borrowing Ruth's teal eyeshadow.

'And the last time *I* put make-up on you was when we were going out for Pride last year,' he says. 'I don't know whether to go this year, though. It's so offensively capitalist isn't it? Are you guys going?'

'I'm afraid I'm part of your problem,' sighs Ruth, applying my mascara. 'I'm helping organise my company Pride float. Hashtag ally.'

She glances at Raphy in the mirror. 'I think it's been really meaningful for some of my colleagues though, so... I dunno... It's complicated.'

We're all quiet for a moment. I'm surprised that R&R aren't being more black and white, like they usually are. Usually it's only me who likes to conclude that everything is 'complicated'.

Then Raphy seems to get distracted by how gorgeous he looks, giving himself a little twirl. 'Do you think I should wear this on my date?'

Ruth's brush hesitates.

'What date?'

'You know,' says Raphy defensively. 'My "not my usual type" date. With a woman from OK Cupid.'

Ruth blinks at him. I blink too, with one mascara'd eye.

'*You* signed up for OK Cupid?'

'We agreed to try something different?'

'But... But you need to fill in forms online to be on OK Cupid.'

'Yes, Ruth,' says Raphy, poking at the eyeshadow palette. 'Sadly I'm not *actually* a mediaeval monk.'

Ruth resumes putting mascara on me.

'Who is she?' she asks after a moment.

'Well, she's...' He glances at her. 'She works in marketing, actually.'

Ruth pokes me in the eye with the wand.

'How long have you been messaging?' I ask him.

'Oh, I don't know,' says Raphy, fiddling with his curls. 'Time is a construct...'

Ruth watches him for a moment, then applies my eyeliner forcefully. She must be jealous that she doesn't have a date. We listen to 'Soulmate' for a moment.

Then Raphy says, 'Actually, I've invited her round for dinner.'

The eyeliner pencil snaps.

'You've invited her *round*?' she hisses. 'For *dinner*? At *our house*?'

'You're welcome to join us too? We could have a little... double date...?'

Ruth folds her arms.

'Sounds great,' she says. 'You bring Cupid girl—'

'Her name is Valentine.'

Ruth's forehead vein pops.

'Of course it is. And I'll bring someone who does *not* work in marketing. Someone I'm going to meet organically, serendipitously, spiritually... from *your* outdoor laughter yoga.'

'How charming,' says Raphy brightly. 'It will do you good to do something calming.'

'That's sorted then.'

'Glorious.'

'Can I come?' I say.

They both look at me, and I'm reminded of my parents fighting before they separated. Raphy pats me on the head and Ruth returns to my make-up, more attentively now.

'Of course, Em. You're always welcome.'

We listen to the rest of the song in silence.

'Ta da,' Ruth says finally.

I look at myself in the mirror. This might sound obvious, but in my pink bob, pretty dress, and gorgeous make-up, I look genuinely unrecognisable, especially when I push my chest out and put a coquettish hand on my hip.

This is what other actors must get to feel like, when they aren't typecast as, well, themselves. It's fun, to not be me.

I kiss R&R's cheeks in thanks, leaving big red splotches that Ruth tells me off about, and leave the two of them to finish their own make-up.

The Mighty Hippo improv show is above a busy pub in East London. I sneak in nice and early and order a lime cordial, surprised when no one shouts 'Hey, you're dressed weird!' The paranoia is exaggerated when I notice my name on the improv poster behind the bar.

Then I hear her laugh.

Shit. Mae's on the door, welcoming people in.

I'm thrown by seeing her again. It feels as though it's been forever, even though the *High School* filming was only a few weeks ago. She's even more magnetic than she is in my memory – her smile's warmer, her eyes brighter, her shirt more ridiculous (it's decorated with cartoon frogs).

She gives me a full-on sunbeam of a smile.

'Thanks so much for coming. Do you already have a—'

She blinks at me, and tilts her head to one side.

'I swear this isn't a pick-up line,' she says, as if it absolutely is, 'but don't I know you?'

God, she's irrepressible. She must have flirted like this with everyone in the queue.

'Umm, no, no, absolutely not,' I say, adopting a Liverpudlian accent and not meeting her eye.

'Oh, sorry,' she says charmingly. 'Well, here you go, hope you enjoy the—'

But as I squeeze past her, congratulating myself on being a marvellous actor, she suddenly grabs my wrist and stares at me. A spark of recognition goes through both of us.

'Cloo—'

I put my hand over her mouth. She blinks over it in surprise. I remove it slowly, my palm tingling from her lips.

'I am but an innocent member of the public,' I say, in my Liverpudlian accent. 'Simply here to enjoy a little improvisational comedy, as is my right. I shall not be any trouble.'

Mae blinks rapidly. Then she nods slowly and gestures for me to go up the stairs. As I remove my hand, she licks her lip.

'Enjoy the show, madam,' she says, threateningly.

I wobble up the stairs and into the performance room.

The audience is currently five people and a reserved sign.

The only person who looks excited to be here is a man who is clearly an aspiring improviser, bouncing on the edge of his seat. He's definitely called Steve. (Not an insult, just a fact.) Then there's a couple clutching beers who appear to be on a disastrous first date, roped in from the pub below. There's a man who looks like he's Daryl's dad and, lastly, a surprisingly trendy student, perhaps here to scout out whether to take a workshop and regretting it.

I roll my eyes at the reserved sign. I swear, every production I ever go to has a front row seat reserved. At Saint Gen's, Thalia and I used to call it the Phantom's Seat, because it was there for every first night performance. Evidence of how many reviewers don't show up to do their jobs, I guess, or maybe it's just there to make the show seem more popular?

Apart from Steve, sitting on the front row next to the reserved sign, we all seem to be fighting to see who can sit furthest away from the stage. I can see the whites of everyone's eyes. We're all having the same horrifying thought: 'What if there is audience participation?'

The doors close behind us, with something that sounds suspiciously like the click of a lock.

The lights go down, and a pre-recorded entrance music plays – a dubstep dance track with a violent bassline. From behind the thin curtain the performers enter.

There is a rule of Edinburgh Fringe performances that a show is a success if you have more audience members than cast members. Five improvisers skip onto the stage.

The music cuts off abruptly.

'Goooood evening, London!' shouts Daryl. 'How are we tonight?'

Apart from Steve, the audience woops limply.

'I can't hear you!' sings Daryl. 'I *said*, how are we doing tonight!'

Steve screams. If I was on that stage, I would have already died of embarrassment. But Mae looks completely at ease.

She's smiling out at the audience, turned away from my corner. Even when she's just standing in a line-up, she stands out. I guess she can't help it – even without the spotlight on her, she glows.

'Well, thank you all so much for spending your Saturday night with us at The Mighty Hippo! To say thank you, we're going to make up some stories and some jokes *just for you*! This is fully improvised comedy, which means that none of these sentences have been scripted, rehearsed, planned, or practised – it's all completely made up in the room! That's right, no one will ever say any of these jokes ever again, however hilarious they are!'

I sink lower in my chair. Steve cheers in ecstasy.

Daryl introduces the line-up, with Mae last.

'And all the way from New York – remember her name folks, she'll be on your televisions soon, it's Emmy Clooney!'

I mime clapping, ensuring I make no sound out of principle. I swear Mae gets a larger applause from the crowd than any of the others, just for existing. She does a little bow, still not looking over at me.

Then Daryl introduces the set-up – they'll alternate longer scenes with short games, three of each.

'And don't worry, yes, the games will include audience volunteers!'

My stomach drops. Steve woops.

'Can we have a prompt from the audience?'

Steve shouts out, 'Banana! Aliens! Donald Trump! Banana!'

Daryl takes Aliens.

The improvisers do a series of scenes about being captured by an alien, a storyline that starts with being probed and ends with a surprisingly moving story about how their home planet was destroyed. Mae stands out as an alien made entirely of thumbs. I have to keep reminding myself I'm not allowed to laugh at her, but it's OK, everyone else more than makes up for my silence.

Look, we know by now that I am not naturally a fan of

improv. But I'm surprised to find that... they're actually really good. I even find myself enjoying it.

My applause at the end of the scene is grudging but genuine.

Then it's an audience participation game (I look pointedly at my lap). Steve acts as a puppeteer for two of the improvisers, who still use their own mouths, narrating Steve's attempts to make them have a 'romantic first date'. Steve is clearly having the best night of his entire life – and it's kind of infectious.

By the time the next audience prompt is asked for, the others join in. I start to feel self-conscious that I'm the only one that hasn't given one.

Then Mae's at the front.

'Can I get a prompt for a style of performance?' she asks. 'For example, musical, Western, sci-fi, romcom...' Steve starts shouting different sub-genres of fantasy – but Mae turns deliberately to my corner.

'This part of the room has been rather quiet,' she says. 'How about a prompt from over here?'

I don't know if, in the dark of the audience, Mae can really see my face, but where I am, it feels like she meets my eye with a cocky grin. I glare, trying to think of what Mae would find hardest.

'Greek tragedy,' I say.

She hesitates for just a fraction of a second, then bows graciously.

'Greek tragedy.'

The lights go down then back up. Mae comes to the front, her mouth pulled into a grotesque caricature of a happy face, looking uncannily like a Greek comedy mask, and holding an imaginary platter. One of the other performers comes on, matching her grin.

Mae pretends to be shocked by their appearance and drops the imaginary platter she was holding. Their faces go from upturned to downturned. Mae kneels to the floor in a desperate stigmata.

'No,' she wails. 'My falafel.'

Everyone else in the audience roars and cheers. The lights flash for the end of the scene.

'Greek tragedy, everyone!' says the other performer, gesturing to Mae. Mae does a little bow right at me.

That's... that's cheating. That wasn't a Greek tragedy. That was mere *word play*. Audience prompts should be allowed to come with a dictionary definition.

I fume for the rest of the scenes. Mae goes from strength to strength. Until, all of a sudden, it's the last game.

'So, for our finale, let's play a classic we like to call Whose Hands Are These Anyway?'

Daryl holds up a battered plastic mixing bowl. Behind him, one of the other improvisers sets up a small table with assorted baking items on it.

'At Emmy's request, all the cake ingredients are vegan.'

My jaw clenches. Damn it, Mae's vegan? I know I should be pleased for The Cause, but really, can't she get her own damn ethics?

Mae opens up an egg box to the audience to reveal it's full of colourful egg toys with cheeky faces. Mae grins with her tongue out in mimicry and the audience laugh as though they're trained to love everything she does.

'For this game, we're going to have our Emmy as the host on a baking programme. All she needs to do is act making a cake from these ingredients. The trouble is – she won't be able to use her own hands. She's going to use the hands of an audience member instead. So, can we get our last lovely audience volunteer...'

Everyone else in the audience turns to look at each other and then, when they realise each of them has already been, turn to me.

I have to leave. I'll have to pretend I need the loo. I stand, crouching, and try to slink towards the exit.

'Wonderful!' says Daryl, relieved. 'A round of applause for our last marvellous volunteer!'

'Oh, no, no,' I say, in my Liverpudlian accent. 'I was just going to—'

'What's your name, ma'am?'

I'm not used to someone gendering me with such ease, then remember my costume. I glance at Mae in panic.

'Mae,' I say.

I watch her flush and feel the corresponding heat rise on my own cheeks.

'Come on up, Mae.'

The audience applaud. I don't move, then realise that he means me. I've never been so reticent walking up the steps to a stage.

'So, Mae, you're going to be Emmy's arms. Just go on in and slot your arms through, like you're the big baking spoon to her teaspoon.'

Oh Christ. Mae and I both hesitate. Then I remember an actor's duty is to their audience. I crook my arms like chicken wings. Mae starts to reach her hands out to me.

'No, the other way round, guys! Emmy, *you're* in front, Mae, *you're* the arms.

Arms bent, Mae and I stare at each other in confusion, then remember our name swap.

'Ooh,' we nod, and swap our roles. She crooks her arms for me to insert my hands. I close my eyes, swallow, and step towards her to slot my arms through.

She's a little taller than me (the bastard) and her ridiculous bouncy shoes add an inch or two more. My face is against the top of her back, my arms stretched in front of her chest like a stiff T-rex. I've never been more careful where I put my hands.

I can feel her breathing against my cheek. How is she barely sweating? I've been seated in the audience and even I can feel myself dripping. But she is barely damp, just boilingly warm. Her heart is beating fast and, as I notice it, seems to get quicker. I don't blame her, I always get short of breath when I'm on stage.

God, I feel as if I can feel her citrussy cologne go straight to my frontal cortex. I'm no perfumer, but I'd say there's top notes of lemon, with muskier undertones – oak wood, maybe, and something unexpectedly like – I breathe in deeply again, through my mouth – cherry. Synthetic cherry. Like in a gateau.

'Mae? Are you ready?'

I feel Mae jump under me, then remember I'm Mae right now.

'Yes!' I say, muffled, into her shirt.

The lighting changes to signal the start of a scene.

'Good evening,' says Mae, adopting a British accent that sounds like the one she mocks me with. 'Welcome to the Good English Cake On. I'm your host, a kooky white comedian from the noughties, and I'm going to show you how to make the *perfect* improvised sponge.'

I can feel Mae's words rumbling under my own body. It's as if I'm the one speaking them. As if I'm the one the audience is laughing at.

Eyes closed, my cheek against her shoulder blades, it's as though I can feel what her phantom arms want to be doing. As she speaks, I gesture as she would. The audience giggle in pleasure.

'So first,' she says, 'you need to pick up the mixing bowl from the table.'

She leans to the table, and, after only a few moments of grabbing the air, I grasp the edge of a bowl.

'Then find the box, and take out two eggs.'

I pat the table for the carton, but run out of hands to flip the lid. I feel Mae's hands twitch under me instinctively to help. Feeling rather pleased with myself, I flip it open with my right hand, and tip them into the bowl.

'Then you need to juggle the eggs.'

I hesitate.

'Only joking,' she says. 'Why would we need to juggle the eggs?'

The audience laugh. I put the bowl on the table, remove the eggs, and, my muscles still remembering the juggling training I did for my stage fighting training, throw them briefly round.

The audience woop.

'Well, would you look at that,' says Mae, irritated. 'I can do tricks.'

I snap the toy eggs confidently on the side of the bowl, and crack their imaginary innards into the bowl. Of course, I can't see what I'm doing, but I can hear the audience, and I can feel Mae beneath me. I feel like I'm the rat from Ratatouille.

'I'm such a professional baker that my hands are acting without my instruction,' says Mae warningly. 'I wonder if they'll follow my order to take the oat milk...'

I pick up the carton, screw the cap on tight, and instinctively give it a shake. Compelled by some hitherto unknown instinct, I unscrew the cap and lift the carton up to where I imagine – where I know – Mae's mouth is.

I feel her laugh vibrate underneath me. I can't help it – I smile into her.

'Of course,' she laughs. 'This baking is thirsty work. Now, I'm just going to pour a *little* into my mouth, aren't I? Nice and gently. On three.'

She counts, and I'm tempted to go ahead of her countdown so that I can pour oat milk all over her. But... I dunno, I'm invested in making this scene work now.

Her head tilts back onto my shoulder. I tip a little into her mouth. I feel her swallow. The audience have gone quiet.

After a silence that feels like it lasts forever, Mae makes an exaggerated lip-smacking sigh of contentment.

'Well, that worked surprisingly well,' she says.

I freeze. Shit. We played the game too successfully. That's not what the audience beast wants from us. I tip the carton over Mae's shirt.

The audience gasp. I feel Mae tense beneath me. But then she laughs.

So I'm hugging Mae Jones while she laughs on a stage and weirdly, I don't hate it.

I pick up kitchen roll from the table and pat her front – but I'm so worried about touching her actual body that I barely make contact. I wonder if Mae's going to call it there, but then she says teasingly, 'The last thing I need to do for this cake is add some flour.' The audience go 'Ooh'. 'Now, this could get messy if I'm not very careful.'

I hesitate. Obviously what the audience wants is for me to throw the flour everywhere. But that means Mae wants that too. Slapstick has never been my preference. Instead, I carefully open the bag.

'More,' says Mae. 'More. Yeah, that's it. Yeah, just like that.'

Her voice becomes euphemistic. 'Don't stop.'

I drop the bag.

The audience laughs.

Mae bends, instinctively, to pick it up. In her movement, my hands graze her hip bones. I twitch to remove my hands entirely from her sides, but the audience are laughing, and Mae clenches her arms to keep them there, directing me.

'I just need to use my *left* hand to – no – yes – forwards – a bit to the left – the other left…'

I desperately grab it and pull my arms up as if I'm steering an unyielding horse's reins. Mae stands, her back knocking my nose so hard I wonder if it's going to bleed all over her stupid frog shirt.

Mae, of course, is relishing the audience's attention.

'Now we just need to beat it all together. And to make sure there are no soggy bottoms, so we're going to have to spank it very hard, like the naughty little cake batter it is.'

The audience is lapping it up like schoolboys. I resent being pulled into her easy euphemistic humour.

I do a bare minimum gesture of whisking.

'No,' she says. 'That was just me giving an example of what a limp, uncommitted whisk would look like.'

I am so tempted to drop the whisk and hold up my middle finger to her instead, but this is theatre. I want to prove to her that anything she can do, I can do better. She wants a hard whisk? I'll give her a hard whisk.

'Yeah!' she says, a little surprised, and then imbues it with exaggerated sexuality, 'Yeah! Harder. Harder!'

OK, I confess. The audience laughing, the whisking, Mae shaking along with me under my arms... I get into the scene. At the moment Mae reaches the peak of her shouts, I dip into the bowl and explode a generous handful of flour into the air, like a firework.

The audience roar and applaud. The light flashes for the end of the scene. I imagine what Mae's face looks like right now – grinning to the crowd, covered in flour. Mine, hidden in her back, is smiling too.

As I separate from her, Daryl gestures for us to both bow.

We go instinctively to hold hands for the moment – then remember who we are, and leave them untouched. We style it out into a deeply awkward gesture to each other.

As I head back to my seat, milky Mae being slapped on the back by the improvisers, and me smiling back at the pats of other audience members, I don't know which of us won that round. I'm not sure I mind.

Mae laughs and pushes open the doors of the pub. Outside, the other improvisers lift pints to us in toast, shouting about cake. Mae does a delighted little half-bow to each of them in reply, but doesn't stop to talk. The couple who were in the audience are now leaning against the wall, passionately making out. Mae puts her hands in her jacket pockets, shrugging in the direction of the main road.

We walk along the empty street. I feel giddy – it must be the after-effects of improv. I'm unaware of anything that isn't Mae – the lamps casting different shadows on her face, her lolloping stride, the waft of lemon cologne and oat milk. I realise that this is the first time we've ever been alone.

'Umm. Thank you, for tonight,' I say. 'You were… so much better than me.'

Mae laughs. 'Thank you, Clooney, I know how hard it is for you to say that.'

We look at each other under the streetlights. Her eyes are doing that twinkling thing again. I can see a flicker of gold around her irises.

'Maybe I… underestimated improv,' I say.

We laugh and look away.

'Look who's learning to like spontaneity,' she jokes. 'You know, I actually am grateful to you for getting me this gig, even if it was by rather unconventional methods. I'd missed the joy of it. That feeling of being completely in the flow, alive to the room.'

'The audience loved you,' I say.

Mae frowns.

'I didn't hog the limelight, did I?'

How can I say 'it was impossible to take my eyes off you' without it sounding like I'm complimenting her? I settle for just saying, 'No.'

'Phew,' she says. 'Well, for what it's worth, Mae was a good audience member. In the end.'

Safely out of sight of the pub, I pull off the wig.

'Everyone likes me more when I'm pretending to be someone else,' I say, trying to sound like I'm joking.

I steal a glance at her face and see she's already looking at me.

'I don't think that's true,' she says.

She wets her lower lip and I find myself instinctively mirroring her. Then I worry she might think I was looking at her mouth. What if she thinks I want to kiss her? What if she—

'How are you getting home?' I ask quickly, to stop my brain.

'I've got my bike.'

'Oh, cool,' I say, relieved and disappointed. 'I'm getting the bus,' I say, pointing stupidly at the bus stop. I cough. 'Thanks for your cooperation tonight. I'll await you calling in your return favour. I'm sure you'll try and make it as awful as possible in retaliation.'

'Was tonight awful?' she asks softly.

I look at her, eyes bright in the dark, searching mine.

'You have a bit of flour,' I say, 'on your nose.'

She stares at me for a moment as if she didn't hear me. Then she shakes her head slightly, laughs.

'Weird, wonder how that got there?'

She wipes it with her hand, completely missing the flour. I roll my eyes and reach out with my thumb to clear it away. Instinctively, I boop the tip of her nose. I regret it immediately. Mae's huge blue eyes blink rapidly, like some kind of Disney creature. It's... adorable. As I stare, her cheeks redden.

'Now you can't resist being my hands,' she laughs, fiddling with the hair at the nape of her neck. No one has ever looked lovelier.

I pretend to be busy wiping the flour into my handkerchief.

What's wrong with me? My heart's racing, my palms are sweaty, I feel boiling despite the evening chill, and I'm mentally complimenting Mae? If I didn't know better, I'd think... I have a crush.

But I can't. I can't *actually* fancy Mae. For heaven's sake, she's my lookalike *rival*. And I'm due to see Alice for a second date soon – and indeed she already booked in a third date in advance, because of requesting review tickets. Now *there's* someone who actually likes me and is a good fit for me!

This must be transference from doing a show together. That's a scientific phenomenon. My physiological response is a natural, fleeting fluke.

'Wellthisismybusstopgoodnight!'

I run off.

'Emmy,' says Mae.

I turn back. For a wild second, I think she's going to kiss me.

'My bike is in that direction too.'

'Oh.'

We walk along the remaining street in silence. The night has suddenly closed in on us. I feel very aware of having a reprieve, one last chance to talk to her, in this strange limbo where it doesn't feel that we're quite as much in opposition as we are meant to be. Where the favour has been completed but normal service has not yet resumed...

I want to ask her about everything. Anything. But I don't know where to start.

'Why do you—'

'What's your—'

We both break off, laughing awkwardly.

'You go first,' she says.

'No,' I insist. 'You.'

'Oh, I just wondered... Can I have your number?'

I misstep.

'Don't get me wrong,' says Mae quickly, 'I'm all for trash-talking on Instagram, but it might be more' – she glances at me – 'professional, for us to have each other's numbers?'

I recover and nod. It was stupid for me to think she could mean it in any other way.

'So that you can call in your favour,' I say.

'Right! So that I can call in my favour.'

She passes me her ridiculously large phone. The case has squishy gel in it that moves like a lava lamp. I shake my head at it and she laughs, running her hand through her curls.

As I'm typing my name in, I try not to notice how many contacts she has. Contacts with just a first name. My stomach writhes. I wonder if she's still in regular contact with any of these – presumably very fun, interesting, and sexy – people.

'For business purposes,' I say.

'Of course,' nods Mae. 'For business purposes.'

I hand the phone back to her and spot my bus on the horizon. Feeling lightheaded, I point at it.

'It is I.'

Mae snorts, but it's not malicious – laughing with me, not at me.

She stops and faces me, and I do the same. Are we meant to shake hands? Or, like, bump elbows? I feel incredibly aware of the heat radiating off her body.

'Well, *Mae*,' she smiles. 'Pleasure to meet you tonight. Thanks for the extended hug.'

'HA HA! Goodbye!'

I run over to the bus, but it hasn't stopped yet. I stare very straight in front of me in the queue, holding my payment card out like a Sim under instruction.

It's only when I am safely seated on the bus that I allow myself to look back. Mae is unlocking her bike, a yellow upright covered in stickers. As if she can feel me watching, she looks up, right at my window. We stare at each other as the bus pulls away.

At the last moment, unsmiling, she puts two fingers up to her forehead and salutes me. I salute her in return. I don't know whether she saw. I don't know whether she laughed.

The whole bus journey back, I can smell Mae's perfume on me. But however deeply I breathe in, it's elusive, as though I can't get the full bouquet without her being physically there, pressed against me.

My phone buzzes and adrenaline thumps through me.

Good night my gorgeous one! Can't wait to see you again soon! xxxxoxoxoxoxoxoxxx

For a mad moment I think it's from Mae. Then I realise, of course, it's my nightly goodnight text from Alice, and put my head in my hands.

Maybe it's understandable for me to be, er... romantically confused. After all, I am dating for basically the first time. Yes, that must be it. My body's just getting confused about where to put that energy. I need to channel it back into the person who actually likes me.

My phone vibrates again. Sometimes if I don't reply immediately, Alice sends another few rows of kisses until I do. But when I flip my screen back over, it's a text from an unknown number.

clooney, just checking, are we still enemies? x

I stare at it, trying to ignore the way my stomach is pirouetting. Mae's clearly one of those people who automatically puts a kiss at the end of a text, even if it's a statement of marking territory to a rival actor.

Of course, I type back. *Until you decide what favour I'm doing for you.*

I send it, then read it back and worry it sounds flirty. I put my head back in my hands and lightly groan for the rest of the journey.

21

'*Emmeline?*'

I look guiltily towards Alice.

'Sorry... Would you repeat that?'

'I *said*, you seem distracted.'

'Sorry,' I repeat.

What's wrong with me? Here I am, on a second date – the first second date I've ever been on – with the kindest, most generous and beautiful girl who has ever said they are interested in me, and I'm not present because I'm thinking about how to reply to in-jokes with my arch nemesis.

Mae and I have been messaging ever since we swapped numbers – trash-talking each other's lack of parts, or what we've been working on that day, or insulting what the other had for lunch. Today she horrified me with her gherkin sandwich and vegan Monster Munch.

Alice has been texting too, with increasing numbers of kisses, and increasingly late. Last night she messaged at midnight asking if I was 'up'. I am not a complete buffoon. I understand what this meant. But I couldn't think of anything more unlike me than deviating from my sleeping schedule to go to Alice's house in the dark on a Monday night, so I didn't reply until the next morning.

R&R reassure me it's OK to be moving at my own pace. The problem is, it's not the same as Alice's, and surely she's more likely to be right?

Our date tonight has been extravagant. We're in the bar at the Royal Opera House and Alice looks incredibly glamorous in a red cocktail dress. I'm feeling underdressed, even though I'm wearing my Red Carpet outfit. I tug at the pinstripe blazer, thinking about how it was cheaper than one of these theatre tickets would have been. The last time I wore it was when I first met Alice, at Thalia's party.

With a start, I realise I haven't thought about Thalia in ages. I feel strangely guilty.

'I forgive you,' says Alice, putting her hand on mine on the table and squeezing it. She sighs wistfully. 'Wasn't that performance *magical*?'

We watched over three hours of opera and I felt nothing. At least my dad was more accepting of me moving my shift tonight because it was the 'proper Italian' *Madame Butterfly*. Dad has never seen an opera in his life, but thinks he's an expert because he sometimes plays the music in the pizzeria. Generally, he's a lot happier about me missing shifts to go on dates than he was when I missed them to do my actual job. I haven't told him Alice is a theatre critic – for him, that's even *more* of a fake job than being an actor.

I bet Mae would have *hated* this evening. I can imagine her, slouched in her seat, using opera glasses to watch the other audience members. To be fair, she would never have agreed to come in the first place. I wonder if I can craft a message to her about the opera that doesn't reveal I'm on a date. Not that she couldn't know that, it just feels weird to brag about romance to a *work* rival. I wonder if Mae's on a date too...

'What are you thinking, darling?'

I start. Alice's heels poke into my calves, trying to footsie.

'I just...' I wave my hand around the room, her, her dress. 'I can't believe this is my real life.'

'Well, get used to it.' She smiles, and toasts my glass. 'My love language is gifts.' She bites her lip in a clearly planned way. 'I want to give you everything. Everything you've ever wanted.'

I shift uncomfortably. 'All I've ever wanted is to just be a working actor.'

She leans in, her dress low over her chest. 'Then I'll get you a part in any show you want. Name it. I'll make it happen.'

She's joking. Feeling loose from the whiskey Alice chose for me, I suddenly recall my run-in with Thalia at The Boards, my fumbled hint that I was going to be performing there.

'The all-queer production of *Twelfth Night* at The Boards theatre this summer. The one being directed by Francis de la Ware.'

Alice nods seriously. 'I know the producer. I'll ring him in the morning.'

I blink at her, waiting for her to laugh. When she doesn't, I panic.

'No! Alice! I-I didn't think you really *meant* it!'

She raises an eyebrow. 'Aren't you serious about your career?'

'Of – of *course* I am, but—'

'Then why aren't you taking every opportunity you can get? Lord knows, if you could open doors for me, I'd expect you to hold them as wide as possible.' Her heels find my legs again. 'I'm sure you'll return the favour for me *somehow...*'

I flush and look down. The heels are digging in and I can feel them making bruises, but I don't want to be rude, especially when she's being so generous.

She's right. I'm meant to be prioritising my career. But I don't want to *cheat*. I want to play by the rules, and earn my place. Maybe it's not really cheating if you're just trying to play the game on a less difficult setting?

'Per-perhaps you could connect my agent with the casting director? If I get into the audition room, then it will be up to me to earn a place or not?'

'Oh darling, you're so *proper,* aren't you?'

She doesn't say it like a compliment. But then she squeezes my cheek across the table.

'It's done. I'll contact him tomorrow and send you the details.'

'Alice… I… I don't know how to thank you…'

Alice smiles at me, and I try to smile back. What's wrong with me? Alice's being so generous – but the nicer she is, the more disconnected from her I feel.

I'm busy wondering if Alice gives the same help to Thalia, or if she already had all the legs up she needed. I'm thinking about Mae, the defiance with which she said she was forging her career without her mum's help. Then I'm thinking about my own mum, whether she'd frown at this, or if she'd root for me to do anything I can to finally be a real actor.

Unbelievably, I can feel tears clogging in my throat. I absolutely can't cry now, I can't, but telling myself that just makes the tears rise faster. I try to get into the character of someone who is not about to cry.

'Oh darling,' says Alice. She stands and rushes round the table, kneeling at my side, and pulls me into an embrace.

'Why are you doing this for me?' I say. 'You haven't even seen me perform.'

I feel so self-conscious, near tears in this stupidly swanky restaurant, my face pulled into Alice's chest. I try to wriggle away but she pulls me in tighter, stroking my hair. I'm finding it hard to breathe.

'You're so unused to someone being nice to you, aren't you?'

Maybe she's right, but that doesn't feel like why I'm trying not to cry right now. I'm not worth being nice to.

'This is just what girlfriends do for each other,' she says.

The tears stop rising.

Girlfriends?

Isn't that the sort of thing couples are meant to have long discussions about? I thought the script was, around date six, you have croissants in bed and one of you says, 'I'm catching feelings,' and the other goes 'me too,' and traces patterns on the other's fingers and says 'I want us to be exclusive,' and the other says 'me too' and then they kiss and two and a half years later get engaged? I know the stereotype of U-haul lesbians (meet on Monday, engaged by Tuesday, living on a barge with their cats by Wednesday) but I thought that only happened by, well, mutual arrangement.

'Girlfriends?'

She claps a hand to her mouth.

'Oh Lord, I'm so sorry, did I make assumptions?' she says sincerely, squeezing my hand again.

I feel so relieved I smile weakly and start to wave the apology away.

'You prefer the word partners?' she says.

The sound of cutlery clattering and wine glasses clinking and champagne being popped is suddenly far, far too much. The lights in the room seem to flare in brightness. The whiskey burns in the back of my throat.

'I need to go to the toilet,' I say, stumbling up.

Alice grabs my hand and stares down at me, her eyes cold.

'No, you don't,' she says.

I freeze.

'I...'

Alice laughs and slaps my wrist playfully.

'You need to go to the *lavatory*.'

I force out a stiff laugh, but still hesitate.

'Go on then,' she says, tucking her dress neatly to the side and sitting herself back down. 'I'll see you in two minutes. I'll order us more drinks.'

I lock the cubicle door behind me and stay standing, staring at the lock.

I get my phone out to message R&R, but I don't know quite what I need to say. My brain feels foggy, my stomach twisted. Two minutes isn't long.

All that time I spent longing after Thalia, wanting more than she was giving, is this how it felt for her? Was I like Alice? Was I this... What's the word? Clingy? Intense? Claustrophobic?

I stare at the blinking cursor.

But it's terrible that I'm thinking this about Alice. It takes two to tango. I must have been leading her on.

I didn't think of myself as someone with commitment issues – except perhaps being *too* committed – but it looks like I must be. Alice's been thinking of herself as my girlfriend, a step towards her dream of beautiful married life – and meanwhile, I've been... well... having confusing thoughts about my rival. It makes me feel like a cliché straight man, messing around while his faultless wife makes him dinner.

I think of the long, sweet messages that Alice sends every day. How she finds an excuse to message goodnight. How she's invited me as her plus one on these fancy theatre trips, and how she's already booked me in for more. And now she's offering to get me these parts in shows, which should be exactly what I want. I'm meant to be serious about my career, and about doing anything I can to beat Mae and get to the top.

I take slow, deep breaths. Clearly I'm just unused to being in a relationship. As with work, I need to commit. Prepare. Plan. I can perform my role better. I will.

I message in my group chat with R&R:

Alice just asked me to be her girlfriend!!!

They reply with characteristic immediacy – I wonder if they're sitting at home together.

Ruth: *Wow, efficient.*

Raphael: *:O :O :O :O Did you say yes ? ? ? :O :O :O*

Ruth: *Does this mean more free stuff?*

I take another breath, feeling better for the decision. It's all going to be OK, I say to myself, and then feel silly. Only a few weeks ago, I'd have been over the moon that someone wanted to be my girlfriend.

I'm about to put my phone away when the screen lights up with a text from Mae. My stomach does its favourite somersault. She's replied to something we had said about what booby traps we could set in the next audition room we're in together.

lots of snakes, and those swinging cleavers from indiana jones
Is he another one of your celebrity relatives, Jones?
hahahahahahaa yeah he's my cousin.

you know clooney, sometimes i think it's a shame we have to
hate each other. do u ever wonder if we'd still hate each other if
we met outside of an acting setting? as in like if we just hung out
as friends or whatever? x

I stare at it. My stomach keep spinning, backwards and forwards.

I put the phone away, feeling the x burning through my pocket. I stare at myself in the mirror.

'Friends or whatever'? *Friends? Whatever?* What would being 'whatever' with Mae mean? She can't mean *more* than friends. She has a million people of every gender throwing themselves at her every minute; why on earth would she choose an awkward, inexperienced, pretentious lookalike version of herself? I suppose she *does* seem to love herself... Understandably.

'Stop it,' I say to my reflection. 'She does *not* like you! She is your enemy.'

I think of Alice, calling me her girlfriend, and her look of disdain when she said, 'Aren't you serious about your career?'

The only thing I have ever been certain about in my life is being an actor. Wanting – *needing* to be an actor. Mae actively hinders me from achieving that ambition.

Whatever I think I might be feeling for Mae right now *is not real*. It's just her dark magic charisma, fooling me. It's fleeting, it's not mutual, and it's holding me back.

It's been more than two minutes Emmeline xxxxxxxxxx

Nausea rises in me. I swallow and splash my face with cold water. Time to be serious.

On the R&R chat I type *So happy!!!!!!*

I delete Mae's message, and I walk back to Alice, my girlfriend.

22

A few days later, I'm working a slow lunchtime shift at the pizzeria when Valerie sends me an email with the details of the audition for *Twelfth Night*. I send Alice gushing thanks and my longest line of x's yet, then slide it back into my apron.

I'm trying to fulfil my waitress duties but I lag behind Dad and Carmella, so there isn't much for me to do except loiter at tables they've already cleaned.

I wipe, thinking about *Twelfth Night*. I'll need to do a great deal of rereading the play and criticism of it. My interpretation of Viola must be original, yet I must be congruent with the text and its traditions. I must not let down Alice, or the producer, or The Bard.

But as I reset Table 13, I find it impossible not to think about the first time I saw the play, with Mum. How we spoke for hours afterwards about the actress playing Viola, and her incredible stage presence.

Checking that Dad's busy attending to a group of Ladies Who Lunch, I slyly open my one-sided WhatsApp chat with Mum.

Her last message was last week, a photo of their dogs sitting neatly by food bowls. Next to them, The Pig has thrown her trough upside-down onto her head, food raining into her mouth. It had made me really laugh, then feel really sad. I hadn't replied.

Setting myself up behind the counter, ostensibly folding more origami pizza napkins, I type cautiously.

Hey Mum, hope you're all keeping well. Guess what? I'm

auditioning for a role in Twelfth Night! *I probably won't get it but it's still exciting. Do you remember when—*

I sigh and delete the message.

Hey, just thought you might like to know I'm auditioning for a role in Twelfth Night—

'Emmeline?'

I drop my phone guiltily. Dad and Pete are looking over the counter at me.

'Dad. Boss. Hi. I was just… napkins.'

They glance at each other.

'We have something important to talk to you about,' says Dad, with unusual gravity.

He's looking teary. Oh my God, they're finally going to fire me. My chest fills with wild panic – and a strange relief.

'Congratulations!' says Pete. 'We're adding the Emmy Special to the permanent menu!'

'Oh.'

Pete's smile wobbles.

'I mean, *oh*!' I correct myself. 'Wow! Thanks, Boss! I'm honoured!'

'It's one of our bestsellers now,' says Dad. 'And we think it's responsible for bringing in a new kind of clientele.' With zero subtlety, he points towards a corner where Mullet and their double denim friends are back. I blush. 'If you have any further ideas for the menu, or what you think your – your customers would want, then we want to hear.'

He pinches my cheek and my heart squeezes.

'I can't tell you how happy I am to see that pizza *is* in your blood.'

I smile back, my ears reddening. Maybe it wouldn't be the worst thing in the world, to stay working here. Maybe if I tried harder, I could even enjoy it.

Dad puts his hand on my shoulder, smiling fondly.

'Your mum would be proud,' he says quietly. 'It took her years to make us try dairy-free dough balls.'

Panic rises in my stomach and I look away, glancing at my phone screen to check it's not showing the conversation with Mum. Could he sense I nearly betrayed him?

'Thanks, Dad, but it's *you* I want to be proud of me.'

He pinches my cheek again and sighs, then picks up the napkins and heads back to the customers.

As soon as they're gone, I open the draft message to my mum and delete it, feeling terrible.

I return from my shift and think the flat is on fire. Raphy's in a kitchen filled with smoke from the multiple pans on the hob, and the too-many tall wax candles he's lit around the room. Oh that's right, it's date night.

He's bringing Valentine from OK Cupid, and Ruth is bringing some non-marketing date. They told me to invite Alice but I said she was busy. I don't really know why, but I feel weird about her meeting R&R. Maybe I just want to keep her to myself for now, until I feel more secure in the relationship. Yes, that'll be it.

Raphy's sweaty and stressed, wearing his sloppiest second-hand tie-dye and holey joggers under a Pride flag apron. He's moved the kitchen around to create space for five people at the table, pulling in Ruth's wheely office desk chair and his own orthopaedic stool as the missing seats. Every centimetre of our IKEA table is covered, Raphy arranging the multiple glasses and cutleries in an elaborate jigsaw.

Raphy keeps glancing at a clock he borrowed from Ruth.

'Anything I can do to—'

'No!' he yells. 'What will be will be!'

I sit at the table, trying to make myself invisible.

At one minute before seven, Ruth's bedroom door opens.

She's wearing the outfit she normally saves for her fanciest marketing pitches, a sleeveless LBD with a high lacey collar and killer magenta lipstick. Her heels have never been bigger. She stands in the kitchen doorway. Raphy stares at her for so long the pitta on the hob sets alight. Ruth calmly takes the tea towel from his shoulder, puts out the fire with brutal efficiency, and slings it back.

Ruth takes the spoon from Raphy's hand. She dips it into the dahl and, never taking her eyes from his, tastes it.

'You could do with more salt,' she whispers, and pushes the spoon back into his chest. Raphy nods dumbly.

She sweeps to the table, sitting at her office chair like a throne. She winks at me. I feel the glow of my friends being incredible. How could their dates ever be good enough to deserve them?

'They're late,' tuts Ruth. 'I expected that from you hippies, but you said "Valentine" works in marketing.'

Raphy twitches. 'There will be a perfectly reasonable explanation.'

Ruth sips her red wine. 'Maybe.'

Ruth and Raphy are practically sitting on top of each other. Reaching for the olives, my elbow keeps hitting both of theirs. It's difficult to tell who looks more uncomfortable.

Twenty minutes later, Ruth's phone lights up and her jaw sets.

'Well, surprise, surprise,' she says. 'He's stood me up. Says he needs to spend this evening "protecting his peace". Urgh.'

I go to hug her sympathetically, but she shrugs me off.

'Oh, I'm not sad,' she says. 'I'm just angry.'

Her acrylic nails tap furiously into her phone.

'I *shaved* for him, the bastard. What a waste of fucking time. I could have been preparing for my promotion.'

Raphy starts to remove one of the sets of cutlery from the table.

'Forget him,' he says, with surprising wrath, 'it's his loss.'

Ruth glances at him. 'Perhaps you should check if Valentine is lost?'

I take over stirring the dahl while Raphy squints at his Chromebook.

'Ru, could you help me with this tech? I must be doing something wrong. Valentine's profile has disappeared...'

Ruth and I exchange a look. Ruth goes to stand behind him.

'Our messages were there…' He points. Ruth blinks.

'That *bitch*,' she says, and starts trying to find her on social media.

'Oh,' says Raphy. '*Oh*, I see.'

He puts a gentle hand on her wrist.

'It's fine,' he says. 'I'm not angry. Just a little sad.'

'Well,' I say brightly. 'Looks like everyone we needed was already here!'

I push Ruth's wheely office chair away, resetting the table to our usual three places.

Raphy serves up three bowls of lukewarm dahl and adds coriander to mine and his. He leaves it off Ruth's (she has that soap gene), and passes her the pot of sea salt flakes instead.

When we're seated, Ruth and Raphy smile tentatively at each other.

'I'm sorry about your date,' he says. 'You deserve better.'

She looks away, smooths her hair.

'Oh, well, like you always say: everything happens for a reason.'

I gleefully snap a huge poppadom and share it out to them, not trying very hard to hide my smile.

23

So here I am, treading the boards again. By which I mean I'm walking into the foyer at The Boards Theatre. But this time, finally, I'm going to be on the stage itself.

Yes, only for an audition, but still.

There's the red carpet, there's the chandelier, there's the spiral staircase leading up to the bloodstained face of Annabel Finch. Now when I look at her, all I can see is the family resemblance to Mae. Even on a poster, I can't meet those familiar blue eyes.

I never replied to Mae's text about us 'hanging out as friends', and she hasn't messaged me again since. Not that I'm complaining. It's good. It's what I wanted. It's easier to remember we're enemies when she's not lighting up my phone. It's good to remove the distraction. Think about how much time I'm going to save, by not constantly checking my phone, waiting to see if she liked my reply! When I finally stop.

I arrived my usual forty-five minutes early, so that I could do my pre-audition warm-ups in the theatre loo. I take deep breaths. I tap my toes. I do my tongue-twisters. A few people come in and out, but I keep going, running through Viola's ring monologue. Even the vivid memory of my first meeting with Mae, and of her twinkling laugh through the wall, won't distract me from my routine.

Ten minutes before call-time, I open the door.

There's Mae.

I scream and shut the door again. I must be hallucinating.

But then I hear her laughter. Evil laughter.

I push the door open slowly. Mae steps forwards, leaning on the open doorway, glaring.

Her shirt is crimson, her cargo trousers are black, her platform trainers are decorated with flames. The playful grin I remember from the improv show has gone and now she's just glaring at me like a vampire whose prey tried to escape.

'Mae – what the hell are you doing here?'

'Clooney, Clooney,' she smirks. 'I thought you were smarter than that. I'm here to audition for *Twelfth Night*. Like you.'

'B-but—'

'Anything you can do, I can do better,' she says. 'Haven't you learnt that by now?'

We look at each other for a second. I wonder if she's thinking about our texts, like I am. About that kiss she put at the end.

'Jones, I – I'm sorry I never replied about—'

She holds up her hand to stop me, then holds it to her chest in remorse.

'Don't apologise,' she says. 'It's my fault, really.' She raises an eyebrow at me, her eyes deathly cold. 'I was stupid to think you were capable of normal human friendliness. But don't worry. I learn from my mistakes.'

My jaw clenches. I'm so sick of people thinking I'm some kind of emotionless robot. I really thought Mae might be one of the few people who didn't think that. But clearly I was wrong too.

I glare at her. Mae languidly reaches towards me and tilts my watch towards her.

'Can't be late. Time for me to crush your dreams.'

Thirty actors are sitting in a circle on The Boards' second stage. It's a more versatile and intimate space than the larger proscenium arch of the main stage, but it also lacks natural light and oxygen. It's a windowless box room with mirrors on every wall, ballet bars covered by black curtains. The combination of this – and Mae's malign aura – are making me lightheaded.

Everyone got the brief that this is a queer production: there's a lot of vests and loose-fitting denim; someone's even in a leather harness. Everyone has a strong individual look, although some people are part of recognisable queer cliques – camp flamboyants, edgy punks, cutesy rainbow dungarees, and a handful of understated monochromes like me.

Francis de la Ware is in the centre of the circle, wearing his trademark blue-spotted neckerchief. He's thirty (he was on this year's list of rising stars, next to Thalia. It's a small industry) but his hair and moustache are grey and stylishly slicked. His eyes are silver too, and steely.

Francis rotates slowly in the middle of the circle, making eye contact with each of us in turn.

'Good *morning*, my little stars,' he says luxuriously, with an east London accent. 'Welcome home. Now the thing to remember about today is that this is a *workshop*. This is *not* an audition.'

My stomach relaxes slightly.

'This is not an audition,' he repeats, twirling. 'This is not an audition. This is not an audition.'

Everyone starts looking shifty.

'As you should all bloody well know, I am Francis de la Ware, and I am the director of this production, which means that inside the four walls of this rehearsal room, I am your God. I am your master and saviour, and what I say goes. You may call me Francis, Sir, Master, or, once you've earned it, Captain Frank. Understood?'

The room replies with his various names. Mae laughs uncertainly, until she catches my serious expression. I appreciate Sir's guidance.

'I want to establish a few things about my vision for the play right away,' says Francis, pacing. 'We have the stage for ninety minutes with no interval, so I shall be cutting great swathes of the script. We also, in order to pay each of our cast fairly on our "limited" budget, will be having a reduced number of performers, some playing multiple roles. I am therefore looking to cast eight actors. Eight, of you.'

The room is very still. Everyone looks round, trying to do mental arithmetic.

'All the parts will be cast gender blind, and the sexuality of the actor does not need to correspond with the traditional sexuality of the role. We may well experiment in rehearsals with what it would mean to shift different characters' attractions.'

He stops spinning for a second, and rolls his eyes.

'Oh my God! Would you all relax? You are all highly experienced young performers who come highly recommended from various casting teams, and have been through several rounds of auditions already…' He hesitates. 'Well, *most* of you have.'

I pray that the blush on my cheeks isn't obvious. Am I the only person who got in without the usual formal channels, or do other people do this kind of thing more regularly and breezily? How did Mae get in?

Francis steeples his fingers.

'But I need the *best*. I need eight actors who are hungry to prove to the theatrical world that they should continue doing productions like this. I need performers who will get us standing ovations and incredible reviews and a place in the Shakespearean canon.'

Mae and I lock eyes across the room.

'I am assuming you have all done your homework, so I won't patronise you with a plot summary of *Twelfth Night*. But what I'm interested in is making this – frankly, ridiculous and unbelievable – story feel *real*. What I want to see today is you bringing sense to Shakespeare.

'For example,' he continues, lost in the middle distance. 'Our heroine Viola arrives on the shore thinking her twin has died at sea. Why does she disguise herself as a man? Why does she go to work for the Duke Orsino? Why does Orsino ask the disguised Viola to help him woo another woman, and why does that woman fall in love with Viola? I want a love triangle as messy and sexy as your own offstage dating histories.'

The group laughs. I force a chuckle, worrying about whether my sexual inexperience off-stage will stop me from getting the part.

'Don't overthink it,' says Francis. 'For this workshop, I just wanted to bring a group of queer performers together to play, to experiment, to be completely safe and free with your ideas. But I shall be watching closely to see who has the *best* ideas.'

He claps his hands.

'Let the games begin! Everyone auditioning – I mean, *workshopping* – for the role of Viola' – he waves the sheets – 'here's the monologue.'

There's a mad rush to grab one. It seems over half of the room are aiming for Viola, including myself. And Mae.

Mae takes two and sardonically offers me one. I refuse it. I've known those lines by heart since I was fourteen. She glares back.

'Now, let's get the work on its feet.'

Francis arranges us in a circle around a microphone.

'When the feeling strikes you, jump in and take the mic. Carry on speaking the lines of the scene as if you're all the same character.'

He sits backwards on his chair – one of those ones with DIRECTOR printed on it – and gestures for us to begin.

Several people step boldly forwards. One wins the race to the microphone and proclaims the first line: 'She returns this ring to you, sir.'

Then, though it's supposed to be that you go in 'when the spirit compels you', people end up taking turns round the circle, cutting the next person off even if they were halfway through a sentence. It's like Quakers fighting to the death.

When it gets to me, I deliberately don't go up. I'm aware of Francis, Mae, and the others looking at me, but I stand my ground. The person who was up before me seems delighted at first, says another line. Then the actor to my right takes over.

More fool them. I'm saving my powder for the first line of Viola's monologue.

Then it gets to Mae, but *she* doesn't go either. My blood boils. What a pathetic copycat. Fortunately, those kind of moves only have their impact once.

Someone is speaking the penultimate line. Here we go. I close my eyes, breathe in deep, and take my confident step forwards towards the microphone.

No one else had incorporated any actions or movement into their lines – amateurs – so I know I'll stand out with my plan to simply bend and pick up the imaginary ring that Malvolio has thrown onto the ground.

I step towards the mic and dip down curiously, as if I really have seen something glinting on the floor by the stand. But as I bend, my head bashes into something. Someone.

I look up to see Mae, doing exactly the same thing. She's even clasping her finger and thumb as if she's just tried to pick up the same imaginary ring that I have.

We rub our heads, looking at the imaginary ring we've now both dropped between us. We look back up at each other. I sense Mae make the decision, see the slightest twitch in her arms. And that's like a starting pistol to me. I start forwards to grab the imaginary ring. She does too. Now we're both gripping each other's fingers. I hear Francis laugh with surprise.

Purposefully ignoring me, Mae grabs the microphone. I have no choice but to step backwards and watch as she says *my* lines.

'I left no ring with her,' she says.

Immediately, there's a sense of history and weight behind that line. She's saying it completely opposite to how I'd practised, but it – it's as if Mae is just chatting. To *me*.

'What means this lady?' she laughs. 'Fortune forbid my outside have not charm'd her!'

I don't have time to be impressed. I don't have time to be awed by her skill at making Shakespearean language sound completely modern. I don't even have time to be angry. It's just me and Mae, arguing.

'She made good view of me,' she says, a swaggering twinkle in her eye.

'Indeed,' I cut in, dryly. 'So much, that sure methought her eyes had lost her tongue, for—'

Mae interrupts me, excitedly playing along, 'She *did* speak in starts distractedly.'

We both pause. Mae shrugs. 'She loves me, sure.'

Francis laughs.

'I am the man,' says Mae, like a stand-up comedian. I snatch the microphone from her.

'*If* it be so—'

She pulls it back, sniggers into it.

'As 'tis,' argues Mae. A few actors in the group laugh now. I snatch it back.

Mae's Viola is so sure this woman is in love with her – it's not even Mae acting, it's just Mae, as usual, thinking the world adores her. I practically spit.

'She were better love a dream.'

The monologue becomes a barely disguised fight. No one else steps forwards for the mic, or maybe they do, but we don't notice them. It's gone so far off my planned versions of this speech that I'm just acting on vengeful impulse now, purely reacting to Mae.

I snap. 'How easy is it for the proper-false in women's waxen hearts to set their forms!'

Mae replies, 'Such as we are made of, such we be.'

Wait. She's missed out a line! Then she does it again, skipping half the monologue.

She's *messing* with *Shakespeare*?

I'm so angry I grab the microphone, but she keeps hold of it too. Both holding on now, our hands clasped over each other's, we say in unison, 'What will become of this?'

We narrow our eyes at each other, breathing heavily. Then Mae grins.

'Thou must untangle this, not I,' she says, and drops the microphone.

There's a sharp clap. We wake, surprised to find there's an audience of other actors watching us. My cheeks flare and I step away from Mae's body.

'Well, this *is* interesting,' says Francis, resting his chin on his hand. 'Do you two know each other?'

I glance at Mae. I don't want to be associated with this unprofessional buffoon, however charismatic she is.

'No,' I say. At the same time, Mae says, 'Yes.'

Francis's grin broadens.

The other performers in the group are now outright glaring, as I would have been.

I return to my place in the circle, and dare myself to glance at Mae. She's already looking at me, but I can't read her expression. I look away first.

It seems like we made an impression on Francis – but which of us will win?

After a short break we split into smaller groups for the other workshop games. I avoid being in a group with Mae, but remain hyper aware of what she's doing. She's quieter, waiting for others to go first before contributing. There's seemingly no difference between her chatting as 'Mae' and chatting as 'Viola'. I want to point at her and shout, 'She's a fake! She's just saying the lines but still being herself! She's not a real actor!' I also want to take her out onto the landing and push her down the stairs.

At the end of the workshop, I'm exhausted.

We all file out and I find myself unsure whether to wait for Mae or not. I know we're enemies, but after today's fracases, can I really leave without saying goodbye?

In the end I don't have to decide, because as Mae walks out, Francis calls to us. To both of us. We silently follow him back into the rehearsal room.

Francis sits back on his director chair, grey eyes flashing between us.

'Well, well. Emmy Clooney and Mae Jones. Your chemistry was really something out there,' he says. 'Are you two...?'

'*No*,' we both say emphatically.

'Interesting,' he says, moustache twitching. 'Then perhaps I should speak to you separately. I only called you in together because it felt as if you were, really, auditioning for each other...'

'Thanks, Francis,' says Mae quickly. 'But the two of us know everything about each other's careers, so we can hear it together. Isn't that right, *Emmy*?'

She says my name so simperingly, I wince. I nod stiffly.

Francis tilts his head at us like we're an odd toy that's fallen out of his cracker.

'In that case...'

He flourishes our printed-out CVs, holding them up to check he's got us the right way round.

'In my career as a director, I have learnt to trust my gut. Well, unless I've had gluten. And my gut has already made my casting decisions for *Twelfth Night*.'

Francis turns to me as though he's on a very long-running daytime gameshow, about to announce whether I've won the jackpot. My heart's thudding.

'Emmy Clooney,' he says, and pauses for a hundred years. 'Congratulations. I'd like you to join my cast.'

I can't help it. I punch the air.

My career has been made. My life has been made. I turn to Mae, all colour drained from her face, and am about to say, 'Suck on *that*, loser!' when I remember the presence of Francis. I shake his hand respectfully in both of mine.

'Thank you, Sir, thank you. I'd be delighted to accept.'

Francis's moustache ripples. 'For the role of Sebastian.'

My hand-shaking pauses. Sebastian? As in, the shipwrecked twin of...

Francis lets my hand go, and turns to Mae.

'Mae Jones,' he continues. 'I'd like to offer you the role of Viola.'

I stop breathing.

Mae smiles slowly, broadly, with dimples. She steps graciously forwards and shakes Francis's hand.

'Thank you, Captain Frank. I'd be *delighted* to accept.'

Hands still clasped, she glances back at me. All the glints in the world are in her eyes. They're saying, 'Suck on *that*, loser.'

24

Superstitiously, I don't tell anyone about the part until Valerie and Louisa send through the paperwork. When it's all signed, they congratulate me.

'This could be your big break!' says Valerie, down the phone. 'And my commission will pay for a whole one week of nursery school fees!'

I try to remind myself that – despite Mae coming along, stealing my dream role, and generally ruining my life – this is still a good opportunity.

I call a flat meeting and tell Ruth and Raphy. They're astonishingly supportive, though when I tell them about Mae being cast in the lead, they wrongly squeal with delight rather than horror.

Raphy bakes celebratory hash brownies ('Don't worry,' he says, 'they're organic') and Ruth suggests we watch *Rocky Horror*.

'It's definitely still positive!' they agree.

'You're still in the show,' says Raphy. 'The same audience will see you.'

'Yeah, it's the same thing on your CV,' says Ruth.

Raphy, tucking into another brownie, giggles. 'It's all in how you *brand* it,' he mimics her. 'Tell public relations that Sebastian is a massive boss and it's a done deal.'

Ruth pushes him and giggles, copying Raphy's witchy gestures. 'The universe says fake it till you make it.'

Then they're wrestling and we're all laughing and I feel blissfully confident that getting this part is, in fact, the best thing that's ever happened to me.

So, in bed that night, high from camp music and lovely friends and, well, drugs, I do something stupid.

I text Thalia.

Hey stranger!!!! How are you!!!! I miss you!!!! Just to confirm lol I AM in the Twelfth Night *at Boards !!!!! See You There on 29th????*

And the wildest thing? Thalia replies.

Omg congrats Emmy! Yeah of course I'll be there. Wouldn't miss it for the world. And drinks after! On me.

The next day I cringe painfully reading my message back. But reading Thalia's makes me feel as if I'm still high.

'Dad,' I say down the phone. 'I've got amazing news!'

'Oooh,' he squeals. 'You're eating meat again? You're going full-time? You're back in touch with your mum?'

'Stop guessing!' I cough and restart, trying to regain the brightness in my voice. 'I've got my big break.'

Silence.

'Well, *a* big break,' I say. 'I've been cast in this production of *Twelfth Night* – you know, umm, Shakespeare? – and I'll be rehearsing for three weeks, and then there are performances at The Boards – you know, that, umm, big theatre? – and they're paying us upfront. So I finally don't need to do any shifts this month!'

I know as soon as the words are out of my mouth that it was the wrong thing to say. Damn it, this is why you should always script conversations.

'I mean,' I backtrack, 'that I won't be able to fit any valuable waitressing work in. Because of my other job.' I try to have more confidence. 'Because of my job. As an actor. Which is what I am.'

More silence.

Then Dad says quietly, 'Some people would be more grateful for this job, Emmeline. For stable money, earnt doing good, honest work. Look at Carmella. She's a... she's like you.' (He means an actor, not a queer.) 'But she still turns up for *her* shifts.'

Thalia's voice in the back of my mind says, 'Yeah, that's because she's not a very *good* actor.'

'I'm sorry, Dad... But when I make it, I'll promote Pete's'zas in every interview I do.'

'Right,' he huffs. 'And what about when this "job" ends?'

I bite my lip. The *Twelfth Night* money is better than I expected, but if I am doing no shifts and no other acting work while it's happening, I'll only just about be able to cover rent and food for this month. I'll start again next month with nothing. Back to square one. Do not pass go, do not collect £200.

I don't know whether to scream or cry. Will it always be like this? Having to sell myself from part to part, paycheque to paycheque?

'When showbiz lets you down again, you'll come running back for more shifts, like you always do,' he says. 'I've been putting your crazy timetable first, over mine, even over the other staff's. But soon, they're going to tire of the favouritism.'

My stomach turns. Indignation has been replaced with indigestion. He's right. I've been taking Pete's'zas for granted, and now it's catching up with me. And let's face it, I'm not a good enough waitress for them to make all these concessions for me.

'As your bosses, Pete and I need some commitment from you. And as your family... I don't think it's unreasonable to expect some mutual respect.'

I drop into my desk chair, blinking rapidly up at my scribbled playscripts and posters.

Dad sighs into the silence. 'I need to know you're not going to just drop all your responsibilities if you get a better offer.'

I clutch the phone in sweaty palms. No wonder he's so upset

with me. He thinks I'm like Mum. That I'm going to leave him for a better life, and never look back.

'Emmeline? Are you still there?'

'Yes, Dad,' I say hurriedly. 'Yes, I am. I'm here.'

'Am I putting you on the rota next month, or not?'

'I… Yes please.'

'All right, then.'

'I'm sorry, Dad,' I mumble.

He sighs.

'OK, Patatina. Want me to bring you over some pizzas for your rehearsal lunch boxes?'

His little potato holds back tears.

'Yes please.'

25

Alice pops a champagne cork and pours it into my glass.

'I'm so proud of you, darling. And no one can say you didn't earn it fair and square.'

She toasts me. I can't help noticing that the neckline of her dresses gets lower on each of our dates.

'Now,' she squeezes my hand, 'don't worry about it only being a tiny little insignificant part. It's like they say, "there are no small parts, only small actors". So just don't be a small actor.'

I nod.

'You can still steal the show. Certainly the record will say you did, if I've got anything to do with it.'

I frown at her over the champagne.

'What do you mean?'

'Well, of course I've put in a request to review it! I'm the only lesbian on the team at *The Atre*, so I'm sure it will go through. Now.' She smiles. 'What's your favourite complimentary adjective?'

I stop my glass on the way to my lips. 'Alice, wouldn't that be a little… unprofessional?'

She frowns. I realise that sounded judgemental.

'I just mean,' I try to make it into a joke, 'surely the reviewing of the show and the reviewing of my performance as a dating partner could get blurred?'

Alice licks her lipstick.

'Then you'd better give me some good reasons to give you five stars.'

Fizz goes up my nose.

'Oh, bless you,' laughs Alice, slapping my hand across the table. 'You're so proper, aren't you? My parents are going to love you.'

Parents?

I force a laugh. Emmy, stop being weird, she's obviously joking.

'Don't you want me to watch you on stage?' she asks. 'See you doing your passion?'

'Of – of course I do.'

'Well then,' she says. 'That's that.'

She shakes out a napkin and places it on her lap with finality. I should let it go, but… it makes me feel sordid. I want to earn my good reviews, not go on dates for them. Besides, what if Mae found out?

'I just think it's… Wouldn't some people maybe think it was… nepotistic? Someone might find out and wave it around online and tarnish our reputations forever, and then our enemies would—'

'Pish,' laughs Alice. 'Do you have many enemies?'

I hesitate. Alice quirks a pencilled eyebrow at me.

'Ooh. An ex?'

Her tone is icy. I tell myself that jealousy is natural and shows she cares about me. But goodness me, dating is an obstacle course.

'No! Not an ex!' I say. 'I told you, I don't have any exes! You have nothing to worry about there! No significant people from my past at all!'

Alice blinks slowly, topping up her champagne. She doesn't top up mine.

I consider lying. But Alice is my *girlfriend*. My *first girlfriend*. I should be honest with her.

'Well, this is going to sound strange,' I say. 'But there's this other actor I've ended up having a bit of a – a rivalry with.'

Alice pauses, her red lip on the rim of the glass.

'What kind of rivalry?'

'We're the same casting type, so we keep competing for parts. And the problem is...' I shrug grudgingly. 'She's really good.'

I find I'm enjoying the excuse to talk about Mae. I don't want to do it too much in front of R&R because when I do, they insist on winking at each other.

'She's the complete opposite to me,' I continue. 'I prepare, plan, research, but she's... she's a natural. *Too* natural, if anything. She's instinctive, reactive, authentic. She's just *herself* on stage. But unfortunately, "herself" is really captivating to watch. She's got that – that stage magnetism.'

Alice is looking at me so strangely, I realise I might have accidentally sounded complimentary about my sworn enemy.

'But she's also incredibly unprofessional,' I say quickly. 'And she's a nepotism baby – her mum is literally a celebrity actress! And she doesn't even do the bare minimum of preparation for a role. She barely learns her lines, and gets away with winging it because she's good at schmoozing. Other people think she's charming, but I see straight through it.'

Alice stares at me, then downs her glass.

'So you're not... You and this enemy girl. You're not close? You don't talk?'

'No.'

'Won't you become friends, now that you're in the same show?'

'No,' I say emphatically. 'We rub each other completely the wrong way. Being around each other just makes it worse. I know it sounds unprofessional, but—'

'No!' she says, banging her fist on the table. 'It's *very* professional of you. She could ruin *everything*.' Alice pours the rest of the bottle into her glass. 'Your career *must* come first,' she shouts. 'You *must* defeat her. Just because you've been cast together does not mean you should fraternise with her. This gives her more opportunity to ruin your career. So you must be on guard. If she tries to become your friend, it's a tactic. Don't believe a word she says.'

She bangs the table again. The glasses tremble. Their scared twinkling and my surprised blinking seem to wake Alice from her frenzy. She gathers herself, and glances up at me.

'That was... not very ladylike of me. But you see, I understand rivalry.' She glances at me again and takes a sip, gripping the stem hard.

'A-another theatre critic. I hardly need tell you that it's not a critic's job to review other critics, but he decided to do some work outside of his job description. Said nasty things about how I was stealing other people's ideas, how I wrote my reviews in advance, blah blah. Ironically, it was rather unoriginal of him.'

I wince, thinking how terrible I'd feel if I was accused of copying someone else's work.

'That's awful,' I say, tentatively taking Alice's hand over the table. 'I'm so sorry.'

Alice squeezes back.

'But you see, that's where you and I are so alike,' she says. 'We're ambitious. We work hard, we strategise and organise, because we know that's the only way to get anywhere in this industry. It's perfectly natural that you'd have competition. In a way, you're in competition with every other actor, aren't you? But don't worry. I'm going to help you. I'll do everything in my power to ensure that you beat...'

She swallows.

'Her name is Mae Jones,' I supply.

'Mae Jones,' she says in a strangled voice. 'This rival of yours, this – this *bitch* will never work another day in her life.'

Alice shakes the champagne bottle, frustrated at finding it empty.

'Now then,' she says, tucking hair behind her ear. 'Are we

going home together tonight, or are you going to say you have to work early again tomorrow?'

'Well, I-I *do* have to work—'

Alice reaches across the table, grabs at my lapels, and pulls me into a deep kiss. I'm so startled I forget to kiss back.

She strokes my ear and says, 'When will you *not* be working early the next day?'

I flinch. She presses her chest more firmly against mine.

'Er… After the *Twelfth Night* performances?'

Alice jerks away, pulling a face.

'But darling, that's *aeons* away.'

'It's only a few weeks,' I laugh awkwardly.

'No,' she pouts. 'I *need* to see you. You can't be rehearsing *all* the time. You need breaks.'

She kisses me again. I feel like I always do when Alice and I kiss – aware of our audience.

To my great relief, she pulls away. Her cheeks are flushed very beautifully, and more blonde wisps have come free from her chignon. What's wrong with me? Any self-respecting lesbian should be agog at a vision like this.

'And now I suppose you're going to call me a cab,' she sighs.

I do so.

I open the taxi door for her, ashamed.

'Thanks for another lovely evening, Alice. And… And for helping me with the part. I really am grateful. Thank you. And sorry.'

She tilts her head at me, her hazel stare steady.

'Can I change your mind?'

I try to look regretful as I shake my head.

'Next time,' I say.

'Promise?' she says.

I swallow, but can't reply.

'You're such a gentleman, aren't you?' she sighs, but there's an edge to it. 'You'll text me, then,' she says, and I nod eagerly. 'And I *will* see you soon.'

She closes the door behind her. As the taxi drives away, I breathe a sigh of relief, then feel terrible and guiltily text her a string of kisses.

26

I close the flat door and hear the fumbling of glasses from the living room. Ruth must have won Raphy over on the music – they're playing some surprisingly sophisticated R&B.

They're sitting on the sofa with a bottle of red and a chessboard between them.

'What ceremony is it tonight?' I ask Raphy, pointing to all the candles he's lit around the room.

'Oh… Moon is in Venus?'

'Cool,' I shrug. 'Budge up.'

In my absence, Ruth had slid into the middle spot on the sofa next to Raphy.

'You're back early from your date,' she says.

'Urgh, I know, I know,' I say, burying my head in my hands. 'I fucked up again.'

They put their glasses down and rub my back, cooing. I nestle into them.

'Alice invited me to hers and I made another excuse. What's wrong with me?'

'Oh honey, nothing is *wrong* with you,' says Raphy.

'I have no excuse,' I say. 'She's intelligent, and impressive, and has been so generous to me, and she is forthright with what she wants and that she wants to do it with me and yet… Urgh! I'm *meant* to want to sleep with my sexy girlfriend!'

'Well,' says Raphy, crossing his legs into a lotus, 'sexuality is fluid and it's allowed to change and grow with you. Are you experiencing *any* sexual attraction at the moment?'

Terrifyingly, my mind conjures an image of Mae. I swallow.

'Sometimes,' I say.

Ruth raises an eyebrow. 'Uh huh. Then babe, you're with the wrong person. When I was with Six-Pack Mike I couldn't get it up, no matter how hard I thought about his presentation skills.'

Raphy gets up from the sofa and starts fiddling with the candles.

'And I bet there are people you've been with, Raphael,' says Ruth, 'where you don't click in the bedroom the same way you click in, I don't know, discussions about psychoanalysis?'

Raphy fumbles with a wick and nearly sets the house on fire. He curses, rights the candle, and then tries to cancel out his swear with a blessing.

'Attraction is interdependent and intersectional,' he says. 'As much as we try to rationalise it, sometimes we have to accept that it's a force beyond our control...'

He takes a gulp of wine, leaving a lipstick-like stain on his lip.

'But surely just because I don't want to leap into bed with Alice, doesn't necessarily mean I'm not meant to be with her!' I say. 'Maybe it just means I-I need to be more comfortable with her first? Or something?'

I'm surprised to see Raphy's blushing a little. Maybe he's embarrassed on my behalf at my lack of libido compared to his.

'It's completely allowed to want to take things slow,' he says.

'Yes, slow can be good sometimes,' says Ruth. I frown at her.

'Really? *You* think that? Miss Efficiency is Best Even in the Bedroom?'

She coughs. I notice she's not wearing her beeping watch tonight. I'm glad she's relaxing, but isn't her big presentation coming up soon?

'Well,' she says, 'it's a big step. Once you've crossed that line, you can't take it back...'

Ruth and Raphy look at each other across me on the sofa, clearly wondering what piece of wisdom to give me next.

'Perhaps it's a good idea,' he says, 'to keep things as they are.'

'But guys,' I wail, and they jump a little, 'if I'm not sexually intimate with her then she'll dump me!'

'Then let her! There are plenty more fish in the sea!'

'You guys are being incredibly confusing!' I wail. '*You* said she was perfect for me! And she is! She actually *likes* me! I might never have a chance like this again! A few weeks ago you were all but forcing me to go on dates and have sex with people!'

They both look at me properly now.

'Yes, honey, but not with someone you don't want to,' says Raphy.

'And not,' adds Ruth, 'not with someone where you really *do* want to if you think it might ruin other important things in your life! Even if you want to, like – God – *so much –*'

I stare at Ruth. Is she… Does she somehow know I've been thinking about Mae?

'OK, so you're saying…?'

'Just don't change anything,' says Ruth.

'Keep things exactly how they are,' agrees Raphy. 'That's for the best.'

'OK…'

We all sit on the sofa, watching the candles burning around us.

27

I'm staring up at the old-fashioned cinema-style lights above The Boards Theatre, imagining my name there. No, it won't be there for my tiny part in *Twelfth Night*, but at least the name of the *show* I'm in will be.

There's a violent shove in my back.

'Wearing black again, Clooney? How fun.'

Mae's wearing an oversized checkerboard shirt and yellow trainers.

'Wearing something stupid again, Jones? How quirky.'

'Wow, you're so original, even with your insults.'

I don't have a comeback, so I resort to mimicking her.

'*You're* so original,' I parrot.

Mae smirks.

'Shall we make sure we don't walk in together?' she says.

'Definitely,' I say, and step forwards.

'Great,' she says, and pushes past me to get in first.

We wrestle with the door handle and end up falling into the foyer together.

The five waiting cast members of *Twelfth Night* turn to look at us.

Mae and I brush ourselves off. She grins and waves.

'Hi!' she says, and goes to befriend everyone. I loiter behind, carefully removing different editions of my marked-up *Twelfth Night*. I want Francis de la Ware to see that at least *some* of us are professionals.

He's wearing a green handkerchief around his neck today. He checks his watch and, on the dot of 9 a.m., opens the rehearsal room, pulls up a box, and stands on it.

'Friends, Romans, queers, lend me your ears.'

We hurriedly huddle. I click my mechanical pencil and hover it over my notebook.

'Congratulations, special few,' he says. 'You have violently beaten hundreds of your fellow gay actors to the ground in order to earn your place on this stage. Now, it's time to celebrate. Let there be foolery! Revelry! Bacchanalian delights! For you have earnt your place in *Twelfth Night*, the play of festivity!'

A couple of performers who seem to already be flirting nudge each other happily.

'But it's not going to be easy,' adds Francis.

They stop nudging.

'We will be rehearsing for the rest of June. Three intense weeks, Monday to Friday, nine to five. Living the Dolly Parton dream. Then we will perform as part of London's Pride Festivities, June 29th and 30th. Yes, in some ways, marvellous, delicious, huzzah. But, as many of you will have no doubt noticed, we only have two performances and no matinees, because that's the kind of trust we get for selling queer-focused shows.'

One of the other cast members – a twink wearing pink flannel – boos, and a few others join in. I'm so unused to being in an all-queer space, I'm astonished to hear someone with authority saying things like this aloud.

'But,' Francis continues, 'if we get good reviews, and sell out – that is, sell out in the good way – then the show might *possibly* be granted a tour.'

We all gasp and look round at each other. Going on tour is like the Holy Grail for a lot of performers. It's a guarantee of more work, positive additions to the CV, and national contacts, while also getting to travel and have fun on the road. I scribble everything down. My desire to prove myself has never been higher.

'Now, usually the play is set on the Twelfth Day of Christmas, but we don't want to be partaking in any of that mainstream Christian tomfoolery. Fortunately, I have a grand *vision* for our production. Our *Twelfth Night* shall be set in the world of... pirates.'

We hesitate for a moment, then 'ooh' and, aptly, 'arr'.

'That's the spirit! Now, I will give this precious piece of eight' – he pulls a prop coin from behind his ear – 'if anyone can tell me why I, God, have decided on this piratical theme?'

I put my hand up.

'Well, Sir,' I say excitedly, 'it's a truly fascinating choice. The play opens, of course, with a shipwreck, so the nautical element is signposted immediately. Then there's historical parallels of pirates as satirists and renegades of the state, which is how actors often saw themselves in Shakespeare's time. And, *Twelfth Night* is a play about disguises, subverting social status, the impact of alcohol...'

But then Mae raises her hand. I lose my train of thought. Francis gestures at her.

'And what does our Viola think?'

She shrugs. 'Because pirates are hot and gay?'

Francis grins and tosses her the coin.

Mae catches it, gives it a spin, winks at me. My jaw hurts.

'Now we don't have much time,' says Francis. 'I'm going to trust that you'll all take the opportunity to – ahem – bond offstage rather than in the rehearsal room. But I won't deny you one ceremonial warm-up game.'

Everyone claps camply. I try not to groan.

I've never gone in for group warm-ups. I value the importance of warming up the body and vocal chords, of course – actors are gymnasts – but we should be able to do it alone, without distracting giggling. Sometimes I think people become actors just because they like Zip, Zap, Boing.

Francis brandishes a toy starfish with a smiley face on it. It's... actually really cute.

'Use this as an opportunity to learn each other's names and, more than that, escalate your familiarity with each other. So get those boundaries down. When this little fella is with you, state your name, pronouns, part you're playing in the show, and something *true* about yourself. Like a fun fact. Or a tragic fact.'

This is my worst nightmare. I'm so busy worrying about what to say for my fact that the actors' names barely register.

'I'm Joe,' says a towering blonde hunk. 'He/him, and I'll be multi-tasking the roles of Duke Orsino and Antonio. My fun fact is that I eat five eggs a day.' He flexes. 'One day I'll be Gaston.'

The starfish is caught by long nails. 'I'm Keiya, she/her. I'm playing Malvolia, and yes, I firmly believe Shakespeare intended her to be a hot black trans woman.'

The others in the circle clap. Keiya tosses her long hair.

'Oh, and I'm a Scorpio, so I might not always be nice, but I am always right.'

Keiya throws the starfish to a short person with a multi-coloured buzz cut. 'Hi everyone! I'm Charlie, my pronouns are they/them, and I'm playing Feste the fool. Ooh, my thing is that I can play lotsa musical instruments, but I'm best at the accordion, the lute, and the penny whistle.'

Charlie throws it to a ginger twink.

'Haiii,' says the ginger twink. 'I'm playing Aguecheek, my pronouns are he/him, and I'm allergic to aloe vera… Oh, and my name is Roger, as in, phwoar, I'd like to Roger him!' He makes a practised gesture with his elbow and laughs for a long time. Roger hands the starfish to the tall bear next to him.

'All right, everyone! I'm Zach, he/him, and I'm playing Sir Toby Belch. Yes, I only got the part because I can burp on command.' He adjusts his flannel shirt and demonstrates, expertly.

'Do you take requests?' jokes Roger.

'If you buy me a pint,' Zach winks. Then he throws the starfish in a cricket-bowler's spin.

'I'm Surina, she/her,' says a pretty plus-size woman with

auburn hair and warm brown skin. 'I'm multi-ing the Lady Olivia and the maid Maria. And I adopted a kitten last week!'

She throws underarm to Mae.

'I must see pictures of your kitten,' says Mae, catching it. 'Like, urgently.'

Everyone laughs. My blood boils.

'I'm Mae Jones, she/her, and I'm so pumped to be playing the role of Viola.' She ruffles her already ruffled hair. 'My fun fact is – oh man, it's so hard to choose, I really desperately want you all to think I'm fun...' Everyone laughs again. Of course she is making a group warm-up into The Mae Show. 'OK. I once made a cake for Dame Judi Dench – and she said it was disgusting.'

The group arrs.

I'm picked last – of course, just like at school – so Mae has no choice but to throw it to me. Still, she manages to surprise me by feinting towards someone else. The starfish hits me in the face.

'G-good morning. I'm Emmy Clooney. No relation. My pronouns are she/her. I'm playing the role of Sebastian and... and...'

I blank. There's nothing fun about me at all.

'This is a safe space,' encourages Francis.

'I... I can name every winner of the Emmy Award since 1995,' I mumble.

The group blinks at me. The disappointment in the room is palpable.

Mae claps me on the shoulder.

'In our twinship, I do the fun; Emmy does the facts.'

Everyone laughs.

I'm so embarrassed that I throw the starfish back to Mae, hard. She catches it effortlessly.

'Woops! Thanks Emmy, but I've already been!'

She passes it to Francis.

'Here you go, Cap'n.'

'Good work, starlets,' he says, putting the starfish into his pocket. 'Take a five-minute fag break.'

Roger mutters, 'Wheey.'

'Then the real work will begin.'

I'm already exhausted.

The saying might be that 'there are no small parts, only small actors' but... Sebastian really *is* a small part, especially in this shortened production.

After our warm-ups, I'm not involved in any of the scenes we rehearse on the first day. But I ensure I'm there taking notes as Francis talks with the other actors about their character work, in case it affects my portrayal of Sebastian.

Mae is in almost every scene. By the end of the day, she has already developed in-jokes with every other member of the cast. I'm not sure who is flirting with her more, Joe (playing the Duke Orsino) or Surina (Lady Olivia). At least it's going to be a convincing onstage love triangle.

At five on the dot – mid-line – Francis stops rehearsals.

'I'm not going to make you work overtime,' he says. 'Go and rest, flirt, I'll see you tomorrow at nine, already warmed up.'

We step out, blinking, into the bright summer light. As always after rehearsals, I'm surprised to find that the rest of the world still exists.

Mae turns back to the group, holds her arms out wide and grins in triumph.

'Pints?' she asks.

Everyone cheers.

'Surely we should be drinking rum?' says Joe, and Mae 'arrs' back at him like a pirate. They laugh together, too loudly.

'Getting drunk is practically method acting for this play,' laughs Surina. Mae laughs with her, even louder.

And here we go again. It's just like in plays at school, where everyone else would effortlessly become best friends, and I'd have to struggle to be included. It would only be by the performance week that I'd finally feel part of a group, but then they'd all return to their cliques. It was the same at drama school, where we spent three years baring our souls (and bodies), and then, as soon as we graduated, I was discarded.

So, this time, do I go, attempt to befriend them, get my hopes up, and then lose them in a fortnight? Or save myself from a double humiliation?

Mae turns to me. 'Coming, Clooney?'

The others look at each other, then at us, then at each other again. Looks like our unconventional dynamic hasn't gone unnoticed.

'I mean, er, "Emmy"?'

'You guys are cute,' says Charlie.

'No, we're not,' we say at the same time.

Mae glances at me. 'Aren't you going to be working tonight?'

I understand her. She doesn't want us to get a reputation as a pair. That would not be good for our careers after the show. So I should say I'm busy, and let Mae go and befriend everyone. I suppose that makes my decision for me. I know I'd had my reservations about going to the pub and humiliating myself, but I can't deny my heart sinks a bit.

'Right,' I say. 'Yeah. I can't make it tonight, I've – I've got another job. Filming in the evenings.'

The others raise their eyebrows at each other.

Well done me. Managed to come across as a complete prick. I swallow uncomfortably.

'Oh. Well, break a leg,' says Mae shiftily.

I stop in the middle of the pavement and turn to walk the other way. Mae stops too. She opens her mouth to say something to me, but I can feel a knot building in my throat and, stupid as it sounds, I think if she were to say one more nasty thing to me, I'd cry.

Behind me, I hear Mae shout to the group, 'First round's on me!'

★

That night, while every other member of *Twelfth Night* is doubtless falling in love with Mae, I do what we *should* be doing: more work.

My play text is already tightly annotated, but I copy out the day's notes and my own developing interpretation of the play into a separate colour-coded notebook too.

I find myself thinking a lot about Mae's role. I mean, about Viola. But of course, everyone knows twins are connected in a mystical way, so it makes complete sense that the actor playing Sebastian would need an intimate understanding of Viola. And if anything were to happen to Mae, I would be the natural understudy.

'*If in our production all characters have queer potential,*' I write, '*then the real question is what stops ~~Mae~~ Viola from intimacy with Olivia? Or indeed with anyone else?*'

Then I find it frustratingly difficult to concentrate on an in-depth academic study of sapphism in Early Modern theatre.

I check my phone instead. I have a new message from Alice, and an alert that Mae has posted on Instagram. Guiltily, I click on the latter first.

It's a selfie of Mae, mid-pint, arms around Joe and Surina, laughing with the rest of the cast.

First Night !!! :D

They look so happy. As I stare at it, my throat knots again.

The thing with this rivalry is, we hit each other where it hurts. However much I might try to convince myself that my way – preparation and professionalism – is the better one, it doesn't make her tactics of charm and charisma any less effective.

I swallow the tears down. I'm well practised in doing that. No use feeling sorry for myself. I can't let Mae see what works, or she'll just do it more. I need to keep my head down and trust that I can impress Francis in rehearsals, and the audience in performances – that's what matters.

I open Alice's message.

I got the confirmation, I'm going to be reviewing Twelfth Night. *Can't wait to applaud you xxxxxxxxxxxxx*

My chest tightens. I still feel grubby about this. But then I click back on the photo of Mae with the cast.

Screw her. She can have friends, I'll have success.

Great news, I reply. *Thank you.*

You're welcome, handsome. Goodnight xxxxxxxxxxxxxxxx

Goodnight, beautiful x I reply, giving myself the ick.

28

When I arrive early for the rehearsal the next day, I'm surprised to see Mae is already there. She's waiting outside the theatre, two coffee cups in hand. My stomach cramps. Presumably one of them is for Surina or Joe, or whoever else she passionately made out with last night.

I blank her completely.

'Clooney,' she says, offering me one of the cups.

I frown at it. She must have spat in it, or is attempting to play some kind of practical joke. I raise an eyebrow at it, then knock it out of her hands.

Her reflexes are so good she catches it.

'Hey! I'm not trying to trick you, dummy. Can I just talk to you for a second?'

'No.'

I turn to leave, but she grabs my wrist. I look at her hand as if it's a particularly gruesome cockroach.

'Please?' she says.

I fold my arms and gesture impatiently. She rubs the back of her neck.

'I'm... I'm sorry about last night. I feel like you would have come to the pub if I hadn't discouraged you.'

She glances at me. My stomach somersaults. I fold my arms tighter.

'Heaven forbid, Jones, have you suddenly grown a conscience?'

She flinches and adjusts her pink shirt. 'There's being rivals and then there's being mean. I hate the thought that I might have made you feel… Look, I'm sorry. You should have been there. Besides, it'll improve the show, right? If we've all bonded together.'

I hesitate.

'Come tonight. I swear you'll have more fun than you expect,' she says. 'I'll even buy your drinks?'

My jaw clenches. Oh, I see. This isn't about my feelings at all. This is about *Mae* feeling bad and wanting to splash some cash for a clear conscience. Must be nice to be able to buy forgiveness.

She smiles and holds the coffee cup towards me again as if the matter is settled. She gestures for us to walk up the stairs together. I don't move.

This is just what Mae is like. Inconsistent. Impulsive. An improviser. She doesn't think twice about the consequences of her actions, or the impact she's having on other people. And she always gets away with it, because she's so bloody likeable. And rich. I can't believe it nearly worked on me.

'I don't need your permission to go to a pub, nor do I need your charity,' I say, not taking the cup. 'I don't want to spend any longer in your company than I need to. Thanks awfully.'

Her grin disappears.

'God,' she says, 'you really love to hold a grudge, don't you?'

'I do,' I say. 'Unlike you, I can commit.'

'Fine,' she snaps. 'Forget it. Isolate yourself. Let the rest of the cast learn to hate you as much as I do.'

I force my face to remain blank, don't let a single flicker cross it.

Mae pours the second espresso into her own keep cup and snaps the lid shut. She tosses the empty cup at my feet.

'Do your worst.'

The only one in the rehearsal room when I get in is Francis. I take my chance. She wants my worst? I'll give her my worst.

'Mae's asked me to send her apologies for her inability to concentrate today,' I tell Francis. 'She's throwing up. Hangover from going out with the cast last night. Her stomach really can't handle that much absinthe.'

Mae walks in at that moment, and her expression, which is unusually pained, furthers my story.

'Mae,' Francis says coldly, in front of the whole cast, 'while it's perfectly understandable to want to bond with your teammates, will you please not get so apoplectic that you can't do your job? You have been cast in the lead role – lead by good example.'

Mae frowns, bewildered, then looks across at me. I stare back, holding the empty coffee cup she littered at me. What did she expect from someone she hates?

Mae apologises so profusely and sincerely that Francis ends up clapping her on the back. Still, I think that's a point to me.

At lunch, the cast collect their bags from the green room, then go together into the theatre courtyard to eat their Pret sandwiches, sharing in-jokes about the pub trip. Mae's words about the cast hating me has made me even more certain they don't want me there. I sit a little distance away and open my play text, pretending I still have to learn my lines.

I open my lunch box to find my pizza has disappeared. My body tenses. It's like school. I look up to see Mae, already watching me, holding the slice of Emmy Special. She bites into it. Then she pauses. She chews. Her expression changes. She looks down at the pizza, as if she can't believe it.

I am not going to sit here and watch Mae enjoy my uncle's cooking.

I go and spend a horrific amount of money on the one vegan three-bean wrap left in Pret. I eat in.

On Wednesday, when Mae's busy on stage, I surreptitiously replace the coffee contents of her Keep Cup with vegetable stock. She spits it out all over Francis's orange neckerchief.

I keep my pizza box about my person at all times. When it's lunch time, I go to my lonely corner of the courtyard, put on my headphones and listen to the *SpongeBob Musical* (trust me, you need to listen to it too, it's amazing) to drown out the laughter of the rest of the cast.

That night, working again while Mae live-streams drinking games from the pub, I text Alice and try to convince myself I'm winning.

On Thursday, Surina and Mae are rehearsing the scene where Olivia tries to woo Viola.

'Something is wrong,' says Francis. 'I want more… chemistry. More spark. Why is it missing, you two?'

'Well,' says Mae, closing her eyes as if reading something behind her lids, 'I think a really important question to ask is… if in our production, all Shakespeare's characters have queer potential, then what stops Viola from being with Olivia? Or indeed, with any of the other characters?'

Everyone else murmurs, impressed by her insight.

I narrow my eyes at her. I *agree* with Mae? Something must be wrong.

Then I notice that my notebook's bookmark is upside down, and in the wrong page, as if it's been hastily returned…

When I look up at Mae, she winks at me across the room. My blood boils like a kettle.

Stealing my food is one thing. But stealing *my ideas about Shakespeare?*

That night, instead of going to the pub, I open my play on my desk and turn to the scene I know Mae will be rehearsing tomorrow. I write something, highlight it in pink, add a few pointing bookmarks, and write I AM A GENIUS, next to it. FRANCIS IS GOING TO LOVE THIS. CAN'T WAIT TO SAY IT IN FRONT

OF EVERYONE. I JUST HOPE JONES DOESN'T THINK OF IT FIRST.

On Friday morning, our rehearsals don't go well. When Francis calls us together before lunch, the mood is tense.

'Time's winged chariot is hurrying near,' he says, marching up and down the box room. 'We're getting dangerously low on rehearsal time. So. No more uncertainty about the meaning of one's lines.' Mae blushes. 'No more pedantry about irrelevant historical details.' I blush too. 'I want the filmset experience from now on. One-take rehearsals.'

Francis adjusts his neckerchief.

'But let it not be said that I am an unjust God. If any of you are desperate to tell me how to do my job, the floor is yours. Any ideas, concerns, questions, or suggestions on where we can lose ten more minutes of performance time, speak now.'

He sits on his director chair, folds his leg over his knee and waits.

I keep my mouth firmly shut. I'm here as an actor, not a director. I would never *dare* to step out of my place.

Mae, however, pipes up.

'I do have a *little* idea, Francis,' she says pleadingly. She's clearly trying to make up for forgetting her lines earlier.

I hold my breath.

'To play with a sense of...' She closes her eyes as if reading lines on the inside of her eyelids. 'Deus ex machina' – she pronounces this wrong – 'we have one of us lowered from the rafters dressed like William Shakespeare but with angel wings, and, for the rest of the production, have him spinning above all our heads.'

The room is silent for a moment. She blinks. In that moment, it's as though she realises what she's actually said and she blanches.

I can't help myself from letting out a snort. Charlie titters uncertainly. Francis looks annoyed.

'Alas,' he snaps, 'that might be somewhat *avant garde* for this production. Instead of spending your precious brain space thinking about Shakespeare as a kebab, how about you learn your lines? You do, after all, have rather a lot of them. Though of course, that can change.'

Mae looks at the floor, nods her head.

'Now, if no one else has any *insightful* suggestions…?'

The rest of the group are statues. Francis waves a disappointed hand.

'Go, feed yourselves. Be better this afternoon.'

I skip out to the empty smoking area. Mae might be winning with the other cast, but at least she's losing in the rehearsal room. All is as it should be.

I open up my lunchbox to find that Mae's stolen my pizza again. I shrug to myself, and pull out the coffee cup of hers I stole too.

A door bangs and I look up. Mae storms over, her hair wild and her open denim shirt billowing behind her.

'How dare you make a fool of me like that!'

'I didn't do anything,' I reply calmly. 'It's your own fault for stealing *my* ideas.'

'Imitation is the sincerest form of flattery,' she snaps.

'That's not imitation, that's theft.'

I open my laptop case to reveal another bag in which I have hidden a spare, larger slice of pizza. Mae glares at it and says, 'I was just trying to even the playing field.'

'Right,' I say, chewing sarcastically, 'I work on those notes late at night while you drink with your friends at the pub, then you steal them. Very even.'

I remember how Thalia used to take my drama school essays. She never thanked me. She didn't view studying as a real part of being an actor either. I swallow.

'No wonder you think stealing is OK,' I mutter, taking a sip from her Keep Cup. 'You've never had to work for anything in your life.'

Mae snatches her cup from me.

'I have to work to try to understand stupid Shakespeare! You don't understand how hard that is for me. We didn't all have your fancy education.'

'We didn't all have your celebrity family.'

'I disowned her! *I* have never got a job through my relatives – unlike you!'

I stop chewing.

'Sorry, are you seriously comparing me working as a waitress in a pizzeria to you having a wealthy showbiz family?'

I put my crust down and stand up to her.

'You want to pretend you're all independent to belong in liberal artsy groups,' I say. 'But can you really kid yourself that your career choice was unaffected by your culturally rich childhood? Acting was *always* going to be a legitimate option for you. You don't have to worry about convincing your parents, or getting money to live on from other jobs. Any second you want, you can just turn around and ask your mummy for a part and you'd get handed something bigger than I'll ever be able to earn, no matter how hard I work. Don't you *dare* claim this is easier for me.'

Stupidly, my throat feels tight. I can't let her see any crack of weakness, so I snatch up my things and move to push past her.

Behind me, she says quietly, 'I can't do this without you.'

I freeze. I must have misheard.

'What did you say?'

She's not looking at me.

'I can't do this part without you,' she repeats. 'I tried researching it, really I did. But it's old and stupid and I'm dyslexic, and the only way I can really perform stuff well is by relating it to my own experience, and I… I only really get it when you explain it.'

She looks down and scuffs the toe of her huge trainers.

'The only reason I could do that monologue in the audition

was because I heard you rehearsing it in the toilet. I knew you'd be there, saying all the lines, so I... I eavesdropped.'

I stare at her.

'When *you* talk about it, it makes sense!' she says. 'The lines are meaningless until you say them. I think because y-you understand it, and all the depth behind. I-it makes the audience get it too.'

I feel my chest heating. I should *not* be letting myself feel so pleased by Mae's excuses.

'Once I'd heard you saying the speech,' she continues, 'or even when I read your notes about Viola, I found it easy to perform it. I could even vary it. It's like a musician doing a cover of a song they already know. You gave me the chords, I just... sang it in a different key.'

I fold my arms, unable to meet her eye. I remind myself that Mae should not be allowed to steal my hard work and then absolve herself just by giving me a complimentary metaphor.

'Are you admitting that I'm a better actor than you?' I ask.

'I... no!'

'Then, are you calling in your favour?'

Mae hesitates, looking at me. Then she folds her arms too. 'No!'

I step up to her and place the crusts from my pizza into her hand.

'Then it's not my problem. Break a leg.'

The atmosphere in the afternoon rehearsal is tense. It's finally time for us to do Sebastian's early scenes, which involve a misunderstanding with his besotted friend Antonio (played by Joe).

I throw my all at the scenes, and thankfully, I execute them just as planned. But at the end, in horrible silence, Francis shakes his head.

'Oh, deary me.'

My stomach convulses. Despite all my hours of research, I've failed.

'Don't look so stricken, Emmy, it's not your fault. You're a bloody impressive actor and you've brought a... frankly unprecedented amount of depth to the character of Sebastian. But the problem is... his lines are dull.'

The stage shakes beneath me. No one else seems affected.

'The scenes with Antonio are only interesting when he is being illegally gay,' Francis continues. 'And that dynamic is lost in this casting. Antonio, of course, is *the* most boring character in the play.'

Joe nods in easy agreement. I glare at him. *He's* fine. He's got all of Duke Orsino's part to rely on. But these scenes are the only ones I have.

'I'll... I'll work on it, Sir. I'm sorry. There will be a solution.'

There's a cough from the rehearsal room floor. The rest of the cast are outside, but Mae's in the seat I usually occupy, watching.

Francis raises an irritated eyebrow.

'Mae, if this is about another human kebab descending from the heav—'

'What if we cut all of Sebastian's scenes?'

The stage under my feet shakes again.

'I mean, Viola is the main character, right?' Mae continues. 'The audience are seeing the story kind of through her eyes. And Viola thinks that her twin really did die in the storm at the beginning of the show. So what if the audience believed this too? What if we don't see him?' She shrugs grudgingly. 'Until perhaps the final scene, where he has to be confused with Viola for the resolution.'

Francis is silent for a moment, staring at the stage above my head.

'Just imagine that moment, Captain,' Mae continues, like a sorceress. 'Emmy walks on, a new unexpected body on the stage, in the final minutes of the play! And suddenly, there are these two twins, truly there, next to each other! What a finale!'

The worst thing is, it's actually a good idea.

'Yes,' mutters Francis. Then louder. 'Yes! Yes! Of course!'

He rummages in his trousers and throws another prop doubloon to Mae. She grins evilly. I think rapidly.

'But… But what about the stage fight scene with Sir Andrew Aguecheek?' I say. 'That's a-a powerful moment too, right? A-and Sebastian has to be the one who does it, because everyone is mistaking him for Viola…'

Francis strokes his stubbly chin.

'We could remove the stage fights entirely,' he muses.

'No!' I wail. Not my one chance to show off on stage! 'Sir, we're *pirates*! Pirates need to fight! Audiences will be expecting it. There'll be riots if there are no stage fights. And I'm… I'm *really good* at stage fighting! Remember my CV?'

He raises an eyebrow.

'You're right too,' he says. 'Damn it all, you're both right.'

He stares at the rafters, his eyes darting wildly. Then he clicks his fingers.

'Fortunately, I am a genius. Emmy, you will still perform the fantastical stage fight scene with Roger.'

I sigh in relief.

'But you will do it without ever showing your face. You will wear a mask.'

Mae applauds. Francis bows. I try not to cry.

'And for the rest of the show, I just… sit in the wings?'

'Of course not!' says Francis, reaching his hand out to help me down from the stage. 'We need you behind the shadow-puppet screen for the squid.'

29

I collapse through the front door, hoping for a massage from Raphy and a cathartic bitch session with Ruth.

But surprisingly, they're both out tonight. I must have forgotten they were doing something. Maybe they're both on 'outside of their type' dates. I suppose it's good in a way, because it means I can go into my room and scream.

I stare at Raphy's manifestation board with its image of Viola, and the ticket from the open air *Twelfth Night* I saw with my mum all those years ago, and the shrine poster of Annabel Finch.

Then I tear them all down.

Mae has taken everything from me.

I *will* have my revenge.

I search through my folder of notes on her from across the Internet and check back through my Google alerts.

I don't know how, but I'd missed that she finally has a Spotlight page.

I click on it – and come face to face with high resolution headshots of her.

For a moment, I'm so startled that I barely recognise her. Mae's wearing black and she's not smiling. Her hair is neat and smoothed away from her face. She's facing a perfect thirty degree angle.

This doesn't look like Mae at all. It looks like Mae trying to be... me.

I must be losing it. But as I tap through, I see the other poses are replications of mine too. One shows her straight on, wearing a white shirt, like mine. Then a full-length body shot, in front of a tree. The only one that's different is her fourth one, which is the original she posted on her Instagram weeks ago. There she looks perfectly Mae-like, grinning her mischievous smile as if enjoying a joke with the photographer. Her eyes are ringed with the lights from the photoshoot, bringing out the colours, the gold flecks around her iris.

The first rule of headshots is to try to capture your neutral personality. If I was a casting director, I would hire this radiant Mae over her blank, serious Emmy-ish Mae any day of the week. What's she playing at? Is this an elaborate prank just to mock me?

I scroll down slowly, scrutinising each line at a time.

As you could expect, our physical details are embarrassingly similar: height 5'7', medium build, dark-brown hair, blue eyes. The only difference is that whereas Valerie advised that my Vocal Type is 'Restrained', Mae's is 'Enthusiastic'.

Mae's agent contact section is blank.

Reading her Credits is like going back through a diary of my unsuccessful auditions. I scroll all the way down to her first credit, the *Tipping the Velvet* short film. Then to the bottom of the page, which lists Mae's training.

Special skills:
Improvised comedy; Stage Fighting (speciality in rapiers).
Training:
MA Classical Theatre, St Genesius (First Class Hons).

Every muscle in my body tenses. I feel like I'm ready to wrestle a bear to the floor. Because that isn't Mae's education. It's *mine*.

I don't waste any time the next morning. I storm into the toilet stalls to find Mae washing her hands.

She sees it's me and smirks.

'We really must stop meeting like thi—'

I grab the scruff of her shirt and pin her to the wall.

'Clooney, what the—'

I hold a printout of her Spotlight page up to her face. She blinks at it far-sightedly.

'What the hell is this?' I demand.

Her squinting eyes focus on it. The colour drains from her cheeks.

'Shit. I—'

'You stole my parts. You stole my notes. You stole my friends and my lunches. But now, on your public record of your identity as an actor, you have stolen my *life*?'

The money. The time. The blood, sweat, tears, and anguish of forging your acting craft. And Mae thinks she can just type a few words online and it's the same thing?

'I did that ages ago. And I haven't technically *stolen* anything,' she says quickly. She swallows under my hand. '*You* don't *lose* anything by me writing that. I was just levelling our applications.'

And to think, for a while back there, I had thought that Mae, despite being my personal rival, was a good person.

I let go of her shirt and walk away.

'Look, OK, now I have seen your reaction, I don't feel good about it,' says Mae, running after me. 'But I didn't know how it all works! The more I met you, the more I saw you had it all so perfectly together, and I thought, well, if I do what she does, I won't go far wrong.'

'Don't try to spin this into flattery, you f—'

She holds up her hands.

'It's true! It was just to get me into the audition room! Wouldn't you agree that it's only fair to judge applicants on merit? So I needed to get into the same rooms, and to do that, I needed us to look equal. I-I thought it was a fair tactic in our rivalry.'

The tap drips. Mae curls a hair at the nape of her neck and mutters, '*You* pretended to be me for your improv job.'

'You *know* that was an accident,' I hiss. 'That was completely different.'

'My agent Louisa said—'

We both freeze. 'What did you say?'

Mae tries to think on the spot. I grab her face and turn it to mine.

'Tell me everything,' I say quietly, and nod towards the door to the rehearsal room, 'or I tell *them* everything.'

'Fine, fine,' says Mae urgently. 'My friend Louisa works as an assistant in a talent agency.'

'*My* talent agency,' I say hysterically. 'Louisa is the assistant to *my* agent.'

I release her face and grasp at the sink for support.

'When did you start working with her?'

'When you started this stupid challenge,' she says. I glare at her. 'I mean, when we *both* started this *necessary competition*, I looked up who your agent was. When I saw that Louisa worked there, I realised I had an *in*. I thought it was a sign, or something. S-so I contacted her, and… I asked her to put me forward for anything that you were going for.'

All I can do is gawp. This whole time Mae has just been piggy-backing my career.

Mae lifts her hands above her head.

'Look, Louisa would be my agent if she was allowed, but she's a junior, she hasn't officially started a list yet. And it's not like I could ask Valerie if she'd like to represent me officially, no way she needs *two* butches on her list.'

My fists clench.

'Valerie isn't the only agent in the world!' I say. 'If you wanted an agent, you should have had to graft for it, like the rest of us did!'

Mae could have had any agent. Mae could have *anyone*. Yet she's deliberately come into *my* home, to take *my* crumbs.

'All I wanted was to get into the audition rooms,' says Mae. 'That's it. Once I was there, it was all fair and square. It shouldn't be about where you trained, right? It's about the director being reassured that you can do everything you need to do. So who cares if I'm winging it, or if I'm learning the skills on the job, if the final performance is good? It's not fair that I should be held back just because I didn't have a fancy school on my resume, just because I hadn't *always known* I wanted to be an actor.'

I hold my hand up and she stops talking instantly. I'm shaking.

'How *dare* you,' I whisper. 'Don't you *dare* pretend you're the underdog. I worked every second of my life for *years*, and you think you can just "yes and" your way to success? You think you don't have to play by the same rules as everyone else?' I jab her chest. 'Stealing. Faking. Networking and nepotisming your way in.'

'Oh yeah?' Mae retaliates, jabbing me back. 'And how did *you* get into the *Twelfth Night* audition?'

I blink at her, and swallow. Mae barks in triumph.

'Oh, you think you're so different from me, Clooney, so much better.' She steps close, sneers in my face. 'But as usual, you're just a poor copy of me.'

We stare at each other, breathing shallow, heat radiating off our bodies. She's so close I can see the gold in her eyes.

'I challenge you to a duel,' I say.

Mae laughs. I don't.

'Wait, what?'

'I challenge you to a duel,' I repeat.

'We're not in a period drama, Clooney.'

'No, we're not,' I say. 'But I see from your acting CV that you have distinction in stage fighting from Saint Genesius School of Drama.'

I shove her with her CV – *my* CV.

'Me too. That means we will have had the same teachers. The same training. We'll know the same choreographed routines.'

Mae has a glimmer of panic in her eyes now. Is this how good improvisers feel? Like I'm immortal?

I pull her out of the loo and into the rehearsal room. Within clear earshot of the entire cast, I call out to Francis.

'Sir? Mae says she has an amazing idea for Sebastian's stage fight scene, and she wants to show me how it's done. Would you mind if we used the rehearsal space during the break? And the weapons?'

'Oh, n-no,' says Mae, but Francis booms over her.

'Splendid! Why not use the main stage? More room up there and we can all watch.'

Mae is sweating. I've backed her into a corner. And I intend to do it again, with a big fucking sword in my hands.

'What's your weapon of choice?' I ask her, like the gentleman I am. 'Knives? Swords? Guns?'

She blanches as if I'm suggesting a fight with real weapons. Maybe she is so inexperienced she thinks they are.

'Oh, I see here,' I say, pointing to the CV she's clutching to her heart, 'that you have a special talent with rapiers.'

I smile.

'What a coincidence. So do I.'

30

The cast are seated in the auditorium while Mae and I are up on the main stage.

Mae's dressed in three layers of padding. I cockily haven't put any on at all.

'You could surrender now, you know,' I say, bouncing on my toes. 'Just confess.'

'It's only waving a bit of metal around,' she snaps. 'If you can do it, I can do it.'

I unsheath the prop rapier and bring it whooshing down. It makes the sound of a whip.

'You're right,' I say. 'It's easy.'

Mae looks like she might throw up.

I toss the rapier between my hands, enjoying its familiar weight.

'How about a little wager?' I say.

Mae's eyes follow the flying blade. 'What kind of wager?'

'The loser of this fight has to give up.'

'Give up what?'

I run my finger along the blade. 'We said it before, Jones. Showbusiness isn't big enough for the both of us. You played dirty, so I have no choice but to play dirty with you.'

I pick up two prop daggers from the box, tucking one into my sock.

'Give up your part in this show and they'll give me Viola.' I hold the other dagger out to Mae. 'Do that, and I won't have to tell everyone about your little CV of lies – or about your mother.'

She growls and snatches the dagger from me.

'Never!'

I point my rapier at her and shout, 'En garde!'

We start to circle around each other, Mae's rapier taut and wobbling, mine languishing casually in my palm.

'I'm the *lead*,' she says, as if to herself, 'because I'm better than you. You only got cast because of me.'

'You only got cast because of *me*,' I snarl.

'You got me into the room, but in the room I beat you!'

'If I wasn't good enough, they wouldn't have cast me at all,' I say. 'They could have twins who look dissimilar, like literally every other production of *Twelfth Night*.'

'I never said you're not a good actor!' says Mae.

I hesitate. Her backhanded compliment catches me off guard. Then Mae drops her rapier, jumps forwards at me, and her backhanded slap catches me on the cheek.

Distantly, I hear the cast gasp.

I clutch my face. Trust Mae to use a slap in a swordfight.

She crouches lightly on her feet, like a feral cat, and grins. 'But you know what, Clooney? You're a better actor when you're opposite me.'

I narrow my eyes and throw my rapier aside. I crouch and hold my clenched fists in front of me, mirroring Mae.

Mae's smile broadens. 'See?'

My blood crackles. I dart towards her. She feints. I spin and we circle each other, faster now.

'You don't want to admit it,' she laughs, 'but I know you have never acted like you have when you're around me. You stood out in this audition because I baited you on the workshop floor. I get you out of your clever little head. Any success you've had since we met is because… of… *me*.'

She lunges forwards, and we click into a full-on wrestle. I push back with all my might, but we're evenly matched. We stare at each other in the headlock. Mae screams in frustration. Staring into her furious eyes, thinking about everything she's taken from me, I scream back. We shout louder and louder until finally, with a supreme effort of will, I push her backwards and she falls onto her backside.

I stride towards her, picking up both the abandoned rapiers. I swirl them in the air between us. Mae shuffles desperately away, patting herself, trying to find her dagger amongst all her padding. Her back reaches the set behind her.

The set is a leftover from the previous show, in the last stages of being dismantled. It's a painting of the lava pits of Hell. Mae's pressed against its ruins as I step over her legs, straddle her, and point the rapier at her chest.

She pants underneath me.

'As the chip on your shoulder keeps reminding me, *I* have trained to do this,' I say, stroking a rapier along the side of her neck. 'I attended the best fucking drama school in the country, and I worked to get the best fucking marks in every fucking exam. And that's how I can do *this*.'

I throw the rapier into the air. I don't need to watch it spin. I catch it by its handle and, in the same fluid motion, push it into the scenery wall above her head. It quivers.

'*You're* the one who's copying *me*,' I spit. 'Any success that you have, is because of *me*. Don't you *dare* forget it.'

And right now, I almost believe myself. I move to the front of the stage to take a bow.

But it's not over yet. Mae, panting, calls behind me. I turn and watch her reach for the handle above her.

'Oh yeah? Well then, I'll just copy—'

She pulls it out and throws it into the air. For a second, we all watch in wonder as it travels upwards. But then, like a corgi trying to jump onto a sofa, it barely gets an inch high. It drops with an embarrassed 'flump'.

We look at it, then up at each other.

I give her a slow clap.

'Wow. Mummy must be so proud.'

Mae stares at me. Then she gives a sudden deranged scream and lunges for my foot.

Still laughing, I hop backwards, continuing to clap, like a renegade Morris Dancer.

'You'd be nothing without me!'

'*You'd* be nothing without *me*.'

She's managed to find her dagger, but it's facing the wrong way. As she fumbles with it, she looks up, and her face is suddenly so horrified and awed, I wonder if she's finally conceding to my mastery. Maybe if she believes it, I can believe it too.

Then I realise quite how far backwards I'd been hopping. My non-hopping foot comes down into blank air behind me.

I flail my arms out to try to right myself back from the edge of the stage. Mae reaches out wildly for my hand.

Unfortunately, some stage fight part of me still thinks she's trying to attack me. So I don't take it. I try, stubbornly, to hold on alone. And for a second, I really think I've done it.

'I win!' I cheer.

Then I trip on a footlight and fall backwards off the stage.

31

Picture the beginning of a medical drama. Life support machines beep as too many doctors and nurses wheel an urgent trolley through hospital doors; a patient in a white sheet, gas mask and tubes.

That's all going on behind us. Mae and I sit mutely in the boring A&E waiting room.

'Does it hurt?' she asks, for the fiftieth time.

Annoyingly, it doesn't, but I grimace and shrug like a very brave martyr.

'You sure I can't get you anything?'

I shake my head.

Mae fidgets, looking more pained than I am. She goes up to the receptionist's desk to ask again what number in the queue I am. I don't know if she's desperate to be rid of me or feeling guilty.

At first, my fall off the stage was so surprising and embarrassing, I thought the cast must be right that I wasn't in pain because I was in shock. But Mae insisted on calling a taxi to A&E and came with me, urging the driver to break the speed limit.

But now we've been here for an hour. Around us, a muddy woman in rugby shorts clutches scraps of tissue to her torrentially bleeding nose. A hunched gentleman hacks into his hands. The guy next to me is holding his ear as if it's fallen off.

At most, all I have is a broken toe. Probably only a little one. I feel inadequate.

Mae returns and I glance at her.

I mutter, 'I can't believe I didn't even break a leg.'

Mae looks stricken. But then we hold each other's eye. Both of us realise in the same moment how utterly ridiculous this is.

Something shifts between us.

We start laughing. Haltingly at first, and then irrepressibly. We slap our knees, each other's knees, howling, weeping, snorting. We laugh, and we don't stop, even as the others in the waiting room look at us as though we're contagious.

My stomach hurts so much I clutch at my aching belly and cling to Mae's elbow, begging for her to stop.

The receptionist comes over and asks Mae if I need sedating. Mae replies sincerely that it won't be necessary, which sets us off again.

Eventually, we do calm down. Mae wipes tears from her eyes, sighing contentedly.

But now, when we look at each other, there's a new tickle of uncertainty.

'Jones,' I say. 'I… I have a new proposal.'

She raises an eyebrow.

'For the duration of *Twelfth Night*, should we have a ceasefire? A truce. For the sake of our other limbs.'

Mae looks at me, and, for maybe the first time since we started our rivalry, she smiles at me with her full, natural, dazzling smile.

'I couldn't agree with you more,' she laughs, and holds out her hand for me to shake.

I grasp it, feeling lightheaded. My hand tingles at the connection. I must still be in shock. Yes.

Mae's still sparkling at me.

'You're very good at stage fighting,' she says.

'And you are absolutely not,' I reply.

Mae snorts like a pig. 'I can't believe I thought I could just wing it.'

What had seemed so galling to me only a few hours ago now seems very funny.

'*En garde*,' she teases, pretending to be me with an imaginary rapier.

I join in, pretending to be her dropping her dagger in shock, patting my pockets.

In the course of our play fighting, our hands come together.

'Genuinely, are you OK?' she asks, squeezing my fingers.

'Yeah, honestly, it's embarrassing how much it doesn't hurt. I reckon all I'll need is some Calpol and to Sellotape my toes together for a few days.'

We smile at each other. Then we seem to realise in the same moment that our hands are interlinked. I pull away and she runs her hand through her messy hair instead.

'Do you want me to ring anyone for you?' she asks. 'Like a… a girlfriend?'

I flush. I texted Ruth, Raphy, and my dad from the taxi, but I completely forgot about Alice. I'm a terrible person.

'I-I don't think I should really expect someone I've been on three dates with to wait with me in A&E.'

We both look at the seat in front of us.

'Well, you can if you really like each other,' she says.

'I-I don't know… She seems to like me, but…'

Mae glances at me, running her hand through her hair again.

'Sorry,' I say, 'I sound like a dick. I just…' I take a deep breath. I don't know why, but it feels very easy to talk to Mae. 'Honestly, I'm not very experienced when it comes to dating, and I'm finding the whole thing very confusing. It's as though I'm not feeling what I'm meant to feel. But I don't know if that's normal.'

'Oof,' she says, 'I'm sorry. I was in something like that for a while. She wanted me to be someone I wasn't, and it's hard not to play along. It makes you doubt yourself. I felt so much better when it ended, like I could finally hear myself think again.'

She catches herself.

'Not that I'm telling *you* to stop seeing her,' she says quickly. 'Date as many people as you want, obviously, it's… that's… not my business.'

'Well, unlike you, I don't have many offers.'

'What do you mean, unlike me?' she asks.

'Oh, come on.' I nudge her playfully. 'Literally everyone you meet adores you. Even the receptionist was flirting with you!'

'What are you talking about?' she laughs.

'Everyone in the cast fancies you. Maybe you're just so used to it you can't see it.'

'Or maybe you're the one imagining it,' she says.

I roll my eyes.

'Why on Earth would I...?'

Mae grins. 'Duh, maybe you're just jealous.'

We both blush suddenly and furiously.

'As in,' she says quickly, 'you know, obviously I meant you're jealous of *them* flirting with me instead of them flirting with you – I don't mean...'

I'm about to feign a searing agony in my toe, but at this moment there's shouting from the A&E entrance.

'*I must be allowed to see her! She's my only daughter!*'

Dad appears at reception, wearing his Pete's'zas uniform. Absolutely no one is stopping him.

'Where is my Patatina?' He bangs the desk. 'I *demand* to see her!'

'Dad,' I say, at normal room volume, a metre behind him, 'I'm right here...'

He wheels around.

'Oh,' he says, 'I thought you'd be in one of those stringy brace things.'

His disappointment that I'm not in a coma shifts to a glint in his eye when he sees Mae, who has stood up to greet him.

'Oh ho!' he says. 'Is this—'

'Er,' I interrupt hurriedly, in case he thinks she's Alice, 'this is Mae Jones. She's one of the other actors in the play I'm in.'

Dad bows to her and puts his hand on his heart. '*Buongiorno,* Mae Jones. Thank you for looking after my daughter.'

'Oh it's – it's my pleasure,' blushes Mae. 'Excuse me, but are you responsible for Emmy's pizza lunches? I tried some the other day and it was so good that, honestly, it made me cry.'

Dad pinches his fingers into a flamboyant chef's kiss.

'Ah! For that, you can get your next one free,' says Dad. 'You have excellent taste in *friends*, Emmeline.'

Dad texts Pete – who stayed behind to watch the pizzeria – to tell him I'm OK, and then talks animatedly to Mae about the merits of thinner and thicker bases.

Ruth and Raphy arrive hot on his heels. Bless them, they're so worried about me that they're holding hands. Ruth sees me and they drop them as they run. Raphy's limping.

'Em!' Raphy coos. 'I was so worried about you! I felt it, the moment the accident happened, like a phantom limb! I fell too! But then I knew you'd be OK because I could feel this incredible libidic energy radiating from you, like—'

Raphy sees Mae.

'Aha! Yes, that'd be it.' He bats his eyelashes at her. 'Gracious me, your aura is *gorgeous*.'

Ruth slaps him and hisses under her breath. She is giving Mae her best bitch glare. It's so effective, Mae steps back.

'Oh,' I say quickly, 'Ruth, you don't need to…' I cough. 'Umm, Ruth, Raphy, this is Mae, umm, who I might have, umm, mentioned briefly in passing about her being my, umm, colleague – but we've recently agreed a new, er, arrangement. We're not, umm, enemies anymore.'

Ruth switches her bitch glare off.

'In that case, hi,' she says, holding her hand out. Raphy gives Mae a huge hug, lifting her off her feet.

He pulls back and gestures between her and me.

'You radiate complementary colours,' he says. 'As I'm sure you know.'

Mae blinks rapidly.

'Gosh! Right! Thank you very much!'

I remember in that moment how different my family and friends must be to hers. Mae has a literal celebrity for a mother, for heaven's sake. She has thousands of cool friends. Of course I think Ruth and Raphy are very cool, in their own way, and Dad is, well, *Dad*. But still.

'Sorry about them,' I murmur to Mae. 'I know they might seem eccentric, but they're, you know. They're *my* eccentrics.'

Quietly, Mae says, 'They seem like the absolute best.'

I watch her, watching them, and realise she's... Jealous? My chest aches.

'Well,' she says quickly. 'You've got your real friends here now, so I-I guess I should head off.'

I'm surprised to find I'm disappointed. I wish I could invite her to stay. But of course, just because we've agreed we're not enemies anymore, doesn't mean I can think of her as my friend.

'Of course,' I say awkwardly. 'Thank you for, you know... Being here.'

'Well, it *was* kind of my fault,' she laughs.

'I really think it takes two to tango.'

She smiles dazzlingly at me again, then waves at the others. 'Lovely to meet you all. I hope maybe one day we'll... Well, yeah, *ciao*!'

To me she says, 'Message me when you... Well, I'll see you at rehearsals. Let me know if I can help with...' She waves to my feet. 'Carrying your books or something. I won't steal them this time.'

'Thanks, Jones,' I say. 'Er, I mean, umm... Thank you, Mae.'

Looking rather pink, she gives me a sort of pat on my shoulder, then another flappy wave to the others, and heads out.

There's a pause while everyone watches her go. Then they look at each other with such outrageously raised eyebrows that I want to slap them all.

'Guys! Stop it! We're just friends! Barely even that!'

'Well, I knew she couldn't be your girlfriend,' says Dad.

I blush and look away.

'I know, it would be way too weird,' I say.

'Weird? In whatever way would it be *weird*?' says Dad.

I blink at them.

'Because of the... You know.' I gesture between my face and Mae's retreated back. 'Because we look the same! That's what you were going to say, isn't it? We'd be put on that Siblings or Dating website for people to vote on and judge us.'

The three of them frown at each other.

'Em...' says Ruth. 'No one else was thinking that.'

'I can assure you,' says Dad. 'You and Mae are not in any way related. No cousin of Clooney has ever mated abroad.'

I groan and wave my hands wildly.

'That's exactly what I mean! I couldn't stand this... This... People thinking we're self-obsessed little narcissists, in love with ourselves!'

'In *love*?' says Dad, wiggling his eyebrows.

'You know what I meant!'

'Yes, we know *exactly* what you meant,' says Raphy cheerily.

'Stop it, all of you! I... I... Opposites attract!'

Ruth and Raphy glance at each other, and then away, but I guess they must decide not to continue the battle with me.

'Besides,' I snap. 'You're the one who started this, Dad. *You're* the one who said Mae could never be my girlfriend.'

'I simply meant she couldn't be Alice,' he says innocently. 'She wasn't cutting enough to be a theatre critic.'

'Oh.'

I shake my head and look out towards the exit.

'Right.'

Dad coughs politely into the silence.

'Pizza?'

32

I hobble into the rehearsal room the next day with a barely necessary crutch, feeling like Hugh Laurie in *House*. I confess I'm playing up to the injury (after four hours of waiting in A&E, the nurse just gave me half a roll of fabric tape) because I don't want Francis to fire me.

Fortunately, he seems to have found the whole thing a great set piece.

'Our wounded soldier!' he says, clapping me on the back. 'Seriously though, are you OK? We really can't afford for you to sue us.'

'Thank you, I'm fine,' I say. 'The show must go on.' I'm barely on stage for longer than five minutes anyway.

'I thought perhaps you could incorporate some of yesterday's heated antics into the stage fight choreography,' he says, as he wags a finger at Mae. 'But perhaps it's for the best if we don't have any more improvised stage fights from the two of you.'

Mae and I catch eyes and grin. It's worth breaking a few bones to have her as a friend.

That lunchtime, I'm about to hobble to my quiet corner of the smoking area to eat alone when Mae catches my arm.

'Please join us today? I swear, we're not *that* bad.'

'I never thought you were...'

I let her let me lean on her, expecting the rest of the cast to be awkward.

'Hi, everyone, d-do you mind if I…?'

'Omigod *please*,' says Roger, budging up closer to Zach.

'Emmy, what you did with those swords was *so* fucking cool,' gushes Charlie.

'And I love what you were doing with Sebastian,' says Joe. 'And honestly, I know you're not on the stage for much time any more' – Mae winces guiltily – 'but all that depth is still coming across in the final scene.'

'Francis brings your notes into our scenes *all* the time,' says Keiya. 'You must be like… properly smart.'

I look around in bewildered pleasure. Of course, it's only because I'm friendly with Mae now that the others allow my company. But still, if this is what being second-hand friends feels like, I'll take it.

'Umm… Do you guys like pizza?' I ask.

The next day I'm up before Raphy and Ruth finish their morning meditation and task-setting. When they come into the kitchen, I hand Raphy a green smoothie and Ruth her coffee. They smile at me, slightly disconcerted.

'You're working hard,' says Ruth.

I hum a sea shanty from the play, packing my bag with several boxes of pizza.

'Yep,' I smile.

Raphy kisses my cheek, then Ruth's. 'It's really lovely to see you happy.'

And he's right. I *am* happy. Deliriously so.

Even though it's only been our routine for a few days, this week of rehearsals has already become a distinct 'era' in my mind. It's as though I'm experiencing them with a present-day nostalgia, idealising and fearing their ending even while they're still happening. I've started counting the days we have left.

Mae and I have formed a series of little rituals. We meet early outside the theatre, her holding out an oat-milk flat white she's made for me herself. (She told me that when her mum found out she had a café job, she bought Mae a professional coffee maker to practise her latte art. I wondered if Mum would have bought me a pizza oven, if it wasn't literally her ex-husband's restaurant I was working in?) The picture Mae made for me this morning has almost faded, but looks a bit like a leaf without a stem?

At lunch, I hand her a full Emmy Special of her own. (Pete seemed wickedly pleased to make double portions when I asked him, which makes me suspicious of how Dad spun the story of meeting Mae at the hospital.) After rehearsals, we religiously go to the local with the rest of the cast, and make one rum and coke last for the evening. Last night Charlie led everyone into an intricately harmonised sea shanty and, even though I can't sing as well as the others, I joined in enthusiastically with the percussion (banging our tankards on the table) until we were asked to leave.

I'm alarmed to realise that, for a long time, I felt anxious about pretty much everything in my life. I used to dread my shifts at the pizzeria, dread preparing for auditions, dread not hearing from Thalia, dread hearing from my mum. Although I loved those rare moments of becoming someone else on stage, the build-up would make me so nauseous that it sometimes didn't feel worth it. The only times I looked forward to wholeheartedly were watching musicals with R&R, and even then I'd sometimes still feel nervous that they'd get bored with me.

Now, though, I look forward to every part of my day. Even though I still want to do a good job in *Twelfth Night*, I feel less terrified about it. And I feel much less cross about not having a large part. Truly, I feel grateful to be any part of it, to collaborate with these amazing creatives.

Even though Mae still hasn't cashed in her official return favour, we can help each other without that now. When she is struggling with the meaning of a line, she asks me, and when I am getting too robotic in my delivery, she helps bring new energy to it again. Ruth may be right that competition makes businesses improve, but I think Mae and I are even better performers now that we're in collaboration.

Although I feel closer to the other cast members, there always seems to be an excuse to spend time with just Mae. It feels, somehow, as though we've been friends forever, but we also have a huge amount to catch up on.

On Tuesday of our final week, before we all head to the pub, Mae says she's forgotten her water bottle in the green room, so I offer to get it with her. The others smirk unnecessarily.

'I don't know how to thank your family enough for my lunches,' Mae says on the way. 'My God. My mum would *die* for them. She's been on a liquid diet since 2019.'

'I don't mean to sound like too much of a fangirl, but what is your mum up to at the moment?'

Mae sighs. 'She's filming a kind of psychological thriller, set in this ridiculously fancy villa in LA. She keeps trying to get me to go and join her.'

I look away from her reflection in the green room mirrors.

'Why wouldn't you?' I ask.

It's not that I'm jealous, although I would commit all sorts of felonies to join Annabel Finch in the sun. But it's a cruel reminder that my new friendship with Mae is temporary. Either she will stay in the UK, take all my roles, and become unavailable to me because of her success – like Thalia – or she'll leave the country entirely. She'll return to the improv scene, or take up her mother's legacy in going from theatre to film. True rising stars will naturally ascend from my level on the audition circuit.

'I want my life to be separate from Mum's,' Mae replies. 'We're always closest when we're furthest apart.'

'Deep,' I say.

'I am *very* profound,' says Mae. 'I love her, but whenever I'm around her I feel kind of like I'm... I don't know, betraying myself somehow?'

'Mmm,' I say vaguely. 'What does your water bottle look like, by the way?'

Mae looks round, blushing.

'Well, isn't that funny,' says Mae. 'I guess I must not have left it here after all... Sorry!'

She shrugs, and we turn back to head to the pub.

'Clooney, do you mind me asking... What happened with your mum? You never talk about her.'

I tense.

'You don't have to tell me,' she says quickly. 'Or you can lie. The best lie you can think of please.'

'No, it's fine,' I say. I realise I do really want to tell her. 'She... she left my dad when I was thirteen. She fell in love with this other man. John has more money than my dad, and a nicer house, and a daughter who is blonde and sporty and straight. I used to see them every weekend, you know, custody laws. But it was always so awkward.'

'You have an evil step-family?' says Mae. 'Very chic.'

I laugh, but feel bad. 'No, they're not evil. That's the problem. They're really, really nice. No matter how much I give them the silent treatment, they're... Unreasonably understanding. Even my dad's nice about them. Which means I have to work even harder to show I don't like them, to be loyal to him, you know?'

She hesitates in her step.

'Why do you have to be loyal to him by being mean to them?'

I blink at her. It seems so obvious to me that I'd never considered someone else might not be able to see it.

'Because Dad was the one who was left behind,' I say. 'It sounds harsh but... Dad was the loser. He doesn't have anyone else.'

Mae nods slowly, holding the door open for me.

'But what about Pete?' she asks.

'What about Pete?'

'Your dad has Pete, doesn't he? And the pizzeria? When I met him at the hospital, he didn't seem lonely, or like he sees himself as a loser. He seemed really—' She swallows. 'Sorry, I don't know what I'm talking about. I don't know him. And famously, I know nothing about stable family dynamics.'

I blush. I feel awkward that, because it was so publicised, I knew how Mae's dad died long before I even met her. He was a shiny young Hollywood producer who had eloped with Annabel when they were in their twenties. He died from complications involving an overdose while in bed with another actress. Mae would have been twelve.

'I know he was a scumbag,' says Mae, reading my mind, 'but if I had the chance to watch terrible films with him, or just talk about nothing with him again? I'd take it.' Her expression is open and earnest. 'Tell people you love them, you know? Life's too short for grudges.'

She holds the pub door open for me and smiles.

'Well, except ours.'

On the bus back from the pub that night, the cast's tipsy sea shanties resounding in my mind, I spend a long time writing and re-writing a text.

Hey Mum, sorry to message out of the blue, but I just wanted you to know I've been cast in a production of Twelfth Night. *I'm only Sebastian, but it's been amazing so far. It got me thinking about all those shows you used to take me to. You probably don't remember, but* Twelfth Night *was the first one we saw together, the two of us. I know I won't have thanked you properly at the time, so I just wanted to say I still think about that show a lot. Hope you're all well.*

I hesitate, then remember Mae's sincere expression. How much it had made me long to be able to talk to my mum.

Hands shaking, I send it.

I try to tell myself that it doesn't matter how or when or if she replies, the important thing is that I'm reaching out, but I'm still so busy checking if Mum's seen it that I nearly miss my stop. She hasn't, but by the time I get home, I do have another good night text from Alice.

Good night darling, I miss you so much. Xxxxxxxxxxxxxx

My stomach twists. In the few days we've spent apart I haven't missed her at all. It's normal, I try to tell myself, that when you're in a show it becomes the whole world. When *Twelfth Night* is over, I'll focus on developing the feelings I'm meant to have for Alice. And without constant proximity, these definitely-not-a-crush feelings for Mae will naturally disappear too.

I reply to Alice with a simple goodnight message, which she tells me to resend with more kisses.

I'm about to comply when the message to Mum turns blue. I stare as the dots that show she's replying dance on the screen.

And then… nothing. She goes offline.

I swallow and throw my phone on the bed. What did I expect? My mother and I are destined to ignore each other, it just sometimes varies as to which of us is in charge.

I try to distract myself by joining Ruth in one of Raphy's metta meditations, but unfortunately the whole point of meditation is being left alone with your thoughts.

My phone vibrates, and Raphy looks at me as if he knows who it's from. He doesn't even tut that I'm interrupting their flow, he just nods at me until I build enough courage to check the first line.

Emmeline, this message means so much to me. Thank you.

Ruth opens one eye from her much-improved lotus position. I'm glad to have them here, and I know if I wanted to talk about it, they'd listen. But I need to do this alone. I go quietly to my room and shut the door to read the rest in private.

Of course I remember Twelfth Night. *It was the first proper conversation we'd had in weeks. You said you aspired to be that captivating on stage one day too – and I said that you already were. I don't think you believed me then. I hope you might now.*

I know it's nothing to do with me, but Emmy, I am so proud of you. Francis de la Ware! The Boards Theatre! So, so well-deserved.

I hope you are having an incredible time rehearsing and that you allow yourself to have some fun in between working as hard as you always do.

Then Mum sends a blurry photo of a very large hog. It's zoomed in on The Pig's chaotic teeth, which are gripping a squeaky toy in the shape of a doughnut.

And if you ever change your mind and want to visit The Pig, she will always, always be here, and so happy to see you.

I read the texts over and over, my stomach knotting and unknotting again. I don't reply. But that night, I sleep better than I have for ages.

33

I'm giving Mae a shoulder massage. It's very relaxing.

We're alone in the green room again. She's stressed after a group rehearsal where they were meant to be settling the way Mae would deliver certain cue lines. Mae's great at being live in the moment, but whenever her actions need to be consistent or finalised, she panics.

'You were right,' she says, tense under my hands. 'I don't deserve to be Viola.'

'Jones, that's not true.'

She looks at me in the mirror, her eyes wet, and my chest tightens. 'But I don't even *understand* Shakespeare,' she whispers. 'Sometimes, I think... I don't even *care* about Shakespeare.'

I laugh and pat her shoulder.

'*No one* really likes Shakespeare. Everyone just pretends because he carries clout. It doesn't make you a worse actor, just because you don't find 400-year-old jokes funny.'

She blinks at me.

'But *you* like him,' she says.

'Oh, of course *I* love him,' I say. 'I've always loved him, because of my mum... But that doesn't mean everyone else is meant to.'

Mae twists round to face me. Her purple shirt is creased from where I've been touching her.

'Emmy Clooney, you continue to surprise me.'

Her eyes are sparkling and warm. She opens her mouth to say something, and instead just wets her lip.

A door slams upstairs. We both jump.

'Rum,' I say. 'Time for rum.'

But Mae hesitates.

'Oh,' I say, heart sinking, 'aren't you coming to the pub tonight?'

'Of course I am,' she says. My stomach sags with relief. 'It's just, I was thinking... Maybe...'

She meets my eye.

'I'd like to call in my favour,' she says. 'Coach me on Viola's lines. Tonight. At my flat.'

I go very still. I feel as though our friendship is sledding fast down a steep hill. I don't think I could stop it now even if I wanted to. And I really, really don't want to.

I bow. 'Your wish is my command.'

Mae says her flat is near King's Cross. But it is not. It is *above* King's Cross.

In the foyer of a towering skyscraper, Mae walks us past the security guard, past the largest vase of rhododendrons I've ever seen, and into an elevator that takes us to the twenty-fourth floor. Mae looks pointedly ahead the whole time.

She hesitates before holding her magnetic key to the lock. 'Please... don't judge me.'

I assume she means not to judge her on her mess. But no.

The lights come on automatically, shining into a futuristic open-plan flat. It has full ceiling to floor windows with the kind of panoramic views you buy on tea cloths.

'Welcome home,' she sighs. She throws her keys into a gold dish that probably cost more than my monthly rent. She glances at me. 'Is it as bad as you imagined?'

I can't even bring myself to say something sarcastic.

'I imagined you'd live in a warehouse, maybe, with all your parties and orgies coming and going.'

'Nope,' she says, looking around distastefully. 'Just another soulless new build. It's actually pretty identical to all the other ones I've lived in, so you'd think it would feel more like home by now.'

I watch her walk through into the spotless kitchen, past her huge coffee maker and an elaborate, empty, fruit bowl. It's like being on a stage that hasn't yet been dressed.

'Water?' she asks, pouring from the fridge cooler.

'I'm surprised that doesn't come out with a slice of lime and a paper umbrella,' I say. I immediately regret it. She flushes, and I wish I could take it back, say something that would allow Mae to be at her usual ease.

But I don't know how, so I just study the walls. There are no photos, only monochrome canvases of phone boxes, taxi cabs, and Big Ben. I can't believe someone so colourful lives in such grey. I remind myself she's only lived in London for a few months. Maybe that's why she wears her personality on her sleeve – so she can take it with her when she moves.

'Horrible, isn't it?' she says, sarcastically toasting the white leather sofas. 'To be fair, I don't spend very much time here.'

I flush. Does she mean she spends most nights at someone else's?

'My bedroom's a bit better though,' she says, and opens her door.

I hesitate. Clearly she's so used to having lovers round that she doesn't question the flow of inviting someone into her bedroom. I act as if I, too, am completely at ease.

It's a sudden burst of light. Her duvet is patterned with sunflowers – very bad choice for a restful night's sleep, no wonder she's so chaotic – and she has approximately one million pillows. A bedside chair is covered in her ridiculous shirts, and there's a painting of a clear blue sky above her bed – presumably it's an original Van Gogh or something. There are two guitars leaning against the walls, and eclectic pebbles in home-made pots, and slightly wilting flowers. The room smells so strongly of her peppery citrus perfume that I feel faint.

I wander to her bedside table, which has a single framed photo of a very pretty brunette – maybe a couple of years older than us – holding a fat cocker spaniel.

Is this Mae's ex-girlfriend? Is she still in love with her? Does she kiss the glass every night before bed?

Mae must see where I'm staring because she says affectionately, 'That's Penny. I miss her so much.'

I return the photo and walk to her chair, hurling her shirts off onto the floor.

'She's a rescue,' Mae continues. 'She still lives in our family place in LA, with my sister. That's her – Avi.'

I pick up her shirts and start folding them.

'She's adorable,' I say. 'Do you visit them much?'

Mae turns her grin on me, and it suddenly feels completely normal that I'm in Mae's bedroom, talking about her family, basking in summer sunshine.

'At Christmas and stuff – my sister's there all the time now – she's an actor too, *obviously*.' She rolls her eyes self-deprecatingly. 'Avi has always wanted to be as close as possible to our mum, but... I dunno. LA never felt like home to me. I mean, I barely spent any of my teens there. We'd move countries every few months for Mum's work.'

I really can't imagine it. I felt so uprooted when Mum and Dad sold the house I'd grown up in and I moved to Dad's pizzeria during the week and Mum's cottage at the weekends. I say as much to Mae.

She shrugs. 'I know that I've had it ridiculously lucky in so many ways. But I always knew wherever we were was only temporary. Moving between schools, you get used to making friends knowing it won't last.'

I swallow. It's a reminder that I'm just another on her long list of fleeting contacts.

'Sounds like being an actor,' I say. 'You know, best friends with the cast while you're rehearsing, then you never speak again.'

Mae frowns.

'I'm sure everyone in the *Twelfth Night* cast would love to be friends with you after it ends.'

'Only if it meant they could be friends with *you*,' I laugh. 'Everyone uses every moment they can to try to win you over.'

'Clooney,' she says slowly, 'everyone is trying to win *you* over. Just like I am.'

I laugh, but she doesn't. She starts plumping pillows.

'You can seem pretty aloof, Clooney' – she sits on the bed and nestles in against the headboard – 'and that's when you're not even someone's enemy.'

I take a sip of fridge water. I remember Ruth and Raphy saying that. That I'm so sure that no one wants to talk to me that it's a self-fulfilling prophecy. But it's unreasonable to think that's the only reason actors don't stay friends with me – I mean, look at what happened with Thalia.

I fiddle with my rucksack, getting out my notebooks and play text.

'Like, in the first week,' Mae continues, 'you'd always sit apart, and not join us for drinks and I know that was my fault too – but sometimes you have an aura that's kind of intimidating. You're… untouchable.'

I sit on the chair, putting as much distance between us as possible.

'That would explain my abysmal dating life,' I try to joke. 'Not that you'd understand that.'

Mae rolls her eyes and flops back dramatically into her yellow pillows.

'Seriously, *where* did you get this idea of me as a Casanova?'

'Because you're so…' I gesture at her. 'You know…'

What's a synonym for 'perfect'?

'… confident.'

Mae barks and throws a pillow at me in faux outrage.

My pulse is racing. Curious as I am about Mae's dating life, it feels like dangerous territory for me to misstep and ruin our newfound truce. I open my book at a random page and try to think of something to say about acting.

'When we broke up,' Mae says suddenly, 'my ex told me that I'd never have a happy relationship because I am "quantity over quality". She said everyone likes me, but no one will ever love me.'

I actually gasp. 'No!'

'Yeah, she had a way with words,' she laughs weakly, hugging a pillow.

'Just because it's pithy, doesn't mean it's true,' I say furiously. I have an impulse to touch Mae, to comfort her, but that would feel too intimate. Instead, I put my hand on her bed frame and speak sincerely.

'Jones, *everyone* loves you. You're objectively the best person I've ever met.'

Mae blinks her bright eyes at me, then shakes her head ruefully.

'You've spent six months insulting me,' she says, pulling her feet up away from me. 'Now I'm meant to believe you've done a full 180 because you broke your toe?'

'Oh, for heaven's sake,' I snap. 'I've *always* thought it. Why else would I see you as such a threat?'

For once, Mae seems lost for words. Then she says quietly, 'Do you still see me as a threat?'

I look at her, surrounded by pillows and sunflowers, the light streaming onto her freckles.

'More and more every day,' I say.

I snap the play text open decisively.

'Now then. Act 2, scene—'

But Mae starts groaning.

'Oh come on,' I say reassuringly, 'Shakespeare isn't *that* bad.'

'How are you so – so composed all the time? I never know what you're really thinking! You're just a *mask*. Don't you feel *anything*?'

I look at her over the book.

'Jones,' I say, 'I feel everything. That's why I'm an actor.'

She blinks at me again. I blink back. Then Mae screams into a pillow. I don't know what I'm meant to do in return, so I start reciting the play until she stops to listen.

34

I HAVE to see you xxxxxxxxxxxxxxx Come to mine and I'll cook you your favourite dinner xxxxxxxxx

You're so lovely to offer that, Alice! I type carefully, stomach churning, *But I'm aware my headspace is taken up by my work at the moment and I don't want to be distracted thinking about* Twelfth Night *when I'm with you! But the show will be finished next week and I'll be back to normal?*

That also means this newfound friendship with Mae will be over so soon. We'll go back to rivalry – or not seeing each other at all. But maybe that's for the best.

Also, I type to Alice, *I'm really sorry if this inconveniences you, but I don't think you should review the* Twelfth Night *production. I know you were trying to be kind offering, and I'm sure I'm overreacting, but it doesn't sit right with me. I'm so, so sorry. Please could you explain to* The Atre *that you know someone in the cast so that you're taken off it? Hope that's OK, and thank you again!*

Just one drink then, Alice replies. *You'll be in bed by 11, on my honour xxxxxxxxxxxxxxxxxx*

She doesn't send anything else. I feel as nauseous as I do before a particularly scary audition.

I'm sorry, Alice, really. But it's only a week? And could you let me know about the review?

She doesn't reply for a moment. Biting my nail, I slip and tear it down to the quick.

OK, she types. *I wanted it to be a surprise, but you leave me no choice. I invited Thalia to join us tonight... And she was really excited for us all to catch up together... X*

My stomach churns in a whole new way.

I can't believe it. Just as I stopped thinking about Thalia, she's returned into my life. That's what they say happens, isn't it? Something in the universe sensed that I might be getting over her and decided to twist the knife again.

Ruth pops her head round my door. Her hair isn't as slicked as usual and has a little ruffled bounce to it. I can see she hasn't even ironed her shirt, which is surprising given that it's her big pitch this week.

'Em, are you in for film night tonight?' she asks. 'Or are you out with your cast again? Completely fine if you are.'

'I'm...' I glance down at my phone and decide. 'I'm actually going on a date with Alice.'

'Oh!' she says. 'So you'll probably be out late? Maybe even staying over at hers?'

'I...'

It's weird. My relationship with Alice feels as if it's moved at an incredibly fast pace, and, at the same time, at an incredibly slow one. I haven't seen her in weeks, but I have to remind myself she's technically my labelled *girlfriend*! It's now past our third date, but we've never done more than a goodbye kiss. I'm meant to want to have sex with her, for God's sake! And I can't help feeling Alice has invited Thalia as a kind of aphrodisiac.

'I might be staying with Alice,' I say. 'Yeah.'

'Great!' says Ruth. 'I mean, that's great for you! Good luck!'

'Ruth,' I say. 'You're not... You're not cross with me, are you?'

'Cross?' Ruth frowns, folds her arms, and tuts. 'No! Why would I be cross?'

I blink at her.

'Are you being passive aggressive?'

'Me? Why would I be pass ag?'

'Well,' I say. 'It is one of your best skills.'

'True,' she admits and unfolds her arms. 'But genuinely, Em, we get it. We're all having a bit of a changed schedule at the moment, aren't we? I mean, *you* are, nothing important has changed with me or Raphael's schedule...'

She smooths her hair hurriedly.

'Honestly. Everything is good, Em. We'll hang out the three of us soon.'

I watch her retreat and call back to her.

'Ruth?'

'Yes,' she says, looking alarmed. I look at her, knowing we both know we're not telling each other something. But she's my oldest friend. My best friend. I think I'm finally at a point where I can trust that we'll tell each other when it's right. Neither of us is going anywhere.

'I love you,' I say.

Ruth's eyeliner crinkles. She walks over on her surprisingly low heels, and hugs me tightly.

'I love you too, bestie.'

35

Our costumes have arrived!

Sebastian wears a white billowing shirt with lace ribbons at the collar, a blue waistcoat with gold buttons (infinitely sexier than those on my Pete's'zas uniform), and a thick bronze belt clasping grey twill trousers. His large brown leather boots have a thick sole that's great cushioning for my healing toe.

The other members of the cast all strip off gleefully to put on their costumes. I see more naked body parts than in the rest of my life combined. As comfortable as I feel with them all in other capacities, the thought of stripping in front of Mae is… Impossible. No doubt along with everything else she has a better body than me too.

I take my bundle into the familiar loo cubicle instead, putting on each item with the reverence befitting the costume designers' care.

I don't have the confidence with make-up to apply my own stage face, but I do put on my pirate hat and the accessories which differentiate me from my twin – a large hoop earring and an eye patch.

I look in the loo mirror. I don't look *at all* like myself. I'm delighted.

I head back, clutching my mufti clothes, and hesitate in front of the green room door. I feel like a debutante at the top of the stairs before entering a ball. I can hear the sounds of hair spray and compliments. My ears pick out Mae's ringing laugh.

When I open the door I see her immediately. She's in essentially the same costume as me, except that her waistcoat is a crimson red. She's wearing an identical billowing white shirt, her ribbons dangling untied. She has rips in her knees, and her trouser cuffs are rolled mismatchedly, as if she's been recently wading in the sea. Her boot laces are unevenly criss-crossed, one tongue flapping. In the same black kohl that lines her sapphire eyes, she has a hand-drawn comic moustache on her upper lip.

Our eyes find each other. I sweep my hat off and we step towards each other, meeting in the middle of the room.

'Ahoy, matey,' she smiles.

'Ahoy,' I say back.

She flicks the piratical earring clipped in my left ear. It matches hers, in her right.

'I'm not gonna lie, Clooney. I'm kind of annoyed at how good you look in this,' Mae says. 'I thought *I* was going to get to be the hot twin.'

I don't have a chance to reply, because Charlie appears dressed as a giant foam squid. They run around, slapping everyone on the bottom with their suckers.

Francis interrupts the chaos by blowing on his conch horn.

'Yes, yes, well done, you're all *very* attractive,' he shouts. 'But I must remind you that this isn't a costume party, this is a rehearsal. For a professional production which shall be performed to paying audience members – and reviewers – in a mere four days' time.'

Everyone hushes.

'Up on the stage. Act 3, Scene 2. Charlie, bring your spare tentacles.'

After the dress rehearsal, we step out disorientated into the muggy outdoors. Mae spreads her arms wide and says, to me, 'Rum?'

I can't help but smile back. For a second, I allow myself to enjoy the ease of going with the flow towards the pub.

'I can't tonight,' I say. Mae blinks rapidly. She still has traces of kohl around her eyes.

'Surely you've learnt all your lines by now!' laughs Roger. 'You're allowed an evening off!'

Zach slaps my back. 'Hear, hear. You're making the rest of us look bad.'

I smile at them. 'What if I promise I won't even *glance* at Shakespeare?'

'Give her a break,' says Keiya. 'Obviously Emmy's got a date.'

'Ooooh,' grins Surina.

I don't want to lie, but I don't want to admit it either. My friendship with the cast is still so young, so easily fractured. I just raise my hands.

'Tomorrow,' I promise. 'Tomorrow, and tomorrow, and tomorrow. I'll be there.'

Zach starts reciting the rest of the Shakespeare speech, and the group drift on, apart from Mae, who doesn't meet my eye.

'I'm sorry,' I mumble.

'You don't have to apologise to me for going on a date!' Mae laughs loudly.

'No, no, I know! I know! But I... Honestly, I would prefer to be with you.'

Mae goes rather pink.

'With you all,' I clarify.

Her hair's post-rehearsal ruffled and her flowery shirt is creased in the breeze.

'Then stay,' she tells me. When she says it, it really does sound simple.

But Thalia... Alice...

I shake my head ruefully. But I'm still kind of disappointed when Mae doesn't fight back. Her smile doesn't reach her eyes, but she fires a pistol with her fingers at me.

'Go get 'em, tiger.'

36

I change outfit approximately fifty times, despite knowing I only have one good enough for a meeting with Alice and Thalia. I decide to mix up my Red Carpet pinstripe suit by wearing a *black* Uniqlo T-shirt instead of a white one. Completely different.

I arrive with my hair in its most careful quiff, my oakwood cologne triple sprayed over my pulse points. I did my warm-up exercises before leaving the house so that my posture would be good.

I catch sight of Alice's tightly plaited hair across the bar. Seeing her makes my stomach clench painfully. That's a good sign, isn't it? Butterflies?

But she's alone.

I reach to kiss her cheek, but she clasps my head and pulls me into a full-lipped kiss.

'Hello again, darling!'

'Where's Thalia?'

'Oh, didn't she message you?' pouts Alice. 'She's *so* sorry but she can't make it. Something unexpected came up. She's *so* busy with all her commitments at the moment, isn't she?'

Alice looks at me carefully. I get the sense she's practised this line. Maybe she's just trying to make excuses for Thalia, to save my feelings. I know I shouldn't feel this disappointed to be having an evening alone with my girlfriend, but I can't help thinking of Mae in her flowery shirt, singing a sea shanty.

'Oh well. . .' I say.

I'd been so expecting Thalia to be here that I haven't prepared for this to be a date with Alice. I feel awkward again, nauseous, as if I'm performing and I want to get a good review.

Alice's dress has a plunged neckline and, as I take her jacket off, she leans into my hands. She turns to look at me over her shoulder and smiles under lowered lashes.

'My gentleman.'

She hands me a drinks menu, which I try not to baulk at. These fancy cocktails add up. I hadn't realised that being in a relationship was so damn expensive. Well, at least it's a silver lining for having been single up to now!

'Alice,' I dare myself to be brave. 'I was wondering if you'd thought about what I said, about not reviewing *Twelfth Night*?'

But Alice doesn't reply. She's looking out at where our waiter is approaching our booth.

I immediately clock that they're queer. Androgynous, tall, sporty, with a surfer's dark blonde hair, and a trouser suit – they look a bit like me, but hotter. They almost look like Mae.

I pat my quiff. It's pretty rare to bump into another butch in the wild. But when they look up at us with a polite smile, they suddenly freeze. They back away.

'Umm, excuse me?' I say, emasculated. 'Please could we order please?'

The waiter pauses, gulps, and returns slowly, avoiding eye contact.

'What can I get you?' they ask, their voice breaking.

I glance at Alice to see if she's noticed this weirdness. Her face has gone absolutely white.

'Old Fashioned, darling?' she says, way too loudly. The waiter's face snaps to look at her in alarm, then looks to me, then resumes staring at the floor.

I look between the two of them and realise what's happening. I can't help it – I start smirking. I put the menu down.

'Actually, I don't like whiskey,' I say. 'Just some sparkling water for me, thank you *so* much.'

'Oh! Of course!' says Alice. 'Silly me. I'll – I'll – I'll have a...'

I lean back, tickled. Seeing Alice flustered is a novelty.

'Martini?' I ask, at the same time the waiter says it. We glance at each other. The waiter now has an edge in their eyes.

'Of course,' says Alice, fanning herself desperately with the menu. 'Thank you.'

The waiter stalks away.

I'm delighted. The whole time I've known Alice, it's felt that she was an angel who could do no wrong, and I was unworthily ruining our image. She seems a lot more human now.

'So, *darling*,' I say, languishing back. 'Who's your friend?'

'We're not friends!' she snaps. 'I mean, we're not anything. We don't speak anymore. I swear.'

'What happened?'

'Nothing's happening! I did *not* know she worked here! I didn't even know she was back in London!'

I pat her hand.

'Alice, it's OK. Honestly.'

She frowns at me.

'You're not jealous?'

I try to plumb my emotional depths. But no, I feel rather magnanimous.

'Maybe I'm not a very jealous person,' I say.

Alice crosses her arms, and something in my stomach clenches in response. Sorry, but how did this suddenly become *me* doing something wrong?

'All I mean is,' I say quickly, 'I believe you! You say you haven't spoken in years, you don't have feelings for her anymore, so... Tell me about her?'

Alice looks around in terror.

'We just went on a few dates,' she says hurriedly, then licks her lip. 'Well... we were seeing each other. For a while.'

'How long is a while?' I ask.

'Eight years.'

I splutter.

'But for two years of that,' she adds, 'we were engaged.'

The waiter returns with our drinks on a shaking tray. She passes me my sparkling water, setting it down a little roughly for such a fancy establishment. Then she sets down Alice's martini and a delicate dish with two of the plumpest olives I've ever seen.

'On the side,' says the waiter quietly. She lingers for just a second longer, then says, 'Let me know if you want anything more,' and runs away. We both watch her retreat.

'You were engaged?' I hiss.

Alice takes a huge sip of her martini and gasps for air.

'Well?' I demand. 'What happened?'

Alice shakes her head.

'Please, Emmeline. I don't want to talk about it.'

She rolls the olives round the pot.

I open my bottle of water with a fizz. I open my mouth and close it again. Then I giggle. Alice stares at me with complete betrayal in her eyes.

'Sorry,' I say. 'Sorry, it's just funny!'

'What on earth is *funny*?'

'Well, you have a type!'

Alice's face whitens further.

'Wh-what do you mean?'

'It's not a problem! I'm just saying...' I gesture between myself and the waiter. 'Me... her... there's a pattern!'

Alice's shoulders lower slightly.

'It's natural,' she says, poking an olive with a stick. 'For someone like me to be with someone like you.'

She pops it in her mouth.

The laugh dies in my throat. I put my bottle down.

'What do you mean?'

'You know very well what I mean,' she says, chewing. 'We might be lesbians, but relationships are still about balance.'

The twist in my stomach starts to writhe.

'You understand,' she continues. 'There's a reason you're

only ever cast to play the girlfriend of feminine women. It's the natural way of things.'

'Otherwise how would we know who wears the trousers?' I say sarcastically.

'Oh, stop trying to be clever, Emmeline, it doesn't suit you.'

It's like a slap. But you know what? A part of me is so relieved. Finally, here's a completely justifiable reason for me to feel uncomfortable dating Alice.

I take a deep breath. As politely as I can, I lift my napkin from my lap, put it onto the table, and stand up.

'Alice,' I say, trying to collate the scripts of romance films into a kind but irreversible break-up speech.

Unfortunately, Alice has seen the same films and clocks my tone.

'No,' she says, grabbing my hand. 'No. No, no, no! Don't start that. I'm sorry. I'm sorry.'

I try to gently tug my hand out of hers, but she clings harder.

'Please!' she sobs. 'I'll do anything.'

'Alice,' I say, glancing around the bar, supremely awkward.

She puts her face in her hands and screams. What is this going to do for the public reputation of lesbians? Awkwardly, I perch back down again.

'I was unacceptable,' says Alice. 'I didn't mean it! Of course I think you're intelligent, I always enjoy hearing your opinions on the theatre. They've even inspired my reviews. I was just so flustered by seeing Sammy again. You don't understand. You've never had your heart really broken.'

I sigh, and think about when I saw Thalia for the first time after the months of silence. How, when she walked onto that stage, I convinced myself she was talking just to me. How she glowed.

I pass Alice a linen table napkin.

'There, there,' I say.

Alice blows her nose. Her mascara has run like squashed spiders. I feel a rush of sympathy for people who wear make-up, how it means you can't hide accidental outbursts. She glances over at the exit, then at me. She looks so crushed, so confused.

'I do understand,' I say softly.

Alice sighs in relief, leans forward over the table, the motion accentuating the low-cut nature of her dress.

'My one true darling,' she says. 'Thank you. I'll make it up to you.'

'You don't need to,' I say, already doubting myself.

'Let's get out of this hellhole,' she says, scrabbling with her bag. 'Take me home.'

I hesitate. Alice pouts.

'We don't have to – we don't have to do *anything* you don't want to do. I'm just asking for us to leave here, and you to keep me company. Please.'

What else can I do? I nod.

She grabs her coat and kisses me. 'I'll wait for you outside.'

I go to pay a different waitress. Sammy has disappeared. The olives on the side cost an extra six pounds.

I can't describe what Alice's flat looks like, because the second we go through the front door, she doesn't turn the lights on, just starts kissing me and pawing at my jacket.

'Woah!' I try to gently push her off. 'Slow down.'

She starts unclasping the top of her dress.

'Alice. Stop!'

She lets the fabric fall.

'I can't do this,' I say.

Alice moves towards me and links her fingers round my belt.

'What about *th*—'

'No.' I push her hands away and look away. 'I mean it. I can't do this.'

'Do you mean *this* this? Or *this* this?'

We stare at each other in the dark. Passing cars light up her face briefly through the window above the door.

God, what am I meant to do? I feel that if Ruth and Raphy were here right now, they'd be telling me I should break up with Alice. But I've never broken up with someone before! I'm always the one broken up with – or indeed, *not* broken up with, because we were never officially 'together' in the first place. Surely I can't break up with Alice when she's had a sad evening. When she's already heartbroken and tipsy and I've rejected her sexual advances? I think of how much Mae's ex upset her with careless words. I don't want to give Alice a complex. If I'm going to break up with her, I'll have to do it right. I'll research it then write a good speech and practise it beforehand.

Thankfully, just as I make the decision, Alice regains control.

'You're not yourself right now,' she says, tying her dress back. 'Your mind is in your character, in your show. I'll see you after the *Twelfth Night* performances, okay? Things will seem different then. You'll be a better girlfriend.'

I don't point out that I had asked not to see her while I'm so busy with the show anyway, but I am at least glad this confirms Alice is not reviewing it anymore.

Besides, maybe she's right. It could all feel different with her in a few weeks. Or she could decide to break up with me, and I wouldn't need to be the bad guy...

Exhaustedly, cowardly, I nod.

'See you after the show.'

37

In rehearsals the next day, Francis, Mae, Joe and Charlie are due to set the final staging for Act 2, scene 4. In this scene, the Duke Orsino is jealous when he thinks that his cute new pageboy (Viola in disguise) has a crush on someone else. But Viola tries to hint that it's *him* she likes, and, listening to romantic music together, they nearly kiss.

I remember Mae and I speaking through the scene in Mae's bedroom. As I watch her up on the stage, I wonder if she's remembering it too.

Suddenly, mid-scene, Joe clutches at his mouth. Visibly green, he sprints off, followed by a concerned Charlie.

'He's throwing up, like, a lot,' they report back. 'Thinks he ate a bad egg.'

'Damn and blast!' shouts Francis, squeezing a prop parrot like a stress ball. 'Is this play cursed? This is a vital tidal shift in the play. I *need* to know where we are going to move the barrels.'

He wheels round. He points at me.

'You. Sebastian. How's your toe? No pun intended, but can you stand in?'

I do know the direction from watching them.

'Yessir!'

'Good show,' says Francis, a twinkle in his eye. 'I merely need you as a body, don't worry about snogging your heart out...'

My heart rate rockets. I hobble up the stairs and get into the position left by Joe, avoiding Mae's eye the whole time.

246

'And. . . action,' says Francis.

Upstage, Charlie's Feste starts singing a sombre sea shanty about a captain throwing himself overboard for a siren's call.

I glance at Mae, unsure whether she'll look as nervous as I feel. But instead, she looks like she's trying not to laugh. She looks so adorable I can't help myself. I flick her nose. Then I remember we're on stage, and I'm meant to be the *Duke*. I style it out into Duke's lines, where he's convinced that Viola has a crush on someone.

DUKE ORSINO
My life upon't, thine eye
Hath stay'd upon some favour that it loves:
Hath it not?

Mae's eyes linger too long on mine. Then she curls the hair at the back of her neck and looks away.

VIOLA
A little, by your favour.

Jealousy flares up in me. I know it's just the energy of the character, but somehow it feels real.

DUKE ORSINO
What kind of man is't?

Viola looks back at me, unblinking.

VIOLA
Of your complexion.

My heart jolts. For a second, I think she means me. Then I catch myself and remember that, for God's sake Emmy, we're both *actors*! I'm getting too into the story

– after all, in terms of the play, Viola *is* talking about the Duke.

DUKE ORSINO
He is not worth thee, then.

But as she puts her hand on mine, electricity courses through me. As she moves closer to me, I forget that we're characters. It's just me and Mae.

Suddenly, the music stops. We reel round. Charlie curtseys with their pink ukulele.

I 'pretend not to be flustered' while also pretending not to be flustered. I'd completely forgotten Feste interrupts at that point. Thank goodness my knowledge of the play takes over on autopilot. The Duke stands, and rummages for some coins in his purse, then pushes the Fool from the room. God, acting does weird things to your nervous system.

The thing that happens next in the play is that the Duke, in their sudden silent privacy, looks over at disguised Viola, someone he's not allowed to be attracted to, and thinks to himself, I mustn't spend more time with him or I'm going to embarrass myself.

I look over at Mae, and realise I know exactly how he feels.

As the Duke, I tell 'Cesario' to leave, to go to Olivia and woo her on my behalf. To win someone he *should* want to be with. But Viola doesn't leave. She comes back, and takes the Duke's hand.

VIOLA
Sir, shall I to this Lady?

She brings his hand to her mouth, turns it and kisses his wrist. The Duke stares at her, then remembers himself, and waves her away. She leaves heartbroken. In the distance, the fool plays another sad refrain. The Duke returns to his seat, and brings his wrist to his mouth, kissing the trace of her lips.

'And blackout!' calls Francis.

The spell snaps away. Francis leaps up to the stage, moving treasure chests and talking to Mae about her delivery. No one else seems to have noticed anything untoward. They don't know that I didn't mean to do that. I wasn't being 'the Duke', I was just being... myself. Myself, desperately wanting Mae to kiss me.

I hobble down the steps. Then Mae's there, offering me her arm. I pull away from her as if she's on fire.

'You OK, Clooney?' she asks, as if everything is normal. 'You look like you've eaten one of Joe's eggs.'

'I'm fine! I'm fine!' I say, but I do then spend some time with my head in my hands in the loo.

This is bad. Very, very bad.

38

I text R&R saying we need to have an emergency flat meeting.

They look surprisingly nervous, sitting on the sofa. Raphy squeezes Ruth's hand reassuringly. They must be feeling my terrified energy.

I close my eyes, take a deep breath, and say it aloud for the first time.

'I think I might possibly... have a crush on Mae Jones.'

R&R start laughing.

'Yeah,' says Raphy. 'Duh.'

I bury my head in the beanbag and scream.

'So what are you going to do about it?' asks Ruth.

'Nothing,' I say immediately. 'Absolutely nothing! There's nothing to do, except ignore it. In one week's time, I'll never see her again.'

'One second you're convinced you'll see her constantly, the next you think you're never going to see her again,' says Ruth.

'Now I know I won't see her in auditions anymore because she's so much better than me,' I explain. 'She might not even have to do auditions anymore – she's so good as *Twelfth Night*'s leading lady, she'll get casting offers off the back of the reviews.'

'OK, so even if you won't see each other in auditions or in productions anymore,' shrugs Ruth, 'you could, you know, arrange to meet outside of your workplace?'

I blink at her. 'Why would she want to see me outside of work?'

'Because she might like you back?' says Raphy.

I laugh hysterically.

'Guys. You met her! She's out of my league! She could have her pick of literally anyone. She doesn't think of me that way! She's literally spent the past months telling me, regularly, how much she dislikes me!'

R&R share a meaningful look.

'Well, Emmy,' Raphy says, in the way of a parent about to give The Talk, 'sometimes we might tell ourselves that someone isn't right for us, or isn't into us, as a defence mechanism to protect ourselves from being vulnerable.'

'What about Alice?' I say. 'She's obviously the one I should be with! She has explicitly told me she likes me! And she's... She's formidable!'

'Your energy is off when you speak about her,' shivers Raphy.

'You've had plenty of opportunities to shag her, but you haven't,' shivers Ruth.

I blush. 'You said it's OK for me to go at my own pace!'

'Yeah, of course it is. But do you want to do it with Mae?'

Flashes of Mae pushing me against a locker.

'Aargh! That doesn't matter! What matters is that, in my twenty-five years on this earth, I've never been in an official relationship! Alice is my best chance to be a real adult. Even... even if Mae somehow *did* like me, it would only be temporary. She's flighty! She's an improviser! I can't handle another situation where I'm devoted to someone who doesn't care and throws me away when they're bored!'

Raphy takes my hand. 'Em... what if you accepted no one can have a meaningful relationship without risk? Yes, she might leave, but she might not. What if it's still worth it?'

But a dreadful, familiar panic rises in my chest. I start hyperventilating.

'Em, it's OK,' says Ruth, putting her cold hands on my cheeks. She holds her forehead to mine, like she did when we were at school, if I was freaking out about whether Dad would be too busy to pick me up, or about the girl who didn't want to kiss me anymore, or about how much I missed Mum.

'It's OK,' she says. 'We've got you.'

I nestle into the sofa between them, and feel my breathing return. I wipe my cheeks.

'Sorry,' I mumble, but they just carry on cooing.

'I love you both so much,' I say. 'I should say it more. I'm so grateful for your friendship and...' I sniff. 'I know I've been absent recently with rehearsals and everything. But soon it'll be over, and we can hang out and watch musicals like always, OK?' I look at them tearily. 'Nothing has changed?'

Raphy and Ruth glance at each other. 'You know Em, change can be a good—'

I hold out my hands for the three of us to shake.

'Best friends for the best time?' I plead.

R&R look at each other for a moment, then nod. They join in the handshake.

39

On the last day of rehearsals for a show, I'm usually desperate to spend the evening with the cast, knowing it will be the last time I'll see them outside the theatre. But tonight, a guilty part of me hopes I'll be able to spend some time with just Mae.

As we gather in the bright, humid evening, we realise our group is depleted. Roger and Zach have officially got together, as we knew they would, and say that as they hadn't had sex in five whole hours they simply *have* to go. (I'm not going to question the maths of having spent eight hours in rehearsals today.) Keiya's got tickets to see Bimini Bon Boulash in concert, and Joe's getting an early night because he still feels a bit eggy. Surina and Charlie live near each other in Peckham, so suggest that, instead of going to the pub, we go back to Surina's.

I glance at Mae – she's already looking at me.

'I...' Mae says, her eyes questioning.

'Well, I live in North so—'

'Me too,' says Mae. I'm not sure King's Cross really counts as North, but I'm not going to complain.

'Right,' I say. 'Yes. So maybe we should—'

'Right!' says Mae.

'Finally!' says Charlie, clapping Mae on the back. Mae slaps their elbow.

'Oops, sorry.'

Charlie hugs me and whispers, 'Remember to use protection.'

They all wander away, waving happily to us. Mae and I start walking. I notice it's not towards the nearest Tube stop.

As usual at the end of June, most shops still have their corporate Pride stickers in their garish windows like a Christmas light competition, ready to take down on the 1st July. I don't dare to look at Mae.

'I *do* really like hanging out with everyone,' I say.

'Oh my God, me too!' Unabashedly, she loops her arm with mine and smiles at me. 'But you're my favourite.'

I have to hope that she can't feel my outrageous heartbeat through her elbow.

'So,' she says. 'What shall we do?'

What's a suggestion that's worthy of a ceremonial, celebratory evening with Mae, but that doesn't sound like a date? Not that I'd know where to suggest if it *was* a date – it hardly feels appropriate to go to the same places I've been to with Alice.

God. Alice…

Don't be silly, Emmy. Just because I might have a tiny, temporary, confusing crush on Mae, nothing factually has changed. It can't be 'cheating' to go on a friendly excursion with someone who doesn't like you back. That would be impossible to police.

'Let's just…' I wave in the direction of the city, and dare myself to touch her tattooed wrist. '"Yes and" whatever comes up.'

She grins and hugs my arm.

What we 'yes and' first is cans of pre-mixed Captain Morgan's which we clink as we promenade along the side of the river, watching the sky turn from blue to gold. Then we 'yes and' a bag of hot vegan doughnuts. When she's licked the last crumbs from her fingers, she loops her arm comfortably round my shoulders. My heart clenches. Does this look like we're on a date? No, don't be silly. People probably think we're sisters. Or brothers. A couple of buddies, chilling. Which, I remind myself, is exactly what we *are* doing.

Mae takes a deep breath of polluted air and exhales contentedly.

'You know...' she says. 'Of all the places I've lived, I think London is my favourite.'

Mae looks at me, her face sparkling like the moonlit river. She nudges me.

'Will you let me stay? Or is it not big enough for the two of us?'

I shrug out from under her arm.

'Honestly, Jones, I don't think we'll overlap much,' I say, trying to keep my voice level. 'You're a star that's rising far too fast for me to keep up. Maybe I can have a career as your lookalike.'

'Clooney,' she says warningly, 'let's not get into a compliment fight – who knows which of your limbs I'd end up breaking.'

Despite everything I'm feeling, I laugh. I look at her under the setting sun, the way her dimples wiggle when she smiles.

Oh God. I've got it bad.

'What are you thinking about?' she laughs.

'Nothing! Literally nothing!'

I pat her shoulder in what I hope is a friendly, matey, no homo kind of way.

'I'm just... I'm going to miss you.'

Mae reaches up to hold my hand on her shoulder.

'Why would you have to miss me?'

I pull my hand away. That's what Thalia said too. Why do I keep doing this to myself?

I try to smile back at Mae but it feels more like a grimace. The reality of it is kicking in. This is probably the last time we'll spend time together outside of the theatre. It's all happened so fast. I wish I could stop it, freeze it, keep this in a perfect still.

I swallow painfully and turn away, pretending to admire the view. My techniques for maintaining a neutral expression aren't working.

'Clooney?' Mae steps in front of me. 'What's happened?'

'Sorry,' I mutter, carrying on walking. 'Just... suddenly tired. I should go home. Sorry.'

I turn away, but she takes my hand.

'Hey,' she says, 'talk to me.'

I shake my head. Mae reaches out her hand and touches my cheek. It's like a jolt of adrenaline straight to my chest.

I finally meet her eyes. They're bright, searching mine, her gold flecks like a kaleidescope.

Fuck, it's going to take a long time to recover from her.

But maybe Raphy's right. Maybe it's worth it.

'I give up,' I say, and gently fist-bump her shoulder. 'You win.'

I take her hand and I start to run.

Mae laughs in wild surprise, but quickly matches my pace. Down the street, we run between couples and tourists, racing, whooping. At a crossroads, she points in the other direction and we sprint again until we come to a breathless stop outside an old-fashioned cinema.

I bend over panting, laughing as I watch Mae clutch her stomach, fanning her star-patterned shirt from her chest. She holds a finger up while she catches her breath enough to say, 'I have an idea.'

She opens the cinema doors for me and looks around. There's a woop from behind the counter. An usher with wild sandy hair and a curly moustache waves at her. Mae runs over and is swept into a bear hug. I smile to myself. Of course Mae knows the staff here.

Mae waves me over. 'Clooney, this is Alex, who used to come into the café to write his amazing screenplays.'

He laughs. 'She'd slide me free mocha top-ups and I'd slide her free cinema tickets.'

'Alex, this is Em. She's in *Twelfth Night* with me. But she's like, a *proper* actor. She knows *everything*. You should totally come to see her!'

'Mae's the real reason you should come to see it,' I insist. 'Imagine *this*,' I gesture to her grin, 'but in a pirate costume.'

Mae and Alex share a look which I can't read, the corners of his mouth curling under his moustache.

'Well, I look forward to seeing you both on one of these screens some day,' he says.

'What's on tonight?' I ask.

Mae raises her eyebrows significantly at Alex, and he looks round at the other staff in the quiet cinema, then nods conspiratorially at her. She grins.

'Em, how about you choose some snacks? Al and I are just going to sort something out.'

I'd happily spend my entire *Twelfth Night* fee on buying Mae cute sweets at the pick 'n' mix. I get mixed popcorn to balance my salt with Mae's sweet. At the till, I spontaneously get a mini bottle of Prosecco too – a sip each to celebrate the end of rehearsals.

Alex waves aside the payment.

'This is on me,' he says. 'God knows, Mae saved me enough on coffee.'

I'm overwhelmed at Mae's magic. 'Thank you,' I say sincerely. 'At least let me get you something for your shift?'

'I can see why she likes you,' he smiles, and I blush as I pay for his Ice Blast.

'You want Screen 5,' he winks, and points me towards the corridors.

I juggle the food to open the screen door, wondering how I'm going to find Mae without bothering too many people.

It turns out not to be a problem. The room is empty, except for Mae, seated in the middle. She turns to me and spreads her arms out.

'They have these rooms for private cinema screenings, but they don't always get booked up,' she says. 'Al and I watched the entirety of *Gilmore Girls* here.'

'This is… surreal,' I say to her.

She grins even more broadly.

'It's all real, baby.'

I sit down next to her, passing her the pick 'n' mix. She

squeals at the huge blue dolphins and pops the cork on our mini Prosecco.

The opening credits start. It's *Carol*.

Mae's eyes twinkle, gauging my reaction.

I laugh and roll my eyes.

'Jones, you cliché! I hope you're being ironic.'

Mae sips the Prosecco and passes me the bottle. 'Oh you just wait. By the end, I guarantee, we'll be taking it very seriously.'

I am astonishingly aware of the warmth of her body next to mine, the way our fingers touch when we pass the Prosecco bottle back and forth, the way she is not careful when reaching into the popcorn.

Mae starts a running commentary, far more enjoyable than any director's cut. When there's a moment that's become a meme, she hurriedly explains her laughter. When the characters' queer longing becomes too much, she clutches my arm. You'd have thought that all this distraction would mean I can't concentrate on the film. But Mae's engagement is infectious. For the first time in forever, I'm not judging the actor's technique, or thinking about how I would have said the lines. I'm just lost in the story.

And Mae's right. It isn't long before we stop laughing. Her hand stays on my arm.

I sit back and watch them fall in love, trying not to cry.

40

I close the front door carefully behind me so I don't wake Ruth and Raphy.

I'm feeling decidedly strange. It was a mistake, I realise, to watch an intensely erotic lesbian film alone with a woman I'm trying not to develop feelings for.

We sat through the credits in silence and afterwards I couldn't look at her. We walked to the Tube in silence and even though we both know where the other lives, I said, madly, that I was going in the other direction. She didn't stop me. We parted with our first, unbelievably brief, hug. My heart rate hasn't returned to normal since.

Although I would love to debrief with R&R about everything, I can't wake them for something as silly as this. Besides, if I asked them 'should I dump Alice over text because I watched *Carol* with someone else and now I have literally every feeling for her?' they might tell me something I don't want to hear.

It's past midnight, so I'm surprised there's music coming from the living room. Hypnotic tubular bells.

I tiptoe in, thinking Raphy must have left his CD player on. But no, he's in there, straddling someone on the sofa. His hair's wild and free and flopping forwards over his lover's face. He pulls back to look at her.

It's Ruth.

Ruth and Raphy. Making out. In my spot.

For a moment, my brain doesn't catch up. I don't do anything except watch. Then it all hits me in one violent surge.

I thought we were a three. I thought I was their best friend. But the whole time, it was the two of *them*, and me alone. The whole time they were encouraging me to date, was it just because they wanted me out of the way?

I watch the two of them; how obvious it is now. The shared looks, the uncharacteristic behaviour, the excuses to spend time as a couple. How could I have been so stupid?

Deep in my core, something jealous writhes in agony.

I step backwards and they turn at the noise.

'Em!'

The two of them look at me, then each other, and, to my utter astonishment, start giggling.

'Well, I guess we don't need to worry about how to tell her anymore,' says Ruth, smoothing her ruffles. Raphy dismounts, tucking coy curls behind his ear.

'Anymore?' I say quietly. 'How long…?'

They look at each other in that familiar way couples do, about who is going to tell the story of how they got together.

'When you went on your first date with Alice,' says Ruth.

'We all made good on our promise to date people outside of our usual types,' laughs Raphy. They're glowing.

I haven't moved from the doorway.

'But that was *weeks* ago,' I say. 'Why didn't you tell me?'

'Well, we had to be sensible,' says Ruth. 'At first, we didn't know if it was going to be a *thing* and we didn't want to rock the boat for no reason. Then when it became evident that…' She looks shyly at Raphy.

Raphy strokes her hair behind her ear. 'That it was what was always meant to happen.'

Ruth smiles back. A stab goes through my chest.

'Then we put it off because we didn't want you to think it would change anything between *us*. We wanted to be able to say – well look, it's already *been* working fine. So… Look!'

I do. I look at the new way they're looking at each other, and moving around each other, touching each other. They have a whole separate life now, one that doesn't involve me.

'But it *does* change things,' I say. 'It's already changed things. We were meant to be best friends having the best time...'

What's it going to be like, being around the two of them, knowing they don't really want me there? Having them always jump apart when I come home. Gradually breaking off promises to hang out as a three. The plaster ripped off the wound over and over again.

I turn away from them, unsure what I'm meant to do next.

'Em, you've changed too,' says Ruth, walking over. 'Maybe the two of us only came together because you weren't around anymore.'

'And that's good!' says Raphy hastily. 'Change is natural! We're both happy for you that you're finally dating!'

Their pity feels like a slap.

'I should have realised I was always second best for you.'

'Umm,' says Ruth, folding her arms. 'Actually, *we've* always been second best for you. First we were second-best friends to Thalia. Now, we're second best to your girlfriend. Both of them.'

My chest feels as though it's caving in. Some actor part of me at the back of my brain tries to take notes for future performances. What is this specific feeling? Like being hit by a very targeted truck?

'Thank you for the confirmation,' I say stiffly. 'You don't want me around anymore. Maybe you never did.'

'Em' – Ruth rolls her eyes – 'no one is saying that.'

'You don't have to say it! It's obvious!'

What couple wants to live with a third wheel? They'll probably move into one of Raphy's dad's beautiful *one*-bedroom homes, and they'll never want to see me again. Ruth and Raphy, the only friends I believed would never leave me. What an idiot.

I go to my room and pack a hasty bag, glad that my monochrome wardrobe makes it easy to leave home in a hurry.

Ruth and Raphy stand in my bedroom doorway now. I try to close it, but Ruth puts her heel-hardened foot in the gap.

'Em, you're overreacting.'

'*Me*?! You think *I'm* overreacting?!'

I pull my underwear drawer out from its cupboard hinges and tip it upside down over my suitcase.

'My best friends have both betrayed me! With each other! I'm reacting in a completely reasonable way!'

I ram the drawer back in and do it again with my T-shirts.

'See?' Ruth says to Raphy. My jaw drops at her. That's how it will always be from now on – Ruth and Raphy having a separate conversation over my head.

'Em,' says Raphy placatingly. 'Ru and I changing the nature of our relationship doesn't have to change anything between ours.'

The way Raphael says 'Ru' sounds different now. Private. Intimate. Special. And this whole time, I thought that *I* was secretly the others' favourite. It's so embarrassing.

'I'll move back in with my dad,' I say. 'Of course, I'll still transfer you the rent for this month.'

'This is your home as long as you want it,' he says.

I shake my head. I can't cry now, not here, I'd never be able to stop. I take a last look around my too beautiful room. *Raphy's* too beautiful room. Maybe they'll convert it into a sex dungeon. Or a nursery.

'I hope you'll be very happy,' I say, my throat tight. 'Maybe you'll consider inviting me to your wedding.'

She throws up her hands. 'This doesn't have to be one of your little audition pieces. Stop being so dramatic.'

I feel winded.

'You always do this!' she says. 'You're blaming us for abandoning you, but you're the one leaving. It's like with your other play friends at school, and the other actors after college, and the girls who tried to date you – and it's exactly like you did with your mum.'

Raphy flinches. He takes a step towards me, but I hold up

a hand. I can't look at either of them. I just walk slowly to the bedroom door, and they both back away, like I have a powerful forcefield.

'Em,' Ruth says urgently, with a softness I haven't heard from her since the bullies got to us in primary school. 'Em, I'm sorry. I'm sorry, I didn't—'

'Please,' I say, my voice unfamiliar, 'if either of you care about me at all, don't message me.'

I close the door gently behind me.

41

We're having pizza for breakfast.

Dad's always in charge of the kitchen in the flat, to give Pete some time off. On top of sourdough bases, he's fried eggs on spicy tomato sauce like an unholy shakshuka, and for me, he's unsuccessfully replaced the eggs with scrambled tofu. I miss Raphy's smoothies.

'Isn't this wonderful?' sings Dad. He's wearing a frilly pink apron my mum bought him twenty years ago. The words KISS THE CHEF have faded into invisibility.

He sits down with a contented sigh, waves at us both to eat, and squeezes my hand over the table.

'You won't need to worry about rent anymore.'

Dad assumed the reason I fought with R&R was because I'd missed a payment, and I didn't correct him. Better than explaining I officially have fewer friends than he does.

'We can do shifts together every night,' he says, rolling his pizza cutter, 'and settle into some immersive three-person board games. Ticket to Ride? Catan? Pokemon Master Quest?'

'Maybe,' I say, pushing tofu round my plate. 'But Dad, I won't actually be around here much over the next few days, remember? Because of my show? *Twelfth Night*? I've got today off, and then the performances on the 29th and 30th...?'

I leave a gap for them to say that they've got tickets, but they've both become very preoccupied with their cutlery.

'Did we restock garlic?' Dad asks Pete suddenly. Pete nods back, egg yolk in his moustache.

I force myself to ask, 'Are you coming to see the show?'

Pete turns to Dad.

'Oh, *mi amore*,' says Dad, 'you know how hard it is to get time off work here at weekends. I'll have to check with the others.'

Dad is literally in charge of scheduling. I put down my cutlery over my untouched breakfast.

'OK,' I say, cheeks burning. '*Other* people are coming to see me.'

Dad and Pete stop chewing and look at each other.

'Like my old drama school friend, Thalia,' I continue, wildly. 'She promised to see it *months* ago, even though she's basically a celebrity now.'

Saying it aloud makes me suddenly realise how soon two days is. When we're back in the smoking area at The Boards, maybe it will feel like this year never happened at all. The thought is enough to make the scrambled tofu look even worse than it does intrinsically.

But this doesn't have any effect on Dad and Pete. They're still staring at each other like they're having a whole conversation via blink semaphore.

So I add even more desperately, 'And my girlfriend, Alice, is coming to see it. She was going to be reviewing it, actually, but now she's just coming to support me. To cheer me on.'

They exchange another significant glance. Oh, I get it. They're thinking of the time I pretended I had a girlfriend. She was called Amethyst, and we were very much in love, even though her mafia parents didn't approve. Dad once made a joke about it at a parents' evening and I had to say she'd emigrated.

'Alice is real!'

'Neither of us said she wasn't! We just haven't had the pleasure of meeting her yet!' Dad snorts.

Dad always knows how to push my competitive buttons. I scrape the breakfast into the food bin.

'Then I'll invite her here sometime!' I snap.

'Do!' he says, calmly biting into his pizza.

'Fine!' I say. 'How about today? Lunch?'

Dad just laughs.

I drop my plate into the sink and, right there, text Alice.

I immediately wish I could take it back. I even hold the text to delete it. But she's already replied.

Yes!! Finally!! I'm going to make your parents LOVE me!! Xxxxxxxxxxxxx

I watch Alice arrive. She looks lost, even though she's clearly followed her map app and is looking right at the Pete's'zas sign. She's wearing another glamorous red cocktail dress, and a smokey eye. Thank God I'm not in my pizzeria uniform.

We're not open for lunch today, so we have the place to ourselves for this regrettable family gathering.

I open the door to her, hoping Dad doesn't see her distaste as she looks at the pizza-coloured bar stools. Oh God, why did I bring her here?

'It's a pleasure to meet you, Mr Clooney,' Alice says to my dad, then turns to Pete and adds, 'And… Mr Clooney?'

For someone who is literally gay, she seems shocked at the thought of me having two fathers. I suppose it shows how little we've talked about our lives outside of theatre.

'No,' I correct her, my neck warming, 'this is my Uncle Pete.'

'You look alike,' says Alice, as they shake hands.

'Oh, we're not related,' I correct her. 'We're… Well, we're just colleagues, actually.'

Pete's eyebrows rise.

'Well then, I'll leave you to it,' says Pete, and bows out to the kitchen.

Dad frowns at me. I try to move my eyebrows in a way that

says, 'what did I do wrong?' but Dad just rolls his eyes back. He takes a breath and then turns to Alice with his waiter demeanour. He flamboyantly pulls out a seat for her, and compliments her outfit.

'Good for if you spill tomato sauce!' he winks.

Dad often makes this joke with red-wearing customers. Alice doesn't smile back. She grimaces and folds her skirt under her as though she's sitting on a damp picnic blanket.

I ask Alice what she'd like for lunch.

'Pinot Grigio please. And do you do salads?'

Dad looks at me like this is a dumpable offence.

'I'm sure Pete can rustle something up,' I say.

Dad barely hides his sneer as he returns with a bottle. He pours a sip for Alice to try, then, when she nods, a full glass for her. He takes the delivery of our order as an excuse to leave the table completely. He too disappears into the kitchen, turning up the TV in there, clearly to cover up their private gossiping. He's meeting my girlfriend for the first time, why can't he act like a dad, not a waiter? It's so rude.

Alice asks me how the last days of rehearsals have been. My mind flashes images of Mae, in a green room, and Mae, in an empty cinema. I'm so scared of revealing something about my confusing temporary crush on her (I know, I'm a terrible person), that I end up telling Alice everything about Ruth and Raphy's betrayal, and explain that's why I'm staying with my Dad again.

'Well,' she sips, 'it's natural that they would prioritise their romantic relationship with each other over their friendship with you, right?'

She squeezes my knee under the table, then raises it higher. I jerk it away, nearly toppling off my mushroom.

Dad walks over, delivering me an Emmy Special and Alice a truly delicious-looking salad. He doesn't have any food for himself or for Pete. He turns on his heel and returns to the kitchen TV.

I can't help comparing my dad's behaviour with Alice to how

he treated Mae at the hospital. How he immediately loved her and joked with her.

As I watch Alice push a walnut round her plate, it all bubbles up in me – the guilt, the longing, the doubt. If I allow myself to imagine being here, with Mae at the table instead... I feel like such a fraud that, despite the terrible timing, I can't let it carry on any longer.

'Alice,' I say, putting down my cutlery. 'I... As you know, I'm not very experienced with dating. I really, really wanted to make this work. But I feel like I must be doing something wrong. I don't... I don't think I'm feeling what you're feeling.'

She smiles at me, fluttering her eyelashes.

'No?' She smiles at me, taking my hand. 'I promise, I feel exactly what you're feeling.'

I'm going mad.

'No,' I say. 'I really don't want to hurt your feelings. B-but... I-I think I might... Like someone—'

And Alice is still holding my hand, astonishment crossing her face, when I hear horribly familiar music.

'Saus-a-ges, saus-a-ges,'

I freeze.

'Saucy fun for all a-ges,'

'No way!' calls Pete from the kitchen. 'Emmeline! You're on the TV!'

'On its own or in a bun,' the commercial sings. *'It's meaty fun for everyone.'*

Dad stares at me through the kitchen serving hatch, then turns back to the screen. Alice runs over and I follow, lightheaded.

We watch as, on the TV screen, a Japanese teenager pushes a bento box aside, and replaces it with an anvil of steaming Saucy Sausages. Two black men do the same with chicken wings. I cringe so hard I feel as if I'm melting into the floor.

'Please turn it off,' I say.

No one moves.

And then there I am. Like I always wanted.

'*Even* I love *Saucy Sausages!*' my voice says.

Arm in arm with my pink-haired girlfriend, our apartment decorated with rainbow flags and cat photos, we push our salads aside to feed each other sausages. Zoom in on my mouth chewing, curry sauce dripping down my chin. A cartoon pop of explosive enjoyment. My 'girlfriend' cheekily wipes it with a finger and then looks to the camera as I lick it off her. '*Mmm!*' says a bass voice.

Then the cast are lined up, standing in front of a green screen of zoomed in sausages, cartoon faces drawn on each one.

'*Saucy!*' we cheer.

There's a blip of bad editing at the end of the commercial which means the line of us is frozen for a long second before the next advert starts.

Dad pauses the TV.

We're all silent for a moment.

Then Dad says seriously, 'Pete, we're removing the Emmy Special from the menu.'

He's disowning me.

He continues, 'We're turning it into a Sausage Fest.'

Pete and Dad laugh heartily.

I know they're only joking. I *think* they're only joking. And for heaven's sake, the advert *is* horrible trash. So why am I feeling like I'm about to cry?

Dad rewinds and plays the horrible commercial again, studying it while polishing a glass.

'So *this* is your "job"?'

I'm blushing as hard as the pizzas. How is my Saucy Sausages commercial the first acting work my dad has seen me do since school?

Alice looks at me.

'Mr Clooney, with respect,' she says, disrespectfully, 'it's incredibly competitive to get a television commercial spot like that. *I'm* very proud of her.'

I stare at her. I can't believe that, even after I tried to give her bad news about our relationship mere minutes ago, she's still standing up for me. She's even willing to fight my own family about it. I'm so embarrassed, so close to tears, that when she takes my hand and gives it a defiant squeeze, I feel so much gratitude it's overwhelming. I squeeze her hand back.

Dad comes through from the kitchen, Pete trailing behind him. Dad's chest puffs the way it does with rude customers.

'Oh, and it's not competitive, selling pizza in London? Everything is competitive. But you don't need to sell your soul away for something that doesn't care about you, that stereotypes you like this. You choose this – this foolishness to a proper family job?'

It's the final straw. Something deep in me snaps.

'You know what?' I say. 'Fuck you, Dad.'

The words echo round the empty restaurant.

'My face has been seen by more people in the past minute than will ever step foot in this restaurant,' I say, shaking. 'I earnt more money doing that commercial than I've *ever* made from being a waitress. What do I have to do for you to believe acting is a proper job?'

Dad stops polishing his glass. Pete takes his chef hat off and worries it round in his hands. I think I feel the power Alice must experience when she summarises someone's flaws in reviews. It's intoxicating.

'You've never come to see my shows,' I gasp. 'Never! I-I got the best marks from the best drama school, and y-you didn't even ask if you could come to my graduation?'

Dad grasps the counter and looks away from me. His frown has collapsed in on itself. He opens his mouth, but now I've started, I can't seem to stop.

'*Mum* wouldn't have laughed,' I say. 'How is the parent who literally abandoned me still more supportive than the one I stayed with? Sometimes I—' I choke. 'Sometimes I wish I'd chosen her!'

My throat is sandpaper, but it's strangely satisfying, how it hurts.

'I have tried and tried to be a good daughter to you,' I shout, 'but you – you've *never* tried to be a good father to me. All you care about is yourself, and your one friend, and your stupid – fucking – *pizza*.'

I pick up the plate with the cold remnants of my Emmy Special to gesture with it, but in doing so, I accidentally knock it off the table. It smashes onto the yellow brick tiles.

My immediate instinct is to apologise, run to the back room to get the dustpan, and offer to sacrifice a week's wages. But suddenly Alice mimics my gesture, pushing her own uneaten salad off the table. The plate smashes next to mine. She comes and grips my hand, triumphant.

'Emmeline, love,' says Pete quietly. 'You've got it wro—'

'Stay out of this please, Boss!' I snap. 'This is a family matter.'

Pete looks like I've spat at him. I feel sick. I've never been intentionally rude to Pete before. But my mouth keeps going.

'And in fact, you're not my boss anymore,' I say. 'Because I quit.'

'Emmeline,' growls Dad, but Pete puts a hand on his arm.

'In that case,' says Pete, 'I can only thank you very much, for your contribution to the company.' He bows, puts his chef hat back on, and leaves the restaurant.

For once in his dramatic life, Dad seems lost for words.

'Well then,' he says finally. 'I'll take you off the rota.'

My throat hurts so much. Isn't he going to apologise? Aren't I? We can't just leave without a reunion, can we?

'We can talk more tonight,' he says.

'No,' says Alice. 'Emmy's going to come and stay with me.'

I stare at Dad, trying to will him to tell me to stay. All I need is one word from him, and I'll stay.

But Dad just nods. Alice squeezes my hand. As he walks away, I feel the world slipping away from under me.

'D-don't come and see *Twelfth Night*,' I call after him. 'Not that you would have bothered anyway!'

At the door, he hesitates and turns back. My heart leaps.

'You should apologise to Pete,' he says, and closes the novelty meatball handle behind him.

42

Alice calls us a cab and strokes my leg. I check my phone, expecting missed calls from Dad.

Instead, there's a text from Mum.

Hi my love, hope you won't mind me texting, but Pete just called to say you fought with your father. You always have a home here, if you need a place. Would you like to talk about it? I'm just a phone call away. I'm sure it feels awful right now but I hold out hope that there's always a chance to forgive the people who really matter.

I swallow painfully. I stare out the window, wondering how I could even begin to reply. When I look back, I have a new message. From Mae. I angle my phone away from Alice.

Yo, Cloons. Feels kind of weird not seeing each other every day now, doesn't it? Before the tech on 29th, are you still on for meeting with the rest of the cast outside Foyles? Oooor I wondered if you wanted to meet you and me before that? Maybe we could get coffee so I can insult their latte art technique?

Alice tuts at me. 'Darling, don't worry about anything else right now. Turn that phone off.'

'I just need to—'

She holds a finger up. She's right. Dad isn't going to contact me, I'm stressing myself out further by seeing these other messages, and I'm being rude to Alice. I return my phone to my pocket and try to enjoy the feeling of her hand in mine.

As soon as we're in through her front door, she puts our bags down and hugs me for a long time.

'Shhh,' she says. 'You're safe now. No one can get you here.'

At first I feel very tense, presumably the aftermath of the fight. I do my calming breathing exercises. I take in the soft-pink walls of her corridor, the white marble tiles.

'That's right,' she says, stroking my hair. 'That's better, isn't it. We'll be all right – now it's just you and me.'

I desperately wish I was with Ruth and Raphy. But they don't want me bothering them anymore.

'Stop overthinking, darling. There's nothing to worry about now.' She rubs my tense shoulders. 'Let's get rid of all that stress. How about a nice bath, hmm?'

Alice steers me to her bathroom. It has elegant hexagonal tiles, a vase of white lilies, and a skylight casting holy reflections onto the huge bath. The only bath I'm used to is the pool of sudsy water at the bottom of our blocked shower, but Alice has one of those freestanding tubs with ornate feet and bronze taps.

She sits me on a wicker chair (begging the question – why do you need a chair in a bathroom?) and runs the tap for me, pouring in salts and oils. It makes me feel like a grimy urchin. She lights a huge candle, making it even more cloying in the room. I go to open the high window, but Alice stops me.

'Cosy and warm,' she says.

So I just watch, the smell of the rose bubbles, the vanilla candle, and the lily perfume heavy in my throat.

Alice produces a large white towel and dressing gown as though I'm at a spa. She ferries treats from the kitchen, lining up a home-made Old Fashioned and chocolate truffles. I feel awful when I remind her that I don't like whiskey and I'm vegan. She whisks up the bubbles angrily and huffs as she takes them away.

'Alice, no one has ever been this lovely to me,' I say. 'Thank you.'

She looks at me for a long moment, and kisses me. The steaming water pounds into the endless bath.

'This is what it will be like, every day, from now on,' she says. 'You don't need to worry about anyone or anything else. I'll take care of you.'

I worry she's going to try to get in with me, but she just adds, 'Risotto for dinner.'

'Alice. . .' I hold her hands, feeling so awed and humbled that the guilt about Mae is kept at bay, 'thank you for being so generous, but please, you really don't need to do anything more. Let me order in some takeaway or something, it's the least I can do.'

But she waves her hand away.

'I don't want you eating trash. I'm going to feed you properly.' She turns the tap off.

'This is just what a good relationship looks like. Get in now, darling.'

I wait for her to leave, but she remains, looking at me. When it's been too long, I start to take off my clothes like it's a game of poker, least vulnerable clothes first. Socks, jeans... I pretend to fiddle for a long time with my shirt buttons.

'Thank you,' I say again. 'I'll be all right from here.'

Alice tuts affectionately and with quick fingers undoes the remaining buttons of my shirt, pulls it over my head. Now I'm just in my pants and sports bra. I cross my arms.

'I... I need a wee before I get in, actually,' I say.

Alice gestures to the loo.

'I... can't... I can't go while you're in here. Performance anxiety.' I force a weak laugh. 'Ironic!'

She sighs. 'What are we going to do with you? OK, darling, I'll put these in the washing machine and get you when dinner's ready.'

'Thanks so much,' I nod, keeping the smile on my face as I force myself to add, 'darling.'

Once she's out of the room, I have a mad impulse to lock the door. I wish I had my phone, but Alice must have accidentally taken it with my clothes.

What is wrong with me? Alice is the only person in my life who has been wholly kind to me – well, apart from Mae. Yet I'm acting so weird around her. Could Alice be right, that I'm just unused to being in a relationship, unused to being treated well?

I sink into the bath. It's scalding, but after the initial pain it's soothing. I dip my head under the water, feeling the foam reform above me. I take a deep breath, then release a long slow breath out under the water, watching the bubbles stream consistently in front of me.

I do start to feel a little better. Perhaps it's understandable that I'm feeling so on edge. It has been a stressful day. And I've barely eaten anything.

I come up for air, then submerge back under the water.

I decide I will avoid the problem of what to say to my mum by simply not replying. It's traditional. There's nothing to say to her anyway.

And as for Mae... I'll invent an excuse to turn down meeting her for coffee. I know rationally that we're only friends – and only temporary friends at that – but my stupid body doesn't seem to be able to remember that when we're alone together. I'll just see her for the performances, and then never again. It's for the best.

A hand grabs my hair and pulls my head up above the surface. I choke on the sudden rush of foam in my mouth.

'Dinner's nearly ready, darling,' says Alice, sweetly.

I cough, little bubbles popping out of my mouth. My throat tastes like rose soap.

'Thank you,' I splutter.

She sits on the side of the tub and strokes my wet hair.

'And... I have a present for you,' she says.

'I... What? No, please, Alice, you've already done so much for me.'

'It's a gift for me, to give a gift to you.'

She hands me a white Pandora box, the size for a ring.

'Open it,' she says.

I can't.

Alice tuts and opens the box herself, angling it towards me. Oh my God, it *is* a ring – a wide silver band.

I meet her eyes, chest tight.

'Darling, it's just a ring! I'm not proposing!' She kisses my temple. 'That would be your job anyway, wouldn't it?'

She slides the ring onto my fourth finger. It's too big, and slides off.

She scowls. 'We'll get it fitted.'

She pushes it forcefully over the knuckle on my thumb, the slippiness of the bath oils helping her get it into place. She holds my fingers, admiring it.

'I want to see you wear it on stage,' she says. 'So I'll know you're mine.' I force myself not to flinch.

'Alice,' I manage to say, 'you're not reviewing *Twelfth Night*, are you?'

She blinks. 'Darling, I'm just supporting you.'

I sigh with relief.

'Umm, Alice? Thalia said she's coming too. To see the show. And have a drink with me afterwards.'

Alice's eyebrows raise.

'Is that so? Well then, we can go together. Toast your success. The three of us reunited at last.'

I look at the ring on my thumb and nod.

In bed that night, I try to kiss Alice back, honestly I do. But I'm queasy from the rich dinner and the clammy bath, and the bed is so hot. It goes on for some time with her touching my bath-soft body, taking my hand in hers and sliding the thumb ring over her chest. Alice's moaning is too loud in my ears.

What's wrong with me? People are supposed to love sex,

aren't they? Maybe especially lesbians? I imagine Mae never has this issue.

I stop kissing Alice and curl up into myself. I can tell she's disappointed and confused, which makes me feel even worse.

When I've been lying in the foetal position unmoving for long enough, Alice seems to accept that I won't be sleeping with her tonight.

'Turn around then, Emmy,' she whispers into my ear. 'You should be big spoon.'

She grabs my arm and gently twists it until I'm holding her back.

43

On June 29th I wake in Alice's bed, feeling sick. This day has been looming in my calendar for so long, I can't believe that it's actually happening, out of my control. Soon, I'll be at London's Pride parade, seeing Mae for the last time as friends. Then in a few hours, we'll be doing the *Twelfth Night* tech rehearsal, and then our actual first performance. And in the audience watching and judging me will be industry professionals, ticket-carrying theatre-lovers, my girlfriend, and a real life flesh and blood Thalia Brown.

I run to Alice's beautiful bathroom and throw up.

When I've cleaned myself up, I find Alice in the kitchen, packing my lunch bag.

'Your favourite,' she says, waving some beef jerky.

I grimace, but I don't want to be a naggy vegan.

'Please, Alice, you're not my assistant, you don't need to—'

But she just raises a finger and kisses my cheek.

Sadly for the Pride festivities, the humid weather we've been having has finally broken and it's now raining. I didn't pack a jacket. Hung up on Alice's coat rails by the door, between Alice's faux furs and silks, is one coat that looks very 'me' – a dark-green denim jacket.

'Darling,' I ask her carefully, 'would it be at all possible for me to please borrow that jacket?'

Alice freezes and my stomach twists. Clearly, I'm not meant to ask for things, she's only meant to give them.

'This one's much warmer,' she says, and passes me a pink cagoule.

We both look from it, to the denim. 'Is there a problem with me borrowing that one? Is it designer or something?'

Suddenly she grabs for it, flinging it on the floor. 'It's not precious to me. Not at all. Lose it for all I care. It's old. I never wear it. I've been meaning to get rid of it for ages.'

'Thank you,' I say, for want of anything else. It fits me perfectly.

Finally Alice walks me to the tube stop, and hands me my phone.

'I'll see you tonight, my star,' she says. 'On the stage! And then I'll bring you home straight after to rest.'

'Umm, Alice, remember, I'm meeting Thalia after the show tonight?'

Her smile falters.

'I mean, *we're* meeting Thalia?'

She hesitates, then kisses me on the mouth. 'Whatever you want, darling,' she says, and watches my bus pull away.

As I wait for my phone to turn on, I manage to pull the ring off my thumb. I'm not used to wearing jewellery, and it's uncomfortable for being too tight.

On the *Twelfth Night* group chat (it's been renamed by Roger to 'Shakesqueer'), Mae has messaged everyone that she's on her way to Foyles. I swallow – of course she is just as happy to meet the cast as to meet me. I didn't need to give her an excuse after all.

As we get closer to central, I spot more overtly dressed-up gays. Some carry signs: No LGB WITHOUT THE T! NOT GAY AS IN HAPPY, GAY AS IN FUCK THE PATRIARCHY! I LOVE LESBIANS!!! Whenever I see other short-haired, masculine-presenting queers we smile at each other. I even see, through the group at the end of the carriage, two butches kissing. I can't help but stare. I spend so much of my life seeing the world through the eyes of a casting director, where it feels that two masculine-of-centre characters are so rarely allowed to fancy or love each other, it's easy to forget it's perfectly common (and hot) for them to do so in real life.

As we file out like gay sardines, swimming off towards Soho, I feel a glimmer of hope. It's surreal, feeling part of a majority for a change. Part of a community, not a competition. My mood starts lifting.

I arrive late and sweaty, but happy, to Foyles. It's waving rainbow banners outside its displays of LGBTQ+ books, but I can't see any of the other cast. I go to send a message on the Shakesqueer chat, but the network is so oversaturated that my mobile data isn't working.

I hesitate and then I ring Mae.

'Clooney,' she says. 'I'm right behind you.'

I spin around, and there she is, waiting by the self-help. She's wearing an oversized chessboard shirt and carrying two coffee cups.

'Jones.' I smile and hang up, going over to her. I desperately, desperately want her to hug me. But she doesn't, of course. She just looks at Alice's jacket.

'I used to have a jacket like that,' she says.

OK, things are definitely weird between us. What did I do wrong?

'I guess we have the same taste after all?' I try to joke. 'The same taste as literally every other queer in London?'

Mae glances up at me and her expression cracks into a small smile. I feel impossibly relieved. She hands me a coffee cup, and I remove the lid to admire the pattern.

'I made it myself in the end,' she says. 'It was a rainbow. A really good one, actually.'

'I'm sure it was,' I say quietly. 'Thank you. And, you know, thanks for waiting for me.'

We start walking and I sneak a look at her. It's so unlike her to be quiet. Is she angry that I'm late? She's never been on time for anything in her life. Is she angry I didn't reply to her? But she messaged on the group chat this morning... Is she still feeling weird after seeing *Carol*? I know I am.

Come on, Emmy, she has a whole life that doesn't involve you. Most likely, whatever she's feeling has nothing to do with me.

'Are you nervous?' I ask. She glances at me. 'I always get pre-show jitters. Do you get pre-show jitters?'

'I usually just feel excited.'

'They say nerves and excitement are the same feeling, don't they? In the belly.'

She doesn't smile back. 'I think they're different.'

I down the coffee.

'Taste the rainbow,' I joke, but she doesn't laugh.

We walk on in tense silence. The hordes of queer folk around us are shouting, laughing, already day-tipsy with their friends.

Mae sighs and says, 'Clooney, honestly, I'm being weird because I'm feeling a bit mad at you. You didn't message me back last night, and it made me feel silly.'

'Jones,' I say, my stomach writhing. 'I'm so sorry, I... I went AWOL. I had a big row with my dad.'

Mae's entire demeanour transforms.

'Oh,' she says, with such a weight of sympathy behind it that my throat tightens. 'God. I'm sorry, Em. I hope you're both OK. Was it about acting? Or your mum?'

She hesitates.

'Sorry, you don't have to tell me, I just... you know you can talk to me about anything, right? That's what friends are for.'

She reaches to squeeze my elbow. My body remembers Alice doing the same thing this morning, and twitches away. We both bury our hands in our jacket pockets.

'Thanks,' I say. 'But I'm fine.'

Crowds of queer folk around us laugh and cheer and toast their cans together. Mae and I walk the rest of the way in silence.

44

Tech rehearsals are always weird – like fast-forwarding through a film and only seeing the story in still snapshots.

Actors are just there to act as markers, standing in the right spots so that the technical team can check the lighting and sound cues are working.

Charlie is doing a terrible job of disguising that they're tipsy from day-drinking at the parade earlier. The others shiftily try to tone them down by patting them on the shoulder when they hiccup.

I'm only in the first and last scenes of the play. After I've done my shadow-puppet shipwreck cue with Keiya, Charlie and Surina, I sit in the wings and watch Mae. I'm so aware of the mysterious awkwardness between us, I spend the whole rehearsal anticipating Viola and Sebastian's 'reunion hug' in the final scene. It then doesn't happen because it isn't a lighting or sound cue.

The next time I am close to her is when we're cueing the finale jig. Mae and I loop arms and start to do our period dance. I feel like Mr Darcy when he can't talk to Lizzy Bennet at the ball.

'Jones,' I finally say, during a ridiculous hop. 'I'm sorry.'

Mae is making wild knee-kicks look natural.

'What about?'

'I've been weird. I was really looking forward to seeing you, and then I've messed everything up.'

I hold my hand out. Mae takes it and spins out, looking back at me at the outward pull. As the rainbow lights flash, she gives me her broad, dazzling smile.

Then she swings into my arms and says, 'There's always next time.'

My chest hurts as we bow.

In the green room, we all get into costume. Mae and I are in the corner together, separate from the rest of the squawking cast (literally, Charlie is practising their parrot sounds).

I catch Mae watching me take Alice's jacket off.

'If that jacket *was* mine, I'd share it with you,' she says. 'You look really good in it.'

'You're so in character,' I laugh. 'Method acting Viola wearing her twin's clothes.'

'No,' she insists. 'I know when I'm acting and I know when I'm feeling things for real. Don't you?'

I look into the mirror. 'This is going to sound so thespian, but sometimes I'm not sure whether I'm really feeling things or just playing along with the script.'

Mae looks up at me from applying stage eyeliner. She passes the pencil to me.

'And what's the scene we're in right now?'

'It's different with you,' I laugh, lining under my eyes. 'I always feel like I'm improvising around you.'

She smiles and nudges me. 'Can't you tell what my character is thinking?'

I gulp. If I didn't know better, I'd say she was flirting with me.

She catches my eye in the mirror.

'If I didn't know better,' she says, 'I'd say I was flirting with you.'

OK, so I don't think I have an *actual* stroke. I don't think I even faint, because presumably that would mean I fall over. But it's as if the world stops. The noise in the room dampens. It's the moment where you pause at the top of a rollercoaster.

I stare at her as she turns pink. But she doesn't take it back. Slowly I turn from her eyes in the mirror to face her.

She must be joking. This must be banter. A prank I'm not in on.

'And if I didn't know better,' says Mae softly, eyes shining, 'I'd say you were flirting back.'

I've stopped breathing. If I don't put a serious brake in this ride right now, I'm going to fall off the edge and embarrass myself.

'If we are,' I say, 'it's only because of Shakespeare.'

Mae blinks.

'I mean, I think it's our acting instincts,' I say breathlessly, fiddling with my shirt laces. 'It's natural for performers t-to transfer the – the high emotions they're enacting onstage t-to offstage relationships. We're mistaking the emotions of a classic romantic comedy with – with reality.'

Mae glares at me. Then she grabs my hand and pulls it to her chest. It's pounding.

'Don't try to tell me *this* is because of Shakespeare.'

I look into her blue-gold eyes. Her pupils are dilated. God, she's the most beautiful person I've ever seen.

'Oi! Emmy-Mae!' calls Charlie. We leap apart. 'We're heading upstairs. You coming?'

Mae pokes out above the line of costumes.

'In a moment!' she calls.

Keiya cackles.

'Take your tiiime,' sings Roger. 'There's a good spot for privacy behind the—'

Zach jostles him, and they all head out.

The door closes and Mae and I hesitatingly meet each other's eyes.

'Can I ask for clarification,' I say, 'on what you mean by flirting?'

Mae doesn't laugh this time. Slowly, cautiously, she reaches out her hand to touch my cheek. It warms under her fingers, and

I feel the same electricity we had when we were filming for *High School*. But this time, there's no camera, no crew, no audience.

'Emmy, I would like us to kiss,' says Mae. 'Like, ideally, all the time. I've been thinking about very little else since we first met.'

Completely unhurried, she slides her hands from my cheeks to my waist. 'In fact, I think number one on my list of urgent priorities is to kiss you, right now.'

With one hand on the small of my back, she pulls my hips close in to hers. 'And I really believe, if I have *any* ability to know what my stage partner is thinking, that you'd like to kiss me too.'

I copy her gesture instinctively, my hand on her back, pulling her in closer. Through the thick texture of our pirate trousers, I feel our hip bones jutting into each other.

Mae laughs, but not as if she's joking. As if she's amazed.

I want nothing in the world more than her.

But not like this.

'Mae,' I stop her. 'No. I'm sorry, but I don't want to kiss you.'

Mae blinks. Then she blows a long raspberry.

'Right! OK! Cool! No worries!'

She lifts her hands away from me and steps back.

She grabs at Alice's jacket lying between us, then remembers it's not actually hers, puts it back, and grabs for her own instead.

'See you on stage!'

'No, I...' I laugh and grab her hand, 'Mae. I'm sorry. I meant... I *do* want that, I really, really do.'

I pull her hand to my thumping chest, and my voice breaks a little as I say, 'As usual, you copied me.'

We stare at each other.

'But...' I exhale. 'Oh God.'

I haven't planned the right words to say this. I never thought this could happen. I never thought she might feel the same way. But I look into those huge kohl-lined eyes, see the curious gold flecks searching mine, and I know I can't lie to her.

'I have a girlfriend,' I say. 'I'm sorry. You have... No idea how sorry I am.'

I brace myself for Mae to slap me, shout at me, and/or run fast away.

Instead, she is still for a moment, then nods.

'Thank you for telling me,' she says. She doesn't even sound sarcastic. 'A lot of people don't.'

I look away. It's a reminder that I'm sure Mae is very experienced at this, has successfully flirted with hundreds of people before me. But still, it's nice, feeling like I've done the right thing for a change. A relief.

Mae ruffles her hair. 'I mean, obviously I'd love it if you were single and we were making out right now, but I guess it's not reasonable for me to expect you to be available just because I fancy you.' She nudges me playfully. 'You're not open then?'

I shake my head, blushing further.

'It has taken me twenty-five years to find *one* person who wants to be in a relationship with me,' I say. 'Polyamory has never been something I have needed to consider. Besides, I'm not sure it's for me, personally.'

Mae frowns. 'Yeah, if your relationship with acting is anything to go by, you're probably too one-track-minded for multiple partners.'

I look away. It's confirmation, as if I needed any further, that any flirting Mae might want to do with me does not equal her wanting a relationship with me. I almost embarrassed myself there by assuming she would want that. For her, this was just for the fun of a show-time crush – and winning the challenge of cracking prim Emmy Clooney.

But then Mae frowns. 'Is your girlfriend the same person you mentioned when we were at the hospital, when you broke your toe?'

I blush and nod.

'You...' She hesitates. 'I really don't mean to sound jealous, but you didn't seem to be that into her back then.'

I shrug awkwardly.

'I-I think she's pretty serious about me.' Mae tilts her head, and I realise how mean that sounded. 'And I'm grateful, honestly I am! I've never had a real relationship before, so I... I should try to work it out with her rather than, you know, have a fling with you. As much as I would really, really like that.'

Mae folds her arms.

'Fling?'

'Oh, sorry.' My cheeks burn harder. 'Don't they have that word in America?'

Mae raises an eyebrow.

'I know what a fling is, Clooney. Flings are nice, but...' She fiddles with her hair. 'Look. I'm not suggesting you break up with your girlfriend for me, honestly I'm not. It's your life, it's your decision. But...'

She meets my eye.

'Em, I really, really like you. If you wanted me to, I'd wait for you. I'm not going anywhere.'

It's as if I've chugged a bucket of espresso. I want to pinch myself, to pinch Mae, to make sure I'm not in a dream. Rationally, I shouldn't believe what she's saying. But I do.

The intercom buzzes violently with the tech team's call for us to go up to our positions backstage. We both jump. I fumble for my shadow-puppet squid.

'Will you think about it?' she asks, and I nod, once, stiffly, in case I let on just how confused I feel. She smiles.

'If I'm getting any better at seeing through your mask now, Clooney,' she whispers, 'I'd say you like me too, but you're scared. You don't trust that I'm not going to just run off.'

Very gently, she kisses my cheek, and says into my ear.

'I'd love to prove you wrong.'

45

The combination of Mae's confession and the first-night performance nerves are doing truly chaotic things to my nervous system. I've never completed my pre-show rituals at a more hyper pace.

Then I'm squinting out at the audience from behind the shadow-puppet screen, Surina, Charlie and Keiya beside me trying to discern the cloudy outlines of audience members.

'Do you have friends in tonight, Emmy?' whispers Charlie.

I shake my head – I'm not sure either Alice or Tahlia count as a friend.

My stomach twists as I see the outline of Alice's upright posture taking a seat in the front row. I even think I see her open her review notebook on her lap, but it must be a trick of the cloudy screen. Even though I'm sure I'd recognise Tahlia's silhouette anywhere, I can't spot her yet.

An alarm sound plays over the speaker system. 'Ahoy, mateys!' says a recording of Roger. 'Please take to your vessels and throw any mobile devices overboard, the show is about to begin.'

Then the lights go down, and I lose all my anxieties to the show.

A seascape plays over the speakers and, led by Charlie, we sing an *a capella* shanty from offstage. The shadow-puppet screen is lit by rippling blue and green lights as if submerged under stormy waves. Surina, Keiya and I move the shadow props across, telling the story of a ship lost at sea, of two twins, thrown overboard, of their separation and arrival on an island...

Lights down on the screen and up on the main stage. The audience applauds generously. The energy is already sky-high. As we head into the wings, we all mime high fiving each other. I'm buzzing.

Then Mae stumbles onto the stage. The audience immediately silences.

She's magical.

I can hardly breathe. I watch Viola look for her twin, refusing to accept he could be beyond her reach. I wonder if everyone else in the theatre believes she's looking just for them.

I don't have anything to do in the rest of the first half except help some of the other actors change costumes, so I hover in the wings and lose myself in her performance. When Mae does her ring monologue, the audience roar with laughter. It's as if she's glowing from the inside. I watch her fall in love with the Count with more sparkling magnetism than I've seen from her before.

Before I know it, there's a blackout. Time for the interval. As the audience lights rise, I glance out to gauge their reactions. Everyone's smiling, engrossed, turning to talk animatedly to their neighbours. Except Alice. She's frowning, scribbling into the notebook on her lap, a reviewer lanyard round her neck. My stomach cramps.

I asked her so many times not to review this show. She said she wouldn't... Wait. What if she's still going to submit a terrible quote about Mae? It would be all my fault...

I think about texting her, but she might not see the message. How quickly after the show will she send in her review? Surely I'd have time to convince her not to turn it in when we're having our drink with Tahlia afterwards, but what if she's incredibly efficient? I can't risk it.

So I slip out of the wings, out the backstage doors, and into the auditorium.

I'm very aware of being in costume. The audience haven't seen my face as an actor yet, so I try to stride confidently to make anyone who is still seated think this is part of the theatrical experience.

Alice's wearing a cropped blazer over a sleeveless jumpsuit, her hair tightly coiled over glittering waterfall earrings.

I apologise repeatedly to the audience on the front row as I squeeze past to get to her. The front row has an empty seat as usual, which I sit in next to her.

'Hello, darling,' she says, kissing my cheek. 'I can't believe you weren't on in the entire first half. You really are a small role.'

'Alice, I asked you not to review the show?'

She rolls her eyes. 'I don't go back on my commitments,' she says. 'And it's my gift to you! Besides, it's really no bother, I've already written it.'

I blink at her. It's as though she's claiming to announce the results of a football match that hasn't been played yet.

'What?'

'"Emmy Clooney – no relation – is going to become more celebrated as an actor than her namesake",' Alice recites, and smooths her hair. 'It takes a lot of work to write a review, you know. I've been awfully nice about the production too. The only person who comes out badly is your rival, Mae Jones.'

My blood freezes. Alice smiles and pats my hand.

'No. Alice, please!' I try to breathe deeply and speak very fast. 'It's not fair. I know I'm responsible, but I should never have agreed to it. I know you're trying to be kind and I'm grateful, but I'm asking you, professional to professional, please don't post that review. It's not objective.'

She talks over me, making air quotes. '"Mae Jones, aka, Mae Finch, nepotism baby of the illustrious Annabel Finch—"'

I stand, fists clenched. 'No! Don't you *dare*.'

It's my fault. I should never have told Alice that Mae had a famous mother. Mae's attempt to separate her career from her mother's would be ruined and it would be all my fault.

The audience around us watch us curiously, eating their ice creams.

Alice finally looks at me properly. It's as though she's seeing me for the first time.

'You don't hate Mae Jones,' she says.

'No,' I say, lightheaded. 'No, I don't.'

It's the first time I've seen Alice look scared. She opens her mouth as if she's about to ask something, but then closes it. It makes me feel even worse, that she seems so upset. But I remember how much of a relief it felt, to be honest with Mae. I should do the same now.

'In fact…' I sit down. 'Alice, I'm sorry, but the truth is, I have feelings for her.'

I take Alice's ring from my pocket and hand it back to her.

'You're a… formidable person,' I say, 'I'm grateful for everything you've tried to do for me. But clearly, I shouldn't be your girlfriend anymore.'

I brace myself for Alice's most venomous insult.

'OK,' she says.

'Sorry?'

'OK.' She shrugs. I know I should feel heartbroken, but honestly? I don't. I feel the weight of the world off my shoulders.

'Thank you—' I start, but Alice carries on over me.

'It's hardly original for an actor to fool themselves they have chemistry with their co-star,' she says. 'But that does not mean we are breaking up.'

Piratical music plays over the intercom. 'All hands on deck!' announces a recording of Keiya. 'We set sail in seven minutes.'

Blank-faced, Alice waits patiently for the intercom to stop, then holds up two long fingers.

'We are not breaking up for two reasons. Firstly, because you want to be an actor – and if you break up with me, you will never work again.'

A buzzing starts in my ears. Alice's hazel eyes flash.

'I will post a terrible review of you,' she says. 'I've already written that one too. Believe me, if you continue with this nonsense, I will send it. And it isn't just about you, by the way. It tears this entire production to pieces. *The Atre*'s review will influence whether this show gets a tour or not. Do you want to be responsible for ruining the careers of every member of your cast?'

My hands are going numb.

'Alice... are you blackmailing me?'

She rolls her eyes in a way that is eerily reminiscent of Thalia.

'It's for your own good!' she says. 'Emmeline, we're *right* together! We make sense! Why would you throw away our commitment for a sordid quickie with Mae Finch, someone you'll then never see again? Unless you're intending to move to America?'

'What are you talking about?' I ask quietly.

Alice licks her lip smugly. She snaps her pen with feigned casualness.

'She's leaving soon, isn't she? To film a television series with the illustrious Annabel Finch. It's about a mother and daughter who are both actors. Twenty-four episodes.' She pouts. 'Oh, didn't your new best friend tell you?'

She laughs.

'Trust me, whatever you think you know about Mae Finch, it's an act. She's a liar.'

'How would you know?' I mumble. 'You've never even met her.'

Alice's expression falters for a second, but she quickly recovers her composure.

'I'm good at my job, Emmeline,' she says. 'I researched. There's plenty of gossip about her. Don't you know about the string of heartbreaks she leaves in her wake? She's manipulative. She love-bombs with flattery and gifts. She overpromises and gaslights. She tells you how you're feeling so that you don't trust your own senses. Can't you see? She's playing games with you! I'm sorry that you fell for it, darling. But think about it rationally... It's not as though the two of you *could* have any serious potential. You're workplace rivals, and you look like… Well—' She gestures to my hair. 'You'd be like a freak show! You'd be a joke to her, and a joke to the world.'

Louder signal music plays over the intercom. 'Abandon ship!' cries a recording of Zach. 'The enemy are boarding in five minutes! Every man for himself!'

But I can't move.

Alice takes my hand.

'You're lucky I like you so much that I'll forgive you. I mean, Emmeline… You're twenty-five, and you've never had a proper relationship. You want to break up with me and wait another twenty-five for someone else to want you?'

She's right. I'm so close to allowing everything I'm most scared of to happen.

'So what's it to be?' She traces circles on my palm. 'Either I come with you to meet our good friend Tahlia, we have champagne, and I post a glowing five-star review of the show, which gets you a tour… And gets you promoted to the vacant part of Viola.'

Bile rises in my stomach.

'Or…' she says, circling in the other direction. 'You break up with me over some strange fantasy with a co-star, and you regret it for the rest of your life?'

She's right. I *know* my crush on Mae is self-destructive. Why am I always so drawn to people who will leave me? Didn't I learn anything from Tahlia? The Tahlia who clearly isn't even here tonight, letting me down *again*?

The intercom music is playing for the final time, but I still can't move.

'Don't worry about anything, darling.' Alice kisses my cheek and whispers, 'I love you.'

Now all feeling has gone from my body. No one has ever told me they love me before. I know I'm meant to say it back, but I can't find my voice.

Alice pushes the ring back over my thumb.

The ushers are closing the auditorium doors. I stumble up to run to the backstage wings.

'Go and live up to your review,' Alice smiles, as the lights go down.

I crouch behind the curtains, trying to do my breathing exercises. They're not working.

There's a gentle tap of leather boots next to me. Mae crouches, rubbing my back. Her touch feels as if she's bringing my body back to life. But I shuffle away.

'I didn't know you got such bad stage fright,' she whispers. 'How can I help you?'

I shake my head. How am I still falling for her act, even after everything Alice told me? Even when I *know* she doesn't mean it, I still desperately want to be near her.

Mae whispers, 'Unique New York. Unique New York. Unique New York.'

My chest aches. I look at her in the half-light from the stage. Then I shake my head and stumble up.

'You're a better actor than me,' I say quietly.

Mae grabs my hand.

'Em, what—?'

But then she glances at my fingers in hers. At Alice's ring.

Her face changes. The change is so sudden and extreme, her expression so full of devastation and humiliation, I stop in my tracks.

'How *could* you?' she hisses.

My breath catches. 'What are you—'

She laughs, not even lowering her volume for the ongoing performance metres away from us.

'Your girlfriend is Alice Sefton? My ex?'

All I can do is stare at her beautiful sneer as everything slots horribly into place. Alice and Mae. This ring was once Mae's ring. Alice's jacket was once Mae's jacket. Well, I knew Alice's type… But why didn't she *tell* me? And even when she insisted on writing this review she was just using it as an excuse for revenge.

Wait! Was Alice the girlfriend who said those awful things to Mae?

Before I can ask her, Mae shakes her head deliriously.

'This was all still some sick competition to you, wasn't it? Screwing my ex to get one over on me? And all the while making me fall for you—'

'Mae, no, I *swear*, I didn't kn—'

She violently pulls her hand from mine and takes one last look at me, her face in sharp shadows from the spotlights.

'You really had me fooled,' she says, then steps out onto the stage.

46

I note vaguely, from my nauseated squat in the wings, that the stage has been quiet for a while. I become aware of the violent hissing of cast and crew around me.

'Emmy! What the fuck are you playing at?' whispers Zach. 'Roger's out there waiting for you!'

Oh. It's time for Sebastian's stage fight.

I try to breathe, pat my side for my cutlass, and step out onto the stage. Roger's eyes are like he's being held hostage.

There's a comic scene preceding this one where Viola and Sir Toby are both forced into a fight they don't want to be in – cowardly and untrained, they fumble their weapons and try to be as far away from each other as possible. I mess up my choreography so badly that my fighting is worse than theirs.

I throw the cutlass into the air, but miss catching it. When I bend to pick it up, my mask nearly slips, so I clutch at it and nearly poke my eye out. Roger is just standing there, holding his sword out. I try to do my jab to hook it out of his hands, but I'm so limp our metal doesn't connect. Roger looks down at his untouched weapon and, a beat too late, fakes a scream and lets it clatter to the floor.

The audience laugh uncertainly. Maybe they think this is a daring piece of Francis's reinterpretation.

Face blanched under my mask, I step into the safety of offstage. Charlie and Keiya, waiting in the wings, stare at me as I put my cutlass on the prop table and escape to the empty green room.

I wish I could shout 'cut' on my life. Take it from the top with a completely new direction, making my character say better lines in a better way. I wish my life was a dress rehearsal so that it wouldn't matter how badly I'm fucking it up.

But I have no time to think, or understand, or plan what I should do next. I don't even have time to process. It's already time for the final scene of the play – the 'reunion' between Sebastian and Viola.

It's my big reveal, the moment where I take off my mask and the audience sees the twins on stage together for the first time. In the scene, Sebastian apologises to Olivia, his secret new wife (Olivia proposed to him, mistaking him for his twin).

Maybe, if I act this *perfectly*, so poignantly and so truthfully, it will somehow solve things. Maybe, through the magic of theatre, I'll be able to communicate everything in this hug with Mae.

SEBASTIAN
I am sorry, madam, I have hurt your kinsman:
You throw a strange regard upon me, and by that
I do perceive it hath offended you:
Pardon me, sweet one, even for the vows
We made each other but so late ago.

I have said these lines a thousand times in my bedroom. I have said them a hundred times in rehearsals. But now, on stage, looking at Mae, I can't say any of them.

For the first time in my professional life, I blank.

After a long silence, a voice speaks tentatively from backstage. '*I am sorry, madam,*' says the prompt.

After another tense silence, I repeat it, like a particularly inept parrot.

The other characters on the stage are trying to be awed, looking between Sebastian and Viola, me and Mae.

ANTONIO
How have you made division of yourself?
An apple, cleft in two, is not more twin
Than these two creatures.

I stare at my other half longingly across the stage. But 'Viola'
is apparently so awed by the reappearance of her ghostly twin,
she can't even look at me.

Falteringly, I open my arms out to her.

'*Do not embrace me,*' says Mae sharply, and then continues
to perform the rest of her perfectly performed lines, '*till each
circumstance / Of place, time…*'

I stare at her. I'm giving the least professional performance
of my life because of fighting with her. Yet she is completely
unfazed.

Whatever she was hiding from me, Alice was right about one
thing. Mae clearly doesn't care about me at all. Surina clasps my
hand to drag me off.

The audience still applaud, but I barely notice.

Charlie starts singing the sea shanty for the final jig.

FOOL (sings):
But when I came, alas! to wive,
With hey, ho, the wind and the rain,
By swaggering could I never thrive,
For the rain it raineth every day.

Surina pulls me back on, tucked into her arm. I get my
choreography so wrong it might even look deliberate. As we
swap partners, I'm swung towards Mae.

Our eyes meet for just a second, our arms crooked to slot
into each other's. Then she effortlessly sidesteps past me, and
hooks into the quickly adapting arms of Surina and Joe. I twist
to watch them. Standing by myself in the chaotic midst of the
other dancers, I'm jostled over and over by their joyous jigging.

Maybe if I was a brilliant improviser like Mae I could make this into a benefit: jig by myself, do the Macarena or something. But I'm not. I leave the stage.

When it's time for me to go to the front to take my bow, the clapping in the audience noticeably diminishes in volume. I don't even bother to dip my head. But Alice, from the front row, gives me a solo standing ovation. She throws a red rose at my feet. I collect it, ashamed.

47

I have a feeling Mae will avoid the green room to try to avoid me, so I take my clothes and wait in the empty second rehearsal room.

I'm right. Mae opens the rehearsal room door carrying her own bundle of clothes. She sees me alone in there, and turns to slam it, but instinctively, I put my foot in the door. My Sellotaped broken toe crunches in agony.

'*Oww*! Mae, please listen to me.'

She glances out towards the green room, where the rest of the cast are presumably talking about how much they hate me. I pull her in, where she angrily dumps her clothes and stands, arms folded. Our matching Viola and Sebastian costumes are repeated in the mirrors around us.

'I didn't know about you and Alice,' I say. 'You've got to believe me.'

She laughs bitterly.

'Why would I believe a professional liar? She's writing a review of the show tonight, is she?'

'I… Yeah, she is. But I asked her not to!'

'It'll be a terrible one of me, obviously,' sneers Mae. 'I already know what it will say. She probably wrote it when I broke up with her and she's been waiting for a chance to use it.' She shakes her head. 'I wouldn't have given a single flying fuck. But *you*, using that? Is getting one good line in a second-tier media outlet really more important than – than…'

'Mae—'

'No, Clooney,' she says. 'You were always on a high horse about acting being about working hard at the "craft". I respected you for that. But then here you are, fucking your way to good reviews.'

'I was *not*... We never—'

'Right,' says Mae sarcastically. 'Just friends, are you? That's why she gave you a ring?'

'You're trying to make me into the villain here,' I say, 'but all I did was go on a few dates with a girl who was serious about me and *nice* to me.'

'Tip for next time you steal someone's girlfriend, Clooney: make your lies more convincing.'

'I did not "steal your girlfriend"!' I say desperately. 'You'd already broken up, right? And I didn't even know you'd been together!'

Mae's unreadable expression is multiplied in the mirrors.

Slowly, she walks towards me and puts her hand to my chest, feeling the racing heartbeat there. She meets my eyes.

We stare at each other like a blinking contest. I feel sure I could prove my innocence if I could kiss her.

But she's going to leave, I try to repeat in my mind. She's going to leave, just like Tahlia, just like Ruth and Raphy, just like Mum. The only person who isn't going to leave me is Alice. She said she *loves* me.

'I quit,' says Mae.

She gathers her clothes.

'What do you—'

'I don't want to be an actor anymore,' she says. 'If, in order to be successful, I have to be as – as cold and fake as you are? I'm out.'

She instinctively picks up Alice's jacket – *her* jacket – then drops it as if it's diseased. She shakes her head deliriously, the kohl of her stage make-up magnifying her wild eyes.

'Tomorrow can be my swan song,' she says sarcastically. 'Congratulations, Emmy Clooney. You fucking win.'

She opens the door. Alice's pressed to it on the other side.

'H-hello darling,' says Alice.

Mae stares at her for a moment, her shoulders tensing like a cat under attack.

Then she pushes past her and says, 'You two deserve each other.'

Alice rushes to me. 'Darling!'

I hold up a hand; I try to push down all the fury, all the confusion and humiliation. My jaw aches.

'Why didn't you *tell* me?' I ask.

There's a long silence. Now that I know Alice is the ex who was so awful to Mae, it's a lot easier to be angry at her.

'Did you give her this ring too?'

'You wear it better,' she says quietly.

I try to pull it off my thumb, but it's stuck.

'You *lied*!' I say.

'I just didn't want to talk about my ex in front of you!' she wails. 'That's normal in a new relationship!'

I hesitate.

'Yes, I have dated other people before you,' she says desperately. 'We're not all virgins like you!'

My cheeks flush painfully.

'But Emmeline, I'm with *you* now. Not Mae, not – not anyone else. I want you to be my everything, my everyone. Tell me what I need to do to make it up to you. I'll do anything.'

I shake my head uneasily.

'It – it shouldn't be like that,' I say.

She throws herself at my costume boots.

'Please. I *love* you. I love *you*.'

She's kneeling in front of me, the straps of her dress slipping off her shoulders.

But now I see through the act. Alice doesn't love me – she loves Mae. To be fair, I understand that perfectly.

I feel a tiny glimmer of sympathy for Alice. Sure, it doesn't feel great to be a poor replacement, but I know all too well how losing Mae could lead to despair.

'I'm sorry,' I say, offering my hand to help her up. 'I can't be her.'

'I don't want you to be her!' she says. 'Look, let's just start this all again. I'll post this nice review of you, then we'll go back to mine and I'll wear the lingerie you got me, and in the morning I'll make you bacon pancakes, and—'

I have never bought anyone lingerie (including myself), but it's the last one which gets me.

'Alice, again, I'm vegan!'

As I see Alice's certainty crack, I realise something.

'And so is Mae…'

And that's when I remember the waiter in the restaurant, Sammy. How Alice shook when she said they'd been engaged.

Just as I think of it, Alice breaks down. And this time, it's real. She claws at her throat, her hair uncoils from her tight plaits, and tears stream through her mascara.

'I try so hard,' she wails. 'Every time I think *finally*, here's the right person for me, she's the *one*. But it's never the same. They're never her.' She thumps at the floor with her fist. 'Why didn't she want me anymore? Why did she leave?'

So Alice wasn't in love with Mae after all. We were *both* rebounds. Alice wanted us both to play the role of someone who broke her heart years ago.

Her ring slides off easily now. As I hand it back to Alice, her fingers snap shut around it like Golem.

'I'm sorry you've been hurt,' I say. 'Honestly, I am. But all you're doing at the moment is perpetuating the cycle.'

I remember how Mae spoke about her ex and rage flares in me. Knowing her experience makes me see my whole relationship with Alice in a new light. I take a deep breath.

'I don't know if you're doing it consciously or unconsciously, but I know you really messed with Mae's head. And… You really messed with mine too.'

Alice goes very still, staring at the ring in her hands. I swallow hard.

'I thought it was my fault,' I say. 'But... You said Mae was manipulative. You said she was a liar, who overpromises and love-bombs... Alice, those are all things *you* did to *me*.'

Alice still doesn't look up at me. I shuffle and offer my hand to help her up.

'I know I am absolutely not a relationship expert,' I say awkwardly, 'but I... I really think you should talk to someone who is. Someone who can help you. Someone who can make sure you don't repeat this again. For your sake, but also for your date's.'

Alice looks at my hand, then stands without it.

'You bitch,' she spits. 'You bitch! Of everyone I've ever dated, you are the *worst*. You don't have the best looks, you don't have the best charm, you don't have the best success. You're a failure. You don't even deserve to get compared to them.'

For a moment, I falter, feeling as if the world's been tipped onto its axis. But then a voice in my head, one that sounds like Mae, says, 'Wow, she really is a critic.'

And the world rights itself again. Much as it makes me miss Mae, it also makes me laugh. Alice gawks at me.

'You're right,' I shrug. 'There's really no comparison.'

I go and open the door for her, like a gentleman.

'So maybe we shouldn't be compared at all,' I say. 'Goodbye, Alice.'

48

The foyer is still busy. The audience cluster round the other members of the cast, now changed out of their costumes (though they've 'accidentally' kept their flattering stage make-up on). I wonder how many people are here to support Mae? The room's more hushed than you'd expect on opening night, especially as half of them have clearly come after the Pride parade, dressed in rainbow glitter and leather. My awful performance has clearly ruined the vibe.

I wonder if I should interrupt the cast's evening to apologise. But what would I say? I let my personal life affect my performance – *our* performance – and that's unforgivable. I've destroyed any hopes I had of us staying friends after it ends. I'm far too ashamed to talk to any of them.

I do search for Francis, but can't find him. Mae is nowhere to be found either. And still no sign of Thalia.

I keep my head down as I pass through the red-carpeted foyer to the smoking area. The ghosts of mine and Thalia's drama school days are still here, but tonight they feel less... haunting.

Still, I pause before opening the smoking area doors, getting déjà vu about seeing her after her show those few months ago. How achingly I wanted her to be there then, for her to finally see me again, for us to be reunited. I remember her pink smoke at our corner table, her gap-toothed smile... And I remember her there a year ago, at our graduation, pouring champagne. I said

I had something I needed to tell her. She said she did too. My heart pounded as I said she should go first. Excitedly, she told me about her offer of a life-changing role. So I never told her how I felt about her. Would it have made a difference?

I've been thinking about June 29th for literally a year. How many hours did I spend planning alternative conversations, trying to script exactly the right combination of words to try to get some reassurance, explanation, apology, closure? But now it's actually happening...

I know before I open the doors that she won't be there.

The smoking area is empty.

I sit down at our table and open up my one-sided WhatsApp with her. She's online.

I message her.

Hey T, I'm at our table at Boards... are you joining?

The tick shows that she's seen my message.

She's typing.

Then she's not typing anymore.

The minutes tick by. A couple of people come and go. Someone even has a pink e-cigarette. But none of them are my old best friend.

Flicks fall on my cheeks, as if the sky isn't sure whether to rain or not. I start shivering and pull Mae's green denim jacket tightly round me.

I message again. *Just let me know?*

As I sit there, watching some theatre lovers laughing and gossiping, I consider what would happen next, in the official script of my life. Would it pour with rain, allowing me to finally cry over Thalia, who would then appear from the clouds and say she misses me too, but [insert twist here that explains why she ghosted me and leaves everyone feeling good about themselves, e.g., she officially comes out as straight]? Or would I send her some angry and poignant voicemail which somehow also redeems me with Mae?

In the Hollywood version, my character probably wouldn't

just sit here, teeth chattering in the drizzle. But alas, that's what I do.

After a bleak hour, I accept that Thalia isn't coming. Once again, she has disappeared and, once again, I will never know the reason why.

I look at the setting sun, the blue turning into gold, and I think… Really, what have I lost? How much of what I cried over was really missing Thalia as a person? How much of it was just the pain of rejection and wounded pride, the relentless torture of trying to solve what's going on in someone else's mind? How much of that pain wasn't really about Thalia at all, but about it making me feel inadequate?

So I imagine, instead, some tentatively optimistic guitar starting to strum. A rainbow would appear through the rain, as my voiceover says: Sometimes, you don't get to have your poignant closure scene. Sometimes things just change, no matter how much you don't want them to. One day, you have to accept that if you're not in their life anymore, maybe they shouldn't be in yours either. Because sometimes people leave, and maybe, just sometimes, that's OK.

Then the guitar would reach its chorus, as I say: But some people… Some people never really left.

The camera zooms to the rainbow reflected in my eyes, and then me looking down at my phone, as I close the conversation with Thalia and instead open the number of the person I most want to speak to.

There's a glorious key change as, for the first time in ten years, I dial my mum's number.

And she picks up.

The fantasy shatters, the rainbow disappears, and I realise what the hell I'm doing. I immediately cancel the call.

Breathing hard, I close my eyes and consider the practicalities of starting a new life in a distant cave. But then she's calling me back. I swallow, and accept it.

'Hi, Mum.'

'Oh! Oh! *Hi*! Emmy? Are you really there?'

Her voice suddenly rises. 'Is everything all right? Do you need me to—'

'Everything's OK, Mum,' I say, my voice thick. 'I'm fine, I'm safe, I'm just at the theatre.' I sigh. 'I-I'm sorry to ring out of the blue like this.'

She pauses.

'My love, you can call me whenever you want. Day or night.'

For a moment, all I can hear down her line is some dogs yapping and a big pig snorting.

'Is this about the… talk you had with your father?'

'I… Kind of. Not just that, but…'

I don't plan to say this. But what slips out is, 'Mum? Why did you leave Dad?'

There's another pause, broken by disgruntled grunting.

'But darling, I *didn't* leave your father.'

'I'm… pretty sure you did.'

Mum barks with laughter, then coughs and stops herself.

'You want the full story? Well, let me see. Your father and I had been stepping out for about a year when I became pregnant. I wanted to keep you, and was happy to raise you alone, but Julius wanted to be involved as much as I'd let him. So he proposed.'

'I know that,' I say impatiently. 'I've seen the wedding photos.'

I used to think they were idyllic. The small, intimate ceremony in a quaint chapel, Mum's bump proudly displayed, Dad grinning in every picture. Pete's wife Sally was maid of honour, and Pete was best man and caterer.

Mum says, 'I should have known the marriage was doomed as soon as I saw that wedding cake made of pizza.'

'You *never* loved each other?'

Is that why I can't seem to love people properly? Some curse of being born to parents who don't really want you?

'Oh, Julius and I had an understanding,' Mum says. 'But sometimes two perfectly lovely people can like each other, and that does *not* mean they should get married.'

She laughs heartily, then stops herself again.

'Your father and I quickly realised we were incompatible as spouses. Emotionally, logistically, sexually—'

'I do not need to know that part.'

'Well, we weren't incompatible enough to stop us from having you, I suppose,' she muses. 'But after the honeymoon all that stopped, to our mutual pleasure. Once you were born, our relationship became something else. We were co-parents. If we hadn't had you, we would have got divorced immediately.'

'So you were both miserable,' I mumble. 'Because of me.'

'Pumpkin, *no*. The opposite. We had you, and, mad as it sounds, having a screaming child shitting herself every second made us love each other more. Because I loved your father being a *father*. And I think he felt the same about me being a mother. We felt lucky because we both had you.'

I swallow painfully.

'You were our whole lives. We both wanted to be there for you. We kept telling ourselves we'd separate one day, but the goalposts kept shifting. First we said we'd wait for you to go to school. Then, we'd wait for you to start Key Stage 3. Then you were twelve, and you came out to us, and we thought, God, the last thing we wanted to do was for you to associate coming out with us breaking up! So we held on…'

I try to keep my voice level.

'So, what changed? You met John?'

'No,' she sighs deeply. 'What changed… is that Sally died.'

I watch the drizzle make patterns on the table. The sounds from the bar rise and fall.

'I *wish* you'd been able to know her more,' says Mum. 'She was – oh, she was the best. Wicked sense of humour. Kindest soul. Adored you, of course. When she got her diagnosis we were all so…'

Dogs whine in the background. I can hear the jangling of earrings as Mum shakes her head.

'It shook us all deeply. Pete just... stopped. Didn't look after himself. Your dad moved in with him to help, but they shut the pizzeria, so they were both out of a job. I was looking after you by myself most of the time, while I was grieving too.'

Her words conjure a memory of Sally's funeral – Mum and Dad clutching each other's hands, whispering out of my earshot.

'I... I got it wrong,' I say. 'I knew Sally had died, but... All I really understood was Dad was moving out of the flat and you were trying to hide that you were crying all the time. I thought he was leaving us and neither of you were telling me.'

She sighs. 'I'm sorry that we didn't talk to you more about it at the time. I see now that I should have done. You were thirteen, old enough to understand all of it, but... To me, you were still my baby. I wanted to shield you from reality.'

She sniffs.

'Somewhere in the heartbreak,' she continues, 'your dad and I decided the time would never be right, so it might as well be now. We were going to divorce. But we wanted to make sure we had all the legal information understood before talking to you. It was all very amicable.'

If their separation was so amicable, why did they stop talking, except through me? I swap the phone to my other ear, so that I can warm my other hand in Mae's jacket.

'Sally died in January,' Mum continues, 'and your father reopened the pizzeria in the autumn so... Eight, nine months later? I dropped you off at school and walked into the office to file for a divorce. And there in the waiting room was this man.'

I sit very still.

'And this man had his hand resting on this gorgeous puppy, a grey Staffy with three legs, and the puppy was gazing up at him with such... such pure *devotion* in his eyes, and then John looked at me and...'

My vision blurs.

'I'd never felt like that before,' Mum whispers. 'Like maybe – maybe I was the main character in my own life, and I was finally getting a love story.'

Silently, I press my eyes with the palm of my hands.

'It just felt… right,' she says. 'Your father and I could sell the house and get some money to put aside for you. Your dad could move in with Pete, where they realised they were both happier anyway, and they could get the business back up and running. He'd still get to be with you every weekend. And you and I could move into a cottage the way we'd always imagined. I was so sure you'd love John and Amy and the animals as much as I did. I really, really thought that you'd be happy.'

I swallow hard, looking around the smoking area, but to my relief, I have no audience watching me.

'I did it all wrong, I see that now,' she says. 'I got caught up in it. I thought it would be this magical surprise, this fairy tale, like it had felt for me…'

Driving down that pathway to the cottage, holding hands with Mum, thinking this was my new home. Then the door opening to John and Amy.

'I'll never forgive myself for hurting you, or making you feel second best,' she says. 'If I had to choose between you and anyone, *anything* else – I would choose you, my Emmeline, every time, a hundred million times. But I… I never thought of it that way.

'I don't believe that love is limited. Love isn't a competition. Everyone can be a winner. I love you and I love Amy, and those loves are *different*, sure – but they don't take away from each other. If you had been a twin, would you think I loved you any less? Or if you were a triplet? Or an octuplet? Or—'

I laugh snottily. 'I think I get the idea, Mum.'

'I suppose my problem has always been that I have too much love to give,' Mum sighs contentedly. 'But oh, what a nice problem to have.'

All this time I could have allowed myself to be happy at the cottage with Mum and her wonderfully wholesome other family, and I wouldn't have been hurting anyone.

I look up at the clouds moving past the bright full moon.

'I thought I had to side with Dad because he was the one who was alone,' I say quietly. 'He was the one who was left behind.'

I stand and start pacing. 'But Dad kept trying to tell me. He kept saying he was happy and that I should talk to you, I should forgive you. I just never believed him. I guess because... I guess because *I* found it really hard to be happy without you.'

Mum sniffs. The sound makes me start sniffing. And then I hear Mum is crying, and I can't stop it any longer. Finally, I let myself cry. For a while we both sob, unabashed and unrestrained, animals wailing along in the background.

'Oh Emmy,' she says. 'I wish I was there with you. I always wish I was there with you. I am so, so sorry.'

'No, *I'm* sorry,' I say, wiping desperately at my nose with the jacket sleeve. 'God, I just feel so *stupid*. I hate myself for doing this to us all. You were always so supportive of me, and I was so scared that I hadn't been good enough for you, that you didn't really want me anymore... Think of all the time we've lost because of me.'

'Emmeline,' Mum says, hoarsely, 'it's not too late. We can start now.'

I sniff, and nod desperately, then realise she can't see me over the phone.

'Mum?'

'Yes, my love. I'm here.'

'Will you come and see my show?'

There's a silence.

'If – if John and Amy want to?'

But Mum doesn't reply. For a moment I feel the same as when I invited Dad and he ignored me. Then Mum starts properly wailing.

'Mum! It's really fine, you don't have to, I'm sorry I—'

'I have been waiting for you to invite me to one of your shows for ten years!' she sobs. 'I bought a front-row ticket to every single one, just in case.'

The world blurs. All those shows at drama school with an empty seat in the front row. The reserved seat at the improv show. The seat next to Alice tonight...

Not caring who might come into The Boards Theatre Smoking Area, I wail too.

'Sometimes,' says Mum, through her tears, 'I felt like I was your own Phantom of the Opera.' She starts singing the opening music. I laugh snottily and join in. Sat there wiping my cheeks and clutching the phone to my ear, I imagine Mum doing the same.

'Do you want to stay at the cottage tonight?' she asks. 'I could come and pick you up? I'd be there in a couple of hours, faster if I manage to escape without The Pig knowing.'

I think about what Mum said, about how love isn't a competition. I've done it again with pushing Ruth and Raphy away just because the love between the two of them has changed.

'Thank you, Mum,' I sniff. 'Honestly, it means a lot and I'd love to visit some other time. But I've messed up a lot of things recently, and I don't want to hold off on apologising and trying to set them right.'

Mum says quietly, 'Well then, I'm proud of you.' My chest feels lighter than it has in years. Then she squeals happily. 'And I'll see you tomorrow! Oh, I can't believe I get to say that!'

I smile broadly to the empty smoking area.

'I can't wait. Goodnight, Mum.'

'Goodnight, sweetie. I'm so, so glad you rang.'

'I'm so glad you picked up.'

'You hang up.'

'No you hang up.'

We laugh.

'Mum!'

'Sorry!' she says, but still doesn't hang up.

I smile, and put the phone on the table, leaving it on. Mum and I sit there in silence together, looking up at our night skies, while a pig squeals happily in the background.

49

When I arrive back at the flat, I know R&R are still awake because of the delicate glow of candles burning through the thin living room curtains. On the windowsill I can see the reflection of a crystal Raphy charges in moonlight. I think that one is for the protection of friends. My chest aches as I ring the doorbell.

'It's her,' I hear Raphy say.

'She'd have a key,' Ruth answers.

'She isn't sure if we'd let her in,' he replies. 'And she wants to do a big apology speech. Also, she can hear us.'

I almost turn away in panic when the door opens.

Raphy and Ruth grab me. Then we're all hugging as hard as we can. I look into their faces and immediately start crying again.

'Jesus,' says Ruth, leaning back in alarm. 'I don't think I've ever seen you cry outside of a self-tape.'

Raphy hands me his handkerchief.

'Let it out,' he coos. 'Let it all out.'

Ruth smooths my hair efficiently and Raphy rubs my back, whispering what sounds like, 'catharsis, catharsis'. This is so not going the way I'd expected.

'I'm sorry,' I cough. 'I didn't plan to just cry at you. I want to do a full apology speech.'

'Of course you do,' says Ruth. 'I'll go and get the popcorn, shall I? Is on the doorstep an important setting for you, or do you want to perform it in the comfort of your own home?'

I start blubbering again.

Before I know it, we're in our old routine, Raphy spooning out herbal teas and Ruth checking her watch against the popping of the microwave.

'Emmy, why don't you go into the living room and choose a musical soundtrack?'

I don't know why I was expecting the living room to have changed in the, like, two days I've been away, but it's the same as I left it.

By the time we're settled down, we're already several songs into *Les Misérables* and it feels slightly weird to bring up the apology. But they deserve it.

I cough and stand before them. They nod, crunching on popcorn.

My old instinct would have been to draw on old films for apology scenes and steal their lines, or at least their expressions. But this is Ruth and Raphy. They're *my* best friends. It should be *my* honest attempt.

'I'm sorry I'm an idiot,' I say. 'I was so scared you guys had chosen the two of you instead of the three of us. I didn't want to watch you drift slowly away from me, so I guess I thought I should rip the plaster off.' I sigh. 'But I was acting as if love is a finite resource, and as if change is inevitably a bad thing. I still *really* want to be your friend, whatever that looks like. I want our friendship to grow together. And just to be clear, I'm *genuinely* so, so happy for you both. You're clearly so happy together and honestly, when I think about it, each of you is the only person I would ever think would be good enough for the other, so really, it's perfect. I love you both so much and I really hope... I hope you'll forgive me... And that we can... still be... best friends?'

After a pause, Ruth says, 'I think that's the longest I've ever heard you talk.'

Raphy does some kind of elaborate bow and hand gesture. 'I hear your apology, I receive your apology, I accept your apology. It was accepted before you'd even left the flat.'

In the same moment, they both reach their hands forwards to do our three-handed handshake. I shake them, crying again.

'Goodness me,' says Raphy, his eyes widening as he seems to read my mind. 'You've had a lot of houses in retrograde, haven't you?'

I nod my puffy eyes.

'Can the non-psychic amongst us be given a debrief please?' Ruth asks.

I take a deep breath.

'Since I found out that the two of you were together, I... fought with my dad and Pete, quit the pizzeria, and went to stay at Alice's. Then Mae told me she wanted to kiss me.' Ruth squeaks. 'I told her I wanted to kiss her too, but I had a girlfriend.' Ruth boos. 'Also, she's leaving for America. Alice told me. Then Alice tried to blackmail me and also told me she loved me. Then I fought with Mae because it turns out she's Alice's ex.' Ruth grimaces. 'Then I did the worst performance of my life, ruined the show for everyone. Fought with Alice, found out she's not over her *other* ex, and broke up with her.' Ruth cheers. 'Then I got ghosted by Thalia – again – but no longer care. Rang my mum, realised I've been separating our family for no reason, and invited her to the show tomorrow. Then I came here.'

Ruth blinks and pops a piece of popcorn in her mouth.

'Busy, busy.'

I laugh. Then I start crying, yet again. God, I've officially broken my tear ducts.

'Sometimes I wish I could just become someone else. Throw away the character of Emmy Clooney and start again. Make a completely new life for myself.'

Raphy takes my hand.

'You're the only person you can't run away from,' he says.

'I know. It's the worst.'

'But honey,' he says, 'that means you're never alone. You'll always be there. So stop trying to abandon yourself. Like, I know "self-love" can be hard; it's the work of a lifetime to feel complete and unconditional love for ourselves – but maybe start with cultivating a bit of self-like? Be your own best friend?'

Raphy's woo-woo is sounding bizarrely rational.

'So,' he smiles, 'what advice would you give to your best friend if she was in this situation?'

I look pleadingly up at him.

'I'd... I'd tell her to listen to her friends, because they're much wiser than she is. And I'd tell her to apologise to everyone. But first, to go to bed.'

Raphy adds, 'And dance under the full moon, naked, clockwise.'

I blink at him.

'Would that help?' I ask.

He shrugs.

'Probably wouldn't hurt.'

'Things will seem better in the morning,' says Ruth, patting my shoulder. 'We'll make a list.'

'It's going to have to be a very long list,' I groan.

'What if not everything that's broken needs fixing?' says Raphy.

'Raphael,' laughs Ruth, 'we both know you're just repeating things with a cryptic twist now.'

'What if repeating cryptic things is itself a twist?' he asks.

Ruth and I tickle him until he squeals.

When we head to bed, they both give me a long hug and Raphy invites me to blow out the prayer candle.

I can't tell you what I prayed for, in case that means it doesn't come true.

50

R&R were right. Things do seem a bit better in the morning… Until I check my phone and see that Alice Sefton has posted a review of *Twelfth Night* in *The Atre* online. She has given it one star.

I pull the duvet over my head and try to disappear into the mattress.

'*Emmeline Clooney is clearly no relation of George – someone who shares a great actor's genes could not have such a complete lack of charisma. Not only does Clooney have the emotional range of a self-service machine, she cannot even remember her (pittance of) lines. One has to wonder if Clooney could possibly have earned this part in a fair audition – did she get into the production through dubious means? Apparently she is trained at St Genesius, which shows that even the finest establishments will let anyone in for a high enough fee. It's exactly this kind of amateurish performance that means LGBTQ+ shows will remain underfunded…*'

I continue to read all one thousand words dedicated to describing every way in which I am inferior.

But… The review doesn't mention Mae.

Ruth pushes open my bedroom door.

'Yoga in the living room, T-minus five.'

I groan and try to hide further under my blanket.

Raphy and Ruth grab me under each arm. After Raphy's soothing voice guides us through power poses, we gather round the kitchen table, drinking something fluorescently nutritional. Ruth sits me at my desk chair and leaves me with one of her terrifying focus playlists.

I write, with tick boxes, all the people I want to apologise to.

Looking around at my half-empty walls, the ripped theatre posters, the pile of scripts in my bin, I nod to myself and get started.

First, I ring Valerie. She picks up on the second ring. Her babies gurgle in the background.

'Valerie, I wanted to thank you for your work as my agent.'

'Are you firing me?'

'Aren't *you* firing *me*?'

She must not have read the review yet. I explain, and admit how truly terrible I was.

'The truth is,' I say, 'it's not just that I ruined the show for everyone, I've also been acting in a deeply unprofessional manner. I believe your assistant Louisa knows about it.'

I explain about my competition with Mae, how I took jobs just to try to get them away from her. How she is quitting acting because of me.

'If I'm being such a menace to work with that I not only let down my colleagues but also make them want to give the craft up entirely, then I can't in good conscience continue to be a part of the industry. I'm resigning.'

There's a pause, with the distant sound of the babies laughing.

'Emmy, believe me, what you are describing is a pittance compared with other people in this business. Some clients take the phrase "kill the competition" too literally.'

I laugh uncertainly.

'Look. Do you still want to be an actor?'

I hesitate. I'm thinking about Mae, alive under the spotlight. 'I still find good acting inspirational,' I say. 'I just don't feel worthy of the title.'

Valerie barks.

'Great, an actor with imposter syndrome,' she says. 'Haven't heard that one before. Look, this happens. People's priorities change, their careers can move with them. People start out wanting to be one of the world's handful of stars, the biggest name in the shiniest lights. And then, if that doesn't happen, a lot of people quit. And that's fine. But sometimes that doesn't happen, and someone doesn't quit – they become a different part of the constellation.'

Babies babble.

'There's no leads without supports. It's no fun for anyone if everyone is so busy trying to be in the spotlight that they ruin the show.'

I look around my room at the tattered posters of all the shows I've loved. How many people were behind each one?

'Acting is a team sport,' says Valerie. 'Actors need other people to exist. You need writers. I'm biased, but you need agents. And, much as you might wish they didn't, you need critics, and directors, and producers, and you *certainly* need an audience. You can't be an actor by yourself. Otherwise you're just... Well, a bit weird. Muttering someone else's words to yourself.

'So think about it. You let me and Louisa know. But for what it's worth, I think you've got something. Not just something fleeting, but something with substance. I think the world of drama would shine less brightly without you.'

I might need to accept that I cry every few minutes these days. I sniff and thank her.

'Talking of Louisa...' I say. 'There's something else you should know. She's a great assistant, but I think she's going to be an even better agent. She scouted some great raw talent, and she's been doing everything she can to get her into the rooms she needs to be in, and that's before she's even getting commission.'

'Huh! So I've been growing my own best competition,' chuckles Valerie. 'Sounds like she deserves a promotion. Then she can make me happily redundant.'

Her laugh is drowned out by babies suddenly fighting over who can scream the loudest.

I thank her again and we hang up.

I know these apologies are meant to be about me accepting responsibility for acting badly, but I already feel better. Am I doing it wrong?

I email Daryl from The Mighty Hippo, confessing that he mistook me for the actually good improviser Mae Jones, and that it was she who performed that night. I give him Mae's contact details and say that if he has future opportunities, he should contact her. I also ask if he has any absolute beginner workshops available, because I'd be interested in taking one.

I hesitate over whether to contact *The Atre* about Alice. If I was her manager I'd want to know that a critic was writing biased reviews about their dating partners, in advance of even seeing the show. But, wouldn't they just see Emmy Clooney complaining about a bad review of Emmy Clooney and ignore me?

The thing I feel bad about is that the review is only one star. Although it doesn't mention any of the other cast or crew by name, my failure implicitly affects them too – and Francis's otherwise impeccable reputation. Thinking about it, I realise I'll have to accept my punishment, and hope that other reviews will be more honest, shining a positive light on the others.

I look at my apology list, take a deep breath, and ring Dad.

He doesn't pick up.

I ring Pete.

Pete doesn't pick up either.

I ring the restaurant, but find, completely unprecedented, that the voicemail says the restaurant is closed today – on a Saturday? The sound of Dad's voice fumbling with the message on the voicemail makes my heart squeeze with regret.

I leave a voicemail.

'Hi Dad, I'm assuming Pete's there with you, so I hope it's OK if I leave a message for both of you. I know this can't make up for what I said, but I wanted to apologise for everything. I've been a terrible daughter and non-biological niece and – and *friend* to both of you, and I miss you.' I swallow and plough on. 'Umm, I wanted you to know that I got in touch with Mum. We had a long call and I... I've been so wrong about everything. Can I come and see you after the show, maybe tomorrow morning? Let me know. I love you. And... I'm getting serious withdrawals for a Pete's'za.'

I decide I'm going to apologise to Francis and the cast in person, before the final performance. I look at Mae's name, circled and underlined several times. The hardest one is going to have to be saved for last.

The only one remaining, then, is Thalia. I go into my conversation with her and start to type out an apologetic text.

Then I delete it and, smiling, archive our chat.

51

My nerves about apologising to Francis and the *Twelfth Night* team are worse than stage fright.

When I arrive at The Boards, the rest of the cast is already assembled. Everyone except Mae.

Francis puts down a copy of *The Atre*. No one moves. I raise my hand.

'Umm, Sir Francis. Would you mind if I said something quickly, before notes?' I proffer my shopping bag, full of what I felt were vaguely piratical jammy dodgers, coconut rings, and ginger nuts. 'I got everyone some ship's biscuits.'

After I tip them out, I take a deep breath.

'Umm, I wanted to apologise. Obviously. I was shockingly bad in yesterday's performance, and I'm so, so sorry for letting everyone down. There isn't an excuse good enough. I shouldn't have let my personal life affect my performance. It won't happen again.'

Charlie silently darts forwards like a crab, grabs a pack, and darts back.

'I wanted to thank you all for your professionalism and flexibility in making my own failure not ruin the whole show. Roger, for improvising our fight scene. Joe and Surina, for ad libbing iambic pentameter when I blanked. The rest of you, for being so aware of the production as a whole that you made the machine work, even missing a part. You're all incredible. And I'm sorry this whole speech is so indulgent of me, but, you know... thespians.'

The group nod earnestly. Roger says a hearty 'arr'. Now everyone is tucking in to the biscuits, I turn to Francis.

'Sir,' I say. 'I'm sorry for not living up to the trust you placed in me. I know I was only cast because I look like a good twin for Mae, but I wanted to surpass that expectation and instead I messed it up.'

Francis frowns, holding a ginger nut.

'You were abysmal last night,' he says, biting into the biscuit. 'Truly, one of the worst performances I've ever seen. And believe me, that's saying something. But don't do yourself a disservice. I could have cast anyone as Sebastian, but I didn't, because I'm never wrong. You've been a worthy addition to the cast, on and off-stage. You've taught us things about Shakespeare which, frankly, I don't think he knew himself. As a former Catholic I applaud your self-flagellation, but really, I think you got enough punishment in that—'

He gestures to the printout of Alice's review.

'To be fair,' I say, 'she wasn't wrong.'

Everyone laughs, and... I'm allowed back in. I can't believe it. These incredible talents, these brilliant people, welcoming me, even when I messed up so badly. I fear my tally chart of how many times I've cried this weekend is going to go up again.

'Now, my notes for tonight,' says Francis, dusting crumbs from his neckerchief. 'Emmy... Well, just do the opposite of what you did last night.'

I salute.

'And as for the rest of you... For God's sake, just have *fun*. It's meant to be a *play* not a *work*. What's the point of us getting together to do a big gay comedy and dressing up as pirates if not even the actors have a good time?'

We all arr enthusiastically.

'Now. How about, as a final show treat, we play a nice round of Zip, Zap, Boing.'

Everyone leaps to their feet to form the circle.

But Mae is still missing. After all the relief of the accepted apology, her absence is creating a new knot of worry. What if she changed her mind and, after her threat of quitting acting last night, she decided not to turn up tonight either? Perhaps she flew out to her mum's set in America already?

I stand between Keiya and Zach, who ruffle my hair affectionately.

'Zip!'

'Zip!'

'Zip!'

I turn from Keiya on my left to pass the 'energy' round the circle to—

Mae.

'Zip?' she asks, with a tentative smile.

'Hesitation!' calls Surina, who is puritanical about Zip, Zap, Boing rules. 'Run round the circle in punishment.'

I run round the circle and slot back into place next to Mae. I feel the tension between us like real Zip, Zap, Boing energy.

'Zip,' she says to me.

'Boing.'

'Boing.'

'You can't boing a boing!' calls Surina. 'You're both *out*.'

We bow from the circle.

Surina, Joe, and Charlie are the last three left, zapping at supersonic speed. Francis umpires.

Dumbly, I offer Mae a jammy dodger. She smiles, and says, 'Can I talk to you? In private?'

I follow her round the corner to backstage, behind the shadow screen.

'Mae,' I say, when we're in the quiet half-light. 'I'm so, so sorry—'

'I've had a very busy morning,' she interrupts me, her voice neutral. 'Louisa rang me. She said Valerie's given her the authority to start representing her own clients, and she wants to be my official agent.'

I blink at her. It's great news, though I firmly believe any agent would be delighted to have Mae on their books.

'Congratulations,' I say cautiously. 'Are you going to accept?'

'Then,' Mae continues, 'I had an email offering for me to teach beginner improv workshops with The Mighty Hippo.'

My cheeks warm.

'I have a funny feeling I know who sent those my way,' she says.

I glance up at her, but her expression is unreadable.

'And I noticed,' she says quietly, 'that Alice Sefton's review didn't mention me at all. But it was pretty... ungirlfriendly about you.'

She takes a step towards me and lifts the fingers of my right hand.

'You're not wearing her ring anymore,' she says.

I swallow, blood pounding in my ears. Tentatively, I bring her hand slowly to my chest. We feel my heart pounding through each other's fingers.

'I understand if I have messed this up unforgivably,' I say, 'but please know that I would do anything – *every*thing – for the chance to try to win you back.'

Mae studies me, her eyes dancing. Her mouth curves into her familiar radiant smile.

'Emmy,' she says. 'You won a long time ago.'

I don't know which of us moves first. Maybe she steps forwards and I wrap my hands round her neck, or maybe I step forwards and she wraps her hands round my neck, but either way the end result is that I kiss Mae, and Mae kisses me.

When you stage kiss, you choreograph the way you move. When you stage kiss, you hold your mouth next to another actor's, both far more attuned to the audience than to each other.

You're counting the seconds, sensing the right moment to break away and deliver your next line, or do a cute leg pop.

This is no stage kiss.

All the electricity that's charged between us for months detonates. I've never experienced my brain completely switching off before. I feel awake. I feel alive. I finally understand why so many stories go on and on about the experience of putting your mouth to another's.

Mae makes a soft noise like a contented sigh and I feel it in my own mouth. I desperately want to make it happen again. I kiss her hungrily and she presses me up against the wall.

Unfortunately, what we'd forgotten is that the wall is not a real wall. It's the shadow-puppet wall, made of a flimsy, translucent material mounted on an even flimsier wooden frame. It wobbles and starts to tip over.

'No,' we say. 'No no no no!'

We try to grab the sides, but they're hidden in the curtains. It falls with the slow inevitability of the *Titanic*. In the chaos, I manage to knock over the prop table, throwing cups, swords, letters, rings, and yellow garters to the floor. Each clatter inexplicably loudly.

The screen thuds to the stage floor with a belly flop, revealing Mae and I on one side, and… the entire cast on the other.

'Sorry,' says Mae, 'we were just, er, rehearsing.'

Roger's smirk is so dirty it should have a Parental Advisory warning label.

'Yeah,' says Zach, 'we could see that.'

Mae and I look at each other, then at the shadow wall. The shadow wall that's translucent when lit from behind.

'Thank you for the show,' says Keiya.

Mae and I, still holding hands, blush at each other. Then we shrug, and curtsey.

52

I wonder what Alice would have written in her review if she'd seen the second performance. If she'd seen the audience roar at Mae's speeches; or me whirling two cutlasses in the sky; if she'd seen the twins embrace with something a *little* incestuous; or the cast roaring with laughter as we jigged together around Charlie dressed in their squid costume.

But the truth is, none of us cared about any reviews. All we cared about was sharing the fun we were having with the audience. Making things up and believing – just for an hour or two – that it's real.

I'm so lost in the world of the play, that it's only when I run to the front of the stage to take a bow that I recognise familiar faces.

There is my mum. She's standing in the front row where she should have been all along, next to John and Amy. Their sincere claps cut through the other applause. Dad and Pete are a few rows behind shouting 'Brava! Brava!' Next to them, Ruth and Raphy woop and wave wildly at me. They're all here for *me*.

I take Sebastian's hat off, point it in their directions, and bow.

When Mae goes forward last, for her bow, the whole auditorium stands. I've never felt more proud of anyone. But as she looks out into the crowd, she hesitates. I follow her gaze, and am astonished to see that, standing at the back, wearing incognito sunglasses and a wide-brimmed hat is Annabel Finch, smiling beguilingly. Annabel bows up to her daughter, and Mae bows back.

Backstage, the euphoria of the show still pumping through our veins, Mae and I don't go straight to the green room. We're too busy kissing.

But seeing Annabel in the audience is a hard reminder of just how temporary this bliss is. A part of me doesn't want to know, wants to be able to kid myself that this can last forever. But how long do I have with her?

I force myself to pull away from her and try to regulate my breathing enough to ask, 'When are you flying back?'

'Clooney,' she says, her lips wonderfully red, 'what on earth are you talking about?'

Mae stares at me, and my mind races with numbers. One month? One week? Do I even have the after-party with her?

'Alice told me you're shooting a TV series in America, with your mum.'

Then Mae starts laughing.

'Emmy. *I'm* not shooting a series with my mum. My *sister* is.'

The news hasn't quite caught up with my brain yet.

'You mean…? You're not leaving?'

'Nope. I intend to stay right here. Bothering you. If you'll have me.'

'You mean…? Is this…? Not a fling for you?'

'You silly goose,' she says, looping her arms round my neck, 'it was *never* a fling for me.'

I study the freckles along her nose, the fleck of gold in her eyes, her perfect dimples.

'Can I just double-check,' I say. 'Is this a joke?'

Mae laughs. 'No, Clooney. I've never been more serious about anything.'

As I stare at her, I try to note how this feels so that I can summon it in future roles: relief, joy, triumph, hope, and a whole dollop of horny.

Then I decide to just live it.

I kiss her nose, her cheeks, her forehead, everywhere I can reach. I run my hands through her messy short hair, and she pushes her hands through mine. I kiss her with more fervour and commitment than I've ever given to a part.

'Shit,' I say, who knows how long later. 'Our audience. We should go and greet our adoring fans.'

Mae sighs dramatically.

'OK, OK,' she says, then leans in to kiss me again. 'But give me one more encore...'

Wearing our own clothes, still holding hands, Mae and I head out into the foyer.

The first familiar faces we spot are Ruth and Raphy, who cheer us loudly.

'God, you two!' sings Raphy. 'You're electric together! Mae, you must come round soon so that I can read your tarot...'

'Raphael,' snaps Ruth, 'don't freak her out *that* fast.'

The three of them laugh in a huddle, already planning when the four of us are going to go for coffee together. How could I ever have thought love was a competition? All my favourite people in the world, friends! *Imagine*!

I'm distracted from joining in with the scheduling though, because across the room, I see my mum.

She's wearing what she's always called her best dress: a well-worn yellow with colourful flowers underneath a long blue cardigan she definitely knitted herself. It has a mud stain by the knees that looks suspiciously like a snout print. She's tried to tie her hair into an updo, which is slightly off-centre, and most of her hair is breaking free in gentle wisps. She looks completely the same as the last time I saw her. She's beautiful.

Our eyes meet across the foyer bar and we both stop. Then

she opens out her arms and I run to her. We hug for a long time, me breathing in her fancy perfume, which doesn't completely mask the undernotes of baking and soil and animals. Then she pulls away from me, holding me at arm's length. Her blue-grey eyes are damp, like mine.

'My goodness,' Mum whispers, putting her hand on my cheek. 'You have it, don't you? You have it. Magnetism. I couldn't take my eyes off you.'

Oh God. I start crying, yet again. Mum pulls me back to her.

'Thank you,' she says into my hair. 'For letting me see you.'

I shake my head, hug her tighter. I say into her damp shoulder, 'I thought you might have brought The Pig along.'

'She tried, believe me. A true patron of the arts.'

Mum pulls away from me laughing, and wipes my tears away. I wipe hers.

A stocky grey three-legged Staffy bounds over.

'Watson!'

He's a big boy now, and when he sniffs excitedly into my leg he nearly knocks me over. I crouch to rub his ears, and he ravenously licks my hand.

Two pairs of practical shoes approach behind him.

'John! Amy!' I say, hastily brushing my hands on my trousers. 'Umm. Hi. Thank you so much for coming along tonight.'

'Thank *you*,' says John, seeming completely at ease. 'What a pleasure to visit the theatre. We really must come more often. What magic! I've always loved Shakespeare's comedies – though, if I may, you'd make a stonking Hamlet. But look at me, doing my own monologue…'

From nowhere, he proffers a bunch of red roses, wrapped in baking parchment.

'From our garden,' he says, smiling at Mum. 'For our leading lady.'

'Hi, Amy,' I say awkwardly.

She doesn't reply, and I am astonished to realise she is star-struck. She thrusts her brochure at me.

I've never been asked for my autograph before. Devastated, I pat my pockets.

'I don't have a pen!'

Amy rummages in her satchel and pulls out a new pack of sharpies. Cheeks blushing, I start writing.

To Amy, love from Emmy x

Amy blinks down at it, and then throws her arms around me. God, could it always have been this easy? Sometimes life can really be as simple as being nice to people?

Adding to the parade of my loved ones, over Amy's shoulders I see Pete and Dad, looking around the foyer, nudging and pointing things out to each other. They're in out-of-work uniform of creased blue shirts tucked into belted jeans. I notice Dad's eyes are puffy and feel guilty about the horrible words I'd said to them both – but then realise he's clutching a fresh tissue. Was he crying at… Shakespeare?

Mum follows my gaze, and I see the moment she and Dad first make eye contact. My stomach twists with a deep, old fear. My legs fill with tension, unsure whose side I'm meant to run to or stay on. But then they stride towards each other with open arms.

'Jules,' says Mum.

'Windy,' my Dad replies, and they kiss each other's cheeks.

My world shakes. They continue as if this is all completely normal.

'Julius, Pete, you remember John, and this is Amy.'

Dad and Pete shake both their hands, as Amy smiles bashfully back at them both.

'Wendy always says your pizza is the best in the world,' she says.

Dad and Pete go as red as their tomato base. Dad smiles from her to me.

'Well,' he says to her, 'please come and see for yourself – whenever. We'd recommend the Emmy Special.'

They all turn, smiling, to me. Dad opens his mouth to say something, then sees the roses in my hand.

'Yeesh,' he squirms, slapping his forehead, then Pete's arm. 'Excuse us for our faux pas, we didn't bring—'

I hug him firmly. 'Thank you so much for being here.' He squeezes me for a long time, before I gently pull away to turn to Pete.

'Uncle Pete,' I say, tentatively reaching for his hand. 'I'm so, so sorry about...'

His hug pulls me up off the floor. For once he doesn't smell like pizza, and I miss it. He puts me down, laughing.

'Christ, she's something up there, isn't she?' he says to the group, slapping my back. 'No wonder she was so good with the Specials. Should have put them in Shakespearean whatsit.'

Mum grins and squeezes Pete's elbow. They exchange a glance, and then, without saying anything more, Pete pulls her in for a tight hug. Dad's eyes crinkle, and then he turns to me. John and Amy start tactfully talking very animatedly to Watson, who seems delighted with the attention.

'Dad,' I say, 'I'm so sorry about everything I said. I... Honestly, I am so grateful to you and Pete for always helping me with a stable job and I'm sorry I didn't give your work enough respect—'

'Polpetto,' he stops me, 'that apology is with me too. I'm sorry I haven't been supportive of your acting. I just wanted a safe life for you. I never wanted you to feel like you didn't have enough. I know what it's like to not have a job, to not have enough money, to not have enough food. I was so scared about that for you. But you told me you were an actor. I should have believed you.'

He wipes my cheek affectionately.

'You're talented, my Cioccolatino, even I can see that. You and your friends bring it to life, you know? And when you did your fight scene...? Why don't you bring that coordination to pizza plates!'

We giggle together.

'But you know, it wouldn't even matter if you *weren't* talented.'

I blink at him.

'I mean, it wouldn't matter if you were the best in the world – if you bring something unique to other people and you enjoy it, then you should do it. And that's why I'm happy you've quit the pizzeria.'

He smiles and squeezes my shoulder.

'Dolcezza, if I'd been a different kind of supporter, I should have fired you long ago. But I understand better now. My best job is your worst, and hey, that's OK.'

He glances round, smiling proudly. I can't believe he's called me chocolate and sweetness in less than a minute.

'But why are you dating someone who doesn't order pizza in a pizzeria? Why aren't you with that nice Mae…?'

I blush and look at her across the room, where she's talking to her mum and Joe, whose tongue is falling out of his mouth at her. Mae catches my eye and we both smile automatically.

'Yeah…' I say. 'That's a great idea.'

Dad squeals, and pinches my cheek.

'I am *delighted* for you both, my little Patata. Pete will be delighted to make you Emmy Specials. Perhaps, in time, a Mae Special?'

Dad looks over at Mum and Pete, pulls the three of them together.

'Our little girl's growing up,' he says, and they smile at me. I hide my face in my hands in pleasure.

'You must finally come over for dinner,' Mum says to Dad and Pete. 'Let someone else cook for *you* for a change. And I'm *not* making pizza.'

'I suppose a minute bit of variation in our diets might please our doctors,' says Pete.

'How about tonight?' says John. We all look at him in surprise. 'Well, why wait? We could give you a lift?'

'Please do,' smiles Amy.

Dad blinks in surprise, then shares a look with Pete, who shrug-smiles.

'We'd be delighted. But we're empty-handed.'

'You'll simply have to bring *two* bottles of wine next time,' smiles Mum. 'And Emmy, you're welcome to join us, but you'll probably be busy celebrating with your friends?'

Feeling dizzy, I blink around at the rest of the *Twelfth Night* crew, introducing each other to their audience friends and family.

I used to assume the after-party would be the last time I saw my fellow cast-members. But I realise it hasn't just been them all forgetting me – I've been pushing them away too. Thalia was the exception, not the rule. But whether or not I stay in touch with the *Twelfth Night* crew, it feels right to spend this evening with them. I feel surprisingly sure that there will be other chances to have dinner with both halves of my family.

'Next time,' I smile at my family. 'Tonight my plate can be an offering to The Pig.'

'Well, if we're keeping the shop closed for tonight...' My dad turns to Pete, who smiles and nods. 'Would you like to have a lock-in, with your cast?'

I blink at them in astonishment. They've never left Pete's'zas in someone else's hands before.

'Th-that sounds incredible,' I say. 'But are you sure you trust me with it?'

Dad hands me a key with several pizza-shaped keyrings on it.

'It's your home too,' he says. 'Just lock up when you leave.'

'And help yourselves to any of the leftovers, for the stars of the show,' says Pete.

I thank them both profusely and then, for the first time in my life, I have a group hug with my whole family. (Except The Pig.)

After I've waved them out of the theatre, happy and bewildered, I send a message on the Shakesqueer group chat.

AFTER-AFTER-PARTY AT PETE'S'ZAS

EXPECT REVELRY, DEBAUCHERY, BACCHANALIAN DELIGHTS, PIZZA

BYO RUM

DRESS CODE: GAY

I watch as the cast, like secret agents, check their phones and look over at me, mouthing 'arr'.

Francis de la Ware, dressed in a tuxedo and black spotted neckerchief crooks a finger at me, and then at Mae.

'As much as I'd love to draw out the tension here, I'll cut to the chase,' he says. 'Mae Jones and Emmy Clooney, I'd like to offer you – and the rest of the original cast – the opportunity to reprise your roles in my touring production of *Twelfth Night*.'

We stare at him, then at each other, then scream.

We're so overt in our jubilant salutes to Francis that it isn't long before the rest of the cast have all cottoned on, been offered their roles, and accepted.

I predict that tonight's after-party is going to involve the wildest game of Zip, Zap, Boing the world has ever seen.

And when Mae pulls me out into the smoking area of The Boards Theatre, I don't feel the ghosts of the past clawing at me anymore. I just look into her bright eyes, and see my own expression of amazement and delight reflected back at me.

Life might not be a competition, but I'm pretty sure I'm winning.

Mae Jones twists my lucky earring, and laughs in quiet wonder.

'My own worst enemy,' she says, and I kiss her.

ACKNOWLEDGEMENTS

Thank You!

(Imagine I'm wearing a good suit, tapping the microphone and wiping away a tear, as charming and deserving as Olivia Colman accepting an Oscar.)

Thank you so much for reading this book!!! I hope you liked it, obviously. If you didn't, please could you just pretend?

Thank you to Janklow and Nesbit and my agent Hellie Ogden (Hello!) for allowing me to write this book. Thanks to my OG editor Laura Palmer for acquiring and championing it, and for her excellent early edits. Thank you also to my new editors, Rachel Faulkner-Willcocks, Martina Arzu and Kim Atkins, for taking over her reins brilliantly, and indefatigably guiding MOWE through its various transformations. Thank you to Nina Elstad for the incredibly camp cover – I love it. Thanks to Kati Nicholl for the copy-edit and to Rachel Malig for the proofread. Thanks to all the others at Head of Zeus who have worked on it, including naive-core queen Bianca Gillam and fellow ex-thesp Ayo Okojie. Thank you to Nathaniel Alcaraz-Stapleton, Janet Covindassamy, and the other stars in the magical behind-the-curtain teams of rights, production, and sales – you all deserve more time in the spotlight. Sorry for the outrageous amount of exclamation marks I use in emails – it's because I really want you all to like me.

It's been a pleasure to make-believe being a real author this year, and to get to know some iconic writing babes – shout out to Emma Hughes, Bethany Rutter, and, of course, to Laura Kay (who is apparently not my girlfriend, despite doing a bloody good job of acting like it?).

I wanted this book to be a love letter to acting, a career I once thought I wanted to go into. Thank Christ I didn't, but still, many of my happiest memories are from amateuring about on a stage. So I'd like to thank, in an appropriately dramatic way, everyone who was part of those productions. I hope we'll Zip, Zap, Boing together again. Special thanks to Will Bishop, Aoife Kennan, and Joe Pitts, who were incredibly helpful about describing the details of drama school and what it's like to be a working actor today. And to Ben Walsh, with no further explanation.

Thank you to My Own Best Friend, Riss Obolensky. You are my Raphy. Thank you for inspiring my favourite character, and for continuing to inspire me in general. I adore you. Thank you to my flat-best-mate, Amy Malone. I shall always be a huge fan of William Shakespeare, because he brought us together. And thank you to Louisa and Kenneth, for use of your beautiful house in Devon, where I redrafted so much of this book. Louisa, a character is named after you, as requested.

To my mum, as always. I'm hoping that this cover will inspire you to knit me some bright pink ensembles!

The original pitch I sent to my editor for this book was 'Can I write a book about the fact I fancy people who look like me?' As I was working on it though, it became clear I wanted to write a fun love story about soft little butches flirting and falling in love, because we never get to see that! We're so rarely allowed to be main characters, and then even less likely to be paired with a fellow masc. So, lastly, I'd like to acknowledge all the gorgeous butches, mascs, and short-haired bois out there. You really don't get acknowledged enough. I see you (and probably have a big crush on you).

ABOUT THE AUTHOR

LILY LINDON is a writer and editor living in London. She studied English at Cambridge, where she was part of the Footlights comedy group. She was a fiction editor at Penguin Random House, then at The Novelry. Her debut novel *Double Booked* ('the bisexual romcom of your wildest dreams' *DIVA Magazine*) was translated into multiple languages and optioned for screen. She won a Comedy Women in Print Prize for 'Funniest Sex Scene.' Yes, she is single.